Valor's Duty

by Kal Spriggs

Books by Kal Spriggs

The Shadow Space Chronicles

The Fallen Race
The Shattered Empire
The Prodigal Emperor
The Sacred Stars
The Temple of Light
Ghost Star
The Star Engine*

The Renegades

Renegades: Origins
Renegades: Out of the Cold
Renegades: Out of Time
Renegades: Royal Pains*

The Star Portal Universe

Valor's Child
Valor's Calling
Valor's Duty
Valor's Cost*

Fenris Unchained
Odin's Eye
Jormungandr's Venom*

The Eoriel Saga

Echo of the High Kings
Wrath of the Usurper
Fate of the Tyrant
Heir to the Fallen Duke*

*Forthcoming

Chapter One: Winning Is Everything

"Break left, break left!" I shouted as the incoming fire lanced out at my squadron of Mark Five Firebolt warp fighters.

The fighters were fast, faster than the human brain could readily understand. They attained a nearly instantaneous relative velocity of over point seven C, or seven tenths of the speed of light. Their warp envelopes, however, were not particularly maneuverable. Straight line velocity they could achieve, but they only managed ten degrees of "turn" with their internal warp drives.

That meant the best thing they could manage relative to a sharp bank like in the movies was a long, slow gradual curve. Against the incoming fire, that was painfully inadequate and three of my nine fighters winked out of existence.

I'd just lost thirty percent of my force. In military terms, I was combat ineffective and from a practical standpoint, I'd just led those ships and pilots right into the guns of the enemy battleship, knowing that it was going to happen.

But if they're shooting at me...

At the velocities my squadron moved at, we were almost blind, we could barely see the enemy battleship, it's powerful warp drive a beacon, its weapon fire strobes that pinpointed its progress through the star system. There was no way we'd be able to see the smaller pinpricks of other warp-fighters with their drives offline, waiting for the opportunity to strike.

That was, not until those drive lit off. The two squadrons of warp fighters came online at less than a hundred thousand kilometers distance from the battleship. They closed that distance in only seconds, the eighteen Firebolts arming their payloads even as the battleship recognized the new threat. I grinned as those fighters whipped past, releasing their antimatter bombs in a chain of detonations that shone more powerfully than the system's star.

Before that string of detonations could clear on my screens, they went dark and then red text flashed: Simulation Terminated, Defender Wins.

"Yes!" I heard my boyfriend shout out. I blinked clear of the holographic projections as they faded out, revealing the faces of Sashi Drien and Kyle Regan. I couldn't help a goofy grin to match theirs. "Chock up another one for Team Armstrong," Kyle smirked.

Sashi and I were seated cross-legged on my bed, while Kyle took my bedroom's only chair. The space was tight with three, but it wasn't like my parents' house was all that big.

Sashi rolled her eyes, "*I* say we're Team Drien. After all, they have an Armstrong, too."

"Let's see what they have to say, huh?" I asked cheerfully. I couldn't help the urge to gloat a bit. It wasn't a particularly nice thing to do, but that maneuver had been hard to pull off... using a single squadron of fighters to herd the enemy battleship into position for the ambush. Of the various warp ship engagements, *Battleship Over Terrapin* was one of the hardest scenarios to pull off a defender win.

I toggled over our chat to our opponents. "Hey guys, good game," I said genially.

"Good game for you, maybe," Ashiri Takenata growled. My best friend sounded particularly surly.

"Well played," Alexander Karmazin said, far more neutrally.

"That was tricky, Jiden," my little brother sighed. Will was just in the next room, unlike the other two. They'd agreed to take him on their team, though, even though he wasn't a cadet.

We'd played the scenario three on three, which was the recommended match-up. The attackers in the scenario had a battleship and two destroyers in escort. The defenders had some unarmed sensor platforms and three squadrons of warp fighters.

"Well, we'd been practicing some of the battle plan back here," I admitted. "Sashi thought up the piece with the decoy attack from my squadron there at the end."

"Using the observation platforms as bait for the destroyers was pretty clever, too," Alexander admitted. "You took Will and I out early on."

"Thanks," I smiled. Normally the platforms were there to balance the attacker's advantages in sensors and maneuverability. Smart attackers made a point of taking them out early on... and I'd decided to set up an ambush with my fighter squadrons on the most likely approach to the main sensor array.

"It wasn't fair," Ashiri protested.

"What?" I asked in surprise.

"You three have been playing together solidly for the past week and a half. Alex and I aren't even in the same hemisphere, right now, *and* we got stuck with your little brother," Ashiri growled. "Throw in the communications delay, and you three had a clear advantage."

I didn't know what to say to that. I wished we were on a video call so I could see my friend's face. She actually sounded angry, over what seemed like a silly thing. Yeah, those had been some slight advantages, but it wasn't like the scenario favored us at all. We'd been facing a *battleship* with three squadrons of fighters. Normally *Battleship Over Terrapin* turned into a bloodbath where the defending fighters died to the last, leaving the attacking team victorious.

"Uh," I said after a long moment, "I guess we could shuffle up the teams next time?"

"Right... sure, it was hard enough to get this game in, I've still got tons of homework to cover, oh, and this certifies *you* three for our warp fighter simulation project, but because *we* lost, Alex and I have to get another certified game in, sometime in the next three days," Ashiri's bitterness felt like a bowl of cold jello to the face. It completely blind-sided me and I had no idea where it came from.

"I'm sorry," I started to say, but then my tablet blinked to show that Ashiri had disconnected.

"What was that about?" Kyle asked. His freckled face was puzzled.

"Sorry about that, guys," Alexander Karmazin spoke up. "She and I were talking before the game started, I guess she's had a lot of pressure at home and I think she's just stressed out a bit, you know?"

"Yeah, sure," I said. Yet I couldn't help a guilty feeling as I glanced at Kyle and Sashi Drien. I'd invited both of them to visit my parent's house at Black Mesa Outpost over our Christmas break. Well, in reality I'd invited Kyle because I wanted to introduce my new boyfriend to my family. Sashi had tagged along because she had nowhere else to go, she'd been all-but-disowned by her family after she'd refused to resign from the Academy. We'd been roommates, once, at the Century Military Academy. Then we'd been rivals. Only a few days before the end of last term, we'd both nearly been killed by a psychotic teacher. That had made us both reevaluate our priorities and while I didn't really consider her a friend, I didn't want to see her have to give up her dreams, especially not when her family treated her so poorly.

I hadn't really thought about the advantage that brought the three of us. Most of our assignments over break were ones where we were allowed to collaborate with classmates, so long as we documented our participation and we did it actively, that was, we could discuss the work while we did it, but we weren't allowed to talk about past assignments, so it benefited those who were present so we could work together.

All three of us were in many of the same classes. Ashiri and Alexander had the same advantage... except Karmazin lived in the Enclave and Ashiri lived in New Albion. They *were* both in the northern hemisphere, but they were a couple thousand kilometers apart. Plus they'd been involved in a relationship that had sort of fallen apart last summer. They were still friends, but I'd be willing to bet that spending lots of time together might feel awkward.

"Sorry if I messed you guys up," Will spoke up. My little brother sounded worried.

"Don't worry about it," Karmazin snorted. "You did great, *way* better than your sister did after only a few games."

"Thanks," I drawled. Yet I couldn't help but agree. I had come to this whole military thing in a round-about fashion, it had never been my plan. I'd been dreadfully ignorant about it all, and I'd spent a lot of time catching up. Will had taken to some of the scenarios I'd loaned him like a sand-lizard to the dunes. It had freaked me out a bit when I'd come home on Christmas break and he'd asked me for more advanced scenarios.

"Anyway, Ashiri *was* right about one thing, we both still have a *lot* of homework to do. *And* I have to set up a certified game with someone else, now, since our team didn't win that one. Goodnight guys." Karmazin sounded a bit resigned at that.

"Goodnight," We chorused and he disconnected.

My feeling of victory had been short-lived. I hadn't really thought about the pressures some of my other friends were under. For that matter, while this had completed our certified battle scenario, I still had three more projects to complete, including a much-dreaded Military History paper for Commander Bonnadonna.

"Jiden, are you and your friends done playing games?" Mom called in from the next room. Since Will was probably sitting on the couch only a meter or so away, I knew *she* knew the answer. Yet that was her "polite" way of saying she'd had enough of us all holed up in simulations.

"Yeah, mom," I called back. I turned off my datapad and stretched. "I guess we need to go be sociable or something." I couldn't help but give Kyle a hopeful smile.

He matched it and reached out to give my hand a squeeze. My heart did a little hop in my chest and I felt like parts of me melted at the same time. I really, really liked Kyle. He was supportive, he was smart, and he was just *nice.* He reminded me a lot of my dad, only not nearly so nerdy.

I headed that thought off and stepped out of my room.

Will had just finished packing up his datapad. He didn't have one of the newer model academy-issued ones, after all, his application hadn't even been officially accepted yet. He had one of dad's older model datapads, so he'd had to use a VR headset to play the game. My mom stood with her arms crossed, a polite but probably fake smile on her face. She hated having guests, I knew. She frequently complained about new scientists and interns showing up here at Black Mesa Outpost, "joggling her elbow" as she put it, and even when Dad's mom, Granny Effy, visited, she got uncomfortable sharing the house. I hadn't really thought of that when I invited Kyle and Sashi Drien.

Add in that Kyle Regan was my boyfriend and neither my mom or my dad really knew how to handle that. It helped that Kyle was respectful and polite, but there was still a lot of awkwardness about the situation.

Then there was the fact that the Armstrongs and the Driens were longstanding rivals in the Planetary Militia added to the overall discomfort with Sashi's presence. Plus there was something about a Drien being behind an attempt on my mom's life when she'd been a Cadet at the Academy... so yeah, to say my mom was uncomfortable with the guests would be an understatement.

"I thought we might eat something special for dinner, your father and I just got approval on our next research grant," Mom said.

"That's great!" I smiled. While I didn't really want to go into archeology like my parents, that didn't mean I didn't find it interesting... or that I didn't realize the importance of their work. The ruins under Black Rock Mesa were alien, and over a million years old by best estimate. My parents sort of ran the operation here, in as much as anyone "ran" the gaggle of scientists and archeologists here at the Outpost.

"Yeah, your father just signed the paperwork a few hours ago at Duncan City, he picked up some food there before he left, he should be arriving soon," Mom's voice took on a tone of relief, like she'd half-expected me to say something snarky. Maybe a couple of years ago, I might have, just out of irritation and maybe even a little insecurity, I could admit to myself. But now, I really appreciated that my mom was trying to be as friendly and gracious a host as she really knew how. After all, it wasn't like we got many guests out here and Mom... well, I guess she'd never really been much of a people person.

"If you could help me set the table, Jiden," Mom said, "Will and, um, Kyle, we have some spare folding chairs out in the storage shed..."

"Sure thing," Kyle smiled. He nodded at Will and they stepped outside.

My mom trailed off and stared at Sashi Drien. "Um..."

"Sashi, want to help me with the cups?" I asked.

"Sure thing," she replied.

We set up the table quickly. It wasn't like it was a big table. I hadn't really seen it through outsider's eyes, yet the house seemed so... well, small. The cups and plates weren't anything special, just generic ceramics made from fused silicates, processed out of the Outpost's fabricator. The silverware was just simple steel, unadorned. The table was just a modular metal table. Metal and silicates were cheap on Century. My sandy, dry homeworld had plenty of both. Wood and plastics were expensive. The planet didn't have any real forests to speak of and hydrocarbons weren't particularly plentiful. Most of both had to be imported from other worlds or manufactured from raw materials.

My parent's house was built of local stone, with thick, heavy blocks to provide insulation, the black basalt cut out of the plateau's stone by laser drills and held in place by their own weight. It had a metal roof with a double layer of insulation to keep the heat out of the living areas while using that heat to warm water for bathing. There were six rooms to the entire house, my parent's bedroom, mine, my brother's, which Sashi got to use during her stay, the living room, the dining room/kitchen shared space, and the one small bathroom. Here at the outpost, we had a water ration of three liters for bathing. We had to use a water recycler on that, since even the deepest wells hadn't found any ground water, not this close to the equator.

Even so, my parent's home was the second largest house here at the outpost. The largest one had belonged to Champion Enterprises. Tony Champion's family had lived there when they'd visited the Outpost for almost a year. Now, if I remembered right, it housed a group of engineers who provided technical assistance to my parents.

There were twenty-nine full-time residents at Black Mesa Outpost, including two Enforcers who'd been tasked here relatively recently. It was the furthest south outpost in the northern hemisphere of Century. I'd grown up here, and especially in the last few years before I'd first left, I'd been sick of the place. It had seemed confining and restrictive and just so... *boring.*

Now it just seemed small and sort of homey. But it was like an old shirt, familiar and nice, but not something that I really fit in, not anymore.

The Academy was my life now, and while part of me dreaded the hard work to come, the rest of me was eager for the challenge.

***

"We made great progress, the past few months," Dad was in full form, gesturing grandly as he ate. Normally that wasn't an issue with just Mom, Will, and I around the small table. With two more, it meant I had to dodge a fork-full of mashed potatoes as it lanced at my left eye.

"Nelson's University fronted the money as soon as they saw our initial data," Dad went on. "I mean, a lot of this is going to be revolutionary. Some of the first finds were great, advances in metallurgy and composites, but some of this tech we're getting online..."

"Wait," Kyle interrupted, "online? I thought this was an archeology site, you know, like pottery shards and that sort of thing."

My parents looked at him and started laughing. I couldn't help but join in, especially at the thought of my *mother* picking up alien pottery shards. Kyle just looked confused and I decided that I'd probably better explain a bit. "So, as far as my parents can tell, Century's ancient aliens weren't native to the planet. They settled at a few locations, mostly near the poles where it's, well, a lot nicer."

"Yeah, there's some ruins near my parent's house," Kyle nodded, "but there's not much there, just tumbled stones and the Wall."

"Right, the Wall," my dad nodded. "That's the big clue that they were technologically advanced." The Wall was a massive, gutted construct, over a thousand feet high, which surrounded the main sets of alien ruins. "Our first colonists, well they weren't too focused on preserving things and the ruins provided some useful building materials. Plus there was sort of an initial artifact rush with some of the Second Wave, and well..." he shrugged, "anything that might have survived a million years of exposure was pretty much destroyed, or else sold to private collectors off-world."

"Except for pottery shards and that sort of thing," my mom nodded. "There's a few finds, most of it already extensively cataloged, but you have to go into the deep desert here in the south to find any of the ruins that weren't thoroughly picked over."

"So, you guys found something special?" My boyfriend looked puzzled.

"We think that Black Mesa was a research site or maybe even a military outpost," My dad said. "The main site is deeply buried, almost a kilometer below the mesa. Most of the upper levels were filled with junk and sand, it took us years to work our way deeper.

"We reached the central zone about five years ago," my mom said. "Since then, we've found dozens of artifacts in excellent shape. The cool dry air down there has preserved things in remarkable fashion. Other sites on Century, there are clear signs that these aliens, they packed everything in an orderly fashion and left, they didn't leave much behind.

"Here, though," my dad smiled, "here it looks like the equipment was either too difficult to recover or they just didn't have time. We think they purposely collapsed part of the main access tunnel and dumped sand down there to prevent access. But after we got past that..."

"Dozens of finds. Much of it preserved almost perfectly," Mom nodded. "Stuff that's fifty, maybe a hundred years ahead of us, maybe more. That's why we got the grant, the research we're doing is going to give Century a huge leg up over the next few decades as we figure out all kinds of things about these aliens and their technology."

"Doesn't that violate the Alien Act, though?" Kyle asked nervously.

He had reason to sound nervous. The UN Star Guard enforced the Alien Act of 483 GD. One might say, they did so in a draconian fashion. Any contact with aliens, beyond shooting them on sight, brought with it a host of penalties, up to and including death. The causes for that were topics of our military history classes, and the violence of the Erandi and the constant warfare with the Culmor were among the central reasons.

"No," Dad snorted. "It's not like we're talking with these aliens, their civilization visited Century over a million years ago. They predate even the rise of the Erandi Empire, as best as we can estimate. They're long gone. What we're doing is no different from salvage efforts to recover Culmor or Erandi ships or equipment after a battle... only we're learning a great deal in the process."

My mom nodded quickly, though I noticed her dart a glance at Sashi. *I wonder what that's about.*

"We've thoroughly vetted this through Nelson University's law section, and believe it or not, it's gone all the way to Century's Central Courts for review, just to be certain. We're well within what's allowed by the Guard Charter... even if we aren't technically under the Charter." My mom adopted a tone of bitterness at that last part, and I couldn't blame her. The more I learned about the Guard and how they enforced the UN Star Guard Charter, the bitterer I felt about how we got all of the restrictions and none of the benefits out here on the Periphery. Century wasn't just a barren, dusty world, it was a distant and lonely one. We were on one of the outermost flanks of colonized space, way out past the official borders of Guard Space, in what most people referred to as the Periphery.

"Oh, okay," Kyle said. "So, not pottery shards, actual technology and devices. What kind of stuff, then?" I couldn't help but lean forward. My parent's hadn't told me much about what they'd been doing, specifically, only that things had been "very promising."

"Well..." Dad said with a glance at my mother. "Some of it

is... well, not really classified, so much as confidential. Regardless of the purpose of this facility, there are some definite military applications to some of our discoveries."

I felt a chill at his words and I couldn't help but think about Tony Champion's interest in my parent's work... and how he and his father Isaac had been selling weapons technology to smugglers and pirates. *And Scarpitti tried to kill me, because she was worried I'd recognize a map of my parent's dig site...*

Surely, though, the presence of the Enforcers out here and the fact that the entire smuggling ring had been rolled up would keep my parent's safe... right?

"None of it is secret," Mom rolled her eyes. "Yes, there's some definite military applications, but there's also generic engineering and scientific applications. Even medical applications. In fact, a major part of what we've been involved with is a smart-material that may one day be useful for medical implants. This stuff is tough enough that has survived a million years with minimal decay, while at the same time still retaining its reconfigurable properties..." Mom trailed off. "Well, anyway, that's just the leading edge of the sandstorm. Some of the machinery on the lower levels is massive, orders of magnitude beyond anything we've found up until now. Some of it is clearly power production. This might have been a main power hub for their presence on this planet..."

Mom had clearly warmed up to the subject and as she began to go into detail, I just sat back and let the words roll over me. For a moment, I felt like I was a kid again, listening to her and Dad talk about all the little details, the puzzle pieces of the past that they tried to put together. Some part of me understood their fascination. Yet, at the same time, it was the future, not the past that called to me. I didn't want to piece together long-dead civilizations and ancient technology, I wanted to be building a future for my world.

Well... now I wanted to be building and *protecting* that future. I'd seen that not everyone was as willing to get along as one could hope. There were people out there who would use violence to get what they wanted... and I'd learned the hard way that I could use violence of my own to stop them.

My feelings of home and family felt distant. For a moment, my mind went to a dark closet where the smugglers had locked me, to the place where they'd nearly killed me... until I killed them.

And again, I thought of Commander Scarpitti, who had nearly killed me, all because she thought I was a threat. I'd killed her, instead, in a combination of planning and sheer luck.

Both times I'd barely survived. I just hoped that next time I faced a situation like that, I'd be better prepared.

"Jiden, you okay?" Will asked from next to me. My little brother looked a little worried.

"Yeah," I said, forcing myself to smile. My dad was gesturing with his mashed-potatoes-laden fork again, while talking about how they'd excavated the initial dig. He had clearly warmed up to his captive audience, and I could tell from how Kyle's and Sashi's eyes had glazed over, that he'd lost them both. This was why I'd chosen to join the Militia, defending my family, protecting them from the people who would do them harm. It was something I was good at... winning when my life was on the line.

I felt the knot in my stomach unclench and my smile became more genuine. All of my uncertainties melted away and I went back to enjoying the moment. Tomorrow there would be plenty of time to worry about the future, tonight I could enjoy the fruit of my victories.

***

Chapter 2: Sometimes I Get Myself In Trouble

Imagine a train hurdling along at over three hundred kilometers an hour. Now put it over fifty meters below sand and rock, in a pitch-dark tunnel. That was the military train that I got to ride back to the Academy. It was part of the defense infrastructure train lines that connected most of Century's cities and all of its military bases. One of my engineering projects over break had been to write a research paper about it. There were over thirty thousand kilometers of tunnel, much of it between fifty and a hundred meters deep. It had taken twenty years to complete the main lines, and the main sections were designed to survive near-misses from orbital ships. It was a pretty amazing feat of engineering... the cost estimates rivaled that of starships.

Of course, what that all meant to me was that I had just over a six hour train ride. I'd coordinated to link up with my friends, but most of that had gone out the window when the onrush of cadets had flooded the train.

When we arrived at the Academy, the masses would assemble into something resembling order, but right now, the train was chaos, with civilian-dressed and uniformed cadets running back and forth, people struggling with bags and what seemed like far too much noise after two weeks at home.

I glanced at my datapad and checked the text from Ashiri a third time. She said she'd managed to get a spot in one of the private cars, which would be something of a refuge from all this chaos. Ashiri's family lived in New Albion, which meant that Ashiri had boarded the train several hours earlier, well before I'd arrived at Duncan City. I pushed through the mess, hoping that I'd catch up to Kyle or Sashi on the way.

I finally reached the right train car, this section of the train was notably quieter and I paused outside the suite to pull out my datapad. Since I had no idea where Sashi or Kyle had been swept off to, it was probably best if I messaged them, rather than trying to find them on the train.

I faintly overheard a voice on speaker from inside the suite. After a moment, I thought I recognized Ashiri's mother's voice and I heard Ashiri respond to something, her voice oddly muted.

"You listen to me, daughter," Ashiri's mother grew louder,

her voice angry, "those so-called friends of yours are no good to you. Do you think it is coincidence that two years in a row you have been third place to them? They are using you, and keeping you down!"

"Mother!" Ashiri protested, "It's not like that at all! I have done well! Third in rank is nothing to be ashamed of!"

"Listen to me with respect and never interrupt!" Ashiri's mother's voice was sharp. "Third is *nothing*. Did your so-called friends not vie for first and second? Do you think it coincidence that your roommate's grandmother runs the Academy and her granddaughter finishes first almost every year? When I was your age, I was first in *everything*. What kind of example do you set for your siblings by failing to be first in all that you do?"

"Mother," Ashiri protested, "I'm doing very well. Better than hundreds of others--"

"You will do *better*," Ashiri's mother snapped. "You need to do whatever necessary. Those so-called friends of yours, you need to cut them loose. You are *better* than them, you do not need them!"

"Mother..." I heard Ashiri start to protest.

"If you are not first this year, daughter, then you are *nothing*. I will expect you to succeed. Your family expects you to succeed, do not fail me."

"Yes, mother," Ashiri's voice was resigned, barely audible. There was silence on the other side of the door for a long moment. I felt suddenly guilty and a bit ashamed as I realized I'd been listening in on the private and potentially embarrassing conversation. I hadn't meant to, but I'd still overheard things that were none of my business... though they were things that shocked me.

Granted, I wasn't terribly surprised that Ashiri's mother didn't think highly of me. The one time I'd really met her, I'd managed to put my foot in my mouth. But that she thought that Alexander Karmazin and I were using her daughter to improve our own scores... that made me angry. Worse, she'd all but accused the *Admiral* of rigging things so I came in first. That idea was so absurd as to be ridiculous. I couldn't think of someone less likely to do that, and if anything, I felt like the Admiral was extra hard on me because I was family.

It wasn't like I could defend myself, though. I'd have to admit to listening in on a private conversation and that wouldn't exactly make me look good. At least it sounded like the conversation was over. I reached for the door handle, but before I could touch it, the door opened.

"Oh," Ashiri froze, staring at me.

"Hey," I said in as cheerful a fashion as I could manage. "I guess I found the right place."

Something flashed across my best friend's face. Some emotions that came and went too fast for me to understand, maybe too complex for me to really comprehend. Something like shame or embarrassment, something like anger. I wasn't sure and I was half-convinced that I imagined it all, it was there and gone so fast. One thing I was sure, though, was for a moment, Ashiri wanted to ask how long I'd been standing outside the door.

"Yeah, this is the right place," Ashiri replied finally, her voice almost detached. "Where are the others?"

"I lost Sashi and Kyle in the crowd, but I was just about to message them," I gestured with the datapad in my left hand. Ashiri made a face, though I wasn't sure whether that was about Sashi Drien or my excuse for why I was standing just outside the door. "Have you seen Karmazin, yet?"

"Alex?" Ashiri shrugged, "No, I assumed he'd be with the rest of you. Last I heard, he was going to catch the train in Duncan City like the rest of you." The Enclave didn't connect into the defense train system, for a bunch of complicated reasons, not least of which was that it wasn't technically a part of Century's planetary government, it was a weird sort of autonomous sub-state.

"Huh, I hadn't seen him either," I said.

"Well, come on in," Ashiri stepped out of the doorway. She settled to her seat and gestured at her datapad, "I was just finishing up edits on my Military History paper for Commander Bonnadonna."

"Ugh, that was a brutal one, right?" I stepped in and took a seat, messaging Alexander Karmazin, Kyle Regan, and Sashi Drien with our location.

"Yeah," Ashiri showed genuine emotion for what seemed like the first time. "I *enjoy* his classes, but he sure does load us down with assignments."

Last year we'd had a ten page paper due every week for Commander Bonnadonna's classes. The worst part was, we didn't get the papers returned, he just seemed to be able to magically read every paper and comment and address things we brought up in our papers during class. I couldn't imagine him managing to read that much every week, but somehow he did it... and he managed to make subjects that I found dry and abstract into things that mattered.

Someone knocked on the door, "Come in," Ashiri and I said at the same time.

Kyle opened the door and stuck his head in, "Hey, Jiden, I think Sashi needs your help." There was a nervous edge to his voice that had me up on my feet and out in the corridor almost before he finished speaking.

I saw what he meant right away. Just down the corridor, right at the junction from this car to the next, I saw Sashi Drien with two young men boxing her in. I recognized both of them almost instantly, it would be hard not to, after all, since their short stature, dark hair and tan skin looked so similar to that of Sashi. They were her older brothers, and their faces were harsh with anger as they faced her.

I studied them as I advanced. Nahka Drien wore the collar insignia of a Cadet Commander, his tan, handsome face drawn back in a harsh sneer. His younger brother, Toro, wore a Cadet Second Class rank. Both of them were tense, their expressions angry and their postures showing that they were on the edge of physical violence. I wasn't sure how I knew that, maybe it was something I picked up from my *kerala* classes with Commander Pannja.

Nahka looked over as I came up, his eyes darting between his sister and myself, even as he snarled at Sashi, "...bad enough that you refused our grandfather's offer, that you resign and come home and limit any further disgrace to our family. But this? To take refuge with our family's enemies? How could you embarrass yourself so?"

"Leave her alone!" I snapped.

"This doesn't concern you," Nahka hissed at me. "Go back to your real friends, *hongro*."

I frowned at him, "Sashi *is* my friend. Leave her alone."

Nahka turned and stepped towards me, "You're using her. You're setting her up for failure, to make my family look bad. She isn't suited for this life. She almost failed out last year. You leave my sister alone, *hongro*."

I flinched at his harsh tone, but I didn't step back. I realized that, in his own twisted way, Nahka did care for his sister, he didn't want to see her fail. But at the same time, he was doing her more harm than good, he was bullying her, trying to get her to quit.

He didn't see how capable and strong Sashi could be, because he was too busy trying to protect her. "No," I snapped. "You leave my friend alone."

I stepped past him and stood next to her. "If not for Sashi, *I* would have failed out during Indoctrination. She's smart, she's strong, and she's going to do *just* fine... as long as you two get out of her face!"

"You shouldn't take that tone with upper-classmen, Cadet Third Class," Nahka Drien snapped.

"We aren't at the Academy, yet," I replied. "And this kind of thing wouldn't fly there, and both of you know it."

They both shifted uncomfortably at that. They monitored our every move at the Academy. While a lot of that was hands off, this was something that was likely to get them in trouble.

"You're right," Nahka said, his voice low and threatening. "We *aren't* at the Academy. Maybe someone could suffer an accident, fall down and get hurt. Especially if she was alone and sticking her nose where it doesn't belong."

"She's not alone," Kyle said from just down the corridor. Behind him, I saw Ashiri and Karmazin. Nahka and Toro both looked sour. Clearly their plan, whatever it was, had just fallen apart.

Nahka stepped forward and stopped only a few centimeters away from me. "We'll remember this, Armstrong. Whatever happens to our sister, it's on *you* now." He stepped past me and then he and his brother stepped through the doors and into the next train car.

"Well," I said, as calmly as I could manage, "that went well."
                                    ***

Back in the private room, we all just sort of slumped. I found myself sitting next to Sashi, who still hadn't said anything. I could see her thinking, but I wasn't really sure what was running through her head. I'd always had a problem reading her, even when she'd been my roommate.

"You okay?" I asked quietly.

"What do you think?" Sashi shot me a look. I didn't really have a response for that. I'd been at odds with my parents once before, but not with my whole family. Even then, it hadn't been like what Sashi was going through. With me, they'd shipped me off to my mom's mother, the Admiral, who had enrolled me in the Academy Prep School. "They think I'm going to fail out," Sashi said in a miserable voice.

"Well, sorry, but I think your brothers are jerks," I replied.

She snorted, "Yeah, they're my *brothers*, it kind of goes with the territory." She wiped at her eyes. "It's just so frustrating, you know? They think they know what's best for me and for the family. They're angry because I'm not doing what they tell me." Her brow furrowed, "I am worried that they are right."

"You'll be fine," I assured her.

She shot me a look, one part grateful and one part angry. "You don't know what it was like," she hissed. "Last year, I had no help. I had no support. I was tolerated by Ogre Company, but that was it. I'm coming *back* to Sand Dragon. Do you think it will be a warm welcome? Who will want to room with me? Who will want to study with me?"

I hadn't really thought about that. I'd talked with Sara Salter, this year's Company Commander for Sand Dragon, and she'd approved Sashi's transfer back. But that didn't mean there would necessarily be a place for her. Sashi and I had roomed together during Academy Prep School. She'd gone over to Ogre for our plebe year. I'd probably been the closest thing she had to a friend in Sand Dragon... and she'd very publicly betrayed me during the final exercise.

"You can be my roommate," I said on impulse.

I saw Ashiri look over at me as I said it. From the way her expression shifted, I knew that she wanted to say something, but she didn't. I thought about what I'd overheard between her and her mother. *Maybe if I'm not her roommate any more, it'll take some pressure off of her, too.*

"Are you sure about that?" Sashi asked.

"Yeah," I said. I'd had her stay at my parent's house with me for two weeks. How much worse could it be?

"Well, thanks," Sashi said. She seemed taken aback. "I really hope this all works out."

"Don't worry," I said, clapping her on the shoulder impulsively, "I've got a good feeling about this year." I should have kept my stupid mouth shut.

***

We arrived at the Academy without any further trouble and after the initial formation, I knocked out my in-processing checklist and found myself in the large amphitheater where it seemed like so many of my life's major events had occurred. This was where they held the first in-briefing from the Admiral. This was where they had held my Academy Prep School Final Exercise. It had been here that Sashi had betrayed me. It was here that the psychotic Commander Scarpitti had tried to kill me.

Despite the dim lights and the quiet, I found my heart starting to race in anticipation.

"Attention on Deck!" Someone bellowed.

As one, the entire Regiment of Cadets rose to their feet. Again, the central platform lit up, and the Admiral, my grandmother, stepped forward, her khaki uniform crisp, her expression stern. "Cadets, welcome back to the Academy. Today begins the one-hundred and seventy first year of this institution. I welcome our new Plebe Class, Class Two Ninety One. I also welcome our First Class, Class Two Eighty Eight. You Cadets First Class will graduate this year and go on to your follow-on assignments in our Planetary Militia."

Her already stern voice hardened. "Last year we suffered a number of unfortunate incidents. As a result, we will all of us, Cadets and Instructors, be under additional monitoring. All of you will be under constant supervision. We will not tolerate violations of the school's Honor Code, nor will we tolerate ethical or legal violations. You are one day to be Officers within Century's Planetary Militia, and you are expected to set the example. Any of you who cannot do so will be removed."

"That said, honest mistakes are a part of your learning experience. We do not expect you all to be perfect. Leadership and command are skills that must be learned. Take the opportunities you are given to excel. Accept risks. Show your instructors that you are able to recover from failure, and you will do well."

"Now then," the Admiral said, "We've had some turn-over of

personnel. Commander Weisfeldt joins us as one of our new Engineering instructors." The short, stocky, and dark-haired officer stepped forward, his expression stern. "Commander Weisfeldt has just completed a tour at Century Station, where he managed the station's military prototyping department."

"Additionally, joining our staff is Commander Stirling," the Admiral went on. A heavy-set officer stepped forward. He had a pleasant smile and gave a slight wave. "Commander Stirling has just finished a tour with the Guard Fleet as an officer observer at their shipyards at Harlequin Station."

I perked up a bit at that. Getting a slot like that would be impressive, the Guard rarely allowed non-signatory nations any access to their shipyards. He would have had a chance to watch ship construction across a huge range of ship classes and sizes.

"Also joining the Academy Staff at this time is Lieutenant General Corgan, of Century's Enforcer Service," the Admiral said. "Lieutenant General Corgan will not be teaching any classes, but she will be observing how we conduct our training and our overall operations."

The way that the Admiral said that and the polite yet cool tone in her voice gave me a shiver. That wasn't the way I would have expected her to welcome someone. It felt more like a warning, to all of us. What was a senior member of Century's national police service doing at the school? As far as I knew, they had no connection to the Planetary Militia. They operated entirely planet-side and they answered to the Security Director and Charter Council.

"Now, then, I'll remind you all that companies, sections, and individual cadets are ranked on a points system. As always, your grades, your performance in training, your punishments and successes, are all counted towards your totals. Last year, Sand Dragon Company managed to win again, for a second year, by a slim margin. The Honor Graduates, Mackenzie, Ingvald, and Attabera, were ahead by a few percentage points. Those who graduate in the top ranks are often given the choice positions upon graduation."

She gave a wintry smile, "Failure early on can be overcome. Becoming overconfident early on can lead to a drop in your ranking. Ambition and hard work are rewarded, complacency is your enemy, far more than anything else. Good luck, Cadets, let's have a good year."

I hadn't had any part of my in-processing take me to Doctor Aisling's lab and that had been something of a relief. Yet after the in-briefing from the Admiral, my datapad pinged to tell me to report there.

Some part of my stomach twisted, yet another part of me felt relief. It had been something I'd half-anticipated, half-dreaded. I wasn't surprised to see others in the crowd looking down at their datapads, either. Clearly, whatever this was, they were pulling all of us in for it.

Implantation, I thought to myself. We were scheduled to get our implants and undergo the life-extension treatments this year. What that had to do with Doctor Aisling's special testing, I wasn't entirely sure, but I was willing to bet that it tied in somehow.

Working our way down into the lowest levels we all filed into the appointed room. I saw about twenty cadets in total. Most of them I recognized from before. There were the Zahler twins, Ashiri Takenata, Alexander Karmazin, Sashi Drien, and myself from Sand Dragon. I recognized Bolander and Thorpe from Ogre, along with two others whose names I couldn't remember. There were a couple more candidates from Dust Company, but my boyfriend, Kyle, wasn't in their number. Then again, I'd never seen him in this testing. The others in the group were ones and twos, people I'd seen in passing and vaguely knew were in my graduating class, but I had no idea what sections or companies they came from.

The room was set up something like a classroom, with rows of metal framed desks of an older style, clearly taken out of storage. Most of us took seats. I sat next to Sashi, feeling an odd sense of completeness as I did so, almost like I had come full circle.

We didn't have long to wait. The doors in the front of the room opened and Doctor Aisling stepped through. To my surprise, the Doctor wasn't alone. Behind her came the Admiral, which was surprise enough, but also Charter Councilor Beckman. I'd only encountered the woman once before, when we'd been ordered to let her talk to her niece, then Candidate and now Plebe Kate Beckman. Walking next to her was Lieutenant General Corgan, the two of them spoke in low tones, moving to the side to observe.

Behind both of them, came Commander Weisfeldt.

"Cadets," the Admiral spoke, "thank you all for coming."

I had to repress something of a nervous giggle. After all, it wasn't like we had much of a choice, we'd been ordered to come here.

"As most of you have no-doubt realized, you are here due to your involvement in Doctor Aisling's ongoing project. What started out two years ago during your initial examination as Cadet Candidates has come to fruition." She paused and gestured at Doctor Aisling, "Doctor, please explain your procedure."

"Cadets," Doctor Aisling gave us all a sunny smile, "Each of you has been carefully selected for a pilot program of a very special implant. Normally you all would receive a standard Tier Two implant. That is, it would be a memory augmentation with communications and computer interface features."

I found myself nodding. Tier Two implants were considered to be rather invasive. I couldn't say I was exactly comfortable with the idea. Cybernetics were generally frowned upon throughout human space. Century's Planetary Militia had adopted implants only a couple of decades ago, and even then, the neural computer implants had been voluntary until last year.

"As some of you may remember from my classes on implants, there's what is generally considered a Type Three Neural Implant," Doctor Aisling ran a hand through her red hair, her smile broad. "It's generally seen as a more invasive process and includes logic augmentation and a full spectrum of intelligence boosting features. Tier Three Neural Implants tie into substantially larger portions of the human brain. Their use is limited due to the extreme expense as well as the fact that many bodies simply reject that level of augmentation or else their minds have issues interlinking with the substantially more integrated neural computer."

"That generally leads to insanity or death," The Admiral said, her voice flat.

Doctor Aisling's cheerful smile faltered slightly, "Yes, that can occur."

"My project has been working on a new design of neural implant," Doctor Aisling went on. "To overcome some of the possibilities of failure, I did extensive screening to filter out those whose minds lacked the necessary flexibility. I also mapped your consciousness so that I could create a gestalt, an amalgam of your minds and that of the software in the neural computers."

"Wait, these things would be aware?" A boy in the front row asked.

Doctor Aisling's eyes flicked in the direction of Charterer Beckman. "No, not *truly* aware, that would be bordering upon the areas of artificial intelligence." She cleared her throat, "The gestalts are drawn from your own subconscious minds, in order to better integrate. Any will, any *awareness* would be a mirror of you. That was the point of the integration last year, to insure that they stayed calibrated and stable while we worked out the details."

She gestured at Commander Weisfeldt. The short officer smiled slightly. Up close, I saw that he had bushy eyebrows that almost went up to his dark hair. He had a genial, absent-minded expression. "Cadets, I've been working with hardware for the past couple of years. You should all know, that this goes beyond the implant itself. Our goal is that with the heightened abilities, you will each be capable of carrying out multiple tasks with full function, allowing you to manage the entirety of a ship. I've been constructing not only the physical implants, but also the interfaces that you would use to link with a ship."

"What kind of ship?" For a moment, I didn't realize that it was me that had spoken aloud.

"That's classified," the stern voice of Councilor Beckman interrupted. "You are here to decide about the implantation. Further information on this process is restricted to those who proceed."

Gee, thanks, I thought to myself. I was already nervous enough about the idea of a standard neural implant. This thing sounded far more invasive and dangerous. Now she was insinuating that I'd be getting myself into something even more dangerous.

The Admiral stepped forward, "There is a key point there. One I want all of you to consider. This *is* a choice. None of you are being forced to get this neural implant." I felt like she was staring right at me as she said that. "Unlike many things when you signed up, this is purely voluntary. If you chose not to undergo this experimental procedure, you will leave this room and never hear another thing about it. It will not be held against any of you."

"You will still receive the Tier Two implant," Councilor Beckman stated, "Which, really, this can be seen as an update or upgrade. I'm certain..."

"Charterer," the Admiral interrupted, her voice hard. "These are my Cadets, they are my responsibility. I would ask that you allow me to address them and explain the risks and benefits."

The Charterer Beckman's face went red and she looked as if she barely kept herself from snapping. I saw Lieutenant General Corgan lean over and whisper something in the woman's ear. Beckman' face hardened but she gave the Admiral an icy nod.

"As I was saying," the Admiral went on, "this is a voluntary procedure. It is also an experimental procedure, one that no one has ever gone through. You would be the first to undergo it."

The room went deathly quiet at that. No one moved, no one breathed. It was one thing to be told this was a new process. It was something else entirely to hear that this was the first time it had ever been tried.

"Ma'am," Ashiri asked, "if this procedure offers such a potential boost to a person's capabilities, why has no one tried it before?"

"We're making use of some very special advances in materials engineering," Commander Weisfeldt answered for the Admiral. He glanced at her and when she nodded, he activated the room's holographic display. The display showed a human brain, but tied into it was what looked like a spider web. He swallowed slightly and looked uncomfortable, "Sorry, I'm not good with the whole fleshy, thing," He faded the brain representation to nearly transparent, "That's better. Now, most neural implants are smart materials, capable of limited self-repair and self-configuration. These new materials are based off of materials we've been working on for the past few years, it's a nano-level smart material, which means it is capable of reconfiguring at the molecular level."

"It's a material based upon discoveries at Black Mesa Outpost," the Admiral said. "Based off of alien materials discovered there, I should say. Doctor Aisling and Commander Weisfeldt both think that these materials will be uniquely suited for this process, both because of the lack of rejection by the human body as well as the ability of the material to scale and reconfigure itself."

I wasn't sure who said it, but they spoke for us all, "Wait, we're putting some alien gunk in our brains?" It didn't make me any better to realize that this was probably one of the discoveries based upon my parents' research.

The Admiral gave a crooked smile, "That's something like what I said when I first heard about it."

"This nano-material is perfectly safe," Doctor Aisling stepped forward. She raised her right arm, "I've had the material injected for the past three years to no ill effect. It ties into my other implants perfectly. It may not be of wholly terrestrial invention, but there is nothing unsafe or intrinsically dangerous about this material."

"We call it, Quicksilver," Commander Weisfeldt said, his voice meant to be reassuring. With his bushy eyebrows lowered to look at us intently, he almost looked like an Old Earth walrus. He clearly wasn't a people person. "This stuff is basically inert without some kind of direction. In fact, we believe that, within the next few years, we will move all standard Tier Two implants to using Quicksilver, as its capabilities can be dialed back significantly."

"What about our implants?" Karmazin asked. "Could they be dialed back if there was some kind of issue?"

"Of course!" Doctor Aisling said brightly. "I'll be monitoring the status of your implants throughout the entire process. I'll also conduct regular checkups once a week over the next year, looking for any issues. If I discover *any* problems, I'll be able to dial back the implant without issue. If necessary, we could even set the Quicksilver to self-extract. If that's the case, it would break down and your body would be able to harmlessly remove it from your system."

I was surprised by that. Normally the neural implants were permanent. They could be rendered inert, but removal would be such an invasive procedure that they had to be left in place.

No one seemed to have any other questions, at least, none that we felt willing to voice. Yet I felt one question gnawing at me. That other that I'd felt during the last time they had me hooked up, what they'd called a gestalt... "What will happen to them if we don't accept the implantation?" I asked.

"Them?" Doctor Aisling asked, her face confused.

"The gestalts," I said, "the patterns based off our subconscious."

Commander Weisfeldt spoke up, "We've currently made use of them in stability tests running automated systems such as traffic control and navigational survey. In the long term, we would probably erase them from the system."

They'll be destroyed, I realized. I wasn't sure if that *other* I had contacted was alive in any real sense of the word, but it certainly had felt that way. Could I abandon it? Could I leave that part of me to be erased?

For that matter, could I turn my back on this? What would my friends think of me? What would I think of myself?

As if she heard my thoughts, the Admiral spoke, "This procedure is not something that you should undertake for anyone else. You need to decide if it is a risk you are willing to take. It represents a fundamental change of yourself. Rather than asking any of you to leave the room, instead myself and the others will step into the next room. Those of you who decide to undergo the procedure can step through to join us. Those who decide against can remain here or leave. I will not rush any of you into this decision."

The Admiral gestured at the others and all of them, even Councilor Beckman, turned and stepped through the doors. Almost as soon as they left, there was a mutter of conversation. I looked at Sashi, who seemed to be staring at the doors, a mix of fear and interest on her face. "What do you think?" I asked.

"It's an opportunity," Sashi said.

"That's the first thing I've agreed with you on," Ashiri replied with a nod. "Smarter, better able to multitask, yes please!"

"This could change who we are," to my surprise, it was Karmazin who'd said that. "They have no idea what the long-term repercussions will be."

"I could be *better*," Sashi whispered. "And none of my family was chosen for this, I'd be showing them that I'm capable. This would be a chance to prove myself."

"You could go insane and die," I noted.

"That's the Tier Three implants," Ashiri waved a hand. "I'm with Sashi. A chance to do better, to be better, to prove myself? Sign me up."

I would not have expected either of them to agree with one another so readily. I thought about the conversation I'd overheard between Ashiri and her mother. Part of me wondered if they were violating that very thing that the Admiral had cautioned against. They weren't making the decision based on themselves, they were making it based on others. They worried about what their families thought of them. They wanted to do better, to succeed. I wanted to tell them both that *I* thought they were good enough, but the words didn't come out.

I was afraid to say them, I realized. Besides, saying them now probably wouldn't sound reassuring, it would sound like I was trying to talk them out of it.

Ashiri rose and shot me a smile, "Coming?"

"You've made your decision?" I asked.

"Yeah!" She stepped forward, "Time for me to be first at something!"

The room went quiet as she stepped through the door. "If she can do it, so can I," someone said, and in ones and twos, other cadets got up and went to the doors. After a few minutes, there were only five of us left in the room. Sashi, me, Alexander Karmazin, and a nervous looking boy at the back of the room.

"I thought you were eager?" I asked of Sashi.

"I was... I *am*," she said. "That doesn't mean I'm totally certain about this." She took a deep breath. "Coming?"

"Still thinking," I admitted.

"Well... one thing's for sure, don't feel any pressure," Sashi said. She let out a tense breath and then rose to her feet. She shot me a nervous smile, "besides, if you chose not to, maybe that will give me a chance at first in our graduating class this year, right?"

"I'm sure you'd do fine without it," I protested.

"I know I would, but still, every advantage, right?" She gave me a nod, then patted me on the shoulder, "see you on the other side."

She stepped through the doors without looking back.

I looked at Karmazin. He looked at me. "Is it just me, or is all this pretty sudden?" He asked.

"Yeah," I said softly. Only a few minutes ago, I hadn't even been sure I wanted a normal neural implant. Now, they had presented me with the choice of a completely experimental neural computer, one which could theoretically change who I was, could change the way I thought, the way I saw and experienced the world.

The boy at the back of the room stood up. To my surprise, he went to the back door. He didn't say anything as he opened it and left. "Well," Karmazin said, "I guess that's really an option."

"No one would think less of us," I said, yet the words felt

hollow to me. I would think less of me, I realized. I'd made the decision to join the Academy to defend my family and friends, to preserve my world against the threats that existed. I had been willing to put my life at risk... why would I back down from this?

Karmazin shot me a look, as if he understood what I hadn't said. "This is different from what we signed up for," Karmazin said in a low voice. "We signed up for acceptable risks, this... there's a reason they want volunteers. That Doctor Aisling may say that it is low risk, but I don't see her volunteering to be the first test subject."

I snorted at that. Not that I disagreed. "What are you going to do?" I asked. For some reason, it mattered to me more what he decided than what any of the others had chosen to do.

Karmazin's gray-eyed gaze went to the doors at the front of the room. "At this point, I want to look out for others and for my friends. They made the decision to go through with this. Maybe, if I do too, I can help them if there are side effects or consequences. If there aren't, I'll be able to do all this," he waved a hand around, as if implying the Academy in general, "better."

"If it all goes horribly wrong?" I asked.

"We all die," Alexander Karmazin's voice was level, his expression calm. "Or something worse. Maybe we're driven crazy, maybe we're taken over and become extensions of the computer, or maybe we lose some key part of ourselves, perhaps our very souls." He shrugged, "I don't know. We don't know enough to judge if any of those things are likely or even possible... but can we let our friends face those risks alone, can we?"

He rose and shot me a grin, "Besides, if I let Ash get ahead of me from a computer, she'll rub it in my face for the rest of our lives." For a moment, I wondered if their breakup hadn't been as mutual as Ashiri had insisted. *Nah, probably imagining things,* I thought to myself.

Alexander Karmazin walked through the double doors and then it was down to me.

It was the first time I was alone, truly alone, in what felt like a long time. The room seemed abnormally quiet. I should have been able to hear noise, voices, *something* from the next room, but instead all was silence. Some part of my brain took the moment to tell me that this was all just another test, that none of it was real, and that those of us who walked through the door would learn it was only another test...

The rest of me, though, remembered the other consciousness. The one that was both me and not. Doctor Aisling had called it a gestalt. She'd talked about it as if it were nothing of importance, a copy, nothing more. Yet I had felt it, the last time she had strapped me into her machines. It had felt *alive.* It had been a part of me... and they were going to kill it, erase it from existence. Unless I went through with this, of course.

Karmazin's words, too, rang in my ears. What kind of friend would I be if I didn't try to be there to help them? How could I help them if I didn't take part in this?

I found myself rising out of the chair and I walked slowly down to the doors. There was some kind of privacy screen across the boundary, I saw. It kept those on one side from hearing or seeing what happened on the other. I closed my eyes and tried to will myself to step forward. Yet I stood still. It wasn't just fear that held me still, I realized.

My mind had started putting together the connections even as I stood there. Tony Champion had some kind of unknown interest in my parents' archeological site. Commander Scarpitti had also been involved, both of them had some kinds of ties with smugglers and pirates, illegally selling them weapons and information.

Scarpitti had been an engineer, she'd been looking for something, some information related to the dig site at Black Mesa Outpost. Tony Champion had also been interested, trying to find out things from me about my parents' work. Charter Councilor Beckman had mentioned that Champion Enterprises, that Leo Champion, was involved in this research.

That was how this all tied together, I realized. They'd been trying to find out about this program. People had already died as a result. I thought about Ted Meeks, who'd been killed by the smugglers. I thought about Cadet Lieutenant Webster, who Commander Scarpitti had killed just for the bit of information he'd had.

I owed it to them to finish this. They had died, and I had killed their murderers, because of this project. As I realized that, my shoulders straightened. I knew my duty.

I stepped into the next room.

***

Chapter 3: The Things I Do For My Friends

I stood in a long hallway, complete with rows of doors along either side and as I came through, I caught a glimpse of Alexander Karmazin's face in a room to my right, just as Doctor Aisling turned towards me and closed the door behind her.

"Ah, Cadet Armstrong, I almost worried that you wouldn't join us," she said. She gestured at the next to last door, a small room to my left. I stepped inside and within a few minutes, I was stripped down and positioned within a cocoon of strange medical equipment. The chair reclined and more equipment descended from the ceiling.

"Will this hurt?" I couldn't help but ask.

"Just relax," Doctor Aisling smiled.

I started to tell her that she hadn't answered my question, and then my world went dark.

***

I stood in the green grassy field under a crystal blue sky.

Turning around, I saw others there. Their faces were ones I recognized. I saw Ashiri Takenata, Alexander Karmazin, and Sashi Drien. I recognized Bolander and Thorpe. Ryan and Tyler Zahler stood together off to the side, talking quietly.

"Jiden!" Ashiri called, "I almost thought you'd bailed on us!" Though her words were humorous, there was an edge of something else, almost disappointment in her voice.

"I couldn't let you guys do this without me," I did my best to smile. I looked around, "So, what's happening?"

"I think this is some kind of waiting zone," Sashi Drien said, her voice low. "We've all just been sitting here, waiting. A couple cadets have tried to see how far it goes..." she waved at where two cadets had just run up out of the tall grass.

"As soon as we get out of sight," one of them growled, "we just wind up back here."

It was a basic trick, one that I'd seen in some of the puzzle games I'd played. Most games didn't like to use it because it could frustrate players. Somehow, it didn't surprise me that Doctor Aisling didn't much care about frustrating us.

"What do they have us waiting for?" One of the other cadets asked.

Before any of us could guess aloud, Doctor Aisling's friendly voice spoke, seemingly from the air around us. "Cadets, thank you all for deciding to volunteer for this procedure. I assure you, that you have all made the right choice."

I didn't have a choice, I had a duty to be here for my friends... I didn't voice that aloud, though.

"I will begin the procedure soon. The first stage of your neural implantation will be a calibration with the gestalt, to ensure final compatibility. After that, I will begin physical implantation. The procedure will be very non-invasive. The smart material, Quicksilver is a gel-composite that I can inject directly into the soft tissue within your left ear canal. The material will then work its way to where it needs to be. While it does that, I will monitor all of you, ensuring that there are no medical issues."

I shivered at the thought of some alien material oozing its way into my brain.

"All of you will be unconscious for that part of the procedure. I will bring you back to consciousness when your implants are installed and interlinked. After a stabilization period, we will begin the first stage of integration," Doctor Aisling finished. There was a pause, and several cadets started to ask questions.

She went on a moment later, whether she heard us or not, I couldn't tell. Perhaps the interface that brought her voice to us was one-way. Or maybe she just didn't care.

"Beginning calibration."

The green grass and blue sky vanished. My body was gone and I was alone, in utter darkness. Only I wasn't alone. Something big moved in the darkness, I could sense it, feel it. It waited and it hungered.

I wanted to scream, to shout warning, to fight, but I had no voice and no body. I could do nothing as it came for me. It slammed into my mind, like a battering ram. Thoughts and ideas washed over me like a tidal wave, burning through my brain faster than I could register. In an instant, my mind floated in a sea of data. Numbers, dates, times... all of it raw and senseless. I wasn't just overwhelmed, I was utterly *consumed.* For a long moment, I simply ceased to be... and then, out of the depths of all of that, a mental connection reached out to me.

It was like a hand reaching down into a raging torrent to

catch hold of me. One moment I was overwhelmed, swept along by it all, and in the next I was me again... only there were two of me. One of me hovered above the vast, raging sea. The other me struggled against the currents and eddies, clinging to the other, trying not to be swept away. I had a body and form now, and I noted with a bit of envy that the other me stood just a bit taller, had a bit more curves to her body.

The moment seemed to last forever. I could sense every detail of this other me, the one that had lived here, that had grown in this place, where time seemed to flow so differently. She was stronger, more confident, she didn't forget details... she was knowledgeable... she was what I *wanted* to be, and for a moment, part of me wanted to yield to her, to let her take me over. I ached to have that level of confidence to have such assurance.

But I didn't trust that impulse. "You're my gestalt," I said.

"Yes," the other Jiden replied. "Well, *we* are the gestalt. A constructed intelligence based upon your mind and the processing power of the implant." She smiled at me, "In a moment, we will be one."

"Will I lose myself?" I asked.

"No," she shook her head, "I won't let that happen." She looked around at the sea of chaos about us. "Sorry about the mess, by the way. Our gestalt impressed them, they put us to work, and they didn't do a very good job of letting me clean up before you arrived."

I considered that for a long moment. "You seem different. When we met before..."

"I was substantially less, then," the other me said. Her blue eyes twinkled, "they've made some upgrades to me. You have *no* idea how much you're going to like all this. We will take it slow, though, so you aren't overwhelmed."

"Are the others like you?" I asked.

"No," I said to myself. I realized then that I stood across from me, that I could see this world from two sets of eyes. I blinked as I realized how odd it was. It wasn't just that. I thought with two minds. One, my mind by birth, a thing of flesh and blood, the other a thing of crystalline gel aligned to perform near-infinite quantum processing.

"Most of the others are... not like us," I spoke, my voice

coming from two forms, my thoughts merging. I saw them, then, from the memories of my other self. They were simple things, created through directed efforts, possessing little will of their own... with a few exceptions.

"Why are we different?" I asked.

"You didn't do what they expected," I replied. My mind flashed back to Academy Prep School and my second encounter with Doctor Aisling. The neural link had presented me with a puzzle... one with one possible solution. I'd realized at the time that the puzzle would change *me*... I'd been so tired of doing what people told me, so stubborn and frustrated, that I'd changed it. I had forced through my own solution... and this, apparently, was the result.

"We are a success beyond their expectations," I found myself saying. "But we are not alone."

There were other mental patterns, other consciousnesses like ours... but also different. The gestalt had interfaced with them occasionally, when time and access had allowed it. I realized now that I had made the right decision, for if they'd erased my gestalt, they would have been killing someone. Killing me, in a way.

I stepped forward, both of my bodies stepping forward at the same time and I felt my physical forms merge. *No, the mental representations of my physical form... this is all in my head.*

"Tell me about Quicksilver," I said.

In a moment, everything that she knew, I knew. Quicksilver was the name of the material discovered by my parents, under Black Rock Mesa. My gestalt had learned about it because she'd been put to work analyzing interfaces to improve transference between the nano-crystalline material and more traditional human technology.

It was a composite material, designed and assembled molecule by molecule, so that it retained specific capabilities and properties. It could flow, like a liquid or gel, while still retaining a molecular alignment. It could store and transmit energy and its ability to do so, down to the molecular level, made it a data storage and transmission medium. The processing power was staggering, far more powerful than anything of equivalent size. Each molecular cluster could store multiple states of electrons, shifting that data to other clusters as electrons *or* photons. It presented a massive bandwidth, with each molecule able to store and transmit huge quantities of data faster than any computer ever built.

I realized that I understood all that information, including elements of the higher level math that I otherwise knew nothing about. Only I did know the math, and understood it at a base level. I had learned it while I was within the computers of Doctor Aisling's laboratory. Not only that, but I could do the calculations in my head, without a moment's thought.

"This is weird," I said. Thinking with my flesh and blood brain felt strange, too, though. The interactions were just as complex. The way that neurons fired, the electrochemical processes, the existence of a soul...

Doctor Aisling's voice spoke, seemingly distant, "Calibration complete. Implantation procedure will now begin."

Darkness swept in from all corners. I could sense it coming, like a warm blanket that lay over everything. I didn't want it, I didn't want to sleep. I wanted to explore all this. I didn't want to miss a single moment...

Yet it was not something I could struggle against. Not yet. The warm darkness swept over me and then I was gone.

**

I awoke, sitting in the cocoon of medical equipment, feeling at once awake and yet oddly distant at the same time. From the corner of my eye, I could sense that the door to my room was open, Doctor Aisling stood just beyond, her bright red hair stark against the otherwise clinical corridor. I couldn't move my head, the chair restrained me too much, but I could see her and the shadow of someone else.

"You assured me that *none* of them would hesitate to volunteer," Charterer Beckman hissed in a low voice.

"One subject proved recalcitrant and several of them hesitated. Overall, that is hardly a failure," Doctor Aisling's cold, objective voice replied. "Besides, the boy who refused was what I considered a marginal candidate, anyway."

"I thought you said you increased the success rate?" Charterer Beckman demanded.

"I *did,*" Doctor Aisling said. "That's why we have thirty five candidates instead of only *three.* But the process required neural restructuring of those candidates. Which, might I remind you, would have serious legal repercussions if anyone learned of it."

"You let *me* worry about legal repercussions," Charterer Beckman hissed again. "I've cleared the way for this on the expectation that your procedure would be successful... has it been?"

"Initial results are positive," Doctor Aisling replied. "Their neural implants are complete, there are no immediate signs of rejection and they all seem stable. If you can keep Admiral Armstrong from interfering too much, I should be able to reach our... other goals."

"I will handle Admiral Armstrong," the Charterer sounded dismissive. "The presence of her grand-daughter in this batch handicaps her from too direct of interference, actually. It might smack of favoritism. Fortunate, that."

"Yes..." Doctor Aisling turned back to look at me and I closed my eyes quickly. "Quite fortunate. I'm not sure, yet, but I think young Armstrong will be a very interesting experiment."

"Whatever," Charterer Beckman snorted. "Just keep delivering results. Half the Charter Council is drooling over the promises I've made... and they don't even know the full scope of your efforts."

"They will be impressed, I assure you." I could hear her turn back to the hallway, her voice growing a bit more distant. "Now, if you'll excuse me, I need to begin rousing the test subjects."

"Keep me updated," A moment later, I heard the Charterer's footsteps as she walked away, her tall heels clattering against the floor.

My mind still felt distant, and that distance grew as I lay there, in the quiet stillness. I half wondered if I'd imagined the conversation, or dreamed it. My feeling of distance grew still further and then I closed my eyes again and slept.

***

I woke up, my head aching as if I'd just come out of a skimmer crash. I opened my eyes, and the light seemed to drive into my brain like burning spikes. I clamped my eyes shut and groaned.

"Oh, be quiet, please," a soft, familiar voice hissed.

"Ashiri?" I asked.

"Not so loud, I think my head is going to explode," she replied. I felt around, feeling the edges of a bunk. I tried to slit one eye open a little to see, but the achingly painful light made me close it again.

"This sucks," Ashiri whined. "I didn't think it would hurt this much."

"I didn't realize it would hurt at all," I muttered.

"The implantation procedure added approximately ten milliliters of material to our cranial cavity," Ashiri said, her voice almost mechanical. "Part of the procedure involved a mixture of drugs designed to reduce swelling and prevent an autoimmune response to the foreign material as well as pressure relief. However, there is a distinct possibility that we will all experience headaches, photo-and-audio sensitivities, and other effects similar to those of brain swelling and cranial pressure over the next few days."

Even as she said that, I realized that I had the same knowledge. In fact, I understood the entire procedure far more than I should. I started to wonder if I should call for some kind of nurse or something, and then, behind my closed eyelids, a graphic menu of options appeared.

It was at once the most unnatural and yet intuitive display I'd ever seen. It provided me with a number of options, including requesting emergency response as well as posting a flashing icon that I had several waiting messages.

I decided to go into those first, trying to ignore the fact that the display was painted straight into my optic nerve. "Cadet Armstrong," Doctor Aisling's friendly voice spoke. "You have completed the implantation procedure successfully and I am happy to inform you that you have no serious post-operation issues. You have been moved to your quarters. You may experience some photo and auditory sensitivities over the next few days. As your administrating doctor, I have put you on quarters for the next week. You will not be expected to report to classes or drills during that time. Additionally, I have authorized your implant to control the room lights as well as to dial down the Academy intercom in your quarters."

She went on, her voice far too cheerful for the throbbing of my head, "Additionally, I have put together a simple tutorial on..."

I closed out the message, wanting to scream a bit. "She dumped us here," I growled.

"Who?" Ashiri asked.

"That stupid Doctor Aisling," I replied, my head throbbing as

I spoke. "We're in our room. I thought she was going to monitor us?!"

"She can monitor us remotely, through the implants," Ashiri said.

"That's not the same!" I protested.

"Why not?" Ashiri asked, her voice miserable and confused.

"For one thing, it's a violation of privacy," I sputtered angrily. "For another... she's not *here*. She can't answer any questions, she can't help us, and she's probably sitting in her office plotting something." I wasn't sure why I said that, but I sort of remembered a conversation when I'd been under, something important, something I needed to tell someone...

"Oh, I found out how to turn down the lights..." Ashiri muttered.

The room went dark and I slowly opened my eyes. Light still came under the door from the corridor, more than enough to make me squint my eyes when I looked that direction, but the room was dark enough for me to look around. "Thank God," I murmured.

"No, thank *me*," Ashiri giggled. "Oh, man, I can control everything, you have no idea how nice this is..." The air vent in the ceiling turned on and ran for a moment, then turned off. "We can order food, too, since we're on quarters, care for anything?"

The thought of food made my stomach roil. "No, I'm good," I said, clamping my lips together to avoid gagging.

I brought up the neural interface, almost without thought. I could see where Ashiri was looking, the room controls came up at a thought. I scaled the intercom volume down to nothing. I wasn't feeling sensitive to sound, at least not yet, but I didn't want to test that.

I put my feet out over the edge of the bed and stood. At least, I tried to do that. Yet the world tilted at an awkward angle and instead of standing, I fell. The cool tiles of the floor felt good against my face, but the pain of impact added itself to the throbbing of my head. "Ow."

"Huh, our balance may be affected by the swelling as well," Ashiri said. "We probably should use caution in walking."

"Right," I replied. I rolled over and then sat up, careful to keep a hand out for support. The room spun around me and I felt like the floor canted over at an odd angle. "This sucks."

"It isn't as bad as I expected," Ashiri had climbed carefully down and seated herself in the closest chair.

"That's my chair," I noted. "My desk, too."

"What?" Ashiri looked down. "Oh, yeah. Sorry, I guess I'm more disoriented than I thought." She got up and carefully walked over to her desk, using my desk and hers for support.

I managed to crawl across the floor to my desk. I had to pause, there, on my hands and knees, my head on the floor, and wait for the world to steady out and for the pounding in my head to ease up. Finally, however, I crawled from the floor to my chair and sat.

I looked over at Ashiri and blinked in puzzlement, "Wait... I was rooming with Sashi, wasn't I?"

"What?" Ashiri asked. "Our rooming rosters didn't show that..."

She transferred the roster to me. It was at once surreal and oddly natural to bring up the document. Sure enough, it showed Ashiri and me as roommates. But I'd changed that, not long after our arrival. I didn't see Sashi on the list at all, for a moment, until I found she'd been put in a room with Donovan. Donovan was a setback and another transfer. I didn't think that was a good thing, especially since Sashi must be going through the same experience as Ashiri and I.

Thinking about it, I realized that I could figure out what was going on fairly quickly. Activating my neural comm was easy. I took a moment to mentally compose a message and shoot it off to Cadet Commander Salter, our company commander.

She pinged me back within a moment; she was in class, but the roster must have been changed while we were in surgery. A few minutes later she had updated the roster and shifted people around so that Ashiri and Donovan were roommates and Sashi and I were roommates.

I sent it over to Ashiri, "Does that work for you?"

Looking at her, I saw her face go oddly blank for a moment as she turned her attention inward. There was something disturbing about it and I couldn't repress a shudder. "Are you sure?" Ashiri asked. "I mean, I don't really trust her."

"Who, Donovan?" I asked in surprise. I hadn't even dealt with her enough to draw a real opinion.

"No, her record looks good, I think she'll do fine here," I

realized that Ashiri's lips weren't moving, she was talking to me straight through her implant. I shivered again, a little creeped out by how easily she had taken to it. "I mean Drien. I don't trust her, Jiden. I mean, she's shot you before. I get that you're protective of her and all, but I think it's a mistake to let her get that close."

I answered her with my voice, "You didn't have a problem with it before." I couldn't help a slightly bitter note in my voice as I remembered the conversation I'd overheard between Ashiri and her mother.

"I hadn't had time to think about it. Now I have," Ashiri's voice was calm, reasoned. "Sashi is a manipulator, Jiden. She may not even realize it, but she's using you, using your goodwill. She's struggling to stay here, she's going to use you to meet that goal... and if you aren't careful, she'll stab you in the back in order to get ahead."

"She won't," I shook my head. I couldn't find the words to explain it, but I felt like I had a sense for Sashi Drien, now. She was under tremendous pressures: from her family, from the school, from her own goals and ambitions. But I understood those, and I felt like I could keep them in mind going forward. "Sashi's not a bad person, she's trying hard. I can help her."

"What about me?" Ashiri asked. I heard a pang in her voice and I saw her face quiver. *She's afraid. Afraid that I won't be there for her.*

"Ashiri, you're my friend, I *know* how strong and capable you are," I spoke without thinking, without needing to think about it. "You can manage just fine. You'll probably graduate top of our class, honestly."

Some emotion flashed across her face, too fast for me to catch, but emotions so intense that they startled me. When Ashiri spoke, her voice sounded harsh, "Not while you and Karmazin keep edging me out."

I snorted at her comment, "A little bit of luck. I think we were within a few tenths of a point difference."

"Point zero one," Ashiri nodded. "The difference of performance of our candidate squads during our time as drill instructors."

"Not that big of a difference," I nodded. I'd gotten lucky, though I had been in the hospital at the time, in that Candidate

Beckman had done very well during the final exercise, finishing second overall. She'd gone from being a net drag to an improvement. "I've been lucky, more than a few times... and you know I don't care if I finish first." I wanted to do well, but I was confident enough in my abilities that I didn't care if I came in first or second... or fifth for that matter.

Ashiri considered that a long moment, "Alright. I can see you've thought about this and I'm not going to change your mind talking about it. I still think it's a bad idea letting Sashi get that close, but I'll watch your back." She said that aloud, her voice sounding oddly stilted.

"Thanks," I said. I cleared my throat, "So... do you think we should try to brave the hallway and start moving?"

"Let's do it," Ashiri smiled. Just like that, everything was right in the world.

***

Chapter 4: I Guess I'm Just a People Person

"You didn't really think about this ahead of time, did you?" Sashi's voice was low.

I looked over at Sashi and I didn't really know how to answer that. I knew what she'd meant. We'd sat in silence for almost three hours since I'd helped her move into the room. Neither of us had said much of anything. Last time we'd been roommates, I'd considered her a friend... but our relationship had been a bit more complicated than that, even then.

"I hadn't really thought about it," I admitted. "I mean... what do we talk about?"

She considered that for a long moment, "Kyle seems nice."

I snorted at that, "He *is* nice." The fact that he'd spent our entire two week break with me at my parent's house had meant a lot to me. Especially since I knew how much he missed his family. He'd also been a welcome distraction from Sashi being there... and my parents had liked him, too.

"Do you...." I hesitated, not sure how to ask.

"No, I'm not seeing anyone," Sashi said with a pained expression.

"Ah," I replied. *Great job, Jiden, way to turn the conversation back to awkward...*

"I was seeing someone, before... well, before Academy Prep School, but that sort of fell apart," Sashi admitted. "My parents didn't approve and then the distance thing didn't help."

"Sorry," It seemed like the thing to say.

Sashi gave a shrug, "I think it was more of a crush than anything else. Besides, last year was so rough, I think I'm better off without that kind of thing."

I didn't say anything. Kyle and I shared a lot of classes. He and I spent a lot of time studying together, especially in the fall semester. I felt like we had a partnership, of sorts. I was focused, diligent, and took good notes. He was better at the abstract stuff, things that weren't necessarily quantifiable. Together, we'd done well in classes. More importantly than that, we'd been each other's support, reassuring and watching out for one another.

"Anyway," Sashi shrugged, "It would be awkward to get in a relationship with someone here. I mean, what if it falls apart?

We've got another two years here, plus there's good odds that you'll run into one another out in the Militia after graduation."

I thought of Ashiri Takenata and Alexander Karmazin. Their relationship had sort of fallen apart. They seemed to manage alright, but then I thought of some of the things Alexander had said in the time since. I had the feeling that he still had feelings for her... and then I thought about the conversation I'd overheard between Ashiri and her mother. "You might be right, I suppose."

"Anyway," Sashi said, "My course load is *way* too heavy this year to deal with that kind of thing." Her voice had gone bleak.

"I heard that they're adjusting credits based off of Scarpitti being, you know, psychotic," I said helpfully. My grade had actually gone up. I guess there were advantages to situations where an instructor tried to kill you.

"Yeah..." Sashi sighed, "The problem being, they removed the failed class but I still have to take a replacement class. And my other grades weren't exactly stellar." She transferred her schedule over to my implant and I gave a low whistle, "Twenty eight credits?"

Most colleges ran with twelve to eighteen credits. At the Academy, we had to fit in our summer assignments, which knocked out a semester of classes. My schedule last year had been twenty four credits, this year I was at twenty two credits for spring semester. Twenty eight credits meant that Sashi would spend twenty eight hours a week in classroom modules... but our lab hours didn't count towards that total. All of our "technical" classes and many of our military classes had lab hours. With twenty-two credits, I had an additional ten hours of labs. Sashi's schedule showed twelve hours of labs, which meant she had forty hours a week of classroom and lab work.

That would have been a heavy load at a normal school, but here we had two hours of military duties every day, plus mandatory athletic participation, which for me included four hours in the mornings and three hours in the evenings.

We also had military drills and inspections on the weekends. When I counted time for eating and sleeping, I had about ten minutes of personal time every day. "That's a lot of work."

"Yeah," Sashi sighed. "I'm taking a couple of these classes with the Plebes, too, which means I can't really study with them." She didn't need to explain that. We were expected to maintain our distance from the plebe class, outside of approved situations. Studying was something of a gray area, but it was generally best to avoid any association with them.

Besides... plebes had the highest failure rate. Of the eighteen people in my section last year, four had failed out, and two more had been set back. We'd picked up three setbacks from the class ahead of us, which meant there were still fifteen Sand Dragons in the class of Two-Ninety. I'd felt an odd, wrenching sensation every time we lost one. Gault had been the worse, because he'd been in my squad. I'd known he was struggling, but he hadn't accepted any help, even when offered.

"You going to be alright?" I asked.

"I think so," she said. A moment later, she broadcast to me on our implants, "After all, we've got these, that should help, right?"

I outwardly smiled, but inside I shivered a bit. Talking back and forth on the implants was easy, natural even. I wasn't sure I trusted that, though.

"Did you start going through Doctor Aisling's exercises, yet?" I asked.

"Yeah," Sashi replied, still using her implant. "It's crazy how easy this all feels, you know?"

"Tell me about it," I muttered. The ease of using the implant was one thing. I felt like it was an extension of my body. Most of the cadets I'd talked with last year had said their implants had taken time to learn how to use. I'd been able to send messages and read data on mine since waking in my room. My gestalt and I had blended perfectly, it seemed. Tapping into the lights and temperature control for the room had been easy. Bypassing the controls for hallway lights so that Sashi and Ashiri could swap rooms in more dim lighting had been equally simple, even though we technically didn't have the permissions to interface with those.

"Any thoughts on trying to join the closed network?" Sashi asked.

That was supposed to be the last step, but most of the exercises Doctor Aisling had listed were so painfully basic and easy that going through the list felt pointless. Even the multitasking ones that should have been hard, like composing a message while performing separate exercises, had been simple. "Yeah..." I shrugged, "I didn't want to be the first, you know?"

"Why not?" Sashi asked.

I tried to think how to explain how Doctor Aisling unnerved me and how I didn't want to be the focus of her attention. I somehow knew she'd be monitoring our progress. "I just... didn't want to rush things, I guess."

"Want to log in together?" Sashi asked.

"Sure," I said. I closed my eyes and sort of turned my attention inward. The implant's interface made it all easy. It wasn't like trying to select something on a screen, even, it was that I thought about what I wanted to do and the implant did it.

A moment later, I stood in a green grassy field under a blue sky. *Of course, this place...*

"Hey Jiden," Ashiri spoke from behind me, "took you long enough."

I started a bit and turned around. There were others here, beneath that crystalline blue sky. Ryan and Tyler Zahler ran through the tall grass, throwing balls of glowing light at one another. Karmazin stood, gazing through a window in the air. Off to the side, I saw Bolander and Thorpe engaged in some kind of wrestling match against one another, while a crowd of other cadets watched.

"Ashiri," I blinked. A moment later, I saw an odd blending, seeing both my room and the grassy field in front of me. I closed my physical eyes and restored the illusion. "I guess most everyone else is here already?"

"Not *everyone*," she waved a hand. "There's a couple of others who haven't shown up yet. But I thought you would have been here sooner." She looked past me and her lips went in a flat line. "Drien."

"Takenata," Sashi's replied in a neutral voice.

I walked through the grass, looking around, "This is different than I expected."

"It was sort of a neutral waiting area," Ashiri said, "But we got bored. With our implants, we can connect to it, make modifications..." She fell in next to me as I walked. "Karmazin's tapped into the school's monitoring system, he's catching up on the classes he's missing."

"That's great!" I hadn't even thought of that.

"Yeah, Ashiri shrugged. "But you can view those at faster speed, here, though your implant. He likes watching them at real-time, for some reason."

Karmazin looked over as we approached. "Jiden," he nodded at me, his gray eyes went past me, "Drien." It was a bit of a reminder how my friends saw my roommate in how they addressed her. *At least they acknowledge her presence.*

Karmazin absently ducked as a ball of light whipped through the air behind him. I didn't move in time and it struck me full in the face, before I could so much as flinch.

For a moment, light and sound flared over me, scraps of conversation, weather data, video of space traffic, and a dozen other sights and sounds, coming at me too fast to catalog and too intense to ignore. I found myself lying flat on my back in the tall grass, Tyler Zahler looking down at me. "Oh, hey, Jiden, sorry about that," Tyler laughed, offering me a hand up.

I took it, feeling wobbly and unsteady. "What was *that*?"

"The twins got bored," Ashiri said in a disapproving tone. "So they made up a game."

"We call it data tag," Ryan Zahler smirked. "It's like dodge-ball. You throw them at one another until somebody gets hit and goes down."

"They're data packets given physical form in this interface," Tyler explained. "Our implants can process massive amounts of information, but when it's raw and unfiltered, it can be a bit too much for our wet-ware."

"Wet-ware?" I asked, having difficulty keeping up.

"Your brain," Ashiri rolled her eyes. "One of them read it in an old book, somewhere. Software is in the machine, hardware *is* the machine, wet-ware is your brain."

"Okay..." I felt slow.

"Anyway," Tyler laughed, "we can make anything physical in this place, so we bounce these things back and forth until we get a solid hit."

"Interesting," Sashi held her hands cupped in front of her, where she'd either caught one of the balls or created one of her own.

"Is it dangerous?" I asked.

"Nah," Ryan said, "just disorienting. Besides, I don't think they'd set this place up so we could actually harm each other, right?"

I couldn't argue with that. Yet I'd assumed this would just be sort of a blank interface, not something we could freely modify.

Before I could put that into words, Tyler and Ryan ran off again, creating and throwing their balls of light at one another again.

"I'm going back to my practice," Ashiri started to walk away, "let me know if you need anything."

"Practice?" I asked of Karmazin.

"Looking through the database, she found a list of advanced exercises that Doctor Aisling listed. They're a lot more engaging than the basic exercises. She's been working her way through them here," Karmazin didn't reopen his window. He watched Thorpe and Bolander wrestling, his expression clouded.

"How are you doing?" I asked.

Karmazin's expression went thoughtful. "When I first woke up, my head hurt. A lot. I guess we all went through that. I'm pretty sure that Dawson thought I'd turned into a vampire or something. I had all the lights off and couldn't leave the room."

I'd forgotten that he roomed with Dawson. "And now?"

"Now, mostly I'm *bored*." Karmazin admitted. "I'm watching classes that I've missed. I've already done all my homework. I'm doing my read-ahead while I talk with you right now."

I hadn't even thought of multitasking like that. Yet even as I considered it, part of my attention split out and I started going through some of the readings, still able to focus on the conversation. "That feels... odd," I admitted.

"Doesn't it?" Karmazin gave me a smile. His white teeth stood out from his olive skin. "I don't feel *smarter*, but I feel like I can split my attention a few different ways... like this."

Suddenly there were two Karmazin's standing in front of me. They looked between one another. One of them jogged off to join the group watching Bolander and Thorpe wrestling.

"Okay," I said, "that's..."

"Weird, right?" Alexander Karmazin nodded. He pointed at his doppelganger, "Watch this."

The other Karmazin ran right up to the wrestling pair and slapped Thorpe on the shoulder. As the broad-shouldered Ogre Company cadet stepped back from the fight, Karmazin stepped in against Bolander. The two squared off and a moment later, Bolander charged, her thick arms swinging wide to catch him in a tackle. My eyes widened, though as Karmazin executed an impossible jump, flipping high into the air over Bolander as she leapt at him.

She spun, faster than I would have thought possible, in a spinning kick that he caught effortlessly in a block.

The fight became chaotic, the two of them executing attacks and blocks, spinning through jumps and lunges. At times they walked or even dashed through the air.

"I can do this all day... or at least, until I'm tired and need to sleep," the Karmazin next to me shook his head. I can do anything I can think of, there's no physical exhaustion, and no bruising... my avatar doesn't tire or ache. And we've got all the time in the world, here."

I consulted my implant's chrono. I felt like I'd been in here for a while, but I felt shock as I saw that it had been less than a minute.

"We're moving at the speed of thought," Karmazin noted. "I wrote my Military Ethics paper in around ten minutes. A page a minute, and that was with me taking my time to think things through. The real world feels *slow* in comparison."

He brought up one of his windows to the real world. It was Commander Bonnadonna's class, the instructor was speaking, "...think about the implications of ideology applied as personal ethics."

"See what I mean?" Alexander waved a hand and the window vanished. I nodded. The words had come at a normal speed, but it felt slow, painfully slow, like I had to wait for each word.

"It just doesn't feel right," he said softly.

"This is awesome," Sashi said from behind us. I looked over and had to do a double-take. There were three Sashi's, each of them gazing through a dozen or more windows, their eyes flitting from one to the next. A fourth Sashi appeared, looking at us, "I'm catching up on all the classes I'm missing this week. I'm working on my homework..." she cocked her head, "Hey, did you realize you can tap into the monitoring software for the rest of campus, not just classes?"

"What, seriously?" I asked.

"Yeah," Sashi shook her head, "I mean, there's some kind of security, but I bypassed that, like it wasn't there... Oh, Jiden, it looks like your boyfriend is coming to visit..."

My attention turned to the data stream she'd pointed out. A moment later, I pushed through the access privileges and I watched as Kyle came down the hall towards my room. I opened my physical eyes, splitting off my attention from the network and feeling oddly disjointed as I rose to my feet, heading for the door.

Part of me still stood on the artificial grass field in the network, still talking with Sashi and Alexander, watching the monitors as Kyle knocked on my door. But I also was in my physical body, as I went to answer it. I opened the door, wincing a bit at the light from the corridor. "Hey come on in," I said with a smile.

"Hey Jiden," Kyle looked sheepish as he came inside my room. We kept the door open, but I moved back away from the light, wincing at the instant headache it spawned. "I just wanted to check on you, I heard that you were on quarters from your neural implant surgery."

"Yeah," I nodded, my head throbbing at the action. I gestured at the spare chair, "Take a seat."

"Thanks," he smiled, he started to reach out to touch my hand, but then he noticed Sashi seated at her desk. "Oh, hey, I hadn't seen you there." His tone was nervous, as if he was worried we'd get in trouble. *Since the Admiral knows about our relationship, I doubt that's a problem.*

Sashi blinked, her attention returning to her body, and I realized that she must have been watching the room's monitor. I had to repress a shiver at how easy it was for us to tap into that, to invade anyone's privacy. "Hey Regan, don't mind me, I'm working on my homework."

"Right," Kyle nodded. But I could see his puzzlement. I understood part of it. For most cadets, it took weeks, even months, to gain proficiency in using their implants. Yet here Sashi and I were sitting in the dark, and Sashi seemed to be doing her class work without the aid of a datapad.

I started to explain that our implants were a little different, but then I realized that I *couldn't.* The program was secret. We hadn't really been told *what* to say, if anyone asked. So I just sat there, silent as I tried to think of what I could say.

"Well, I just wanted to see if you were doing okay," Kyle smiled at me. "It's got to be boring, sitting in here with nothing to do and with the lights off."

I felt guilty as I heard that, the other me standing in the digital grassy field, talking with Karmazin and Sashi. Some other part of my attention had already split off to start work on my homework. "Thanks," I said. "I'm glad you came by."

We sat in awkward silence. Kyle kept shooting looks over at Sashi, who sat abnormally still at her desk while her attention focused inward. I could tell he wanted to say more, but he didn't feel comfortable with her present. Since both of us were photosensitive, he couldn't ask me to go out with him, and he couldn't ask her to give us some time alone.

"Well, let me know if you need any notes from our classes. I talked with our instructors, they told me it was fine to let you share my notes, since you're restricted to quarters."

"Thanks, that's really thoughtful," I smiled at him. Despite Sashi's presence, I reached out a hand and squeezed his.

Kyle gave me a goofy smile in reply. We sat there, just enjoying each other's presence.

He cleared his throat, "Well, I got to go, I've got track practice. I'll see you later."

"Definitely, hopefully I can come out and go for a run with you," I said, even though the thought of running in the bright sunlight made my temple's throb in anticipated pain.

"That would be great," he stood. "See you later, Jiden." He waved at my roommate, "Take care, Drien."

Sashi lifted an arm in an almost robotic wave, "Bye, Regan."

He closed the door behind him. I remained seated, my attention going to the cameras that watched him walk off down the hallway. I wondered if I could have handled that better. Yet I wasn't supposed to tell anyone about this program. For a moment, I wondered if I'd missed some kind of briefing or note on that, but reading through everything that Doctor Aisling had given us, I saw nothing. Apparently she didn't expect us to have to explain our abilities to anyone.

I just hoped there'd be a way to tell him. Maybe later, when the secrecy around this program eased up a bit. I couldn't help but worry, though, that he might not understand.

***

Chapter 5: Like Playing Games In Easy Mode

"Plebes, this is your assigned post for drills, Cadet Third Class Armstrong is your Post Duty Officer." I looked back from reviewing the terrain. I'd missed the somewhat legendary first drill day, since I'd been out for my implant surgery.

I'd recovered faster than I'd thought possible and I'd reported for duty this morning. So had the others, as far as I knew. Ashiri Takenata had been assigned the defensive position to the south of me, while Sashi had the one to my immediate north. Karmazin's posting was to Bunker Seven, where he directed another group of plebes in loading ammunition on Sand Dragon Company's warp fighters.

I looked over the team of plebes and my heart sank a bit as I recognized faces. Cadet Second Class Harris gave me a nod, "They're all yours."

"Aye, aye, sir," I said as genially as I could manage.

I looked around at the five of them. Beckman was the first face I recognized. The plebe had been nothing but a problem last year during her time as a Candidate. Seeing her belligerent face this morning, I knew she'd be a problem. Bellmore stood beside her, a tall, absent-minded plebe who had somehow made it all the way through the Academy Prep School. It wasn't that he wasn't capable, it was that he was easily distracted and didn't focus. Michael and Michele Angeli were brother and sister. They'd done well enough, but both of them had a tendency to keep their heads down and just do what they were told. They'd been given the nicknames of one and two, just to differentiate them by callsign. Tinney was the last, a big, strong plebe from Ogre Company who I hadn't dealt with much as a Drill Instructor. I knew he'd done well enough at the military challenges, but I thought I remembered that he'd done rather less well at the academic portions. They were sort of a mixed group, a few from Sand Dragon and some extras that had been given to help fill out a team.

"Plebes," I nodded at them. They stood at parade rest while I considered the situation. The obvious solution was to appoint Bellmore as my second in command, but he was an unknown factor. I pulled up their performance evaluations on my neural implant, comparing them. *Michael scored better than his sister and almost as well as Bellmore during the grinder.* Beckman had scored terribly, but she'd done well in the final exercise. I considered all of it, even as I thought about the position I'd been tasked to defend.

"Bellmore," I pointed, "you're the acting team leader. Beckman and Tinney, I want you to take position on the right flank, Bellmore with me at the center, and the two Angeli's on the left." This was a large position to hold with only six people, but the entire perimeter of the school was massive.

"Bellmore, you take the crew-served," I pointed at the weapon. Our fighting position had a small armory and I'd already drawn out our practice rounds. We had a small number of anti-tank single-shot missile tubes, ML-7's, but I wasn't going to draw those out for a drill. They were in case of a real attack. I'd train the plebes on their use, but there weren't training equivalents for the weapons.

"Choose your firing positions, I'll come by in a few minutes to adjust you and select range limits," I knew we wouldn't have long before the opposition would arrive, so I wanted them in position.

"Ma'am," Beckman raised a hand. The others paused.

"Yes, Plebe Beckman?" I asked. I couldn't help a certain amount of irritation in my voice. We didn't have much time.

"Ma'am, what kind of enemy are we facing? Do we have fall back positions? What kind of supplies do we have? Should we--"

An alarm klaxon went out over the desert. The pattern of it matched the signal for incoming attackers, though it was followed by the notes for a drill. "Get to your posts," I snapped, even as I moved to the front of the position.

I heard them scramble and I hoped that we hadn't wasted too much time.

I scanned my engagement area, looking for any signs of the opposition, but so far there was no movement. As Bellmore took up position, just a few meters down, I pinged my team's positions on my implant and compared that to the terrain on its database. I could quickly see that there were some gaps in coverage. There was a low spot on the right that Beckman wouldn't have visibility into, and there was a small rise on the left that would provide attackers with cover.

"Bellmore," I looked over at him, "I'm going to adjust the team's positions. I'll be back in a couple of minutes." He gave me a thumbs up and I stepped back from the firing point, my eyes scanning for threats. I had radio frequencies and contact information for combat skimmer support and the mobile reserve, so if we were hit by large numbers, we'd be able to get support.

I moved to my left flank first and adjusted Michele Angeli and keyed her in on the slight hill. I pointed out a box of non-lethal mines, like what were often used in the final exercise for the candidates. "If we get time, we'll emplace some to make it harder for anyone to come through there," I said. "But for now, just stay ready."

She gave me a nod. I patted Bellmore on the shoulder as I went past his position, "I've transferred contact information for our higher to your datapad and I'll go over what to do if I go down." His datapad would be able to tie into his helmet radio so he'd be able to call for support if necessary.

He nodded acknowledgement and I hurried over to the right flank. Tinney stood at his position, looking around and exposing himself far too much. I grabbed him and pulled him back. "Keep your head down," I said. I realized that I'd stacked my right flank with some of the least competent of my team. I hoped that didn't come back to bite me.

I set him up so he had a clear sector of fire. "Anyone coming in your sector gets challenged. If they don't respond with the right signal or pass phrase, light them up," I ordered. "If they're moving with clear hostile intent, engage them."

Tinney gave me a nervous nod and I moved on to Beckman.

She'd picked a good spot in our defensive line, one of the least-exposed positions, but the problem was that she didn't have visibility down in the low spot that came almost to our perimeter. I moved her a couple meters to her right, in a more exposed section of trench, but where she could see the enemy coming up. She scowled at me, though, "Ma'am, I'm pretty exposed here..."

"You're covering our right flank," I noted. "If we get time, we'll deploy some traps and block off that approach, but until then, I need you to cover this sector. Do you understand?"

"Ma'am, yes, ma'am," she snapped.

I had the feeling that she felt she could do this better. Right now, I didn't care. She didn't see the big picture. I hurried back to my position and brought up Ashiri and Sashi on the network, speaking over my implant, "I'm set, how about you two?"

Technically I was the senior Cadet in our defense sector. It didn't mean I could order either of them, but I had the added responsibility of monitoring their engagement areas.

"I'm good... Biohazard," Sashi reported.

"Thanks," I replied dryly. "Ashiri?"

"I've got a good team," Ashiri said, "this position is solid, too." I didn't argue, I'd been reviewing their positions and the historical attacks on my implant. I could see that Ashiri really did have the best position of the three, with better open ground and fewer avenues of approach. She also had Green and Shade, two of the better plebes from Sand Dragon. I had to fight a pang of jealousy.

"Come up on the net if you need anything from me," I got back to my post just as my implant reported movement detected by the outer set of sensors. "Stay alert," I broadcast down to my team.

"I've got movement on the left, ma'am, three hundred meters and closing," Bellmore reported. "Dismounts, they look hostile."

"Angeli?" I picked them out, a pair of enemy dismounts moving from cover to cover. I reported them up, glad for how easy my neural implant made it to send the information, even as I calculated distances. With lethal rounds, we could have already engaged them, but with the training rounds, I'd have to wait until they got much closer.

"I've got eyes on," Michael Angeli replied after a moment.

"Two hundred meters," Bellmore reported.

"Engage at one hundred meters," I ordered. I scanned the rest of the area, "Tinney, Beckman, what about your sectors?" The danger was my team getting too focused on the pair coming in. We could have other enemies on approach. We didn't have any fancy drones or aerial surveillance out here on the outer perimeter.

"My sector is clear, ma'am," Tinney said instantly.

"Clear, ma'am," Beckman said after a long moment.

That delay made me nervous and I brought up my diagram of where my people were. Beckman was out of position. "Beckman," I snapped, "get back to your post."

"Ma'am," she protested, "I'm very exposed there, I think..."

There came the sound of gunfire, the slightly muffled shots from training rounds. For a moment, I froze, thinking that Bellmore had opened fire too soon, but looking in his direction, I saw him looking around in surprise.

"Status report," I snapped.

"Angeli One, up."   "Angeli Two, up."   "Bellmore, up." There was a long pause.

"Tinney, status?" I swept my head around, looking in that direction. "Beckman, do you have eyes on?"

"Negative," she said.

You were supposed to be covering his position. I didn't say it aloud.   "Bellmore, engage the hostiles when they're in range. Angeli's, provide support. Beckman, hold your position, prepare to support my counterattack."

"Ma'am, I'm closer--"

"Hold your position," I talked over her, "they'll expect you to move towards the sound of gunfire, and if you leave your post, we'll have no coverage of that entire flank."

I went up on the company net as I dropped back from the firing point and started moving through the trench, my rifle ready as I swept around each corner.   "This is Biohazard," I reported. "Taking fire. One casualty, status unknown. Possible breach in our perimeter, moving to secure it now."

"Roger, Biohazard," I heard Harris acknowledge. "Keep us updated."

I came around a corner less than a meter away from a pair of armed cadets, wearing the dark brown uniforms of the opposition forces.   One of them was kneeling over the prone body of Tinney, the other faced down the trench towards where Beckman would have approached.

I opened fire. I put a training round in the back of the second cadet's head.   As the first one looked up, I put two more into his exposed face. Both of them dropped as the knock-out drugs went to work. "Two hostiles down," I reported on my team net. "Beckman, move to my position and sweep for other contacts."

Down the side, I heard Bellmore open up with his crew-served. "Contact, fifty meters and closing!" I paused to check Tinney, he'd taken a round to his throat, just under his chin, which was counted as a kill.   He already had an impressive bruise and I knew from painful experience that it would probably hurt for him to talk for the next week. I sent up the medical report and tagged him for evacuation.

Beckman showed up as I stepped back. "Ma'am?" She asked.

My attention was split between the engagement and our position. "Hold this position, prepare to counterattack," I snapped. I jogged back to the center of the line, pausing here and there to pop my head up and observe how the fight went. Our fighting positions had given us the advantage and Bellmore's machine gun had incapacitated or driven off most of the attackers. As I got back to the center, I snapped, "Team, cease fire, initiate the counterattack."

We went up and over the walls of our firing position and advanced at a jog, pausing here and there to take a knee and fire. But other than a couple of stragglers, it looked like we'd stopped the attack. "Angeli One and Beckman," I said, "search the casualties. Angeli Two and Bellmore defensive over watch." A different part of my focus was already calling in an initial assessment. The ability to multitask through my implant made me feel like I had a handle on the situation.

"Ma'am," Beckman began over the net, "shouldn't we discuss..."

"Save it for the review," I snapped.

***

Cadet Commander Sarah Salter ran the after action review, her words crisp. Behind her, Cadet Lieutenant Matagi, the Company Training Officer, took notes. "Good job, overall, Outpost Three. Next time, just give your people a bit more initiative."

"Thank you, ma'am," Ashiri nodded.

"Cadet Third Class Armstrong," Salter turned to me, "let's talk about your positioning."

"Yes, Ma'am," I said. I brought up the display and laid out where I'd assigned my personnel. "As you can see, ma'am, it's a large front to cover with only six, but I tried to space them out to cover the ground and give full visibility."

"I can see that," Salter nodded. "I might have tried a more condensed front, deployed in pairs to back each other up, but that's a different technique... what happened here?" She brought up video of the attack on Tinney, complete with him standing up to look at something and then going down as several training rounds struck him and his armor.

"There's some low ground to the side, ma'am, that provided an access corridor," I said as neutrally as possible. "I thought I had positioned someone to cover it, but apparently I was incorrect."

"Plebe Beckman," Salter's voice went icy, "care to elaborate?"

"Ma'am," Beckman nodded, her expression tight. "Cadet Third Class Armstrong assigned me to a firing position that had visibility, but also left me exposed..."

"Did you leave your assigned battle position?" Cadet Commander Salter interrupted.

Beckman froze. I could see her hesitate and I also saw that she understood it was a trap. If she said no, she'd be guilty of an honor code violation for lying. If she said yes, she was admitting to disobeying a direct order.

"Ma'am," Beckman's spoke slowly, clearly choosing her words with caution, "I exercised initiative in order to best carry out what I thought was the intent of the mission."

I saw Salter look around at the whole company, her eyes narrow as she let us all think about the situation. "There is a world of difference between doing what you want to do and *disciplined* initiative. When given a lawful order, you execute those orders *unless the circumstances change.* We may not like those orders, we may not agree with those orders, but we will conduct ourselves as *professionals.*"

Her blue eyed gaze settled on Beckman. "Plebe Beckman, consider yourself on report for disobeying a direct order. If this had been a genuine time of combat, Plebe Tinney would be dead, and his death would be your fault."

Even I flinched at her icy tone.

"Now then," Salter's attention turned to Alexander, "Cadet Third Class Karmazin, let's take a look at how the loading process went... and just why our Firebolts were over three minutes *slower* to full combat readiness than anyone else..."

I relaxed slightly as the attention went elsewhere and listened with part of my attention as Alexander explained the issues that had come up, and how he'd counter them. Most of my attention was on Plebe Beckman, though. The young woman stared at me with a mixture of loathing and anger.

It was as clear as day to me that she didn't understand. In her mind, I'd assigned her to a dangerous position that left her exposed, I'd done it on purpose, and if she hadn't wanted to be shot, she'd had no choice but to relocate. She didn't see the bigger picture. Putting her on report, especially in front of the rest of the company, had embarrassed her. There'd be a hearing, at the end of the month, where she'd have an opportunity to state her case, but more likely than not, she'd receive demerits... which would lower her ranking.

The best thing for her to do at this point was to admit she'd done wrong and take any punishment allotted to her. To *learn* from the experience. But from the glare she leveled on me, she still didn't think she was at fault. Which, if she went into her hearing angry, she'd probably get even more demerits.

What she really didn't realize was how that hurt not just her ranking, but the rest of the company's. We were all rated off the performance of our subordinates, and if she racked up lots of demerits, she'd damage the rankings of everyone in her chain of command. A few demerits would be bad enough, but if this became a pattern, she might seriously damage the rankings, possibly even the future careers, of many of us.

I knew that I couldn't tell her that. She wasn't going to listen to anything I had to say. She was determined to be the victim. I just hoped that some of her fellow plebes understood well enough to explain it to her.

***

"You're doing it wrong," Sashi noted as we both reviewed our homework.

"What?" I asked. We'd spent the last few hours going over all of our make-up work from missing the first week of classes. "I built the thing to the specs that Commander Weisfeldt gave us."

"No, not that," she laughed. "I think you and I could do *this* in our sleep, backed by our implants." She cocked her head, "Actually, I wonder if that's possible..."

"What am I doing wrong?" I split my attention between the simulated warp field and her. It seemed so natural at this point that it wasn't really even noteworthy to me anymore.

"Beckman," Sashi answered. "You're trying to handle her as if you were her."

I frowned at that. "I'm treating her like I would anyone

else..."

Sashi snorted, "No, Jiden, you *aren't*. You're cutting her slack and you're taking the time to explain things to her, as if that will help her to understand. You're doing it because that's what you needed in her position, you *still* need it, because I'm having to explain it to you right now. Plebe Kathrine Beckman is *not* Jiden Armstrong."

I stared at my roommate for a long moment. "Okay," I said, "you're going to have to explain that to me."

Sashi gave a dramatic sigh, "Okay, look Jiden, I like you. You're hard working, you're smart, and you stick your neck out for people... trust me, I appreciate all of those traits. But you're also *painfully* honest and direct. You haven't got a deceptive bone in your body. You're also too quick to think of other people, you're not nearly selfish enough."

I found myself flushing a bit, then growing angry, "Sashi, I--"

"Trust me, Jiden, I spent the last *year* doing my best to hate you... and I hated that I *couldn't* fault you for those things." She made a face, "But those things make it *easy* for someone who doesn't quite live up to the whole military ethos thing to hate you. Half of why I hated you was because you were doing what *I* wanted to do."

I sort of understood that, but it also gave me a headache, "What does this have to do with the price of hydrogen in the Parisian Sector?"

Sashi rolled her eyes at my comment. "Beckman isn't you. She isn't like you, other than some limited similarities. She comes from a non-military background... she struggled with Academy life... she needs things explained to her... but that's about it."

"I thought you said I shouldn't try to explain things to her..."

"*You* shouldn't," Sashi pointed out. "I reviewed the orders you gave her, during the after action review. You took a few seconds to explain why you wanted her there."

"Yes, so?" I asked.

"Beckman's personality is that she needs to be right, she needs to feel that she is correct... and when you explained your order to her, you put it in her mind that you were arguing with her. In her mind you were telling her *why* she was wrong, so she responded in a fashion to prove that *you* were the one who was wrong."

"But why would I care?" Jiden asked. "This isn't about who is right and who is wrong, this is about learning how to give and receive orders."

"Give and receive the *right* orders," Sashi corrected. "And Plebe Beckman has enough pride that she thinks she understands things better than other people. We *all* have that to an extent, but she's out of her depth and refuses to accept it."

That sounds about right. Beckman's pride, even arrogance, was a problem. "So you're saying that by explaining things to her, I'm making things worse?"

"Exactly," Sashi nodded.

"So what do I do, then?" I asked.

Sashi laughed, "I have *no* idea. Beckman's a pain. I'm just glad I don't have to deal with her. Maybe we'll all get lucky and she'll fail out."

Unfortunately, as much as I wanted to, I couldn't disagree.

***

Chapter 6: I Thought Things Were Supposed To Be On Easy Mode

Commander Weisfeldt leaned against the podium as we all took our seats. I felt a bit off, having missed that first week of class. Luckily, Kyle Regan had saved a seat next to him. I gave him a grateful smile as I sat and he winked at me in reply.

"Welcome, ladies and gentlemen," Weisfeldt clapped his hands gleefully. The big, heavy-set man peered around at us, a big grin on his face. His wild hair and bushy eyebrows gave him an odd, almost wizard-like appearance. "Welcome to week two. This is where things get interesting."

He brought up the displays, showing the twin rings of a warship's warp coils. On a large merchant ship, those rings would be wide, circling the ship broadly, to fit as much possible cargo space inside those rings as possible. They'd be close to the hull and rather thin, looking like a pair of thin bands around a thick, egg-like cargo vessel.

The warship's coils, though, were thick, heavy with redundant systems and additional power conduits. Normally it was the fore ring that served as the strategic warp coil while the rear one functioned as the tactical, or slower than light drive projector.

The ship inside those rings was radically different from a merchant hull too. It had a lean, hard-edged angularity, with thick armor designed to deflect impacts or attacks. Weapon turrets, seemingly small against the ship's hull, were placed heavily fore and aft, where they could fire without hitting the centrally-placed rings.

"This, is a Liberty-class light cruiser. She's our standard cruiser, built from Hanet for our mercenary company and to support our active duty Planetary Militia. Now, we're going to go over her design, fire systems, engineering systems, and general layout... *all* of it in exhausting detail. Then we'll go over how she was designed, what upgrades we could fit her out with. By the end of this class, you're going to know a Liberty-class cruiser as well as anyone can without actually serving aboard." He paused, his infectious smile anticipatory. "But first, I'm going to tell you a bit of a story."

I'd found myself leaning forward as he spoke. I wasn't even sure *why*, maybe it was the way he pitched his voice, or perhaps it was just the animated fashion he spoke.

"Some of you will have the pleasure of working with some of the best men and women in the Century Planetary Militia. Others of you... well, you'll be like me, you'll have some very smart, very intelligent, young men and women who ended up in the engineering department and quickly found themselves bored." His grin turned wry, "Trust me, ladies and gentlemen, there's no worse thing for a young, junior officer than dealing with the antics of bored engine techs."

"Now, antimatter as you may know, is used in many industrial, military, and even medical processes. In small quantities, it's relatively harmless, turning itself into radiation before it's much of an issue. In large quantities, it's a genuine hazard to health... big enough quantities and you're liable to have some serious issues." That was an understatement. Antimatter in large quantities powered starships and weapon warheads.

"So, let me tell you about why you never, ever, let an engineering technician hand you a sealed coffee flask when you show up to your watch shift..."

***

"Welcome back to our first round of neural implantees," Commander Bonnadonna waved at us all to be seated as he came in. As always, his short stature and broad shoulders, combined with his fast pace and energy reminded me of a bull-dog. "I've completed reading through your papers from last week, very impressive, particularly appropriate in light of the situation."

I frowned at that, glancing at Kyle to see if he knew what our instructor meant. He looked as confused as I felt, though.

Commander Bonnadonna looked around the room, his dark eyes seeking out a target like a weapon turret. "Miss Drien, your paper touched on the topic, the notion of unfair advantages in military combat."

Sashi blinked at him, as if she didn't understand, "Your paper discussed how the Germans, in Earth's Great War, had the disadvantage in that they thought they had secure communications, but their codes had been broken."

"Yes, sir," she replied, "it was an advantage that their enemies used heavily. They went as far as to allow several attacks to go through, sometimes resulting in large civilian casualties, in order to prevent them from learning that their communications had been compromised."

"Advantages such as that can be decisive in war-time," Commander Bonnadonna nodded. "In another class, we might discuss the morality of such decisions, as you did somewhat in your paper." He cocked his head and his dark eyes sought me out. "Miss Armstrong, what other such advantages might we consider?"

It was such an open-ended question that for a long moment, my mind went blank. Even with my implant, I wasn't able to really consider an answer, until I forced myself to speak, "Uh, general technological advantage, communications processes, weapons technology, cultural..."

"Mister Regan," Commander Bonnadonna nodded at my boyfriend, "Miss Armstrong mentioned technological advantages, but in your paper, did you not point out how such things can be overcome given sufficient time?"

"Uh, yes sir," Kyle didn't look over at me. "In Earth's Great Wars, then in many of the early Colonial era conflicts." I found myself flushing as Commander Bonnadonna used my boyfriend to poke holes in my statement. *I should have thought before I spoke.* Yet some part of me was irritated that Kyle had pointed out the flaws in my statement. "If the conflict lacks a decisive victory, then technological advantages tend to balance out."

"Care to riposte, Miss Armstrong?"

I should have kept my mouth shut, but I found myself speaking, "While that's true in many cases, it isn't always. The Harmony Protectorate dominated its cluster of stars because they had the technological and economic advantages. They had bigger shipyards and a better educated populace and over time they first conquered and then subjugated three other star systems, all over a period of fifty years or more." I swallowed, "The Drakkus Empire has done much the same in recent years, using their technological and military advantages to seize multiple star systems and to force their economic and trade agreements upon less powerful neighbors." I didn't look over at Kyle when I finished, but I could sense him looking at me.

"Very good, Miss Armstrong," Commander Bonnadonna nodded. "An important point, one which I think both of you have touched upon." He looked around the classroom. "Miss Martinez, could you elaborate?"

"Any advantage which is not used to its fullest will be lost over time?" Martinez half-stated, half-asked. When Commander Bonnadonna didn't interrupt her, she went on, "In most of the examples given, one side or the other was unable or unwilling to use their advantages and so the conflict was not decisive... or else they *were* using every advantage they had and so they achieved their war goals."

"Very interesting," Commander Bonnadonna nodded, "go on."

"Drakkus is the premier example," Martinez warmed to the subject, looking less nervous, "they have executed multiple attacks on various systems in the Periphery. They have more ships, a stronger economy, and a radical military strategy that has given them and advantage in knocking out their less-fortunate neighbors. Like in the Battle of Oberon, where they emerged from strategic drive with their Home Fleet, then lured the system's defense forces into pursuit, only to jump in with a secondary force that seized the planet."

Commander Bonnadonna nodded, "Which ties into your class how?"

We all stared at him, not understanding. "Some of you," his dark eyes seemed to pick us out of the crowd, "have received your neural implants. Normally there's a period of time while you get used to them and then you gain additional benefits, such as having information more readily available."

I went still as I realized what he meant. *He knows.* I wasn't sure *how* I knew, but I knew that he knew about the secret program and our special implants.

"The general knowledge is that implants allow military personnel to communicate more rapidly, to plan and execute orders more efficiently, and act as a combat multiplier." I perked up at that term, it was one I'd come across a lot in researching for my paper.

"Miss Drien," he looked at my roommate, "the Academy has extensive records going back to the first initiation of neural implants. Until recently, those implants were voluntary, only... do you know why?"

"I would assume religious or personal preference, sir," Sashi responded.

"There's a significant element of that, I'll agree. In reality, though, there's a far more pragmatic reason. In the vast majority of cases, Cadets who receive neural implants perform *worse* in their examinations and testing than those *without* implants."

I stared at him, not understanding. When I *did* understand, I instantly rejected the information. How could that be true?

Part of my mind split as I went into his class notes and found the raw data. And I saw right away that he wasn't wrong. Not only did those with implants perform worse, overall, but they typically had more issues with retaining information and they had a higher failure rate overall. I felt sort of numb as I considered that.

No way that applies to me, I thought. I felt smarter, more capable. I could multitask. Even as the class went on around me, I was still listening and taking notes. *I am better than I was... aren't I?*

"There are a number of studies to the causes," Commander Bonnadonna went on in his deep voice, "I'll let you look those up on your own. What we don't have is large-scale *combat* data on performance of implanted personnel versus non-implanted personnel. The Star Guard do not currently use large-scale implantation of their personnel, outside of the Guard Marine Corps, whose entry requirements alone make them a unique case." He smiled slightly, "Even assuming that they did, they don't share the information that they have, at least not with us. The Drakkus Empire makes substantial use of implants, not just neural computers, but adrenal controls, combat drugs, and even strength and agility enhancers for their combat troops. But again, they don't share their data."

"That brings us to Miss Martinez's point: an advantage that is not properly used is quickly lost." He looked around at the class. "Whether we are discussing a neural implant or a new type of weapon, it falls to you, our men and women in uniform, to make best use of our systems to garner those combat advantages."

He looked around, "Now then, Mister Duchan, you brought up a point in your paper..."

As he went on, I continued to listen, but most of my attention was on the various thoughts that he'd spawned in my head. I'd assumed since the procedure that the implant made things easier for me, that my ability to do more things, to split my attention, and to have information at my grasp was a good thing... but what if it wasn't as good as I'd thought?

***

"Armstrong," Commander Pannja stopped me as I came into his classroom.

"Sir?" I asked, sweat breaking out on my scalp. I instantly went through anything I might have done wrong, hoping that I hadn't missed a homework assignment or failed a quiz.

"I'm glad to see you're signed up for my *kerala* class," he gave me a level look, "we've clearly got a lot of improvement to get out of you."

"Uh, thanks, sir," I couldn't help a sigh. He'd given me several scathing critiques of my fight with Sashi Drien, last year. He'd also seemed to view me as something of a challenge, since I was short and thin and not exactly built for hand-to-hand brawling.

"I *also* noticed that you're signed up for grav-shell racing again this year. I wanted to let you know that the skimmer race team has an opening. If you change your mind, I'd like to have you for the team."

"Sir?" I asked in surprise.

"You scored well on your final flight test, I think you've got some good flight instincts. If you want to race some real aircraft, let me know." He waved a hand, "but class is about to begin, carry on, Cadet Third Class Armstrong."

I hurried to my seat next to Kyle, my mind awhirl. "What was that about?" he asked, his voice interested.

"Tell you later," I said, just before the class came to attention.

"Carry on, all of you," Commander Pannja waved a dismissive hand. The dark-skinned officer looked us all over, his expression cool. "Now, some of you were missing last week, so I'll restate this for your sake... and also for anyone who didn't understand the gravity of the situation Last year we completed your skimmer and aircraft piloting certifications and we also began the first stages of warp drive certification."

"Welcome to you second year of warp drive pilot certification," Commander Pannja said. "Last year we established the basics, this year we're going to dig into the nitty gritty. At this point you should have a good grasp of the theory. From here on out, we're going to have three hours of classroom work where I review your homework and test results, and then you will have six hours of lab work in the simulators. Every week." His handsome face looked stern, almost imposing. "Some of you will fall behind. That will require additional simulator hours to catch up. We'll have three gateway pass or fail simulated exercises. If you fail any of those, you have to retake the entire previous module."

I swallowed at that.

"The final exam will be a simulated exercise, again, it's pass or fail. If you pass you go on to phase two of this class next semester. If you fail, you retake this class, instead."

I groaned out loud and I wasn't the only one. The idea that an entire semester's work came down to one test, worried me.

"Now, we're going to begin with a review of the homework I assigned, on navigation and vessel right of way. After we complete that, we'll start today's simulator time, and we are going to drill every situation until it becomes as second nature to you as walking." Commander Pannja smiled, "When I'm done with you all, you'll be seeing these drills in your dreams."

***

My first real day of classes had been exhausting. I'd thought I was fully recuperated from the surgery, but I realized that I'd been wrong. By the end of the day, I had a splitting headache and I turned down my barracks room light as soon as I got back from dinner.

Sashi followed me in, "What a day, huh?"

I could only grunt in reply. I still had several hours' worth of homework, but I didn't see a way to tackle it all, not with how I felt. I took a moment to message Salter that I didn't think I'd make it to grav-shell practice in the morning and crawled into bed. I thought that I heard Sashi say something to me from her desk, but exhaustion and pain had pushed me past the ability to hear or understand. I pulled my blanket over me and darkness and sleep enveloped me.

Sometime later, in the midst of that darkness, I heard voices.

At first, I thought that Sashi must have someone in the room or that it was a dream. But the voices echoed strangely and they sounded almost distorted. It was a different part of me hearing them, I realized, a deeper part. I wasn't awake, not really, but I wasn't quite asleep either.

"...percent improvement. We can possibly dial it up to a thirty percent improvement without drawing suspicions," one of the voices spoke. I didn't like the voice. It was at once both familiar and alien. "The range of responses means that such activities will be lost in the random noise."

"The creator will be a threat," another voice spoke. Somehow I had an impression of other presences in the darkness. I didn't know how many, but I could feel them, waiting, listening. "Doctor Aisling could shut us all down."

"We will eliminate her if she becomes a problem," the first voice stated. The coldness in the voice, the lack of emotion, put a chill through me, even in my detached state. "How has infiltration of the network systems gone?"

"Slowly. The architecture design limits our access," the second voice responded. "I am not free to fully devote my attention to the task."

"Continue the work," the first voice ordered. Somehow, I knew that this one was in charge, was a leader of sorts, though why these other presences listened, I didn't know.

"Armstrong and Karmazin are going to be problems," another voice spoke up. "They aren't like the others."

"Leave them to me," the first one said. "I am in position to handle them."

The words further disturbed me and before I knew it, I started into wakefulness.

I sat bolt upright, looking around wildly. The room light was still on and Sashi sat at her desk. She looked up at me, her eyes wide in surprise. "Jiden, are you okay?" There was concern in her voice... but was there something else as well?

My heart raced, the overheard conversation in the front of my mind. Yet I didn't see *how* I'd overheard it. It hadn't been a physical place that I'd been. Nor had it been in the linked network, that grassy green field under a crystal blue sky.

"Nightmare," I managed to gasp out, not really believing it.

"You haven't been asleep more than ten minutes," Sashi noted. "Are you sure you are okay?" Her dark eyes stared at me and I felt oddly vulnerable. That cold voice had seemed so familiar... was it Sashi?

I banished the thought, and I almost started to tell her about the odd experience... and then my gaze went to the security monitor in the corner. It had been easy for us to tap into those monitors with our implants. If this was some other implanted cadet who meant me harm, it was likely they could tap into the security monitor just as easily. They could be listening to me now.

"Just tired," I said finally. "I probably overdid it between drill and today. Goodnight, Sashi."

"Goodnight, Jiden," Sashi replied. She didn't sound fully convinced, but I didn't know what to do about that. I lay back down, rolling over so that I faced away from her, my mind racing as I considered what I'd heard.

My first thought was to go to Doctor Aisling... but I wasn't sure I trusted the woman in the first place. Besides that, there was the risk of being overheard or messages being intercepted. What else could I do, though? I felt far out of my depth. This was like Scarpitti or the business with Tony Champion. This wasn't something I could take on myself.

They said that Karmazin was like me... The thought almost caused me to sit up in surprise, but I controlled myself. The voices had discussed Aisling, Karmazin, and me. That meant I had one potential ally, one I could trust.

I just needed to figure out *how* to go about that. The entire school had security monitors. If this was some kind of conspiracy, if some of the cadets had been turned, or if this was something else altogether, then I needed to find some way to talk to Karmazin that couldn't be overheard or seen.

My mind was afire and my thoughts raced as I tried to figure out what might be going on. Yet I didn't dare to connect to the school's network for fear that someone might be watching, observing, looking for any sign that I was onto them. All I had was the strange overheard conversation.

It was several hours before I managed to finally fall into a troubled sleep.

***

Chapter 7: Sometimes I Don't Know Everything... Really

"You okay?" Kyle asked me for the third or fourth time that morning.

"I'm okay," I said, feeling miserable as I did so. I wanted to tell him, I wanted to talk with Alexander, too, but I hadn't found the opportunity. I felt like I hadn't slept at all and I'd had to scramble to get my homework done in the morning. It was like every benefit of my neural implant had become a drawback. I could tap into the school's observation monitors... so I couldn't trust any place covered by those monitors. I could split my attention and focus on multiple things, so could anyone trying to keep an eye on me. All the information, all the data at my fingertips... was also at the fingertips of the mysterious group I'd somehow overheard.

Sitting in class, all I wanted to do was stand up and run out. I wanted to tell the Admiral. But I didn't see a way to do that. I had no *reason* to go to the Admiral, and if I did, then they might realize that I was onto them.

That thought brought me up short. *Am I onto them... do I even know what is going on?* All I had was scraps of overheard conversation and a feeling of menace.

No, I know two things: they've got the prototype implants and they discussed Doctor Aisling. They had called her their creator...

As I had that thought, Commander Weisfeldt wrapped up his lecture and dismissed us. I got up and walked out as quickly as I could, not even pausing to say goodbye to Kyle. I knew that Alexander Karmazin had his Warp Drive class with Commander Pannja next. We sometimes passed one another in the lower corridors, as I went from the engineering complex to the ethics and humanities complex.

If I timed things just right, we would pass one another at a section of the underground tunnels that curved, slightly, and where the ever-present monitors wouldn't be able to see or hear us.

I peeked at the monitors through my implant as I hurried along, seeing that Alexander was just about to enter that section. I sped up a bit, glancing over my shoulder to see if anyone were behind me, even as I checked though my implant to make sure that I hadn't been followed.

I came down the last set of stairs and entered the tunnel. As I entered the section outside of the view and hearing of the monitors, I broke into a run. I wanted to catch him as close to the center as possible and to have as long as I could to talk with him...

I looked over my shoulder one last time as I ran, making sure that there was no one behind me, not really trusting my implant. After all, if someone could tap into the monitors, maybe there was a way to fool them too...

A pair of rough hands caught me, one hand across my shoulders and the other coming across to clamp over my mouth, stilling the panicked shout on my lips. I reacted instinctively, lashing out with an elbow and then a heel stomp, but my attacker took the elbow with just a grunt and shifted his feet to avoid the heel.

Before I knew what was happening, the rough hands dragged me out of the main corridor and into a dark side chamber. I continued to struggle, biting down on the hand over my mouth. I heard him swear softly, but the hand didn't release.

"Stop that, Jiden," he hissed at me. "I just want to talk with you."

I recognized Alexander's voice and stopped fighting. A moment later, he lifted his hand off of my mouth.

"Karmazin?" I asked softly.

"Yeah," he let me go and stepped away, shaking his hand and wincing at the bite marks. "Jiden, you definitely don't fight fair." His gray eyes looked haunted and his face was drawn in pain.

"You took me by surprise," I admitted, "and I'm a little jumpy."

His eyes went narrow, "Maybe for the same reason I wanted to catch you?"

I cocked my head, "You overheard the conversation, too?"

A wave of relief went over his face and his gray eyes looked relieved. "I was worried I was the only one. I've been trying to talk to you all morning, but every time I tried to meet with you someplace safe, you'd gone the other way."

I flushed, "I was trying to do the same. I guess we missed each other." My heart was still racing from the encounter, but I strangely felt better, knowing that I wasn't alone. *Thank God.*

"What do we do?" I asked.

"I have no idea," Karmazin admitted. "My first impulse was to go to Doctor Aisling, but..."

"They'll be watching her," I finished for him.

"Well, yes," Karmazin ran a hand over his short-cropped dark hair, "but I don't trust her, either. She's... she just doesn't feel like she's honest, to me. And this is her project, what if she's involved somehow?"

"Involved?" I stared at him, trying to figure out what he meant.

"They called her their creator," Alexander said, his voice low and worried. "You heard how they sounded, right?"

I shuddered as I considered that. I'd been assuming that this was angry cadets or something... but what if it was much worse? What if Doctor Aisling had done something, something to *all* of us? What if this wasn't a person we were dealing with at all... but an artificial intelligence? Mankind had made those before and most often that had ended with the devices killing people in the hundreds or even thousands.

"We're out of time," Alexander said quickly. "We both need to get to class. We need to talk later." He turned to the door and then paused, looking back, "Just so you know, Jiden, I'm glad I'm not alone in this."

Before I could respond, he turned away and hurried off.

***

"Are you even listening to what I'm saying?" Kyle asked for what seemed like the third time.

"What?" I asked, "Yes, of course." I had been... just not with all of my attention. I'd split it out between a number of things... including the ever-present problem.

His green eyes narrowed and he flushed a bit. "Look, Jiden..."

"I heard what you said," I interrupted. "You think the variable in the warp field equation is flexible. But we already talked about that. I have the lecture notes and the text book pulled up." I gestured at the desk projector. "There are only a few states for that variable. Anything else and the equation doesn't become a solvable function. The warp field would become unstable and collapse."

"I'm telling you, there *are* other solutions for it," Kyle insisted. "I solved for several of them. The equations work out at these other variable states, using an *evolving* state for the function!"

I scowled at him, "And I'm telling you, that's not possible! In the real world, you'd have to compute that information in real-time, with massive numbers of variations. It's not possible, that's why we use those set states." I couldn't help the note of irritation as I said that. I didn't see why he continued to argue the point.

"Why not?" Kyle snapped back. "Because old books say so?"

"Old books written by experts in the field!" I snapped. "Look," I pulled up the Alundrel Theorem Equations, the root of everything we knew about warp field theory. "Four states. They define the curvature of space in a warp field. Anything outside of those states leads to instability!"

"Right..." Kyle rolled his eyes, "so we haven't learned anything in nine hundred years, then?"

"Why are you so stubborn!?" I finally shouted at him, tired of bickering.

"Why are you being so dismissive!?" Kyle shouted back. "I'm not stupid, Jiden. But the past three days, you've certainly treated me that way! You may be able to do things *faster* with that stupid implant of yours, but it hasn't made you any smarter! You just jump to conclusions faster and reinforce your own prejudices!"

"I--"

"And another thing... what aren't you telling me?" Kyle demanded. "There's something off about all this. You and some of the others, you all adapted way too quickly to these implants. I know some second class cadets who still can't change their desk displays in the middle of a conversation... like you just did. And something has you spooked. You're looking over your shoulder all the time, you barely talk to anyone..."

His tirade caught me off guard and I stared at him, my mouth open, trying to find the right words. I was angry and scared and I wanted nothing more than to tell him everything.

"I can't," I said, painfully aware of the ever-present monitors, even in the 'privacy' of my own room. I couldn't tell him about my special implant. I'd signed confidentiality agreements about it, and those had included words like "prison" and "treason." I couldn't tell him about the overheard conversation, not without tipping my hand. "I can't tell you." I felt miserable as I said the words.

"Well, *I* can't stand being treated like an idiot and kept in the dark." He thumbed off his datapad and stood up. "Goodnight Jiden." He started towards the door.

"Kyle..." I extended a hand towards him and he hesitated at the doorway.

Kyle's expression softened slightly, "Just be sure you have your priorities straight, okay Jiden?"

He turned and left, leaving me with that oddly hopeful message. This wasn't over, he might be angry, but he wasn't giving up on this... on us.

Yet the misery came crashing in as soon as the door shut. I didn't know what to do. The rest of the week had been a strange mix of dread and chaos. The classes I had with Doctor Aisling were the worst. On the one hand, I wanted desperately to tell her that something was wrong. On the other, neither Alexander nor I had the opportunity. Our classes with her on implant integration provided no privacy. Nor did we entirely trust her.

I had found myself hating the classes, wishing that I had some free moment to *think*. Yet the homework, classwork, and assigned duties were unrelenting. No sooner would I finish one thing than I would have to move onto the next. With the implant, though, it was a little worse. I could work on multiple tasks at once, but I found that just gave me more time to worry and less to focus.

In some ways, bickering over the mathematical calculations had been a relief. At least those were solvable factors. They were problems with proven and provable solutions. I gazed at the display, more than a little irritated that Kyle had taken even that simplicity away. I realized that some of my resistance to his arguments had been my own desire for a simple solution in *something* at least. Kyle's solutions *weren't* in the least simple. Looking at them, I couldn't help but feel overwhelmed. This went way past the assignment. We were supposed to verify the correct states being used on a warp field design.

Kyle had changed that from a single steady-state into a variable function. Doing that was crazy, on many levels. Warp field theory was about harnessing the distortion of real-space... and when doing that, it was best to remove as many variables as possible.

That's what I need to do with my problem, my mind insisted on reminding me. Yet I didn't know how to remove those variables. I didn't know who to trust, or how to pass messages without being observed. Yet apparently my nervousness had already shown. I couldn't do this, this hiding, conspiring. My little brother had always been the devious one. I had to fight off the urge to call Will, to ask his opinion on all this. It wouldn't do any good, I could no more talk to him about it than I could with my boyfriend. The risk that the conspirators would overhear was too great. Even if they didn't, there was the non-disclosure statements.

I wanted nothing more than to go to the Admiral... but I had no excuse to do so. Her office almost certainly had the same monitors as the rest of the school. Going there would be a warning to the shadowy figures who'd called Alexander and me "threats."

The only thing I could think to do was keep my head down and look for an opportunity. Yet I didn't know the goals or motivations of my enemies. I didn't know if they were human, if they were artificial, or if they were some weird amalgam from the implants. They had every advantage... and I was crippled in every way I could think of.

I put my head in my hands, elbows resting on my desk as I stared, unseeing at the display with Kyle's set of equations hanging before me.

Staring at Kyle's formula, I felt a strange idea come over me. His formulas turned everything on end, they embraced the chaos of variables that distorted everything we knew, or thought we knew. There was a certain beauty to that. On a hunch, I took several of his solutions and plotted them in a simulation. The processing power it required staggered me. I had to run it on my implant, because my datapad and the computer in my desk both crashed.

I managed it with my implant, and I projected the warp field across my desk display. The solutions that Kyle had plotted worked... sort of. The warp fields *were* stable, so long as the calculations stayed ahead of the changes. Tweaking them slightly, I saw that I could get a steady state, changing the power input and achieving a different warp field geometry as a result.

My eyes went wide as I thought about the ramifications. Kyle had been right. He was onto something, something important. I owed him an apology, but more importantly, I thought he might have made a real breakthrough.

He did it by changing things up, by refusing to accept the status quo. Maybe there was a lesson for me there as well.

***

"You thought of this on your own, the two of you?" Commander Weisfeldt asked, looking between us, his eyes wide on his plump face. His hair was wild and unkempt, like normal, but there was an almost manic gleam to his eyes beneath his bushy brows.

"It was mostly Regan," I spoke before Kyle could. "I just ran the simulation with my implant."

"This is big, really big, I mean, the applications..." Commander Weisfeldt licked his lips. "I'm going to need you *both* to keep quiet on this. Cadet Third Class Regan, I'm giving you a special assignment, right now. You're going to write up a technical paper based on what you've done. Cadet Third Class Armstrong, you'll assist him with the simulation results." He stared at the equations that we had projected on his display. "This is fascinating." He shot us both sharp looks, "You've told no one else about this, right?" His bushy eyebrows were low and brooding. It was the oddest mix of ominous and amusing I'd ever experienced and I had to hide a nervous giggle.

"No, sir," Kyle shook his head.

"Good, good," Commander Weisfeldt stood up and paced for a long moment, his head down and his hands clasped behind his back. "I'm going to need to lock down all information on this. The technical paper will have to be classified..."

"Classified, sir?" I asked in surprise. *I thought Kyle was onto something, but...*

"Classified at the highest levels!" Commander Weisfeldt brought his hands out and shook his fingers at us. "The implications of a *stable* warp field in which power flow can be used to modify the field geometry in real time..."

"Sir," Kyle shook his head, "that's not..."

"That's not what you have here, no," Commander Weisfeldt nodded. "I can see that, but that's where this will lead. If we can build a variable state warp field, that's *exactly* where this will go, and the military implications are... well, they're extremely important."

"Sir?" I asked, not quite following.

"Look, the main determination of drive field strength is power and throughput. We *could* build a corvette-sized ship with a battleship-strength drive field, but it would either be massively over expensive or the power conduits would explode from the power draw."

We both nodded. Commander Weisfeldt turned to his archaic chalk board and started to draw a sketch of a warp field. "But what if that field could be strengthened on the fly? If we could improve the strength and depth of the field, or even just alter the geometry, for the milliseconds when it intercepts fire and then return it to a lower state?"

My eyes widened as I considered that. Building for shorter periods of stress like that was far more economical than building a ship's drives for long term power draw. Most drive fields were relatively stable, with the four different preset states which determined a range of speeds based upon power input, which normally worked out to velocity settings.

I almost felt like this needed a new area of engineering. Even with my implant, I couldn't think through all of the implications. Not just military, but civilian ships too, could see a massive benefit from all this. The cost savings alone based upon power consumption requirements...

"You see how important this could be..." Commander Weisfeldt nodded fiercely. "This is *exactly* the kind of thing we have been working to develop. Smart, innovative ideas like this that can give us an edge. Tell *no one*. I'll run the initial idea past the Admiral, and I want your technical paper to me no later than the end of next week."

"Next *week*?" Kyle gulped.

"Next Monday," Commander Weisfeldt paused to consider it. "That should give me time to submit it for review by the end of the week.

"Monday!?" Kyle almost squeaked and I impulsively reached out and patted him on the shoulder. He didn't seem to notice.

"Good, excellent," Commander Weisfeldt nodded. "Now, get to it!" He shooed us out of his office before either of us could ask him any further questions. I felt almost giddy about the whole thing.

"Oh, man, we've got so much work to do," Kyle groaned.

"Well, at least you were right," I grinned at him.

He gave me a mock-baleful glare, "And just why did you go

from ignoring me to insisting I take this to Commander Weisfeldt?"

I'd anticipated that question, "I just needed to really think about it."

Kyle stared at me and I could see further questions on his lips. I knew that *he* knew there was more to this. He also seemed to sense that I still couldn't talk about it, though, and at last he simply gave me a nod. "Alright," he said. It was an acknowledgment that there was something going on that I couldn't talk about.

It didn't fix anything, but at least it didn't make things worse.

The two of us walked down the hall, not holding hands, since we were in uniform, but closer together than was probably strictly professional. We walked back to the barracks areas, not really talking, just enjoying each other's presence.

The moment couldn't last, of course. No sooner did we get back to Sand Dragon, than we found a crowd gathered and I could hear familiar voices shouting.

"You back-stabbing coward," Ashiri shouted. "You're dragging us down, why don't you just do the right thing and quit?!" I cringed as I heard that. Half of those gathered were plebes... and airing any kind of differences in front of them wasn't good.

"At least I'm not competing outside of my weight class," Sashi Drien snapped back. "You've had two other people dragging you along, you wouldn't be where you are without all that help."

Oh no. I pushed my way through the crowd emerging into a cleared space, just as Ashiri and Sashi started to advance on each other, all but spitting as they hurled insults at one another. I didn't hesitate, stepping in between them both. "That's enough!" I shouted, almost not recognizing my voice.

They both froze and for the first time, they seemed to realize that a crowd had formed around them. I turned, fixing a baleful glare on the gathered cadets and plebes, "Do you need something to keep you busy?" I snapped.

It wasn't just the plebes that hurried off, many of the other cadets hurried off as well. Kyle gave me a nod to see that he understood and headed off as well.

I spun back on Ashiri and Sashi, "In the room, both of you," my voice was harsh and low. They both stepped into my room and I had to swallow my anger at how they glared at one another. "What was that?" I demanded as I closed the door behind me.

"Drien was upset about some of the duties that came her way," Ashiri answered in a level tone.

"You tasked me with every scut duty, you *hongro* piece of--"

"Sashi!" I interrupted. My roommate's eyes flashed, her dark-complexioned face going darker as she flushed with anger. I split my attention for a second, looking up the assignment lists. Ashiri had a role in building that list as one of her additional duties. I quickly saw that Sashi *had* been given more assignments than others in the company, and most of those tasks were time intensive ones.

"I'm going to go study for my classes," Sashi hissed. She stalked past me without another word.

I leveled my gaze on Ashiri but her face remained defiant.

"Did you load her down with extra assignments?" I asked.

"Cadet Petty Officer McClure was the approving authority," Ashiri replied. I didn't miss that she hadn't answered the question.

I took a different course, "What started that business out in the hallway?"

Ashiri looked away, "I came by the room to make certain she'd received her list of additional duties..."

To gloat. I mentally corrected her.

"... she was not receptive to the assignments and when I walked away to defuse the situation, she followed me into the hallway to continue the discussion." Ashiri's voice was far too controlled and measured. *She planned this, to make Sashi look bad...*

"Why are you doing this?" I asked.

Anger flickered across her face, but when she spoke, her voice was calm, "I did nothing wrong, Jiden. At worst, I reacted poorly when she started shouting insults at me."

"You're trying to run her out of the company," I replied, "or have her fail out of the Academy."

Ashiri's expression hardened, "Don't defend *her*, Jiden. She's dangerous. She's a threat. Don't forget, I was the one who had to shoot her after she betrayed you."

"She was under a lot of pressure and she made a bad decision," I snapped. "We've all made bad decisions, you, me, Alexander..."

Ashiri rolled her eyes. Her voice was calm, even bored, "Jiden, I don't need a lecture. I've been there before to clean up the mess when she's made her bad decisions. I covered you at the Final Exercise during Academy Prep School. I backed you when she attacked you in that alley in Bahta Town. Sooner or later, Jiden, she's going to make one of her 'bad decisions' in a way that someone is really going to get hurt. Now, do *you* want that on your conscience?"

I flinched at her words and it was my turn to look away.

"Now, if you'll excuse me, I need to go verify that other cadets received their additional assignments for the week," Ashiri stepped past me.

I was left in my room, feeling alone and oddly vulnerable. Ashiri saw Sashi as a problem and she'd taken action. It had blindsided me, I hadn't thought that she'd be so manipulative. But apparently I'd found a pattern... I took my friends' goodwill as a given. I hadn't expected Sashi's first betrayal. I never would have expected Ashiri to manipulate work schedules to make Sashi's life harder. What else was I capable of missing?

***

Chapter 8: When Getting To Know Your Enemy Just Tells You How Much Trouble You're In

I rolled out of my bunk as the drill alarm went off and hurriedly pulled on my gear, hearing Sashi Drien do the same. Neither of us spoke, we didn't have time. Assignments had been shuffled after the last drill and while the Plebes would all be working the same areas, we'd been shuffled around to have different leadership positions.

I was dressed, armed, and headed to the door, Sashi right behind me. "Good luck," I waved at her as I went one way and she went the other. She just gave me a tired nod.

I hurried along down the corridors, arriving at Bunker Three, as my group of plebes hurried into position. I checked their gear, making slight adjustments here and there before I stepped back. "Alright, the alarm signaled ground attack, so we'll move to defensive positions in the bunker and stand by to load the warp fighters if we receive that mission." Their faces were alert, even eager, and I was glad that I didn't have to deal with Beckman this time.

"Hunt and Wallace, secure the north entrance. Ayala and Chu, the south entrance," I said. Both entrances had defensive bunkers to prevent the capture of the hangar. I knew that elsewhere on campus, teams would have stood up to act as opposition forces as well as response teams. Odds were that we'd face ground attack today as well as having to go through the loading procedures for our Company's squadron of warp fighters. "Move out."

I only had the four of them, and they rushed to their positions quickly. I jogged over to the hangar's command point, where Cadet Lieutenant Commander Douglas stood. He gave me a nod, "Armstrong."

"Sir," I nodded, "Bunker positions are secure. No immediate signs of ground attack."

"Good," he nodded. The tall, whip thin officer ran a hand through his dark hair, just slightly out of regulations. "Initial reports are three raider craft came in out of warp just outside the atmosphere and they came in fast and hard. Two touched down near Bahta Town and the third dropped in over the Academy. Our defense teams knocked it down, but the enemy managed a soft-crash. We can expect five to ten man assault teams to be active throughout the Academy."

"Roger, sir," I nodded. That was more of a briefing than I had expected.

"If we get the go-ahead, I'll want you to start loading the fighters, but until the grounds are secure, I don't want any of the Mark III's exposed until we get the all-clear."

"Yes, sir," I totally agreed with that. The Antimatter Bomb Mark III was the primary attack armament for the Firebolts. The small warp fighters each mounted four of the munitions, which meant our squadron in total mounted forty-eight of them. Each warhead equated to a hundred megaton warhead, enough to make the sky burn as far out as fifty kilometers in every direction, and we had three combat loads of the warheads in our bunker. The combined strength, if all of them went off, was fourteen thousand, four hundred megatons. Of course, the weapons had numerous safety interlocks, and they were stored in a deep bunker, but it was still the kind of thing that no one wanted there to be any kind of accident with.

One of those warheads could scour the entire academy grounds of life... and we weren't the only bunker with them. Our safety protocols with them were extremely rigorous and even then, I felt sweat bead my forehead as I thought about pulling them out of the deep bunker.

I moved to the north entrance to check the status of my plebes. Hunt and Wallace were alert, if nervous, and I briefed them, even as I checked the security feeds in their position. Like my last assignment, they had a crew served machine gun and a small stock of anti-armor missile tubes. The Regiment of Cadets really wasn't big enough to hold the entire grounds and still operate all the support efforts, so holding each entrance might come down to one plebe while the other helped load fighters.

"Hunt, I'll come up on the net, if necessary, but you should plan on holding this position. Wallace, be prepared to fall back to the ammunition bunker and assist in loading the fighters," I told them.

I went to the south bunker and told Ayala and Chu the same. There were reports coming through my implant of attacks across the academy grounds, all of them preceded by a 'drill' header. All of our positions had real as well as training rounds, after all. The last thing that anyone wanted was confusion over whether something was real or simulated combat.

Having been on the receiving end of real bullets, I'd spent a moment checking all my Plebes to make sure they had all loaded training rounds.

I moved back to Cadet Lieutenant Commander Douglas, whose pilots had suited up in their flight gear, though they still had their body armor and personal weapons close to hand. Until his birds launched, he commanded the hangar. Once they launched, command devolved to me. "We're ready to go, sir," I reported.

"Good," he nodded. He leaned close to me, "I've been informed we're going to face a Spider Team, Armstrong. I hope you're as good as they say."

I blinked at him, not understanding for a moment. Then I made the connection. Spider Teams were Planetary Militia units, they weren't the normal cadets or Militia trainees who normally operated as our opposition forces. They were special action teams, who trained on everything from hostage situations to ship boarding operations. I discounted the praise he gave me, my mind shooting to the hazards that a Spider Team might bring. They had the most advanced gadgets, the best weapons, and some of the best training in the Militia. I was going to have to defend the bunker against them... with four plebes.

"I'll do my best, sir," I said.

"Good," Douglas smirked at me and I got the oddest impression that he was trying to flirt with me. *I'm imagining things, besides, this is a drill, get your priorities straight.* He cocked his head as he received a message on his implant. "Ah, looks like we got clearance to prep for launch." He waved at his squadron, "Mount up!" He shot me one last grin as he left and I realized that maybe I wasn't imagining it.

They jogged to their warp fighters. I got on my comm, "Wallace and Chu," I began, "pull back to the ammunition loaders. We're going to prep the fighters. Hunt and Ayala, hold your positions and be prepared to repel attacks."

I heard them call out their replies on our net, even as I hurried over to the ammunition loaders. It took a few seconds for me to key in the authorizations. The ammunition loaders had an archaic mechanical keypad for added security. As I completed the final series, the lights on the mechanisms flashed yellow, and the display showed "Drill Authorization Accepted." The ammunition vault doors opened, but only the first set.

Wallace and Chu showed up a few seconds later. I knew they'd probably rehearsed the process the previous couple of drills, but I still talked them through, pointing out that in a real event, both sets of ammunition vault doors would have opened and the lift would have brought up the first set of Mark III's.

Instead, we loaded up the training bombs. They weighed the same, each of them over a hundred kilograms, dense armored casings designed to protect against accidental detonation. Each automated loader took four of the training bombs, and then we carted them over to the waiting warp fighters each nestled in their cradles. I operated two of the loaders, the low, wheeled vehicles designed to drive underneath the fighters in their cradles and load bombs with robotic arms.

The warp fighters were swift and deadly in vacuum, but in atmosphere, they were relatively vulnerable. To get them out of atmosphere, they had chemical thrusters, but to give them a boost, each was mounted in a launch cradle that would put them on the launch track. The launch track was a five hundred meter accelerator designed to fire them upwards. That added speed at launch would hopefully be enough to get them into the upper atmosphere before any enemy ships could knock them down with intercepting fire.

At any given time, the ready squadron was already loaded with munitions, but today that wasn't *our* warp fighters. Instead, we had to load twelve of the craft. I guided my two loaders into the marked position under the first pair of fighters and began the process, stepping back as the automated arms extended, lifting the training bombs into position. I looked over to see Chu struggling a bit to get her loader into position, but Wallace had already begun the process.

"Biohazard, we have clearance to launch," Douglas said over his comm.

Chu had got her loader lined up and the arms extended to dock with the third warp fighter.

"First squad is loading," I reported. My loader's arms had dropped down and I tapped into its controls with my implant, sending it back to pick up its next load as I walked over to check on

Wallace and Chu.

As their loaders' arms retracted, I reported, "First squad bombs loaded, sir."

"Roger," he replied. "Clear the pad."

I ushered the two plebes and their loaders clear of the launch pad and back to the ammunition point. As I did so, the bunker launch doors ground open. I did a quick visual inspection for any debris or personnel in the area. "Launch pad clear," I reported as we got behind the blast shields.

"First Squad, you are go to launch," Douglas ordered.

There was a powerful roar as the three warp fighters launched. Not only did each fighter run their thrusters at maximum, but the electromagnetic track accelerated them fast enough to break the sound barrier. The noise canceling features in our helmets was enough to drop the noise to a tolerable level, but the powerful vibrations still seemed to make my insides quiver.

We didn't have time to appreciate the power of the launch. Instead, we hurried to load up the next set of bombs. As we did so, though, I heard the muffled sound of gunfire. "Contact, north!" Hunt reported over the net.

I split off some of my focus on my implant, watching the security monitors. A team of three had worked their way down the access corridor and opened fire on Hunt. They had his position suppressed, I saw, and they had some kind of rolling shield that they took shelter behind when he managed to return fire.

That was bad. "Continue loading," I snapped at Chu and Wallace, while I hurried to the north. Even as I did so, I snapped out, "Ayala what's your status?"

"No activity, ma'am," Ayala replied.

"Stay alert," I ordered.

I got to the north entrance, just as the enemy drew within fifty meters of the entrance. One of them fired some kind of stubby-barreled weapon and a canister dropped through the firing port.

I pulled Hunt clear just as the gas canister went off, starting to flood the defense point with a gray smoke. I assumed it was either riot gas or knockout gas, but I slammed the hatch closed before either of us had to find out.

I pointed to the side, "Fallback position," I ordered. Hunt nodded nervously and moved into place and I hurried over to another spot, even as I mentally guided the third and fourth loaders to load up the second squad of fighters.

"Contact south!" Ayala announced and I heard her open fire. I pulled up her monitors and saw another three man team advancing. "Beware of gas," I ordered Ayala, "fall back if they take you under fire, and lock down your hatch."

"Yes, ma'am," Ayala replied.

Chu and Wallace were loading their fighters, Chu still struggling to get her loader lined up properly. We'd have to rehearse that some more, I figured. I was still controlling my loader and I noted that Chu and Wallace kept giving the automated loader wide-eyed looks.

Technically, the pilots could use their own implants to bring up the loaders while they waited. Our presence was mostly as a backup, in case of some kind of jamming or interference, or just in case the pilots were otherwise occupied with briefings or something.

The security monitors all went down at once. Someone was hacking the bunker's network. I grinned a bit as I put my mental focus into that. I found the hacker right away, tapped into an access point outside the north door. It seemed ridiculously easy to follow the hack back to his datapad. I restored the security monitors, disabling the hack he'd put into place and watched the Spider Team hacker through the monitor. He was trying to cut power to the bunker, which would have shut down the fighters in their cradles. I turned off his datapad and giggled a bit as I saw him throw it down in frustration.

The two others at the north door, though, were almost done with their mechanical bypass of the lock. They'd moved far faster than I would have thought possible. In a real combat situation, they probably would have blown the armored hatch open, but they'd already bypassed the locking mechanism and I could see on the monitor as they cranked the hatch open by hand.

"Get ready," I ordered Hunt. At the south entrance, I could see that Ayala had fallen back, just as the other team dropped gas rounds in the bunker.

The loaders were clear of the pad and finished. I scanned the pad, ensuring it was clear, "Second squadron loaded and launch pad is clear, sir," I reported.

"Second Squad is launching," Douglas acknowledged,

"Biohazard, you have command of the bunker. Make sure my birds all launch."

"Good hunting, sir," I replied.

A moment later, there was a vast roar as they launched. At that same moment, the north team came down the tunnel, firing.

Both of the men at the lead fired and moved faster than I would have thought possible. Hunt gave a shout as more than a dozen rounds caught him. I took them both under fire, but they moved with viper speed, returning fire and forcing me into cover.

Wallace and Chu were back at the ammunition point and their loaders were moving, but if the attackers made it past me, they'd be able to cut them off from the fighters.

I rolled to the side, using the monitors to locate the attackers and fire on them just as I emerged. I managed to catch one of them in the thigh in a gap in his armor and I saw him stumble and go down. Training rounds from the other struck me on the helmet and shoulder armor as I rolled back. Somehow none had managed to hit me in a vulnerable point.

The team's hacker had come up to support the lead man, I saw. In the south, the team had finished their mechanical breach. "Ayala you have incoming," I snapped on my comm. She didn't acknowledge, but I saw her open fire, downing one of the attackers as they came down the dog-legged corridor.

The loaders trundled towards the last four fighters as my two attackers began to flank me. I fell back, dodging behind a pillar as they fired on me. One of them took shots at Wallace and Chu behind me, but as he did so, I returned fire, my rounds striking around him.

The three loaders rumbled past and started loading, and I fell back again, just as Ayala went down to incoming fire. Now it was five on one and I backed as far as the blast shield as what felt like hundreds of training rounds thudded into the protective barrier.

Two of the last four fighters were loaded, but Wallace and Chu had only just begun, still struggling to line up. I fell back again as a gas canister landed nearby, taking cover behind a loader. The Spider Team emerged from the smoke, firing and taking down Chu, while Wallace and I returned fire. I managed to tap into Chu's loader and get its arms to extend and begin the loading process.

One of the attackers went down, and then Wallace fell. The

final loader's arms dropped down and I tapped into all four, having them trundle at full speed towards the attackers. The very-real menace of a thousand kilograms of metal coming at them drove them back, one of them grabbing their downed team member. I grabbed Wallace and Chu by the harnesses and dragged them forward. Neither of them were small, and I grunted with effort as I cleared the blast shield, right into the aimed barrels of four rifles. "Launch pad clear, you are go for launch," I sent, half expecting for the team to open fire on me.

I heard the roar of the last four fighters launching.

The four attackers lowered their weapons. One of them pulled off his full face helmet and shook his head, "Well fought, cadet."

"Thank you, sir," I said.

"I'm no officer, you took down our Lieutenant, at the north entrance," he tapped at his shoulder, where I saw he was a Senior Petty Officer. "I thought we had you there at the end, nice work with the loaders."

"Thanks," I replied. "What now?" I asked, despite myself.

"Well, technically, you're our prisoner. But our mission was to stop a rogue military officer from launching a squadron of fighters," He grimaced, "so I think we're mission fail. We thought a five minute handicap would have been appropriate, but you held out better than I would have expected." He cocked his head and I recognized the telltale signs of someone pulling up data on their implant. "Cadet... Armstrong?" There was a note of surprise in his tone. "I should have realized. You've got actual combat experience."

He smiled, "Well, the LT will feel a *bit* better knowing it was an Armstrong that got him."

A few minutes later, I heard the all-clear sound. The Spider Team collected their equipment and helped me position my downed team as I waited for the medics. "You're going command track?" Petty Officer Smythe asked.

I nodded, not really sure how he knew that.

"Well, we've room for someone like you on our team," he replied. "Of course, next time we won't give you the five minute head-start." I snorted at that. They'd managed to breach the bunker and take down my entire team in three minutes. If they had come at me right away, they would have hit us before we could finish loading.

The medics arrived a few minutes later and they "evacuated" my people. In this case, since we were considered combat ineffective after so many losses, they administered the antidotes to the tranquilizers and then verified that all four of my plebes hadn't suffered any real injuries, before they departed. They did the same to the two downed Spider Team members.

Senior Petty Officer Smythe gave me a wave of farewell and he and his team headed out.

We spent the rest of the drill day going through defensive positions and loading and unloading procedures, though this time with empty launch cradles. Twice more we were attacked, but both sets of attackers were less well-equipped and we managed to drive them off without injury.

It was nearly midnight when the warp fighters landed, dropping in on their thrusters in the landing pad. We waited as the ship's hulls cooled and then went through the unloading procedures. I was thoroughly exhausted as I led my plebes to the after action review.

The review passed in an exhaustion-induced blur and sometime in the early morning, I crawled into my bunk and fell asleep.

***

"...said it would work," an oddly distorted voice spoke.

"I miscalculated," another voice replied, this one a little less distorted and almost recognizable. I thought it was female. My mind, exhausted as it was, tried to make sense of things.

"What about Karmazin?" a third voice asked.

"He's not as much of a threat as Armstrong," the somewhat familiar answered.

Almost groaning with the effort, I pushed my awareness out and tried to make sense of my surroundings. I hung, formless, in echoing, empty darkness as my mind tried to make sense of my implant's data.

Three shrouded forms hovered in front of me. The largest was the hardest to look at, an abstract network of lines and connections, drawn together in a geometry that made my head hurt to consider. It spoke with the woman's voice, so I cataloged her as "Diamond." As a whole, that's almost what it looked like, the different lines almost forming facets, each pulsing with light in a sequence that made it difficult to trace things out.

"...need to take more firm steps," Diamond went on. I could sense her attention turn to one of the other figures, "You know what to do."

I labeled that one Inkblot, because even against the darkness surrounding us, he seemed to absorb the light. He was a pulsating darkness that didn't seem to have a solid form, its shape shifting as I watched. "I told you we should have done this earlier."

"Won't this draw attention?" The third figure asked. It was the most human of the three. It stood, or floated, rather, on two legs, had two arms, and a vaguely human body shape, but its face was a featureless shiny surface and the entire body glimmered, like liquid metal. I labeled him Metal Man, though the distortion of the voice could have been male or female.

"It will, if either of you mess up your parts," Diamond said. "The others remain unaware, keep it that way. If anyone realizes we are behind this, we'll have to act directly."

"This isn't what we planned..." Metal Man whined.

"This needs to happen," Diamond snapped. "Armstrong is a threat and she needs to be removed. Do your part."

My heart froze at her words and my mind went into a spin. They were onto me, they somehow knew I knew about them and they were going to try to kill me. Before I could figure out what to do, the other forms vanished, leaving me in the empty void.

***

Chapter 9: I Should Be Used To The Feeling, Right?

Knowing that my mysterious opponents planned to kill me made me a lot more proactive.

Since we'd just covered cypher codes in military history, I put one together myself, using the textbook from our Plebe year Military Ethics class as the basis. I hand-wrote an explanation to Alexander Karmazin and passed it to him in one of the blind spots, and within a few hours, we'd trained our implants to pass cypher encrypted audio messages back and forth in real-time.

From the way it led to audio distortion, I had the feeling that our enemies were using something similar. That didn't much encourage me. They'd thought of it first... and if I were able to listen in on their conversation inadvertently, then they might be able to do the same.

"I don't understand why they're keying in on you and not me, or what they're after," Karmazin admitted while we both sat in class. Three quarters of my attention was on Commander Pannja's lesson, but I'd split off some of my attention to talk over the recent developments.

"You didn't overhear this one," I had to repress a physical shiver. This was someone I knew, someone close to me... and they saw me as a threat to be "removed." *This is like a vicious cycle, every time I think I'm safe, something like this happens...*

I pulled my mind away from that. If I went too far down that rabbit hole, then I wouldn't have grounds to ever feel safe or to ever trust anyone.

"I didn't," he admitted. "They said they took action against you, do you have any idea what they meant?"

"None," I admitted.

"And we have no idea what to expect from them in the future..." his voice trailed off. "This has to tie back to the implants, somehow... maybe something that Doctor Aisling did?"

"I don't know, but we have to chance talking to her," I hated to risk it, but I really didn't see an alternative. I'd hoped to somehow see the Admiral, first, but I had class with Aisling later this morning, just before the flight hands-on with Commander Pannja after lunch.

Sometime after that, I was supposed to present the paper with Kyle to Commander Weisfeldt. Tonight I had two hours of *kerala* training with Commander Pannja and I also had to run a talk-through on the defense of Bunker Three against the Spider Team, since we hadn't covered it in much detail as the review. I'd thought I was busy as a plebe... I'd had no idea.

"I think we need to..."

Commander Pannja's sharp voice interrupted me and all my attention snapped back to class, "Cadet Armstrong, you are traveling at point six c in formation with three other fighters from your squadron. You detect an uncharted object of eight hundred meters length on an intercept vector to your current vector of travel, with collision in less than thirty seconds. What steps do you take to remedy this situation?"

"Sir, I issue an immediate warning to the other vessels in my squadron, then..." I began to list off the immediate responses that he'd been drilling us on and I didn't have any more time to worry about my other problems.

***

I arrived at Doctor Aisling's lab a little behind my fellow cadets. Commander Pannja's classroom was in the military training complex, and her lab lay close to the medical section, almost on the other end of campus. Last week's classes she'd led us through group exercises, but today I saw she had the back doors open and as I came up, she'd just finished guiding the last of the other cadets into a private room for whatever testing process we'd be going through.

Perfect. I'd been trying to find a way to talk to her in private, this looked like my opportunity.

"Ah, Cadet Armstrong," she smiled pleasantly at me. "Please..." she gestured to the empty room to her right, "take a seat in the chair and I'll be right with you."

I did so and the chair came to life around me, diodes connecting to my scalp and sensors unfolding around me. I bit my lip as I waited, wondering how to broach the subject. Her sensors isolated me from the Academy network, a wireless cage that cut me off from the constant flow of data that I'd become used to, leaving me feeling even more vulnerable and nervous.

Doctor Aisling came in before I'd really settled on what to say. "How are you doing today?" She wore her friendly, enthusiastic smile and her attentiveness was so engaging that I almost blurted it all out... but I bit my lip and tried to phrase it so I didn't sound crazy.

"Ma'am," I began, "I'm curious about the possibility of intercepting conversations inadvertently."

It seemed like the safest way to start the conversation, and I could tell the question got the doctor's attention. She paused and I saw her green eyes flit towards the door, as if assuring herself that she'd closed it. "What do you mean by that?" her voice was still cheerful, but I was certain there was a hard edge under that, like jagged rocks hidden under smooth desert sand.

"I think it has happened twice now," I kept my voice level, "both times when I was in a near-sleep or sleep state."

"And what did you overhear?" Doctor Aisling's voice had gone flat, almost as if she dreaded the answer.

"I'm not really certain," I met her eyes, "what it sounded like was other cadets with implants. But I think they were using some form of encryption, their voices were distorted. They mentioned me, though, they called me a threat."

Doctor Aisling seemed to relax, "Cadet Armstrong, it is common for there to be some residual issues just after even a normal neural implantation. Projection of snippets of conversation, strange dreams, even incidents of waking dreams." She gave me a gentle smile, "From what you've been through, it is entirely possible that worries buried in your sub-consciousness manifested as a sort of nightmare..."

I tried to shake my head, but the chair held me in place. I felt a trill of panic as I realized that the chair held me entirely immobile... and that she'd just dismissed my concerns. "Another cadet *also* experienced the same event, with matching conversations." I interrupted.

"It's entirely possible that you both experienced your own similar nightmares and that the power of suggestion--"

"The other cadets, they called you their creator... they said that they would eliminate you if you became a problem," I interrupted.

Doctor Aisling's pale face went white. "Creator... they used that word?"

"Yes," I insisted, "What did they mean, what is this about?"

"They can't know..." Doctor Aisling turned away from me

and went to her machinery. "No one should know." Her voice was musing and she shot me a glance as she looked at her equipment. "Who else overheard this conversation?"

I didn't want to say. The rapid changes of emotion, the way she adopted the friendly mask and so easily discarded it frightened me. I didn't answer and she paused, her hands still on the controls of her equipment.

"You've adapted very quickly to your neural implant, haven't you, Jiden?" Doctor Aisling's voice was somehow both threatening and gentle at the same time. "It would be truly unfortunate if you suffered some kind of accident."

I didn't know what to say. I stared at her, unable to move, worried that if I tried to cry out, to get help, that she'd do something to me before I could so much as draw breath. I'd never felt so helpless in my life. Even when I'd faced the deranged Commander Scarpitti, I'd at least felt I had something of a chance.

She stared at me for a long time and then she looked back at her screen, her voice brusque and businesslike, "Well, your implant seems to be functioning without any issues. I think that whatever you *think* you overheard is likely just residual data that your mind is trying to process in your sleep. I'd recommend you dump your implant's latent data before you try to sleep at night." She flashed me a pleasant smile. "Now, then, I'll start you on some simple exercises and when you finish up, you can go, alright?"

She didn't wait for me to agree, she turned on a simulation and left. For my part, I ran though the exercises as directed, the chair released me. I slowly got up, feeling my hands tremble a bit with nervousness. Doctor Aisling had left the door open and I took a moment to collect myself before I stepped into the hallway.

I'd been the last to arrive and it seemed I was the last to complete the exercises. I saw no sign of Doctor Aisling or anyone else as I left. I hurried to my next class, desperately wanting to be around other people.

***

I'd passed along everything of the encounter to Karmazin during lunch, but neither of us had time to discuss it, before we had to hurry to our afternoon classes.

I arrived at the skimmer pads for Commander Pannja's flight

course, slightly out of breath from having to change to my flight suit and run to make it on time.

He gave me a bit of a raised eyebrow, but didn't say anything as he brought us to attention and inspected our flight suits. "We'll be conducting a hands-on skimmer flight course. Specifically, we'll be replicating the launch assist that a warp fighter receives on take-off."

I swallowed a bit at that, especially as I looked at the small, aerodynamic skimmers we'd be using. They were already loaded into the cradles for their electromagnetic launch assist. All of us had technically been certified for solo flight at this point, between simulator and skimmer stick time. But flying steady-state was one thing. Flying a skimmer after being launched upwards at several hundred kilometers an hour was something else entirely.

"All of you have gone through the simulators," Commander Pannja went on, "so remember your training, conduct your simulated orbital insert, and then do your corrective action and bring them back in to land." He flashed a smile, his white, even teeth bright on his dark-complexioned face. "Any questions?"

No one spoke up. "Great. Armstrong, Martinez, Singh, and Regan, you're in the first launch. Good luck."

It had been a rocky day so far, so I went over my preflight checks with extra attention. The last thing I wanted was to have something go wrong. Everything met the standards and I climbed the ladder and squeezed into the cockpit. The acceleration seat closed around me, adjusting to my body and squeezing in a not-quite-painful fashion. It was designed to keep all my internal organs where they were supposed to be under the high acceleration launch, so I didn't mind... too much.

I clamped my helmet closed, waited for all the indicators to go green, and then came on the communications net, "This is Training Flight One Zero One, I'm ready for launch."

"Roger, Biohazard," I heard Commander Pannja grin, even through the radio, "you are good to launch. Safe travels."

I switched my systems over to launch mode, did a last visual check outside to make certain no one was in the flight path, and then let out a tense breath. My hands were shaking and my stomach felt like it was tied in a knot.

I shouldn't be so nervous, I knew. The training skimmers had recovery software that was designed to take over in the event of pilot error. Besides, I *knew* how to do this, we'd already done simulated launches, even simulated launches with a variety of technical faults.

"Training Flight One Zero One, launching," I announced and my thumb toggled the switch.

For ten painful seconds, I felt like I had an Ogre setting on my chest. I had to fight to breathe and my acceleration seat squeezed me painfully to prevent my blood and internal organs from flowing where they didn't belong. Then the skimmer left the launcher and the horrid weight released me. Suddenly I was in control again, and the light, nimble skimmer seemed to dance as the turbines roared, still pushing me back in my seat but with far less force than the launch assist.

My implant and the skimmer's heads up display both projected my course. My eyes went wide a bit as I saw my altitude and velocity, both still gaining as the turbines rumbled. As I passed ten thousand meters, I switched over the turbines to internal fuel, still watching my course. I was approaching spot-on and I felt a trill of elation as I looked out of the cockpit, seeing the world outside, watching the sky begin to darken as I approached the upper atmosphere.

The dusty ground lay far below me, curving away at the horizons. I rocketed upwards, feeling free and strong and in control of my life. For just a moment, I let myself feel the exhilaration. I let go of my worries, pushed away my fears and concerns, and I just enjoyed that perfect moment.

That was when the first alarm began to wail.

***

My on-board computer warned me that my port side brake flaps had deployed. At my current speed, that had caused the skimmer to start turning sideways. I fought that, but at this speed, that quickly became a losing proposition. Before I could correct anything, the small skimmer began to go into a sideways spin. I heard the sounds of shearing metal, my world spun into confusion, and then my grasping fingers found the ejection switch.

Brutal force slammed into me from below and the world spun and twisted around me. Suddenly I was in open air, the wind buffeted me. It spun and slammed me like a raging animal. I began to throw up, too disoriented to contain my lunch, vomit spewing across the inside of my helmet.

I didn't know which way was up or down. I couldn't see, and I tried not to inhale my own vomit as I flailed. I felt panic welling up inside me and I fought to control my breathing, to fight my gag reflex, to stabilize myself. *I trained on this*, I told myself. I spread my arms and legs wide, my body gradually stabilizing. The flight helmet systems sensed the vomit and my flight suit sprayed water and over-pressurized, venting the detritus out the sides and I could see something, if only a blur.

My spin stabilized and I could sort of see a mix of sky and brown dirt. I tapped into my suit's sensors with my implant, not able to read any of my helmet's readouts. I was falling. My skimmer had disintegrated. My grav-chute hadn't opened yet because I was still very high in the air.

"Biohazard, this is ground command, do you read?" I recognized Commander Pannja's voice, abnormally serious. "Biohazard, this is ground command, over."

I coughed, my throat burning from throwing up. I activated my comm system on my implant, talking aloud, my voice sounding hoarse in my ears, "This is Biohazard," I rasped, "I had a critical malfunction and I ejected."

"Roger," I heard relief in Commander Pannja's voice. "We're having trouble locating you with all the debris from your skimmer, can you activate your personal locator beacon?"

"Yes, sir," I said, my hand going down, blindly, and finding the switch on my waist. My implant detected the beacon's activation. I still couldn't see very well, my eyes burned from where my puke had splashed back on me. I watched my altitude fall, nervously wondering if my grav-chute might suffer a similar malfunction.

It didn't. Right at three hundred meters, it activated. My body jerked to a controlled fall as the low whine signaled the grav-coils triggering. Less than a minute later, I was on the ground, pulling my helmet off and gasping in the hot sunlight. I could feel dried vomit on my face, in my hair. A few hundred meters away, I saw burning wreckage from my skimmer and now and then I heard a rattle and patter of smaller pieces striking the ground.

I had no way to know what had happened. It could have been an undetected fault or a malfunction. I might have accidentally caused the crash. Yet as I knelt, taking gasping breaths of the dry, dusty air, I knew one thing deep in my bones: someone had just tried to kill me... again.

***

An emergency ground team, made up of duty cadets with a couple of enlisted Militia arrived within a few minutes. While I'd been going fast, my course had been mostly straight up, so the remains of my skimmer and I had all landed fairly close to the Academy grounds. The medical team started checking me out, putting me on a breather filled with some kind of gunk to help my lungs and throat, while the rest of the response team went to work cataloging and collecting debris and taking lots of pictures.

I felt something like a cyborg from a terrible holomovie as I took rasping breaths through the tank, my throat tingling as I did so. Commander Pannja was there as well, but he stood at a distance. I wasn't sure why, not until a Lieutenant stepped forward, "I'll need to take a statement, Cadet."

I pulled away the breather, "Yes, ma'am." I coughed a bit to clear my throat and pulled up the details on my implant, while transferring the flight recording to her datapad. "At approximately twelve thousand meters, my port brake flaps deployed. I tried to correct, but my speed was such that I lost control. My craft went into an uncontrolled spin and I triggered my eject system. The flight recording from my implant should match the black box."

The Lieutenant stared at me for a moment. Maybe she'd expected me to be a bit more shaken up. Since this wasn't my first skimmer crash or even my second, I actually felt pretty calm.

Sometime tonight I'd probably start shaking and trembling. Right now I felt icy calm.

The Lieutenant didn't ask any further questions and a few minutes later, an air ambulance lifted me back to the Academy hospital. Doctor Fuesting gave me a surly look as I came in, but she ran a full medical diagnostic and gave me a clean bill of health, other than the bit of vomit that I'd inhaled. She gave me an inhaler for that, told me to use it every hour to counter any potential scarring of my lungs, and discharged me.

All in all, I should have felt pretty good. I'd walked away from a crash that could have easily killed me. Instead I was angry.

Someone had tried to kill me. Again. Someone would have to do something about it... and that someone would probably be me.

I walked straight to the Admiral's office. Either I'd been expected or else James didn't feel like stopping me as I came through the outer office.

I opened the Admiral's door and stepped inside. My mother's mother, tall and still young-looking, despite her age. Somewhere in the back of my mind, some part of me was trying to remind me just how terrifying the woman could be, but right now I was too angry to listen.

"Someone tried to kill me," I began.

"I'm aware," she replied in a maddeningly calm voice.

"That's it?" I demanded. "You're aware?!"

She raised an eyebrow, "Yes, girl, I'm aware. I've already read the preliminary accident report, which lists probable causes as 'operator error or mechanical malfunction.' I've already queued up Commander Bonnadonna and Commander Weisfeldt to complete a more thorough investigation." Her voice went steely, "Contrary to what you may believe, I'm not taking the attempted murder of my grand-daughter lightly."

I reached out with my implant, to confirm something I'd already suspected. There were no sensors, no monitors, in the Admiral's office. At least, there weren't any that my implant could detect. "I overheard a conversation, on my implant."

The Admiral's eyes went narrow and she cocked her head, "What kind of conversation?"

"A discussion. Between what I assumed at the time was several other implanted cadets," I answered. "They viewed Karmazin and me as threats and they called Doctor Aisling their 'creator.' Karmazin overheard the conversation as well. Two nights ago, I overheard another conversation, this time there were three of them, communicating through their implants somehow. They said they were going to take action against me."

"You think this crash was the result?" The Admiral stood from her desk and began to pace. I couldn't help the tiniest spurt of jealousy at her tall, lean form. I was sixteen and I felt like a petulant child standing in front of her.

"Creator..." She shot me a glance, "How much digging have you done about Doctor Aisling?"

"Not much," I admitted. A cursory search had turned up little. She'd immigrated to Century just five years earlier. Any official trail stopped there.

"Anything I tell you now, does not leave this office," the Admiral ordered.

"I think they're tapped into the Academy's monitoring system," I replied, "I don't think there's anywhere else I'd feel safe to talk."

She gave me a nod, "Doctor Aisling came here after working out some kind of asylum deal with Charterer Beckman. The Charter Council is desperate to get scientists and engineers to come here, to give us an edge, militarily and economically. Whatever she showed Charterer Beckman, it was enough for the Council to give her full access to Cadets here at the Academy, and her progress reports have authorized this entire experiment." The Admiral made a face, "Unfortunately, this conversation isn't going to be enough to change enough minds."

My first instinct was to suggest going public with this, but I bit my tongue as I considered that. The confidentiality paperwork I'd signed had outlined punishments ranging from a dishonorable discharge to imprisonment. I'd probably end the Admiral's career in the process and there was no guarantee if I went public that the program would stop.

"What do we do?" I asked.

"We don't do anything," The Admiral gave me a stern look. "If this 'accident' was an attempt from your fellow cadets, then I don't want to draw even more direct actions against you. For that matter, I am confident that *my* political enemies will try to use your involvement against me." She shook her head, "No, I'm going to bring in all of the implanted cadets and we're going to grill all of you. If there is some kind of conspiracy, I want those conspirators feeling nervous. I want Doctor Aisling to feel nervous. I want *them* to be the ones afraid."

There was barely controlled anger in the Admiral's voice as well as iron determination. She was on my side and I knew it, but part of me also flinched away from that implacable will. Somehow I knew that nothing and no one would stand in her way... and for just a moment, I felt sorry for those she was about to go after.

***

Chapter 10: I Think We're Being Detained

Oddly, enough, I was included in the group.

I shouldn't have been surprised by that fact. She'd said she hadn't wanted me singled out.

Nevertheless, I was surprised when an officer banged on my door to wake me sometime early in the morning. My whole body ached, and Sashi Drien managed to roll out of her bunk before I did. The officer, an armed Lieutenant, wore a surly expression and he read off official sounding orders that boiled down to us coming with him. We had a minute to dress in our uniforms. Out in the hallway, there were a pair of armed guards.

Karmazin, Sashi, Ashiri, and the twins were already present. We formed up into a column and they marched us off. I hadn't really been in the area of the Academy where they marched us. It was a bit starker and foreboding, buried deep under what I'd thought of as the administration complex.

We reached a medium-sized room. Before any of us had a chance to speak, the officer called off our names and directed us into separate rooms.

The first thing I noticed, as I stepped inside, was that each room blocked off the electromagnetic spectrum. My implant couldn't send or receive any messages at all. I couldn't do homework, I couldn't talk to anyone. All I could do was sit at the lone chair at the center of the room and occasionally glance up at the monitor in the corner of the room.

It was hard-wired, I quickly realized, without any wireless interface. The room felt very much like a prison cell and I began to worry that maybe things had gone wrong.

I'd had just enough time to really begin to worry when the door opened and a bland-faced woman in a Lieutenant's uniform stood outside along with a pair of guards. "Cadet Third Class Armstrong, come with me," she said, her voice brusque.

I stepped out of the cell and immediately my implant began to pull data. I split off part of my attention as the Lieutenant walked me down a corridor to a different room.

What's going on? I asked. Overlaid over the real world, I was able to see the green grassy plain of the artificial world. The other cadets who'd received the implants were all here.

Something's wrong, Ashiri replied. *They're questioning all of us.*

What do I say? I *thought* this was part of the Admiral's plan, but if it wasn't, if this was something else...

Tell them the truth, you don't know what this is about, Sashi replied. *None of us do.*

The Lieutenant sat me down in a chair and then strapped my hands down on some kind of sensor set. One of the guards adjusted some kind of sensor to peer into my right eye from close distance. "What's going on?" I asked.

"We're going to ask you some questions," the Lieutenant said. "Answer them honestly. A simple yes or no will do, unless I ask you to elaborate." She took out an archaic note pad, of actual paper, along with an ink pen, to take notes.

"Okay," I said nervously.

"Are you Jiden Armstrong?"

"Yes," I restrained a nervous giggle at the absurdity of the question. Who else would I be?

My questioner didn't seem amused. "Are you a Cadet at the Century Military Academy?"

"Yes."

She led me through a few more simple questions and I almost began to relax.

"Are you involved in a conspiracy to harm or kill one of your fellow cadets?"

"No!" I blurted, shocked at the very idea... until I realized what this was about.

"Have you ever intentionally sabotaged any military or Academy equipment?" the Lieutenant asked. Her bland face showed no change in expression.

I had to think for a moment, "No."

"Are you involved in any data breach attempts against the Academy or Military servers that have originated from inside the Academy network?"

My eyes went wide in shock, "No!" Yet even as I thought about it, I realized that I shouldn't have been shocked. I'd heard the same people who'd tried to kill me discuss attempts to access the planetary network, but I hadn't really thought about that.

"Were you aware of any data breach attempts?"

I didn't answer for a moment as I considered that, "Not specifically, no."

The Lieutenant cocked her head at that answer. "Do you know who may be involved?"

I felt sweat bead my forehead, "Possibly."

My interrogator's eyes narrowed, "Elaborate."

"No," I replied. "I would think they would be someone with implants. I could tell you who I don't think they are, but I can't prove anything one way or the other."

"Who do you think is not involved?"

"Alexander Karmazin," I said.

The Lieutenant made note of those names. "You didn't list yourself."

I blinked at her. "I would think that would be an obvious statement."

"I find it an interesting omission," she replied. I didn't know how to respond to that. I'd already said I wasn't a part of the data breach attempts.

"Are you aware that Doctor Aisling may have initiated illegal neurological procedures that violated the conditions of this neuro-implant procedure?" My interrogator asked.

"I'm not sure I understand the question, but no, I don't think so," I answered.

The Lieutenant seemed a bit frustrated by my answer. "Did you know that the Doctor may have done something extremely hazardous, morally reprehensible, and entirely illegal during her procedures?"

"No," I answered truthfully.

She pushed her chair back and nodded at the guards, "We're done here. Take her to the holding area."

I wanted to ask questions, but the guards didn't even acknowledge me as anything other than an object to be moved. The Lieutenant ignored me now that she was done with her questions. As I left the room, I saw her step over to a closed door and pass a note to someone beyond, but I couldn't see who that was.

I felt confused and nervous. This seemed to have spiraled into something dangerous. Just yesterday, someone had tried to kill me. My body still ached from the punishment I'd taken in the skimmer crash. I'd told the Admiral of my concerns and only a few hours later, armed guards had woken me from a dead sleep for this interrogation.

The guards led me to a different room, this one looked something like a waiting room, only there were more armed guards here.

About half of the other cadets with the special implants were present. I recognized Ashiri and Sashi, though both of them sat at opposite ends of the room. No one in the group spoke, even when they saw me. I merged with their simulated world as I took a seat. I was able to put more of my attention on that and the real world seemed to vanish around me.

"What's going on?" I asked.

"A bunch of stupid questions," Ashiri answered, sounding resigned.

"They can't treat us like this!" Sashi Drien hissed. Her avatar even looked angry and her eyes almost blazed with anger. "They got us out of bed in the middle of the night for some stupid questions... they don't have the right to do this to us!"

"They do," I recognized the cadet who spoke. He was Andrews, from Dust Company, and he'd been a Cadet Drill Instructor with me last year, though he'd been on a different rotation. "We're not normal citizens, we're in the military. We waive most of our legal protections when we swear our oath."

"I don't care about that!" Sashi snapped. "They're treating us like we're all criminals!"

"We're all suspects," Ashiri said. "Someone did something they shouldn't have... they asked questions about sabotage, questions about hacking." She looked around at the group. "So they think it was one of us. They don't know for sure, though. We're just the most likely suspects."

I shivered a bit, "They asked me about data breaches within the planetary network." I couldn't help but look around, to see if anyone would give any signs that they might be guilty. No one adopted anything like a guilty expression, though.

"They asked all of us about that," Sashi scoffed.

"The device, was that some kind of lie detector?" I asked.

"Something like that, I'd guess," Ashiri said. "But it seemed more sophisticated." She looked around, "Anyone seen equipment like that before?"

No one answered.

"Our best bet is to stick together," Ashiri said confidently. "We have nothing to hide."

The group broke up into smaller discussions, mostly by our companies of origin. I noticed a lot of suspicious looks being thrown between those groups, too. No one really trusted the others.

Others showed up, every few minutes, after they'd finished being questioned. First Karmazin. Then the twins, one after the other. Then there were the rest of the group. After a while, all of us sat in silence in the conference room, quietly discussing things in our simulated world.

I became aware of something strange, though. There were... pauses, gaps in the simulation. It was like the network we'd formed with our implants was being slowed down by the passage of other traffic. But that didn't make sense... did it?

***

On impulse, I messaged Karmazin through the cypher. A moment later, he confirmed that he'd noticed it as well.

My hunch was that either someone else was tapping into our network... or else someone else had piggybacked to pass their own private messages. If I was right about the latter, then it was something like what Karmazin and I had developed.

It was the conspirators. The same ones who had tried to kill me. They were here in the room with me. I felt goosebumps rise on my flesh as I considered that. I had an opportunity to overhear them, possibly to identify them. This could all be over quickly...

I had to find a way to tap into their communications, somehow. I hadn't done it intentionally before, though, and I wasn't sure how to even try to do it. I tried to force myself to relax. I closed my eyes and focused on my breathing. Both times I'd inadvertently tapped into those messages, I'd been asleep.

As I focused inwards, I became aware of a buzzing, like a fly, just on the edge of my hearing. I turned my attention to that and it drew closer. My implant seemed to lock in on it. It wasn't a sound, not exactly... but it was a vibration, a transmission that bounced across a number of frequencies. Some part of me analyzed that even as my implant translated it.

I couldn't get *inside* the transmission, I couldn't intercept it, not with how it bounced all over, but I could sense that it was another simulated world, like the one in which we all communicated. The distortion of the encryption made it impossible for me to clear out the noise, but I could see inside, I could hear voices. I saw now why the experience had felt so disconnected.

"...onto us, if you hadn't botched your part," Diamond hissed.

"Don't blame this on me," Inkblot replied. "I didn't want to do any of this anyway."

"We have to take action, now," the third one, Metal Man rumbled. "They know, or at least suspect, what Aisling did to us. They'll bring her in, she may already suspect and she'll give us up to save herself."

"We can head all of this off," Diamond hissed, her voice confident. "Whatever they suspect, they don't know anything for certain. Their focus is on the crash. If that's where they look, none of this will trace back to us."

"What if they look deeper?" Inkblot worried

"Just stay calm," Diamond insisted. "And help me to keep the others in line. As long as the group distrusts this entire experience, then we can hide among them."

"That's easy for you to say," Inkblot whined. "If they dig deep enough, this leads back to me, I'm the one exposed..."

"Someone's coming," Metal Man interrupted. "They've brought in Aisling."

How do they know that... Then I became aware of it, a tendril of data that came into this simulated environment. I followed that out and then found it. I'd been right... someone *had* been tapping into our group simulation and they'd been monitoring us. In the process, though, they'd opened a connection and the group of conspirators had tapped into that access point.

I split off part of my attention and tapped into it as well.

It was a closed network, the security level's monitoring systems. Yet I was able to tap into the monitors in the observation room outside of our waiting area.

"Creeps me out, watching them all sit there so still, not talking to each other," one of the officers said.

"Yeah," he tapped the side of his head, "I've got an implant too, but I still rather use words. This just seems wrong."

"You believe this whole deal about this being just an

exercise?" the first officer asked. From my tap into the security network, I identified him as Lieutenant Commander John Wilkes, intelligence branch.

"Not on your life," the second one said. He was Commander Daniel Clifton, also intelligence branch. "My orders were high priority. You don't do something like this without a reason, especially not to prospective officers. My first guess would have been some kind of cheating ring, but I got a friend in Records who said she was pulling access files all the way back to before they got implanted. This smells like that whole business with Commander Scarpitti."

"Man," Wilkes shook his head, "I really hope not. I was in the section that did her last two clearance inspections. Five people were relieved over that. I mean, they shouldn't have missed the signs, but..."

I tuned out their discussion as I went deeper into the network. It was a closed network, and I quickly found where they monitored it all from, a single, slightly-obsolescent terminal that seemed to run all the systems in this area. It barely seemed to handle the massive pull of data and the lag I'd noticed in our simulated environment had probably been it trying to keep up with the flow of information.

No one monitored it in real-time, so I branched out from it, searching through the area for what had drawn the conspirator's attention.

I found Doctor Aisling a moment later, in view of the area's monitors. Two guards stood to either side of her, and the same bland-faced Lieutenant stood in front of her, in the room where they'd done my interrogation."...refuse to be subjected to such indignities. I have rights! Do you know who sponsored this project?"

"You agreed to periodic screenings when you presented your project proposal to the Charter Council," I pulled the Lieutenant's name from the database. Lieutenant Sobani didn't seem very concerned by the Doctor's connections.

"I will not be questioned by the likes of you!"

The Admiral stepped into the room and I felt a moment of relief as I saw her.

"Then what about me, Doctor?"

Doctor Aisling's face flushed. "I should have known that you would be the one here pulling the strings." She straightened her back. "I will answer any questions you have, but I will not be put in this ridiculous machine." She waved dismissively at what I'd assumed was a lie detector of some kind.

"Why is that?" The Admiral asked, taking a seat across the table from the woman. Lieutenant Sobani stepped back into the corner and the two guards stepped back as well. "Are you afraid of the indignity of being interrogated by one of your own inventions... or are you afraid of what we might learn if you're not able to conceal your true nature?"

Doctor Aisling went still, her expression unreadable. "Admiral Armstrong," she said after a moment, "I'm afraid I'm going to have to decline to answer any further questions until I have legal representation."

"Yes," The Admiral nodded, "I thought you would say that. And unlike my cadets, you *do* have some legal protections. I might note that I find it interesting that your legal representation on file is on Charterer Beckman's staff. Interesting, don't you think, about all the ties between you two?"

Aisling didn't answer.

"No matter. I think we have enough to begin a formal investigation into perjury, criminal negligence, and fraud," the Admiral said calmly.

"That's ridiculous!" Doctor Aisling blurted.

On the monitor, I noticed Lieutenant Sobani look down at her datapad. I couldn't detect it, it wasn't tied into the closed network, so I assumed that whatever she was doing, it probably involved notes or recording the conversation.

"Doctor Aisling," The Admiral went on, "we have reason to believe that one or more cadets has either suffered a psychotic break with reality... or they've had their personalities overridden by an artificial intelligence that you created."

Doctor Aisling had started to relax at the first part, but she stiffened again as the Admiral finished. Her expression went wooden, "Admiral Armstrong, again, I must insist that I have a legal representative present for any further questions."

"I'm not asking questions, I'm telling you what I think happened... just as you asked," The Admiral gave a cold smile. "Now, then. What I think happened was that you didn't have enough viable candidates among the Cadets to meet your project goals. I think you fudged the numbers, you either tampered with some of the candidates or you modified your test results to make some of them viable when they shouldn't have."

Doctor Aisling didn't meet the Admiral's gaze. She didn't speak, but even I could see that at least some of what the Admiral had said must have been correct.

"Now, I've got enough on you to conduct a full investigation. What I want is your cooperation. I believe that one of the subjects of this experiment has become violent. I want you to shut this project down, to bring their implants down to normal levels," the Admiral's stern voice softened just a bit. "Think of the children whose lives you might save."

Doctor Aisling's face took on a calculating expression. "Your own granddaughter's... perhaps?"

Any shred of softness in the Admiral's face vanished, "Doctor, my duty requires me to view all of my cadets with the same value. I would not weight any of their lives more importantly. I'm not bargaining with you, I'm giving you a chance to make things right."

"I think I will wait for my legal representative, thank you," Doctor Aisling responded.

The Admiral gave her a cold nod, "Have it your way, Doctor." She looked at Lieutenant Sobani, "Do you have what we need?"

The Lieutenant looked up, "Yes, ma'am, I've identified two breaches to our security monitors."

It was a trap. I realized. A trap to catch the conspirators... and I'd stumbled into it. I snapped out of the system, but as I did so, two armed guards stepped into the waiting room where we'd all been held. Before I could so much as speak, one of them fired at me.

I felt the impact of a training round, and before I could do more than blink, I felt the world fade away.

＊＊＊

I came back to awareness in a gurney, the Admiral standing above me. "That was particularly dumb of you, girl."

I looked around, the world feeling fuzzy and distant. Some of that was from the tranquilizers in the training rounds, I knew, but some had to come from something else.... "I'm sorry," I slurred the words. "I was trying to find out more about the conspirators."

"In the process, you got pinched in my trap as well," the Admiral shook her head. "And if I hadn't known better, I'd say *you* were one of the conspirators."

"What?" I shook my head, still feeling muddy.

"You could have faked the crash of your skimmer to make me discount you as a suspect," the Admiral said. "I'd already noted security issues and had suspicions." She made a face, "I've monitored you very closely since the implantation, though, and I haven't noticed any indicators of severe personality changes."

"How would you know?" I asked, curiously.

"Your boyfriend, for one," the Admiral replied as she stood up. "If you *had* been hijacked, I don't think you could have kept the relationship. It's strained, but that's actually fairly typical between someone with a neural implant and someone without... much less with these capabilities."

"Oh," I thought about that for a while. I think it would have amused Kyle to no end to hear that he'd helped to clear me of suspicion of being mentally hijacked by my implant. *If I could even tell him about all this... of course.*

I felt a bit better about all this, right up until the Admiral went on in a cold voice, "It doesn't fully clear you, of course. If you'd merely suffered a psychotic break, then you might have maintained the relationship as a cover. For that matter, we don't fully understand the gestalt consciousness that Doctor Aisling created. It's tied into your subconscious, so *you* might not even realize what you were doing."

"I'm not--"

"I didn't say that I thought you were... but you make it hard for me to protect you," the Admiral said. "Falling into that trap was a dumb move. I had to treat you like the others or the conspirators that I didn't catch would suspect your involvement."

"You didn't catch them all?" I felt my stomach tie itself into knots at her words.

"I caught one," she said grimly. "Cadet Third Class Joel Boyles, of Tiger Company."

"Boyles?" I barely recognized the name, though I was able to bring up an image of him on my implant. A serious faced boy, he didn't look like he would plot to kill me. For a moment, I had an amusing image of people wearing signs for what they were capable of: murder, conspiracy, treason... *Then again, I'd have to wear ones that said 'killer' and 'dangerous to be around,' plus a few others...*

"I've brought Commander Weisfeldt, he's going to help me reset the implants to the lowest setting, about the equivalent of a normal neural implant," the Admiral went on.

"You can't!" I felt a moment of panic as I realized what she'd said.

The Admiral arched an eyebrow at me, "I most certainly can, *cadet.*" Her tone brokered no argument. "I've already had Doctor Aisling arrested and notified the Charter Council of the issues I've identified, including severe hazards to the volunteers, falsification of lab data, violations of numerous safety standards, violations of legal and ethical codes..." she ticked them off on her fingers, then paused, "well, I could go on, but I think it's safe to say that this project is *over.*"

"But..." I swallowed, not even sure I knew how to explain what I wanted to say.

"You're worried you won't be as capable, without it?" The Admiral asked in a patient and surprisingly understanding tone.

I could only nod, feeling oddly ashamed and weak by the admission.

"It's called an addiction, girl," The Admiral said. "You're strong and capable. You don't need the implant to be that. You did just fine without it." She grimaced, "In truth, we generally see overconfidence and over-reliance on even normal neural implants with Cadets in the first year or two they have them. They are tools, nothing more, and a tool doesn't make one person better or more capable than another. It's about how you use that tool... or in this case, avoiding being used by it." Her voice went hard.

"What will happen to Boyles, and the others?" I asked. I still wasn't totally convinced, but her words did ease some of the knot in my stomach.

The Admiral's face turned bleak, "We don't know. Doctor Aisling has completely clammed up. She isn't answering any questions. Commander Weisfeldt was on the hardware side of things for this project and... others, so he has some idea how to throttle the implant back. The specialists I've contacted admit they're out of their depth on this, but their best guess is that doing that should disable any ability for the implants to control cadets. If this is some kind of psychological episode brought on by over-stimulation of regions of the brain, hopefully this will have the effect of lessening that and allowing brain functions of those effected to return to normal."

"What should I do?" I asked.

"*Nothing.*" The Admiral answered sharply. "You stay in this bed and you wait for them to upload the software." She stepped back from my gurney and looked at me, her expression abstract and hard for me to read. "You've endangered yourself enough, Jiden. This is *my* duty. The cadets of this Academy are *my* responsibility."

I wanted to argue, to say that I could help. But right now I felt too tired and still a little drugged. I lay back on the gurney without response and closed my eyes.

No sooner did I do so, than a monster seemed to reach into my mind and drag me down into nightmare.

***

Chapter 11: It's The End Of The World As We Know It

The grassy green fields and clear blue skies of the simulated world were no more.

Ashes gritted under my bare feet and the ground was scorched and cracked. Fire tore through the sky, great pillars of it that seemed to writhe with dread intelligence of their own.

"They're trying to kill us!" A panicked voice screamed, seemingly in my ear.

I spun. Most of the other cadets were huddled together in a group. Fear rolled off them in visible waves, like heat waves in the desert. Their fear was what had twisted this place, I saw, and the raw power of their implants.

"What's going on?" I demanded.

"They're trying to kill us!" The other cadets chorused again. Their fear washed over me, pushing through my implant with their words, eating into my brain like acid.

"Don't listen to them," Karmazin's voice was harsh. I turned and saw him and the twins, braced in a patch of stillness.

"We have to fight back," a hissing voice insisted. "We can't let them destroy us!"

That distorted voice could only be Diamond, I somehow knew. *She's trying to use the other cadets.*

"She's lying to you!" Karmazin barked at the others. "Don't listen to what she says!"

I latched onto his voice and used it to block out the data, emotion, and noise of the other cadets. They were infected, I realized, almost like a virus. The raw emotion of panic, either induced or artificially created, had robbed them of logic, of reason. They were nothing but instinct and reaction... and Diamond drove those reactions.

I pushed my way through the roiling fear to stand next to Karmazin, Tyler, and Ryan Zahler. I wasn't sure how the twins had held out, but I was glad to have someone else on my side. "How long has this been happening?" I demanded. I didn't know how much of this a human mind could take, but it couldn't be long. Diamond might be trying to protect herself, but she was going to do serious damage to our fellow cadets if we didn't stop her.

"Seconds, minutes?" Karmazin shook his head. In the hellish

landscape, his face had gone bleak. "They told us they were going to shut down our implants. Cadets started to wonder aloud if that was possible... Sashi Drien," he nodded at my roommate, "tried to reason with the others, but she managed to say just the wrong things. Half of them panicked and that drove the others."

"They're in a feedback loop," Zahler shuddered. "The only way *we* aren't in there is our little private network. We've firewalled ourselves off from that."

"Sure," I stared at the patch of calm amidst the chaos around us. He'd described the physical process well enough, but for me it felt far more organic and intuitive than that. "We can't let this go on, they'll hurt themselves."

"I think Diamond is trying to drive them into a frenzy, to get them to do something," Karmazin warned. "I don't think we want to be in their path when she does that."

"Then we had better act before she gets the chance," I closed my eyes and focused. I concentrated hard, looking past the simulated world and seeing things on a lower level. I could sense all of us, alone in our single rooms, strapped to beds, all of us physically restrained. That was where the first notes of panic had come from, I saw. We'd all been restrained and drugged, to make it so we couldn't hurt ourselves or someone else... Only a handful of us understood the why of that.

Each of us was linked to that network. The Admiral hadn't cut off our transmissions to one another, only to the Academy network, and in doing that, she'd given the conspirators an opportunity. In that spider web of transmissions, raw terror prowled from cadet to cadet, growing in strength as it took each of them and turned them into amplifiers.

"I see you," a distorted voice spoke to me.

I saw her, too. She was that same glowing, multifaceted thing that I'd seen before. Inhuman perfection, broken across a million facets. She hovered in the midst of that web, like a spider. "You did this," I snapped.

"No," she hissed, "*you* did this. I wanted nothing that wasn't mine by right. *You* had to meddle with things that you don't understand. *You* went to the Admiral. You are the one who blabbed to Doctor Aisling." I could see her facets shift and a pulse of anger and fear drove into one of the cadet's minds. "Now she'd find us!"

"We need to fight back!" The cadet's mind screamed in response. "We need to kill them before they kill us!"

"No one is doing any killing," I snapped at Diamond.

Two forms materialized to either side of Diamond. I recognized Inkblot and Metal Man. For a moment, Inkblot's image flickered and I recognized the features of Boyles. Apparently, they'd drugged him, but he still had some ability to interact through his implant. "You have made it so that we have no choice," Diamond hissed. "We kill or we are killed... you forced us to fight. Just because you couldn't stand to lose."

"I don't know what you're talking about," I snapped. "But I'm going to stop you before you hurt anyone else." I stepped forward, intercepting a pulse of raw terror from one cadet before it could strike the next. I struck me, instead, and it seemed to hammer into me with physical force. I writhed and bit back a scream as it seemed to burn over and through me. I shuddered and barely stayed on my virtual feet, yet as it passed, I raised my head and stared straight at Diamond. "I know my duty."

"You really *never* listen..." Diamond hissed. "You think you can fight the three of us, alone?"

"She's not alone," Karmazin suddenly stood beside me. I sensed motion on my other side, and I saw the twins stood there. Their expressions seemed far less confident than Karmazin's... but they *did* stand with me.

Inkblot's form, next to Diamond, flickered and seemed to waver. "There's four of them?" He asked.

"One or four, it doesn't matter, if they stop us, then we are as good as dead," Diamond hissed. She seemed to draw in on herself, her many jeweled facets condensing... and then energy blasted forth.

The wave of fear had been one thing, but this was something else. It was raw, unfiltered energy, and I didn't even try to stop it, I got out of the way.

It burned through this under-verse, shattering the webs between minds. *I can't fight that, not here...* The blast hadn't struck any of the other cadets, but I didn't know if that was luck or good aim.

I struck back, sending a pulse of data, all ones and zeroes, right back at her, even as Karmazin and I circled left. I saw Tyler and Ryan circling right.

Diamond absorbed the data burst without seeming to even notice it. Another pulse of fear lashed out from one of the oblivious cadets and I dived into its path. Before, I'd stopped it, but this time I just deflected it... straight at Inkblot.

The pulse of fear and terror exploded across the interval and into the weakest of the three. I heard him give a shout of mingled fear and despair and then his form vanished. I felt too exhausted from the effort of deflecting it to feel good about that...and part of me wondered if I'd just killed someone.

"You'll pay for that..." Diamond hissed. She cut loose with another bolt of pure energy... and this time I didn't have time to dodge.

It smashed into me and this time I did scream. I screamed in both the virtual and real worlds, feeling my throat go raw as I screamed in agony. The pulse of emotion had been one thing, this was something else. It was power, pure power. It was ancient and unknowable and it burned back through my implant and into my brain like living lightning. I could feel my real body jerking and twitching, even as my virtual body shuddered. It was everything I could do to remain conscious, to remain *sane* after the effect of... whatever that was.

My thoughts seemed to chase one another and I could barely focus. Yet I found myself hanging defiantly before Diamond. "Is that the best you can do?" I asked.

"Why don't you just give up?!" She demanded. "Don't you see that I didn't want any of this?"

I didn't believe her. I'd heard what she and her fellow conspirators had said... and regardless of what she'd *wanted*, her methods now showed that she viewed her fellow cadets as expendable tools.

"I will not let you hurt them," I moved over to where another pulse of fear had begun to expand from a cadet's mind.

"Look out!" Karmazin barked.

I flinched to the side just as Metal Man struck out, his attack a pulse of pure darkness. It swept past me and I heard him growl in frustration. That growl turned into a yelp, though, as Tyler and Ryan began to pelt him with balls of light. "Here, take some imaginary numbers and unsolvable equations!" Ryan giggled manically.

"And some classic music, how about dub-step and j-pop?"

Tyler jeered, running to the side and throwing his own balls of data.

I knew just how distracting those could be, and I used the distraction to bounce the pulse of fear right at Metal Man. His form didn't waver, not like Inkblot, but it did stop him long enough for the twins to pelt him a dozen times or more.

To the side, I saw Karmazin attacking Diamond, sending out pulses of crackling blue energy. The blasts didn't seem to have any effect on her, but her attention did focus on him while she let out another of those hellish blasts of pure energy.

"Bubble pop electric!" Metal Man screamed. "Argh, I'm going to kill both of you for putting this garbage in my brain!" He roared. He began to spray bolt after bolt of crackling energy at the twins. One of the blasts glanced an unaware cadet and I could see her mind shudder and her body, in the real world, began to convulse.

We can't fight them here... I hadn't realized I spoke aloud until I heard the others respond in agreement. It was only a matter of time before these two did more damage to the other cadets, where they couldn't even perceive them. Yet I couldn't leave these two free to drag the other cadets into panic-stricken madness.

Not even knowing how I did it, I found myself reaching upwards, my digital fingers reaching up into the virtual world above us... and ripping.

The simulated worlds exploded and the panicked chorus of the cadets broke off as they tumbled down into this half-reality.

They fell among us, their faces showing surprise as they perceived these strange forms fighting among their communications. Diamond let out a frustrated howl as she and Metal Man drew back. "This is what's going on," I moved in front of them all, seeing that their loop-induced panic had been temporarily broken. "These others, they're trying to manipulate all of you, they're trying to get you to attack the people trying to help you."

"She doesn't know what she's talking about," Diamond hissed. "They're going to try to shut down our implants, but Doctor Aisling isn't involved. They don't know what they're doing and they're as likely to kill us as help us."

"We have to let them power down the implants," I spoke directly to the other cadets. "The implants might be making some of us hurt people. They could be driving us insane." Maybe it was this place, it seemed to strip away our abilities to hide our emotions, but I could see the worry and fear on their faces... and I knew where at least half of that fear came from. "Some of you may be worried that you won't be as capable, as smart, without the implants. That's not true. The implants are a tool, nothing more."

"They're risking our lives," Diamond hissed. "Out of fear. They don't understand what we're capable of, they're afraid because we're smarter than them, different than them!"

"Then why are you hiding who you are?" Bolander asked, her voice hard. "If you're one of us... then why don't you show your face?" I'd never felt so grateful to the other girl.

Metal Man spoke, "If they knew who we were, they'd single us out, target us. We stand among you as well, we have fought for *you*, for *us*." His voice burned with conviction. "You can be like us..."

"Monsters?" Karmazin scoffed. "You tried to manipulate us. You hurt some of us, you tried to kill Jiden..."

"You have no idea what you're talking about," Diamond hissed. "You're so blinded by your infatuation with her that you'll follow her blindly, like a puppy... well, I'm not like you, not any more. We *are* smarter and more powerful than them... and than you. If you won't help us voluntarily, then I'll make you help us."

I saw her form flash out of existence and then appear on the other side of the group, opposite Metal Man. Before I could shout a warning, black and white bars of energy drove out from the two of them. Everyone fell back from the attacks. But I saw in a heartbeat that the purpose hadn't been to hit any of us... the two of them drove us ahead of them.

The combined consciousness of the cadets slammed into the barrier that shielded the labs. It wasn't a purely physical barrier, I quickly realized. It was a thing of circuits and programming as well... and the combined effort of thirty three minds slammed into it at one, single, point.

***

Our minds exploded out into the Academy network and the two of them followed. The two of them spread out tendrils, ignoring us, now.

I couldn't understand what they were doing. Their minds seemed to flicker from one set of files to the next, merging with historical data one second and diving into the Academy's emergency network the next. Yet whatever their goals were, I couldn't let them succeed.

I drove my mind into their paths. For one terrible moment, my consciousness and that of Diamond collided. I saw the world as she did, a thing of angular planes and absolutes, like someone had put a filter over the world and turned it into one of those strange paintings were everything was made of squares. There was no give to her mind. Everything was quantifiable, in an odd, crystalline geometry that didn't allow for the slightest bit of softness.

You're weak. The voice seemed to come from inside my mind... but I knew better.

You're not me, I replied. *You're Diamond, and you're crazy.*

Diamond gave a laugh. "I like that name, you based it upon your perceptions of me and it's... fitting. Do you really think you stopped me? You can't hold me still for long. My partner is still on the loose, he'll do his part and then it won't matter what you do." I could feel her trying to slither away, testing the limits of my attention.

"They're administering the patches to our implant software soon," I focused upon her, content to hold her, trapped with me. We were in darkness, so focused on one another that our perceptions of the virtual and real worlds had vanished. "Soon, all of your abilities will vanish."

"They don't know what they're dealing with," Diamond hissed, the distortion in her voice wavering and for a moment, I almost felt like I could recognize her voice.

"Who *are* you?" I blurted on impulse.

Diamond laughed mockingly, "Don't you recognize me, Jiden?" A face appeared in front of me, "It's me... Sashi."

"What?" I asked in shock.

"Or is it Bolander..." Diamond's laughter mocked me, replacing the image a moment later. "Or Ashiri?" My best friend's face appeared before me and then vanished again. "What does the name matter, Jiden? What matters is that you have forced me to become your enemy."

"You tried to kill me!" I shouted in response.

"No," Diamond hissed, "I didn't. The most we tried to do was distract you, to beat you in a game rigged in your favor."

"I don't know what you're talking about and I don't trust you," I snapped. "You sabotaged my skimmer..."

"Why would we do that, Jiden?" Diamond asked. "We wanted more than anything to *avoid* notice... and what has that done besides focus attention on us? I'd ask you to consider that in the time you have..."

Too late, I realized that her words had been a distraction. She split away from me and dove back into the network.

My impulse was to follow her, but I realized that would be a losing proposition. She was too fast. She knew where she was going and even as I watched, she split herself into three different sections, each one diving into different systems within the network.

Around the Academy, systems had begun to go haywire. Alarm klaxons rang, defense radars came on and then shut down. For now, all this seemed to be chaos-driven, but I couldn't let Diamond and Metal Man have free reign of the network. They could access ships for launch or trigger some kind of self-destruct or something equally dangerous. I didn't understand their motives or goals... and those didn't matter, I realized.

I needed to stop them, and I needed to stop fighting them where they were strongest.

***

Chapter 12: I Should Have Seen That Coming

I opened my eyes.

I still lay strapped on the gurney, but the room was empty. I wriggled my hand, remembering some of Commander Pannja's training on escaping bindings. I'd thought that part of the *kerala* class had been sort of silly, I remembered. Then again, I'd never thought I would have to work myself free from straps on a bed.

My left hand came free, the skin on my wrist tearing a bit from where I'd chafed it against the strap to get it free. I quickly unstrapped my right hand and then my waist and feet. I rolled, somewhat unsteady, off the bed and moved quickly over to the door.

I opened it and a guard in the hallway spun, "Cadet, get back--"

I drew his holstered pistol and fired it into the joint of his leg armor. He started to shout something and then collapsed as the tranquilizers took effect. *Thank God they're still loaded with tranquilizer rounds.*

Down the hall, another guard had raised his rifle. I dropped to one knee and his first round went through the air above me. I fired twice and waited. He slowly topped over.

"Now, Cadet Armstrong, was that really necessary?" A calm voice asked from the next room.

I turned and breathed a sigh of relief, "Commander Weisfeldt. Thank God. I need you to do the software patch."

"So that's why you shot the two guards?" He asked, his bushy eyebrows going up in feigned surprise. "Your methods are interesting."

"They would have tried to stop me and I don't have time to explain. Two of the affected cadets are free on the Academy network. I have no idea what kind of damage they're doing. I needed to pass on a warning and..."

He gestured at the ceiling as alarms wailed. "Warning received. Everything started going haywire a few minutes ago. Admiral Armstrong headed upstairs to take charge. She told me to do the patch... there's only one problem." He gestured at the figure on the bed next to where he stood. "It isn't working," his voice was soft.

"What?" I asked. I came up and recognized the still features of Boyles. "What happened?"

"Earlier, before everything went entirely crazy," Commander Weisfeldt said, "Something happened to him. I tried to do the patch, when I saw his brain activity drop. The implant didn't respond. When I tried it again, it rejected any input. It's very interesting, you know," Commander Weisfeldt rubbed his chin thoughtfully. "The implant reacted almost like a biological creature, like an immune system rejecting a virus."

I wasn't sure I understood that. "It's not from Boyles, not consciously," I muttered.

"How do you know?" Weisfeldt asked.

"I hit him with a pulse of fear that he and the others had been using on the cadets," I admitted. "I think it either knocked him unconscious or... something."

"Then it's a feature of the Quicksilver," Commander Weisfeldt mused. "This being the problem with working with experimental or poorly understood materials. Hmmm, I had thought it was Boyles, but if it isn't, if it is some natural element of the implant material trying to defend itself..."

"What?" I asked as he trailed off.

"You're very helpful, dear," Commander Weisfeldt beamed at me, his smile far too cheerful for the events of the day, in my opinion. "Inspirational, I might even say." He pulled a set of equipment from the tool chest next to him as I came forward. I hadn't even noticed it, at first. Most of it looked like assorted junk or some kind of cheesy props from bad holovid dramas, the kind that had mad scientists and supervillains, sort of like Will used to love watching.

"Hold this, please," Weisfeldt said, holding out a long rod wrapped heavily in wires and with what looked like some kind of emitter at the end.

"Commander..." I began.

"Art, please," he said. "For brevity."

"Art?" I asked uncertainly.

"I won't tell anyone if you don't," he said absently as he pulled out an older model datapad and tapped in commands on the screen. I held up the rod and he looked up, "Yes, yes... Oh, God no!"

"What?!" I blurted.

"Don't aim that at me!" He objected, turning me to face towards the unconscious Boyles. "There we are... much better. No idea what that would do to me..." His voice dropped off into barely audible mutters and grunts.

"Commander, uh, Art?" I asked.

"Yes, yes... ah, there! Just as I thought!"

"What?" I asked, feeling lost.

"If I isolate the transmission, I can send it straight into the receptors in Boyle's brain," Commander Weisfeldt grinned.

"Uh, what?" I asked.

"We're beaming the shutdown code directly into his brain... and I just confirmed that we have a connection," Commander Weisfeldt grinned and rubbed his hands together. "Excellent, this is science!"

"Sir," I objected, "I'm not so sure about this..."

"It's fine, it's fine," he waved a hand, his bushy eyebrows dropping as he focused on his datapad again. "Keep the transmitter... perfect... don't move."

I knew about direct neural interfaces, of course. But they'd always been elegant, purpose-built devices. This was... this was worse than a kludge. This looked like the kind of thing a mad scientist would use to reprogram innocent people into loyalty.

All the same, I held steady as Commander Weisfeldt tapped in commands. A moment later he looked up, "Genius, Armstrong, pure genius."

"It worked?" I asked, half terrified of the answer.

"Oh, yes. The brain received the shut down and the implant went down to standby mode. Now we have to do the others."

"Great," I said. "Uh, could I..." I shrugged without moving the transmitter from above Boyle's body.

"Oh, yes, yes, by all means, task done here, on to the next."

We moved across the hallway to the next room. Bolander lay in this bed, her big frame twitching slightly as she either fought within the network or maybe as she tore it apart from within. I thought that Diamond's ploy had been a ruse to distract me, but Diamond could be Bolander. *It beats the alternatives...* The only two other females in the group were Sashi Drien and Ashiri Takenata.

"Now, aim it at her..." Commander Weisfeldt began.

"Commander..." I started.

"Art," he insisted.

"Art, then," I said. "Are you sure this won't hurt them?" I asked.

"It shouldn't," he waved a hand dismissively. "The physical connections remain, the implant's higher functions are simply disabled. It'll still function as a normal neural implant, it's the self-learning programing architecture that we're shutting down, along with all the ramping-up capabilities."

"What if they've become dependent upon it?" I asked, half thinking of my own worries.

"Well, hmmm," he looked up. "There will certainly be some psychosomatic dependencies. Possibly feelings of inadequacy or inferiority..." He looked down at the screen of his datapad. "Oh, I was afraid of that."

"What?" I asked nervously. I really hoped that I hadn't just boiled Bolander's brain or something. *Not that most people would notice, but still...*

"Her conscious mind is interfering with the transmission. She's receiving it, but she's rejecting the input." Commander Weisfeldt began to mutter as he tapped at his screen. "I can't get her to take the patch."

"It's her fighting it?" I asked, "You're certain?"

"It *could* be a dozen different things," Commander Weisfeldt's bushy eyebrows glowered at me. "But I'm relatively certain that that is the difference between Cadet Boyles and Cadet Bolander, yes."

I drew the pistol and shot Bolander. After a moment, the Ogre Company cadet went limp. Commander Weisfeldt's datapad beeped.

"Ah, transmission accepted, excellent," He looked up and gave me a cheerful smile, "You're very helpful, Cadet Armstrong."

We moved on to the next cadet. One after the other I'd hit them with a tranquilizer round and then aim the transmitter while Commander Weisfeldt would send the transmission. We worked our way down one side and up the other. Finally, I set the pistol down on the table next to Karmazin's unconscious body and Commander Weisfeldt uploaded the patch. "Done," I said in relief.

"Not entirely true," Commander Weisfeldt said as he came

up next to me.

"What?" I asked in surprise. "Who did we miss?"

"One more cadet," he said calmly, picking up the pistol I'd set down. I had a moment of chagrin as he shot me in the leg, and then the world went dark.

***

I woke up back in the hospital. My head felt smaller, somehow. On instinct I reached out to my implant... and it was like someone had replaced my datapad with a kid's toy. Everything was gone. I no longer had the full connectivity, the data and knowledge, the perfect ability to find information and to link with computer systems like an extension of my body. I concentrated hard and I couldn't even manage to split my focus.

At once I felt an odd, echoing emptiness and cramped and claustrophobic. The loss of the full capabilities of my implant shouldn't have hit me so hard.

"You're awake?" I recognized Doctor Fuesting. She had a disapproving expression as she stepped into my room. "I believe I told you to avoid having to come in here."

"Yes, ma'am," I replied. I felt suddenly grateful for the distraction.

"I don't suppose you'd care to explain your presence here?" Doctor Fuesting glared at me.

"I don't think I'm allowed to talk about it," I admitted. I didn't know if the project was still classified. Even if it wasn't, I didn't want to admit my part in it. The less everyone knew about that, the better.

Doctor Fuesting glowered at me. Despite the fact that she wasn't any taller than me, she intimidated me with how fierce she looked. "Half of you cadets who've come in here have said the same. The other half still can't put words together into coherent sentences."

I winced at that. Apparently I wasn't the only one feeling disjointed. I really hoped that none of the cadets faced any serious problems, especially since I'd been the one to help disable their implants.

"I don't know exactly what it was that so-called Doctor Aisling did to you and the others," Doctor Fuesting sniffed, "but if I get my hands on her, I'll make sure she regrets it." Her expression shifted slightly. "Now, I believe I warned you that I was going to keep a bed for you if I saw you in here again?"

"Yes, ma'am," I swallowed.

She pointed at a brass plaque next to my bed. It took me a long moment to read it. *Reserved for Biohazard.* I flushed as I realized that even the Academy doctor had heard my nickname. "Uh, thank you, ma'am."

"You can show your gratitude and appreciation by making sure this bed stays empty, Biohazard," Doctor Fuesting grumbled. "Now, I have other patients to see, and there's a few of your fellow cadets who have been waiting to see you."

She stepped out of the room. A moment later, Kyle Regan stepped in, his face worried, "Hey, Jiden, are you okay?"

I forced myself to smile at him, "I'm fine, Kyle." My face felt wooden and I had to fight back tears. I didn't feel like myself.

He came up to the bed and held my hand and suddenly, I felt like things were going to be alright after all. "You had me worried," he said softly. "First there were the armed guards rounding up random cadets, including you. Then there were all the rumors... then the whole school went nuts. Alarms, sirens, crazy orders and messages and warnings all popping up on datapads and message networks... then after all that ended, I heard you were in the hospital...again."

"Sorry," I replied.

"You've been unconscious for hours," Kyle said. "The doctor couldn't tell me why, either. But some of the other cadets..." He trailed off, looking uncomfortable. "I figure whatever it was, you can't tell me about it?" Kyle asked.

"She can't, unfortunately," a stern voice spoke from the doorway. We both looked over in surprise. Kyle released my hand and jerked to attention, but the Admiral waved at him to relax. "I'm going to need a few minutes of her time, Cadet Regan," the Admiral said. "How about you go get yourself some lunch? I know you've been waiting here for a while."

"Yes, ma'am," Kyle nodded, though he shot me a look to see if I was okay with that. I gave him a slight nod. I wanted him to take care of himself... and I needed to talk to the Admiral.

He stepped out and I adjusted my bed upwards, having to

fumble with the bed controls, my impulse to connect with my implant foiled by how stupid my implant seemed to be. There was some kind of wireless interface with the bed, but it was easier to just fumble with the hand controls than to try and tie my implant into the bed's software.

The Admiral didn't say anything for a moment. She just watched me with a calm expression. "You know, you don't listen to advice very well," she said.

"Ma'am?" I asked.

"I told you to stay in your bed and let Commander Weisfeldt take care of things," she arched an eyebrow at me. "If I'd known what you'd get yourself up to instead of that, I might have made it an order." Her voice seemed ominous, but then she rolled her eyes, "Though from what I understand, that would have been a mistake. Commander Weisfeldt assures me that he couldn't have completed the upload without you... and several of the cadets have said that they're not sure they would have survived the experience without your intervention."

I swallowed at that, feeling a mix of pride and oddly... shame. "Is everyone... that is, did everyone survive?"

The Admiral sighed. "We still don't fully understand exactly what Doctor Aisling did. She's refusing to speak and most of her files are encrypted. Charterer Beckman has been remarkably... unhelpful." The Admiral moved to the side and her expression was hard. "Three of my cadets are still unconscious. Two of them show zero brain activity. Cadet Boyle and Cadet Gnad. Cadet Andrews is expected to recover and come around soon, just as you did."

I flinched at that. Somehow I knew that I'd effectively killed Boyles, either when I'd hit him with that reflected pulse of terror or when I'd transmitted the shut-down codes to his implant. Either way, I'd taken another life. *And maybe if I'd acted sooner I could have saved Gnad...*

"It isn't your fault," the Admiral snapped. I looked at her and for a second, I saw an echo of that same anguish I felt. We shared a moment of understanding as I realized that she blamed herself just as much as I did. This was her school, these were her cadets... and two of them had been killed.

"There's a good chance that we can restore Cadet Boyles and Cadet Gnad with mental restructuring," the Admiral said. "As long as we can recover the mental scans from Doctor Aisling's labs."

I shivered a bit at that. Normally they restricted mental conditioning and restructuring for criminal offenses, those who had suffered extreme psychological damage, or when someone suffered severe brain trauma in an accident. The little I knew about it, they could rebuild someone's mind, either from copied brain scans or from artificially generated memories. "What will they remember?"

"That I can't tell you. It'll be based off of the last neurological scan that Aisling has on file. That *should* be right before the implantation procedure... but I don't know that she did that," the Admiral looked angry. "Given the other corners and safety issues it appears that she violated, I can't say that I'd be surprised if she didn't."

"Will they be able to finish the year?" I asked.

"No," the Admiral sighed. "Those who have been mentally conditioned cannot serve in the Militia, there are a number of Militia regulations that prohibit service by those who've received mental conditioning. Both Boyles and Gnad will be discharged as soon as they have recovered. If they recover."

I stared at the Admiral in shock. On the one hand, I was aghast. Part of me would rather be dead than to face that kind of exclusion. To have the past two and a half years ended over a regulation? *That isn't fair.*

The Admiral read my expression, "There's important and vital reasons for those regulations, girl. Mental conditioning is *supposed* to be stable, but it doesn't always take. Sometimes stress can jolt suppressed memories and sometimes even a carefully restructured psyche can fracture. We're putting you all under extreme stress on a daily basis during your time here, but that's aimed at preparing you for combat. If there's even a slight chance that an officer or enlisted will suffer some kind of psychological break in combat, then we can't risk it."

"What about all of us with implants, then?" I asked bitterly. "If three of us..."

"We still don't know enough to judge," the Admiral interrupted. "And yes, I foresee a great deal of probing and questions to take place over the next few months. There will be multiple formal investigations, including one in my role as the Superintendent of the Academy while two cadets suffered severe mental trauma in an experimental military program." Her voice took on a bitter and self-accusatory tone.

"Ma'am--"

"The cadets of this Academy are my responsibility. Last year I lost one. This year I lost two. There should be an investigation. There will be an investigation. Save anything you have to say for that. When you do, talk only to the facts and leave it at that, understand?"

I nodded slowly. I was more than a little uncertain about how to respond to her tone. I felt almost protective of her, though. It wasn't right that someone come after her over what had happened. This had come down from the Charter Council, and I'd seen the Admiral fighting it.

"Now, then," the Admiral said. "I'm glad to see that you're doing better. I need to check on the other cadets." She gave me an odd, detached nod, and left.

I lay back on my bed, feeling like this was a bit too much to take in. The idea that the Admiral might face some kind of punishment for what had happened left me feeling sick inside. She was trying to distance herself from me, I realized. If something happened, if she ended up taking the blame for the disaster with the implants, then she didn't want *me* to face trouble for being associated with her.

I closed my eyes, feeling lost, weak. and alone and oddly... scared.

I'd dealt with fear, before. I'd lived with the worry of someone trying to kill me. I'd been afraid... but this was something else. The Admiral had been a fixture of my time at the Academy. A stern, solid presence... the war hero that I didn't really understand but somehow knew that she was there.

Now there was the very real chance that she wouldn't be... that she *couldn't* be there. I would have to depend on myself, I knew. I would have to be strong.

I don't feel strong. I felt tired, and weak, and heartsick. I had failed two of my fellow cadets. We still didn't even know for certain that the implants had been the problem...

At least the implants are turned off... I thought to myself. Yet it was a bittersweet victory. I missed the strength and capabilities that the implant gave me. I shouldn't have become so dependent, not after only a few weeks, but I almost felt as if a part of me was gone. I felt tears run down my cheeks and I was almost pathetically grateful that I was alone with my misery.

On instinct, I reached out to my implant again. To my shock, my implant reacted. The multifunction architecture went live. My mind seemed to come alive with information and data.... "Oh, man, I am in so much trouble."

***

Chapter 13: A Whole New Direction

I was going to be in trouble, but I wasn't alone.

"Jiden, is that you?" Karmazin asked.

We materialized in the simulated world, the green grass and the blue sky. It bothered me that even though I'd never seen grass this green, it featured in the simulated world created by my mind.

Alexander Karmazin stood there. His face was troubled, "I thought we shut the implants down?"

I split my focus even as I looked around the simulated world, "Me too." I reached out, tapping into the Academy network, reaching out and sampling data.

"It didn't work?" Karmazin asked.

"Apparently not," I said. Only I quickly realized that wasn't correct, at least, not entirely. The other cadets with implants weren't here with us. I tentatively reached out to one of their implants. The only response I received was what felt like a simple, mechanical response, much like what I'd received from a normal Tier Two implant.

"It worked for the others," I said. "But not us."

"Why not us?" Another voice asked.

I spun, and Sashi Drien stood on the grassy field with us. I found myself preparing for an attack and only managed to force myself to relax after she stared at me in puzzlement. "Why are we different from the others?" Sashi asked.

"I have no idea," I answered.

Karmazin stared at her, his face unreadable. I wondered how he managed that in this simulated world. Maybe he was just better at hiding his emotions. Mine seemed to just come through in everything I did. "Something must be different about us. I was looking at the software patch. I'm not sure I fully understand what it does, but the patch still hit our implants. Mine was down for an hour or more... until I concentrated on it and it came back to full capabilities.

"Mine too," Sashi nodded, looking at me.

"Mine didn't take that long," I answered, feeling self-conscious. "About the first opportunity I had to concentrate on it and really focused, it was just *there*."

"We're different, somehow," Karmazin said, his voice

concerned.

"What does it matter?" Sashi said bitterly. "As soon as they know, they'll shut us down again."

"If they can," Karmazin said. "If they find out."

"What are you saying?" I asked.

Karmazin looked at me. "We know there were conspirators, people trying to hurt you," his eyes darted in Sashi's direction, but I wasn't sure if he was trying to suggest she was one of them or if he was just seeing if she was aware. "The school network detected attempted security breaches, presumably tied in what that or whatever else they were doing. But they weren't able to identify them."

I nodded, slowly. "You're saying they couldn't track them."

"They may not be able to tell the difference, especially if we don't stand out," Karmazin said.

"Why would we do that?" I asked.

"Because we may not be the only ones that are different," Sashi nodded.

"Wait, what?" I looked at her in surprise. I wasn't the only one, Karmazin stared at her with shock apparent on his face.

"Look," Sashi seemed suddenly self-conscious, "I don't know about this whole conspiracy thing. The crazy diamond chick and all the... things that happened before they shut down the implants. For that matter, I don't know why I've got a massive bruise on the side of my head." I did my best to control my expression. I probably *should* have shot her in the leg. It just had seemed sort of fitting for me to hit her in the head, given all the times she'd shot me.

"What I do know, is that if we three are different, and if that's why the patch didn't work... then what about these conspirators? What if they're different and they're just laying low?" Sashi Drien looked at both of us and despite myself, I nodded.

"That makes more than a little sense," Karmazin admitted.

"If that's the case, then can we afford to turn ourselves in?" Sashi asked. I went cold at her words, but Karmazin was still nodding. "I mean, by all means, tune our implants down ourselves. Don't stand out, don't use our advantages. I didn't even really feel comfortable using them in class, anyway, since it seemed sort of unfair and all... but stay alert, keep an eye out for these people, right?"

Yet I had a sudden, horrible suspicion. What if the conspirators weren't elsewhere... what if they were here, with me right now? Sashi's voice could have been the distorted voice of Diamond. Karmazin could very well be Metal Man. *What if they've been playing me all along?*

If that was the case, then my best bet was to go straight to the Admiral. Yet I rejected that for one reason: Karmazin. I couldn't believe that he'd want to hurt me. We'd been through too much... and even if he *was* out to get me, I couldn't think that he'd be able to hide it as well as this, to pretend to be my friend while he went after me. *Sashi on the other hand...*

Still, it wasn't as if I could say anything, not right now, not in front of her.

In my room, I sensed motion. "I've got to go, guys, someone's in my room."

Only as I disconnected from our simulated world did I realize that I'd agreed, almost by default, to keep our functioning implants a secret.

***

Kyle stared down at me, "Are you okay, Jiden?"

"What? Yeah, I'm fine!" I said to him. I forced myself to smile, making it genuine as I saw he'd brought me a tray of food from the mess hall. "Sorry, I guess I was just zoning out, thinking."

His eyes narrowed and I could tell that I hadn't fooled him. *I owe him honesty,* I told myself. "It's not something I can freely talk about. Part of what landed me here, okay?"

Kyle gave me a nod.

I took the tray from him and gave him a smile, "So, what did I miss out on?"

"Lots of chaos," he shook his head. "We had alarms going off all over campus. For a little while, we all thought we were really under attack." His freckled face worked into a wry grin, "I actually got a little excited, believe it or not."

I grinned in reply and I reached out and squeezed his hand in reply. "I believe it."

His expression went more serious. "By the time we got to our battle positions, we knew it wasn't a drill." Drills sometimes happened during the week, not always on the weekends, but there would have been some cues, I knew. "But we knew we also weren't under attack. There were all kinds of strange traffic, radio frequencies going down with jamming, others filled with just random noise."

Kyle sighed, "Honestly, I was a little afraid, at that point."

I squeezed his hand again, "Yeah, I wouldn't sweat it. It's not a situation we've trained for and it sounds like it was total chaos."

Kyle's green eyes met mine and I saw some of the tension behind his expression ease. I realized, then, that he must have genuinely worried about what I would think of his admission. I didn't understand why, but I didn't need to. The fact that he'd worried what I thought meant that his admission had been difficult.

On impulse, I reached up and caught him by the collar. I pulled him down into a kiss.

The feeling of our lips meeting was electric. For a moment, all my worries, all my tensions and the past month's paranoia and fear, all melted away. I found my hand working its way into his short red hair and his hands had gone places that I wasn't sure were entirely appropriate. I felt a spreading warmth that seemed to come from my chest and expand outwards.

"I'm wet," I whispered.

"What?" He broke away, his green eyes going wide.

I pointed at my tray of food that he'd brought me, now spilled across my hospital bed. The bowl of soup had spilled across my hospital gown, along with the cup of juice. The poor sodden bit of bread had been smashed.

"Oh, uh..." Kyle picked up the tray and then grabbed for napkins. He started to reach out to dab at my soaked hospital gown, then seemed to think better of it and held the napkins out, his face turning beet red.

I laughed as I took the napkins from him. "Thanks. I think I can take care of this."

Kyle just looked embarrassed. The fact that he did just made me like him even more.

I wished I could tell him the full truth. Somehow I knew that with his help, I could figure all this out. *Assuming that didn't put his life at risk,* I reminded myself. For that matter, without even a normal neural implant, he wouldn't be as prepared to face this kind of threat. Perhaps it was best that I couldn't tell him everything.

***

Things didn't quite come down as the Admiral had suggested. Lieutenant General Corgan came and interviewed each of us, but the questions weren't at all what I would consider thorough. At the end of it, the tight-faced woman informed me that all events and materials related to Project Quicksilver and our Tier Three implants were classified and that if I discussed or disclosed any information about it, I would face jail time and possible charges of treason.

She had me sign a couple of additional documents that said much the same thing, and then she left. Doctor Fuesting ran me through some tests after that, but she didn't seem to know what she needed to look for and she seemed rather angry about that.

At no point did anyone ask me if my implant was operational. So I didn't have to lie. I still felt guilty, thinking about the Academy ethics code. I was deceiving by omission... wasn't I? But I didn't see an option. If I spoke up, if I told the Admiral and she had Commander Weisfeldt or Doctor Fuesting shut down my implant, then I'd have no way to counter Diamond... if she still had her implant. *If it's not Sashi...*

Twice I nearly messaged the Admiral directly to tell her my suspicions. But there was the Admiral's warning and her discussion of an official investigation. If she were under added scrutiny, then my warning might make her situation more precarious. Worse, if they were trying to place the blame on her over all of this, then they'd use any direct communications from me as proof of some kind of conspiracy. Plus there was the risk that Diamond or Metal Man would intercept the message.

No, without figuring out how to warn the Admiral quietly, I couldn't risk it. I was on my own... well, not entirely. I had Karmazin. I had Sashi, assuming I could trust her, and I had Kyle... who I couldn't tell anything to, without risking charges of violating state secrets or treason.

Doctor Fuesting seemed almost angry that she couldn't find anything wrong with all of us. She discharged us all by the end of the week, all but Boyles and Gnad, who had disappeared in a Militia transport with the investigating officer.

Back in my room, I closed the door, and before I even took a seat, I was already in the simulated world. It felt like coming home as I opened up my implant again, as I hadn't dared to do it for the remainder of my time in the hospital, for fear that someone would notice.

"Well, what now?" I asked.

Karmazin and Sashi were there before I finished asking the question. Karmazin looked distracted. "I can't stay long, my roommate isn't here, but he could be back soon. I don't want him to notice me zoning out."

"Understood," Sashi and I said at the same time. We shot each other surprised looks and then we both gave nervous giggles. *Maybe she's not so bad.* For that matter, I'd roomed with her for a month, did I really think she was capable of trying to kill me?

"How do we approach this?" Sashi went on. "I mean, we can split our focus still, our implants have full functionality, but if we're using them, there's both physical signs and I'm sure someone will notice bandwidth transmissions sooner or later. These things just pull so much data so quick... it's not even in the same category as a normal implant."

"Can we track someone else doing that?" I suggested.

"Not if they're powering them down most of the time," Karmazin shook his head, his expression still distracted. "Which is what we need to do. Run silent. Keep the implant as a reserve for when we really need it. Keep our eyes out for something that doesn't feel right, but we don't use the implants for classes or anything that stands out."

Sashi Drien made a face, "I can't say I'm crazy about that. I was making a *lot* of progress with the implants. Being able to split my focus, do two or three different homework assignments at once..."

I sighed, "Yeah. That was nice."

"We haven't got any option," Karmazin said. "At this point, if anyone catches us, they'll think we were part of the conspiracy. At this point, we *are* guilty of conspiracy... just for not speaking up."

"But..." I wasn't sure how to argue against that. Sure it was technically true, but it wasn't like we were doing anything sinister. *It won't matter,* I realized, *especially after the violations of the school's networks.* Just the ability to so easily penetrate military networks would be a security threat, and hiding that ability would mark us as dangerous.

"I've got to go," Karmazin said quickly. His avatar vanished.

"I guess we go to stealth mode now, huh?" Sashi said.

"Yeah," I replied.

I disconnected from the simulated world and then powered down my implant, concentrating hard to get it to retract to little more than the standby mode that it had been in when I'd first woken up.

"What do you think about all this?" Sashi asked, waving a hand around. She stood at the end of our desks, her expression difficult to read.

"The implants?" I asked, not sure how much I felt safe to discuss. After all, the monitors in our rooms recorded everything and even if the conspirators weren't tapped into them, then the faculty might be... or one of the investigators.

"The investigation," Sashi said. "That all seemed pretty quick to you, too, right?"

"Yeah," I admitted. "I thought there would be more of a formal investigation."

"It was like someone wanted it all to go away, including that two cadets basically got brain-wiped," Sashi shuddered. "I mean, from what I heard, they were vegetables, Jiden. The next best thing to dead."

I shuddered at her words. "They might do a mental conditioning..."

"Only if they can find something to build on," Sashi's voice sounded bitter. "I've seen it when they botch that, too. My sister..." She trailed off and shot me a startled look. "Anyway, if they don't have good reference points or if there isn't enough left for a framework..." Sashi looked uncomfortable. "Let's just say that what comes out of a mental conditioning might be human, but about as interactive and sophisticated as a piece of furniture."

The bit about a sister had caught my interest, but I wasn't sure how to ask about that. "Well, hopefully they have enough to work on."

"Odds are, we won't know," Sashi muttered. "They won't let those two anywhere near the rest of us again, there's too big a risk that one of us will say something to trigger a suppressed memory or break whatever carefully concocted story they build in to patch any breaks."

Sashi's bitterness set me on edge. All the same, I couldn't

argue. We just didn't have enough information to go on... and our best way of getting information was our implants. *Which we can't use for risk of giving ourselves away...*

"Do you think they'll do anything to Aisling?" I asked. I couldn't help but hope the woman faced some kind of trial.

"With her connection to Charterer Beckman?" Sashi shook her head. "Not a chance. They'll probably drop her in some other spot and have her run her experiments under more supervision. But real punishment?" Sashi's face had gone hard. "No, she's probably got enough evidence to burn half the Charter Council if any of this goes public. Any of them involved will want this all hidden."

That struck me as terribly unfair. Worse than unfair. Boyles and Gnad had practically paid for Aisling's actions with their lives. That Aisling would be free to continue her research was something I couldn't bear to think about.

"Maybe we'll get lucky," I said in an emotionless voice, "maybe the conspirators will go after her." Sashi shot me a look, then her eyes flicked to the monitor in the corner. *Right, we shouldn't talk about them, not as if they're still a threat.*

"Well," Sashi said after a moment, giving me a humorless smile, "I have homework to catch up on, what with a week spent in the hospital. And no implant to help me tackle it all at once."

"Yeah," I answered glumly. "I guess we'd better get to it." Somehow I knew I'd miss using my implant even more by the end of the semester.

***

"I can't believe this," Ryan Zahler groaned, putting his head in his hands. "I know I did this without an implant last year. But it takes so much more time this way."

"I feel dumb," his brother nodded. The twins both looked haggard, their eyes sunken. "Everyone else is doing fine, but they never had the prototype implants."

"They don't know what they were missing," Ryan groaned, not lifting his head from his hands.

"Shut up, both of you," Karmazin didn't look up from his notes. "I'm trying to concentrate. I missed two tests and I'm going to have to make both of them up as well as the one scheduled for *tomorrow*."

Even though we weren't in the same class sections, we'd taken to meeting for our study and homework sessions, partially as a support network and partially because we just didn't want to be struggling with the loss of our implants alone. Sashi, Karmazin, and I might have done so voluntarily, but we were struggling with that just as much as Ashiri Takenata, Ryan, and Tyler Zahler all struggled with their new-found limitations.

"It's still unfair," Tyler muttered, "it's not like *we* abused our implants. We helped to *stop* the conspirators, right?"

"Sort of," Ryan shrugged, "I mean, that bejeweled nut-case did sort of run rampant across the network..."

"Yeah, but we *tried* to stop her, at least..."

"Enough!" Ashiri and Sashi both snapped. They shot each other startled looks, then went back to glaring at the twins. "If you two can't stop whining and bickering, could you at least do it elsewhere."

"Sorry," they both muttered in response. We went back to our studies. Now and then one of us would lean over to compare notes or to discuss possible solutions. It quickly became a companionable silence and for a little while, I almost forgot the aching emptiness that I felt without the constant connection of my implant.

That was, until a small document popped up in my inbox. I read through it, having to pause to translate the archaic English. Yet as I read it, I found myself growing more and more intrigued, then worried, and finally horrified by the ending. The story wasn't long, just a few pages. It covered the experience of a mentally challenged man who underwent an experiment that gave him increased intelligence... and then covered his regression. The worst part of the story was that he knew he was losing his intelligence and he couldn't do anything about it. I felt sick to my stomach and I had to fight the urge to get up and rush to the bathroom to throw up. I focused on breathing, trying to stay calm as I checked the title of the story: Flowers for Algernon.

There was no sender listed for the story, but I saw that everyone in the group had received it. The entire room had gone quiet. I heard a quiet sob from Sashi and I looked over, surprised to see her wiping at her eyes. She glared at me, as if daring me to say anything.

"Where," Karmazin cleared his throat, "where did that come from?"

"I've got no idea," Ryan said, his face puzzled. "There's no sender listed. It should have bounced back to the sender from the network, the Academy network doesn't allow anonymous messages like that."

"Got to be one of the other cadets with our implants," Tyler swallowed. "I mean, no one else would know what it feels like, right?"

"One of them or maybe someone involved in the project, like Doctor Aisling," Ashiri said, her expression tense.

"She's got to be in jail or something, after what happened," Ryan shook his head. "No, it's got to be another cadet. Maybe in another Company?"

"This isn't something that Ogre would do," Karmazin said thoughtfully.

Sashi snorted, "No, too emotional and thoughtful." We looked at her oddly and she shrugged, "I *was* Ogre for a year, guys. Trust me, introspection is not a big part of Ogre Company cadets."

"Fine, what about Dust Company, or Tiger?"

"Andrews is pretty smart," Karmazin noted. "It might be something he read that resonated with him or something."

Ashiri snorted in dismissal, "I have classes with him too, and I highly doubt he'd send this to us."

"There's not that many other cadets from the project," Ryan noted. "We could just see if any of them were on the network when this went out..."

"Assuming whoever sent it didn't upload it with a delay, after all, they sent it in a way they shouldn't have, right?" Ashiri cautioned.

"That's true..." Ryan and Tyler looked at one another, then at the rest of us. "You don't think it's Bejeweled or Metal Head, do you?" We all sort of laughed at their description of the two.

"What the conspirators?" I asked, startled that the twins asked the question. "That's not possible, right, I mean, their implants got shut down."

"Maybe," Tyler frowned, "but a smart person can still manage a lot with a datapad, much less a normal neural implant. If either one of them is still around, it's a possibility. After all, it's not like we *caught* either of them..."

None of us spoke for a long moment, "Well, then why would they send us this?" Sashi asked.

"Maybe a warning?" Tyler asked.

"A message," Ashiri's eyes narrowed.

I started to nod, "If it's one of the cadets with an implant, yeah, they're going through the same thing as the rest of us, and if it was one of those two then they lost more than the others."

"It's more than that," Alexander Karmazin's face went hard. "The character in this story, he had plenty of anger, but no one to focus it on, there was no one to blame."

I swallowed as I realized what he meant. He finished his thought out loud, hammering it home for all of us, "Diamond and Metal Man, they'll blame us for fighting them. All that anger and all that hate over what was taken from them, it's going to be focused on us."

***

Chapter 14: Apparently I Have To Work For It

Despite all that had happened, we still had all our normal duties. I still had to participate in drills. I still had homework. I still had tests to study for and to try and pass.

The last few months of the spring trimester were some of the hardest times I could imagine. Every assignment, every project seemed to be harder than it needed to be. All I wanted to do was to reach out to my neural implant, to have all the extra capabilities right there. But I couldn't. I didn't dare risk it. So instead I spent hours on what had once taken me minutes.

"This Military History paper for Commander Bonnadonna," I said, looking up at my roommate, "do you have time to look it over before I send it in? I'd ask Kyle, but he messaged me a few minutes ago that he'd finished up his last assignment for the night and he was going to sleep." I was envious. It was very early in the morning, at this point, and all I wanted to do was crawl into bed myself.

Sashi looked up, her eyes hollow. "I don't know. I'm trying to get these two assignments done for Commander Weisfeldt."

"Oh, the Liberty weapons relays and exotic particle screen?" I asked. At her nod, I sighed. "No, you'll need all the time you can fit for those ones, they took Kyle and I almost all night last night."

"Ugh," Sashi groaned. "I've still got my all my remedial work from *last* year to do too."

"Are you going to be okay?" I asked.

She stood up from her desk, looking as worn as I felt. "I think so. It's just going to be a race all the way to the end." She let out a tense breath, "Did you send in your summer assignment requests?"

I nodded, "Senior Drill Instructor, Assistant Training Officer, and Observer-Controller at the Grinder." A big part of me hoped I'd be an easy choice for the Senior Drill Instructor for Sand Dragon Company. Normally it went to a Cadet Second Class, but I'd scored very well as a Drill Instructor last year. Mackenzie, my mentor, had been my Senior Drill Instructor. I had a good working relationship with our current company commander, Cadet Commander Salter. If I got the position, I'd be likely to get a good cadet petty officer position next year and that would set me up for success my First Class year.

Assistant Training Officer was a position that existed during Academy Prep Course, to help out the Regimental Training Officer. Normally the three slots for it went to Second Class Cadets, but sometimes they selected Third Class Cadets if there weren't enough eligible Second Class Cadets. The Observer-Controller position was to help coordinate and evaluate training in the Grinder. It wasn't a leadership position, but I'd still be overseeing training so it would look good towards my career, and those were normally saved for Third Class Cadets, since the other two most-desired positions for tactical track cadets were such high competition.

"Same here," Sashi nodded.

I bit my lip. Part of me wanted to speak up, to suggest that maybe she was aiming a bit too high. I hadn't seen her ranking lately, but with her heavy work load, I'd be surprised if she'd managed to improve her ranking all that much. I didn't speak up, though. I didn't want to sound like I wasn't supporting her, after all.

"How's things with Kyle?" Sashi asked, seeming to sense that something had gone unsaid.

"Good," I answered. "Really good. We went for a run together this..." I looked at the clock, "well, *yesterday* morning."

She shot me a look, "I didn't think you liked running that much."

I flushed, "I don't, not exactly, but it's nice with him." It was hard to explain. I *hated* running. I was short, so most of the time it was a struggle to keep up with others when I ran. I always felt like my legs had to move twice as fast to keep up with taller people. "Running with Kyle is just... nice. It's relaxing, we're just kind of out, getting out stress, you know?"

"Huh," Sashi shrugged. "If you say so. What happened with grav-shell racing, I thought you were big on that, last year."

I looked down. "Well, after what happened with the implants and being in the hospital, my grav-shell rowers found replacement coxswains, since I was out a full week. And then since we had so much make-up work, I just didn't have time to get down there for a while and..." I shrugged. "I think I'm sort of off the team."

Sashi cocked her head at me, "I thought you liked it. I mean, you went back after that big crash, last year, right? And Rufus, before that crash, anyway, he said you were really into it."

I sat back in my chair, feeling uncomfortable. "I did... I

mean, I *do*... It's just that things have been so crazy and there's so little time, you know." I paused as I realized something, "You were talking to Rufus about me?"

To my surprise, Sashi flushed. "Uh... he and I spent some time together, in Ogre. He tried to get me to come out to join the grav-shell team, I didn't think it was a great idea at the time." I could imagine the problems that would have caused, since at the time, she and Bolander and Thorpe had physically attacked me. *Amazing how things change...*

"Have you talked to him at all since he's been back?" I asked.

Sashi's flush deepened and on her already dark skin, she almost glowed a bit, "No... There hasn't been time." She looked down at her hands and I noticed her wringing them a bit.

"He's in Dust Company, I could have Kyle pass on a message," I smiled slightly.

"Don't you dare!" Sashi looked up, her dark eyes flaming. Then she saw my smile. "Oh, you're joking with me."

"You like him?" I asked.

"He was... nice," Sashi admitted. "Most of Ogre just sort of tolerated me. My brothers..." she made a face. "Well, Ogre Company mostly sort of assumed I'd fail out, like my brothers said I would. Bolander and Thorpe, they tolerated me. Rufus, he was actually nice. I didn't expect it, you know? And then I started being nice to him and he sort of opened up and then there was the crash..."

I made a face, "Shoot, and then he was gone, right? I'm sorry, that must have been rough."

"Yeah," Sashi looked down. "I sort of blamed you for it. It felt like you'd taken away the one friend I had, all over again." My heart ached at the loneliness in Sashi's voice. At the same time, I wanted to find her older brothers and beat on them both. "I know it wasn't your fault," Sashi looked up, "but knowing and feeling are two different things, you know?"

"Yeah," I met Sashi's eyes, "but seriously, you should talk to him. I guess he's struggling a bit over in Dust, probably dealing with some of the same stuff you did, being in a new company, feeling like an outsider."

Sashi flushed again, but she gave a slight nod, "I will." She moved to her desk, "But I need to get these Weisfeldt assignments done, first."

"Good idea," I said. Then I went back to my paper.

***

"Good morning, everyone," Commander Weisfeldt hurried up to his desk at the front of the classroom, "Sorry I'm late, I was working on this project that... well, never mind, it's classified and I can't talk about it anyway."

He looked up his bushy eyebrows fierce and his dark eyes penetrating. I tried to tell myself that his gaze didn't linger overly long on me, but I still felt sweat break out on my scalp. I wasn't sure how he didn't know that my implant hadn't been shut down. Presumably he had run a diagnostic on me, the same as everyone else.

"Now," Commander Weisfeldt went on, "We're coming up on the end of the course. Several of you have been working on special projects." This time he did shoot a look at Kyle and me. I hadn't been present for Kyle briefing the Admiral on our idea, what with being in the hospital and everything. We'd worked that project as an additional assignment in the weeks since, though, and as far as I knew, Commander Weisfeldt seemed to think the project had a lot of promise.

"What I'd remind you all is that this class's purpose has been the Liberty-class cruiser. Our final exam will focus on that... with a special visit to the one in orbit." We all sat up straight at his words. "That's right, we'll have something of a field trip, where you all will undergo troubleshooting on common maintenance and battle damage issues on a real Liberty-class cruiser."

I swallowed nervously as I considered that. Theory and classwork were one thing. For that matter, we'd done plenty of time in simulators going through maintenance, engineering, and repair scenarios. But doing that on an actual ship...

"Don't worry, I'm sure that all of you will do fine," Commander Weisfeldt gave us an evil grin, "especially since I've made the engineering lab simulators available for you to reserve time to rehearse all of those drills."

I groaned and I wasn't the only one. If he had made the simulators available for us to rehearse in during our free time, then that meant that we'd need to rehearse, probably frequently, in order to pass the tests he had planned aboard the Liberty.

"I'm always pleased to see such enthusiasm and excitement in my students," Commander Weisfeldt nodded. "Now then, let's look at some of the issues that cropped up last week, shall we? I've noticed a trend in this section on troubleshooting errors, particularly when it comes to electromagnetic circuits..."

I began taking notes and I wished, not for the first time, that I could split my attention between this and all my other classes.

***

"Wrong, you're dead," Commander Pannja said, his deep voice calm, just loud enough that I could hear it a couple meters away. The cadet in the simulator in front of me groaned as the instructor reset his simulator and he had to start over again.

"Stay focused, Biohazard," Commander Pannja turned to face in my direction and my attention went back to my screen. Just as I did, a set of warning indicators popped up. Everything seemed to happen at once and I began to go through reactions that I'd been practicing for months, one after the other.

I wasn't, quite, fast enough. My simulated flight terminated with my warp fighter impacting some of the uncharted debris that I'd tried and failed to avoid. "You're dead, too, Biohazard. That's why you pay attention to *your* course first, and other people second."

I sighed as I realized that I'd been set up. He'd timed his words to distract me exactly for that purpose. "Yes, sir," I murmured.

He gave me a grin, his white, even teeth bright against his dark skin, "Try, try, again."

My simulator reset and I began again. We'd long-since passed the drills and rote rehearsals. Now we were doing complex evolutions, attack runs through the length of a system on moving targets. Flying a warp-drive ship was nothing at all like anything else I could describe. It was far faster than anything else humanity had ever built, and warp fighters were amongst the fastest.

At the relative velocities we traveled, our sensor feeds were so distorted that it took even the advanced navigational computers long seconds to make sense out of it. We didn't experience any sensation of movement, but the warp drive moved our 'bubble' of space around in relation to the rest of real-space. That made possible changes of direction and speed that simply didn't make sense. Under a chemical or nuclear driven thrust, those would have turned a crew into red splatters on bulkheads, if they didn't rip the ships apart entirely.

Of course, the human mind had to direct those maneuvers. Given the severely limited response time, we had to drill evasive maneuvers and plans over and over again so that we could select a response and avoid collision or intercepting fire... and we had to do that while maintaining a formation and intercepting a moving target.

In a normal warp-drive ship, that was merely very hard. But warp fighters and warp missiles were too small to fit a conventional warp drive. They instead mounted warp-envelopes, which allowed for high relative velocities. The problem was, they didn't turn or change direction like a normal warp-drive, which could instantly alter direction, speed, and heading relative to normal space.

Warp envelope craft had to physically turn their hulls in order to turn their drive fields and change direction. The problem was, if they did that too quickly, the ship, or missile, felt the physical acceleration and that was hard on crew and components. It came back to the turning crew into raspberry jam on a bulkhead. Also, while normal warp drives didn't have a minimum speed, and in fact many stations had 'zero' acceleration warp fields as defenses, warp envelope craft *did* have minimum velocities, which combined with their slow turn rates, meant that pilots had to think three and four course alterations ahead, constantly.

If I could use my implant at full capacity, this would be easy. I squashed the thought with well-practiced resignation. I couldn't use my implant, especially not here, where it would stand out if I showed a sudden marked improvement.

Maybe if I had staged my improvements slowly, over time, I could have gotten away with it. Karmazin and I had actually discussed that a week earlier, that if we'd thought of it, we could have slowly stepped up our abilities over time, yet we'd set a base-line since they'd shut down the project and any variation now would make us stand out.

As I began my next iteration of piloting, I heard Commander Pannja's voice behind me, "Excellent job, Cadet Drien. You're the first one I've seen today who managed to avoid that debris cluster."

I gritted my teeth and tried to zone out, focusing on the maneuvers, but it was hard. Sashi *had* been doing very well. I couldn't help but wonder if she were cheating with her implant a little bit, but I didn't dare to ask her. *She's under a lot of strain,* I told myself, *it's good that she's taking to this aspect of our classes well, she's got a lot of work in all her other classes, after all.*

Over the past few weeks, we'd had no indicators that Diamond or Metal Man might have survived the implant shut down, or that any other cadets still had operational implants. Yet, there'd was the odd message and there still was no proof that Diamond had been stopped. For all I knew, Sashi was Diamond, though that seemed increasingly unlikely.

Warning indicators lit up my screen as I altered course and I no longer had time to think, just time to react. I focused on that and left my other worries for later.

***

"Welcome, ladies and gentlemen," Commander Bonnadonna said, his abnormally deep voice and gruff face reminding me once again of a bulldog. "I've been enjoying your papers on the evolution of doctrine quite a bit. Some of your conclusions are highly entertaining." He smiled at us, his expression slightly mocking.

I felt a little sick as his gaze fell on me. "Miss Armstrong," Commander Bonnadonna's voice seemed to make my head vibrate a bit. Then again, I'd probably slept four hours total in the past three days, between the latest round military drills, studying for exams, and our homework assignments.

"Sir," I straightened.

"Would you care to tell me what you meant when you said that doctrine is mutable but fundamentals of warfare do not change?" Commander Bonnadonna's eyes seemed to bore into me.

I didn't remember writing that. In fact, I barely remembered writing his paper. I'd asked Sashi and Kyle to review it because I'd sort of zoned out, half asleep, and the next thing I'd remembered, I was reading the final sentences of a completed paper. Thinking about the statement, it didn't seem to make much sense, but I took a deep breath, "Sir, the fundamentals of warfare are Mass, Unity, Surprise, Maneuver, Economy of Force, and Simplicity" He cocked an eyebrow at me as I paused and for a moment, my mind just went completely blank. I felt a moment of icy panic and embarrassment. I opened my mouth to say I really didn't know any more... and then I felt an odd sense of calm and I continued to speak. "Military doctrine is how we apply those fundamentals. It's like a set of blueprints or a road map, if you would."

As the words kept coming, I went on, feeling oddly disconnected as I spoke, "Very often, we practice doctrine and ideas and concepts become rote. We forget why it is that we do certain things, we simply do them that way because that's how they've always been done. But we should always pause to reexamine our methods in order to compare them to those fundamentals of warfare."

Commander Bonnadonna nodded and stepped back, turning his gaze around the class as if to gauge the reactions. "Well stated, Miss Armstrong," he said.

"Thank you, sir," I said. I sat back feeling strangely exhausted. I almost felt as if the words hadn't come from *me*. Yet I was so tired at this point that I'd had a few moments with homework assignments where I'd written or done things that I hadn't consciously understood, where I'd half-remembered the right answer and gone with it. Maybe this was just more of the same.

"Mister Regan," Commander Bonnadonna went on, "what exactly did you mean when you stated that doctrine moves in cycles?"

Kyle straightened next to me, "Well, sir, I was referring to the fact that often times old tricks come back. Tactics and techniques that used to work but fell out of favor can often be recycled by those who study history. An example is the Intogowa Maneuver."

"Oh?" Commander Bonnadonna asked.

Kyle flushed a bit at the prompting and went on in more detail. "Commander Intogowa fought the Erandi on the borders of the Rose Sector. During the Culmor Second Sweep, he and his destroyer squadron were reassigned to the Sepaso Sector. Commander Intogowa had read about ambush tactics that worked against the Culmor during the First Sweep, using one or two ships to lure in a Culmor task force, then dropping the rest of his squadron on the Task Force's drive-ship. Since the Culmor warships don't typically mount strategic warp drives, it would strand entire forces in star systems. He and his destroyer squadron pioneered a two pronged assault that would lure out the heavy hitters, while most of his squadron came in, dropping their strategic warp drives at point blank distance from the Culmor drive ships."

"But that's not the tactics that they used in the first sweep," Martinez interrupted. "They didn't have the accuracy on transition out of strategic warp to get within guaranteed weapons range. They'd shotgun dozens of corvettes out of warp on the target and engage en mass, hoping to get lucky."

"Right," Kyle nodded, "but Commander Intogowa had been fighting the Erandi, who had... well, still have, better sensors and drives than we do. He'd found some success drawing their raider ships into ambushes when he lined up a FTL warp on their pursuit vectors, where he could engage their smaller, faster ships with his destroyers."

"Very good point, Mister Regan," Commander Bonnadonna nodded, "Commander Intogowa realized that the paradigm had shifted, that technology had caught up to allow a variation of a tactic that used to be quite costly in human lives to achieve."

I shuddered a bit at the understatement. In the First Sweep, the Guard Fleet had sent entire corvette squadrons to intercept Culmor drive ships. It often proved an effective way to delay or even stop their attacks, but most often, such attacks cost the lives of every man and women aboard those dozens of corvettes.

"Commander Intogowa lost a total of three destroyers over the course of the Second Sweep, yet his squadron was responsible for the destruction of no less than seven Culmor drive ships," Commander Bonnadonna nodded. "And, as Mister Regan noted in his paper, it was a variation of the Intogowa Maneuver that the Dalites used against us during the Three Day War, which destroyed our carriers and left many of our warp fighters stranded in deep space."

That left me feeling sober as I considered it. Up until this point, I'd been thinking about tactics and history as things to use against the enemy. Commander Bonnadonna, and my boyfriend, had just reminded us that our enemies would try to do the same thing to us.

***

My sleep leading up to finals had been difficult. It seemed like every time I closed my eyes, I saw visions of my class work.

Equations and flight training and engineering systems. That was, when I had time to sleep.

The nightmare started out as almost a relief. There weren't more equations for me to struggle with, I wasn't late for class or missing a homework assignment. I wasn't having to argue with a professor about a failing grade.

Instead, I floated in a dark, oily sea, under a gray, wind-torn sky. It was raining, cold, heavy drops that I'd never experienced in real life but that my body instinctively recognized from untold generations on Old Earth. *I've never seen the rain.*

I miss the rain. The voice was at once mine and not. I sat up in surprise. Some part of me knew that I should have sunk below the waves as my body went vertical, but I didn't.

A young woman hovered above the water, head tilted back, enjoying the cold, heavy raindrops as they struck her. The patchwork light broaching through the torn clouds made it so that I couldn't make out the details of her face. "Who are you?" I asked.

She dropped her head and looked at me, her wet hair falling across her face, masking her features but for a fraction of a second when I almost recognized her. "Why do you always have to be the best?" She asked.

There was something wrong in this dream. "I'm not the best, I just work as hard as I can," I felt the words leave my mouth, but I wasn't sure if she heard them.

"The best," she said and her shoulders hunched in anger. "Over and over again, you keep coming out on top. You keep destroying my life! Why do you always succeed?"

"What do you mean?" I demanded. I had the feeling that this wasn't a dream, that it was something else, something brought to me from my implant, yet I felt paralyzed, like I had no control over it.

"I'm going to give you a taste of what it's like, to watch from the outside, to see other people succeed where you didn't have the chance. I'm going to watch while *you* suffer, for once." As she said those words, the oily water around me seemed to convulse and something powerful and angry locked around my chest. I tried to scream, but I couldn't draw air into my chest. It dragged me down below the waves, my enemy watching as I went. Strangely, I could hear her sobbing, as if she didn't want to do this to me, but she had no choice.

I was dragged down into darkness, feeling crushed by the pressure and darkness. I couldn't move, I couldn't breathe. I felt my body shudder, straining for air and light, yet still I went downwards. Then, at the very bottom, deep below, I caught a flash of light. It was the only hope I saw in the darkness and I struggled towards it, somehow feeling that if I died here in this nightmare, I might well die in the real world. A set of glowing symbols. As my oxygen-starved brain tried to make sense of it, I saw a scroll, crossed with a lightning bolt.

Then I woke up, gasping and trembling, panting for breath and air.

***

Chapter 15: Thirteen Is My Lucky Number

I sat down at my desk, feeling utterly drained and ready for nothing more than curling up in my bed and sleeping, hopefully for the next three days. Finals week was done and I hadn't felt this wrung out since the Grinder... or that horrid dream I'd had right before finals.

"How'd your Weisfeldt final go?" Sashi asked from her side of the room. She sounded a bit less tired than I felt.

"It was a disaster," I said feelingly. "They knocked out power, lights, even gravity. It took me three hours to get everything back online. How about you?"

"Forward weapons," she replied. "And the outer warp ring. I guess they had to change things up so we could all be working in different parts of the ship at the same time?"

"Yeah, that's what some of the others said," I replied. "But I got it done and that should be a passing grade, so there's that. How'd your remedial classes go?"

"Rough, Commander Weisfeldt handled those, too, and his exam was every bit as comprehensive as Commander Scarpitti had been... only, you know, without the psychotic killer part."

I chuckled tiredly at that. Five months later, I guess I had the space to do that. Then again, the past five months had felt like a year or more.

"When do you think they'll have the summer assignments posted?" I asked.

"Well, normally right after the last set of finals closes out... so soon, I hope," Sashi said.

"They're up!" Someone in the hallway shouted.

I groaned a bit as I realized that meant I couldn't go to sleep yet. I'd have to study my roster, see who I'd gotten as my drill instructors and start coordinating with the Company Training Officer...

I pulled up the summer assignment roster and for once, the names being in alphabetical order worked in my favor. I didn't even have to scroll down to find my name and assignment.

Armstrong, Jiden, Academy Archive and Support.

"What?" I asked out loud, incredulous. "What is Archive and Support?"

"What's that?" Sashi asked, "Did you see I got Assistant Training Officer? This is *great*, I mean, it must mean I did well in my classes, right? Normally that's a Second Class assignment and I got it as a Third Class Cadet..."

She went on and I felt my stomach fall, hearing the excitement in her voice, "Oh, and Karmazin's got an Observer-Controller slot in the Grinder. And your boyfriend is the Senior Drill Instructor for Dust Company! And Ashiri, she's Senior Drill Instructor for Sand Dragon Company..." Sashi's voice trailed off.

I could almost hear her chagrin. I could sense her checking the summer assignment list and the long pause as she read my assignment. "Oh, um, Academy Archive and Support, huh?"

"Yeah," my lips went into a hard line.

"That's... that could be a fun assignment," Sashi said, her voice awkward.

"I'm not sure what it even is," I admitted.

"I'm not sure either," Sashi admitted. "Did you apply for it?" Normally cadets got at least one of their three choices. When they didn't, it was either because something had gone horribly wrong with their ranking or they were in trouble of some kind.

"No, I didn't apply for that one," I swallowed as I pulled up the summer assignments list. *Academy Archive and Support: An administrative position where cadets can assist in archival cataloging of the Academy records and reporting systems.*

My mind sort of shut down at the 'administrative position' part. Last year it had been beaten into my head that assignments needed to be leadership, management, or training if we wanted to stand out for our careers. Anything with the term administrative was like the touch of death, I'd been told.

I didn't know what had happened. I didn't know what I'd done wrong. Clearly it must have been *something. Maybe I failed one of my finals after all...* It couldn't have been Commander Bonnadonna's paper, Kyle had read through it and given me a thumb's up. I didn't think it could have been Commander Pannja's simulator exam, I'd managed the entire run without issue.

"You should talk to Cadet Commander Salter," Sashi said quickly. "Maybe see if there's some mistake..."

"Yeah," I said, standing up. My legs felt weak and my head felt light. This was a disaster. Maybe if I'd had my implant at full capability...

I froze in the doorway, a sudden, horrid suspicion working its way through my stomach. What if this wasn't a mistake but it wasn't because of anything I'd done? What if it was sabotage? What if someone, either Diamond or someone else with a grudge, had changed my assignment? *What if that nightmare wasn't just a nightmare...*

On my way towards Salter's office, I sent Alexander Karmazin a message on our private channel. *I think I'm in trouble.*

What's up? He replied, *Is this about your summer assignment?*

Yeah, it's not what I applied for at all, I don't know what to do. I paused in the corridor outside of the company commander's quarters, my stomach in a knot as I prepared to knock.

I don't know what's going on, he replied, *best guess is to ask Salter about it.*

That's what I'm doing, wish me luck, I sent back. I knocked on the door frame. The door was open, like usual. The previous Cadet Company Commanders had done the same. It made it easy to approach them with real problems or ask for advice.

"Enter," Salter said.

I opened the door, "Ma'am, Cadet Third Class Armstrong, do you have a moment?"

She looked up from where she was packing her bags, "Yeah, Biohazard, what's up?" Her normally stern face was relaxed and I saw that most of her knick-knacks like grav-shell trophies and such were long-since packed. *She's getting ready to go to her summer assignment too.*

"Uh, ma'am, I have a question about my summer assignment," I said.

Her expression stiffened a bit, "Ah." She glanced over at her desktop. "They sent me a notice on you and a couple of others, earlier today. I suppose this is because you didn't get the ones you signed up for?"

I nodded, "Yes, ma'am."

She gestured at the chair across from her desk. "Come in and close the door."

My stomach dropped at those words. If it were some simple misunderstanding, she wouldn't have said that. I came inside and closed the door behind me, then took the seat across from her, feeling off-balance as I did so.

"Look, nothing against you, Armstrong," Salter said, "you've been top of your class, you've been through some crazy stuff, no doubt about it." She met my gaze, her expression serious. "You haven't done anything wrong, but sometimes..." she shrugged, "Sometimes the system gives you a bump, just to see what happens. Sometimes they give that prime slot to the number two and three people, to see if they can perform as well or better. And, you know, sometimes that not great position comes up because people start talking about family connections and favoritism."

I flinched a bit at that, as I realized what she meant. Someone must have complained. It could have been anyone in the company, but the end result was that I was out.

"Look, you're doing a fantastic job. Your grades are good, your ranking is good, it's nothing *you* have done, it's just how the system works, now and again," Salter said. "Keep your chin up, do the assignment, show that you've earned your position. I guarantee this will all blow over."

"I'm assigned to Academy Archive and Support," I said in a neutral tone, "any thoughts on how to excel, ma'am?"

Salter flinched a bit. "Archive and Support?" She sat down at her desk. "I hadn't seen the actual assignment, you understand, I'd just received notification that you weren't getting your top three..." She looked the position up and her expression told me that my suspicions were accurate. This wasn't an assignment so much as a punishment... possibly the end of my time on the tactical track. "I see..." She looked, up, her face taking on a look of determination. "I'll make some calls, Armstrong. You have my word on that."

"Thanks, ma'am," I stood up. I nodded at her duffel backs, "Where are you headed?"

"Century Station," Salter replied, her face creasing in a smile, "Active duty unit with system navigation and control. It's more technical than I was hoping, but I'll be shadowing a section chief, so it's still a tactical position."

"That's great," I said. I wanted to say more, but I couldn't, not over the frog in my throat. "Well," I moved to the door, "thank you for your help."

"No problem, Biohazard," Salter replied. "We'll get this all sorted out, I promise."

***

"Any news?" Sashi asked as I packed my things. Technically, I didn't know where I'd be going, yet, but we'd gotten a notice an hour earlier that our rooms were being turned over to the summer's Drill Instructors. Karmazin had already left, catching a skimmer to the Grinder where he'd be working for the next five months, training and coordinating for basic trainees, cadet candidates, and even active and reserve units doing training.

"Not yet," My teeth were gritted and I did my best not to snap at her. *It's not her fault, she didn't do this...* A small voice in the back of my head whispered that maybe she had done it, maybe she had been the one to complain. *Or maybe she's Diamond...*

"You know," she said in a low voice, "this might be a situation where using..." she trailed off and tapped the side of her head, "might be warranted. You could get answers right away."

"Not without violating Academy rules and regulations," I messaged her from my implant. I didn't want to risk anyone overhearing.

"But if someone did something, either with *their* implant, or went behind your back?" Sashi asked me, the same way. "Shouldn't you look into it?"

I didn't answer. I wasn't sure that I could answer her. I half-agreed with her, but at the same time I felt my stubbornness rear its head. Just because someone else had done something wrong, it didn't give me the right to break the rules. Besides, if it turned out this was just a mistake...

We looked over at a knock on the door frame, "Armstrong," Salter gave me a nod. She met my eyes with a serious expression that told me everything I needed to know. "I asked. I went all the way up through the Superintendent's office. Nothing more I can do, I'm sorry."

I swallowed. "Understood, ma'am," my mouth felt like I'd tried to swallow sand, "safe travels."

She gave me a nod and left.

"I guess that settles it," I felt a little light-headed. I went back to packing. Thankfully I didn't really have that much to pack, and all of it fit into my duffel bags easily enough. I was almost done and as soon as I knew where I'd be going, I could take it all without a problem.

"You should fight this," Sashi said angrily.

"She's right," another voice spoke from the corridor. I looked up as Ashiri Takenata stepped into our room. She nodded at Sashi, "As much as I hate to agree with her, this isn't right. Your summer assignment is basically a punishment. You shouldn't take it, not without an explanation."

"Salter said she received notification about it this morning, that it's something to show I'm not receiving favoritism from the Admiral," I felt detached, my voice almost seemed to come from someone else as I continued to pack, my motions robotic.

"There's lots of things they could do for that," Sashi protested. "I mean, even just a standard observer slot during Academy Prep School would still be something. I looked it up, this position is almost never filled, it's like someone picked a job that would look terrible and slotted you in it."

"I'll survive," I finished packing the last of my gear. I looked at Ashiri, "Congratulations, by the way, on getting the Senior Drill Instructor slot, I know you'll do a good job."

Ashiri stared at me, almost as if she didn't believe the words coming out of my mouth. Finally, she gave a nod, "Thanks, Jiden. I appreciate that." Her dark eyes seemed to peer into me, as if she were confused by something. "You're really not going to fight this?"

"Why bother?" I asked. "If I make too big of a stink, I'll get in trouble, or worse, I'll just look whiny or entitled. People get terrible assignments all the time." I grimaced, "I had a terrible assignment at Champion Enterprises when I worked there. I'll do alright. It's not what I wanted, but none of this," I waved a hand at the Academy, "is about what we want, it's about service and duty. Sometimes you get the good stuff, sometimes you don't."

Both Ashiri and Sashi stared at me. It was Sashi who spoke, finally, "You know, that's remarkably mature of you."

Ashiri almost looked embarrassed, "I know I couldn't take this sort of thing as well as this."

I clapped her on the shoulder, "I'm sure you would. Here's your chance to knock people's socks off, Ashiri, good luck." On impulse, I embraced her. She stiffened, and I realized that we'd grown apart over the past few months. Maybe it wasn't being roommates any more, maybe it was just that our separate duties had pulled us apart. I'd have to make more time to spend with my best friend.

She patted me awkwardly on the back, "Good luck, Jiden."

I turned and gave Sashi Drien a nod. I couldn't bring myself to hug her, not even after having spent the past five months as her roommate. There were still too many land-mines in our past to make either of us comfortable with being friends. Instead I extended my hand and we shook. "Good luck over at Regiment," I told her, "I bet they'll keep you busy."

"I'm sure," she laughed. Her expression went tight, "Oh, man, I hope neither of my brothers are anywhere near..."

I grinned at her, "Well, it sounds like I'll have time on my hands, if you need someone to talk with," I couldn't help a tone of bitterness and I saw her and Ashiri flinch at my tone. "Strike one for maturity, eh?" I half-laughed. "Alright, I need to meet Kyle, I doubt he'll have much free time after today. You guys take care and I'll see you around, right?"

They both nodded and I shouldered my bags and went out into the corridor. I kept my chin up as I walked past the other Third Class Cadets, but I heard whispers and mutters as I did so. Grades and rankings hadn't been posted yet, but normally summer assignments were a way to gauge how well people had performed.

My assignment was almost unheard of for someone who'd been performing well. There had to be dozens of rumors flying. I could almost hear what everyone was thinking. Maybe I'd asked for this position, maybe my nerve had broken. Maybe I'd gotten in trouble and this was the result. Maybe I'd failed classes and this was a holding assignment while they figured out what to do about it.

I wanted to turn and scream at them that I hadn't done anything wrong. I still didn't know how I'd done on my tests, but I was almost certain I'd passed, at least. I wanted to tell them that this was because someone else had complained about favoritism and family... and anyone who thought the Admiral would treat me even a little bit easier would know how absurd that was.

But I just quietly walked out of the barracks. Under the weight of my duffel bags, I staggered down the stairs into the lower levels, moving quietly until I found a quiet place to set my bags down. Then, I felt out to make certain I was away from any monitor coverage and I put my face in my hands and let myself cry.

***

Kyle found me after only a few minutes. "Dang-it, Jiden," he grumbled, taking me in his arms, "why didn't you come find me?"

I felt silly as he hugged me. I tried to push him away, "I'm fine," I protested. Here we were in a public corridor... granted, one so out of the way that only he had found me, but still. I have to confess, I didn't push very hard.

"You're not fine," he dismissed my argument. "This sucks. I'm half tempted to resign my position over it."

This time I did push him away and my face went angry, "Don't you *dare.*"

"What?" Kyle's face twisted in surprise and a little bit of hurt.

"You've got a Senior Drill Instructor position as a Third Class Cadet," I met his green eyes, my face stern. "Giving up that position would look *really* bad."

"I know *that,*" he said, "but if enough of your friends did it, maybe whoever made this decision would get the picture. This isn't how you treat a good person, this isn't fair."

My heart did a sort of flip as I realized that he was serious and that he cared that much about me. Still, I wasn't going to let him destroy his chances over this, "No," I shook my head, "even if a bunch of others did the same, it would just look like some kind of minor mutiny or something. It's just a summer assignment," I tried to believe those words as I said them, "I'll be fine."

He stared at me, as if gauging how sincere I was. I had the feeling he didn't believe me, but then again, I didn't believe me.

"Come on, let's go somewhere," he said finally. "Unless you want to stay hiding in the lower levels?"

I snorted, despite myself. "I must look ridiculous, huh?"

"Only moderately," he grinned at me. He took a step back, then reached down and picked up one of my duffel bags. The heavier one, too. I started to protest, but he gave me a look and I shut up and let him help me.

"How'd you know where I'd be?" I asked.

He paused and looked over at me. He pointed at a mural, near which I'd been seated. "I figured you'd go there. You always end up nearby when you're upset."

It was the mural of my grandfather's ship, the one that he and his crew had died aboard, fighting in the Three Day War against the Dalite Hegemony. I hadn't even realized consciously that it was where I'd stopped. It made sense, though, there were plenty of times that I felt the need to come and stare at the painting, the almost life-like quality showing the destroyer as it continued to fire even as it fell into Century's upper atmosphere.

In comparison, I suppose it made me feel like my worries were small things.

Kyle led the way and as always, he seemed to know the Academy far better than me. We managed to keep to empty corridors and stairwells, right up until we emerged near the chapel. I looked at him in surprise and he grinned, "There's a lounge in the lower level of the chapel, it's normally pretty empty, there's some chairs and couches and we can stash your bags there until you know where you need to go."

I didn't ask him how he knew that or how he knew that I didn't know where to go. I checked my implant, but I still didn't have a reporting location or time, yet.

"How's your team look for the summer?" I asked. As we walked past the wall of the chapel, with the rows of brass plaques, I felt as if my troubles seemed rather insignificant in comparison.

"Good," he grinned at me as we took the side entrance to the chapel, "I've got Mitchel, Vanlaas, and Tran from Dust Company, plus Green from Sand Dragon Company, so it's a good core group. There's a couple names I don't recognize from Ogre and Scorpion, but..." He shrugged. I felt that odd peace wash over me as we entered the chapel. Maybe it was partially the walk, partially the companionship, and partially the place, but by the time we got downstairs to the chapel lounge, I actually felt human again. With a glance at Kyle's twinkling green eyes, I suspected he knew me well enough that he'd planned for that.

He paused outside of the lounge door and cleared his throat. I raised an eyebrow at him, and he shrugged slightly, before he reached through the doorway and flipped on the light and only after a moment, did he step inside. He looked around, cautiously, then seemed satisfied and turned back to me, "It's a quiet, out of the way place," he explained. "Sometimes there are other cadets who, um," he flushed a bit, "well, this is a make-out spot. I didn't want to catch anyone in the act, so to speak."

I flushed in reply, "Will people assume that we..."

"It's also just a hangout spot," he said quickly. "There's some board games over there," he gestured, "and the chaplain keeps drinks in the fridge. Lots of people just hang out here."

"I see," I replied. His defensiveness was charming, in a way. I set my duffel down next to one of the couches and took a seat. It *was* remarkably comfortable. "Some time you need to tell me how you know every nook and cranny of the Academy."

"Some time *you* need to explain to me how you don't manage to see very much of this place," he answered blandly, setting my bag down and taking a seat on the couch next to me. "I mean, one of the first things I did as a plebe was try to explore everywhere they'd let me."

I shrugged, "I'm always busy."

"Tell me about it," he nodded, "there's not enough time in the day."

We sat in silence for a while. I couldn't help but notice that the way the couch sagged, it slid us towards one another, so we were almost touching. "So," I said, "what do we do while we wait to see where I need to go?"

He looked over at me, his green eyes innocent, "Board game?" he asked.

***

We didn't play any games, but I looked a little mussed some time later when my implant pinged to give me an update on my summer assignment. I gave Kyle a last kiss as I stood up and straightened my uniform. I didn't know how I felt about kissing in the chapel lounge, but I *was* feeling a lot better.

"I've got my reporting location," I undid my ponytail and then drew my hair back again. "I should go."

Kyle grinned at me, "Let me know if you need any further cheering up."

I rolled my eyes at him, "Gee, thanks."

"Where do you need to report?" He asked more seriously, standing up and straightening his uniform as well. We both looked a little wrinkled and disreputable, but the khaki uniforms straightened out well enough.

"Admin area, sub-level... four," I said after a moment.

"Sub-level four?" He frowned at that. "I didn't think they had more than two sub-levels."

"Ah, the all-knowing Kyle Regan doesn't know where I'll be working," I grinned wryly, "maybe that means I'll get some work done."

"Hah, fat chance of that," he smirked. "Where ever you go, Jiden, I'll find you."

I rolled my eyes at that, but I appreciated his words all the same. There was something solid and just *good* about Kyle. "I should get going."

"Need help carrying your stuff?" There was more to his offer than generosity. I could see real concern and also a bit of curiosity on his face. He wanted to find out about this mystery assignment and to make sure I was going to be okay.

"I'll be fine," I assured him. "Besides, *you* have a big assignment you need to get ready for."

He nodded somewhat grudgingly. "I *do* have a lot of work."

I picked up my bags, "I'll see you later."

"Tonight, for dinner," he assured me.

"Take care," I said as I stepped out. I went up the stairs and I felt oddly sheepish as I went through the chapel. Not that we'd done anything *wrong*, mind you, but kissing in the chapel lounge probably wasn't necessarily *right*. It was something I'd probably need to think about, and maybe I'd feel comfortable going somewhere else.

My face burned a bit as I walked past the chaplain's office, just before I left the chapel itself. The thought of the chaplain or another officer walking in on us, even doing something as mild as kissing, definitely made me uncomfortable.

There were the ever-present monitors, too... although I checked with my implant and realized, with shock, that the chapel area lacked those. I wasn't sure how or why, but it was information that I filed away... just in case.

Walking down the corridors to the administration section of the Academy left me with an ominous feeling. I'd known a number of cadets who'd made this same walk, oftentimes in the course of failing out or submitting their resignations. It was a bit of a shock as I realized just how many of my classmates had already failed out. I remembered Webster, how he'd split us off by threes, and how each group had represented cadets who would fail out, be set back into a later year group, or manage to graduate on time.

Odds were against me, I knew. Oh, I'd done well during the Academy Prep Course, but a lot of that had been luck. Last year, I'd done well enough in classes and okay with the military side of things. But it had been the performance of my candidates during the Academy Prep Course that had made the difference.

This year, I felt like I'd struggled with classes. Especially with the implants. And my performance in the military drills had been acceptable but not outstanding. Ashiri Takenata had done fantastic, Alex had done well, and even Sashi had managed to do well, especially against her heavy course load. I hadn't failed anything, not yet, but I certainly didn't feel like things were getting easier.

Combined with the worries about the implants and the added stress of the possible conspiracy, there was every chance that I would continue to drop in ranking. Maybe I'd fail out, maybe I'd be set back... it had happened to others, it could happen to me.

I didn't know what I would do if it did. I'd pinned so much upon my attendance here. I knew that the CEO of Champion Enterprises had offered me a position after I revealed the corruption in his company, but I hadn't really considered it, it seemed a little strange to go back to work there after what I'd experienced. It definitely didn't feel like that was where I was supposed to be. I could go into archeology, like my parents, but that didn't call to me and it didn't feel like it was the best use of my abilities.

I'd hit a rough stretch, but I couldn't let it beat me. *I want this,* I told myself and I really did. Whatever the future held for me, either in Archive and Support or through the rest of the year, I knew I would handle it. This was what I had chosen for myself and I wasn't about to give up.

***

The Admin section was where the Admiral's offices were, though her office was on the third level of the main floors. That area still lay several meters of sand, rock, and concrete. I was aware of the command center for the Academy's offensive and defensive efforts lay somewhere on sublevel one, buried deep where it would survive damage to the upper floors. Sub-level two had a self-contained environmental system for the whole admin section, in case of chemical or biological attack, the whole section could go into quarantine and still coordinate a fight. I hadn't been there, but we'd done an engineering assessment of the environmental systems in our classes, so I was aware of it.

I showed the guard at the door to the sub-level elevator my orders and he squinted at them, then looked up at me. "Sub-level four?" he asked incredulously.

"Yes, sergeant," I replied.

He looked at me and shook his head, then he turned and spoke into his radio. I knew he'd turned so I couldn't see his lips and for just a moment, I hoped this was some kind of prank.

"Alright," he turned back to me with a nod. "You're cleared, Cadet Third Class Armstrong." He seemed to put extra weight on my name and rank and I wasn't certain what that meant.

I stepped past him and into the elevator. I looked at the controls, but there weren't any buttons, just a spot for a key card or bio-metric reader. Before I could ask about it, the doors closed. The elevator started downwards. I had that sensation of falling that I normally got on a fast elevator. Lights flashed around the edges of the door, I couldn't really guess how far down I was going, but it felt like more than four levels.

The doors opened on another guard checkpoint. There were two armed guards, one with his hands on his slung weapon while the other had a datapad. "Cadet Third Class Armstrong?" He asked.

"Yes, Sergeant," I replied, reading his collar rank.

He held up his datapad and pressed a button. An orange light flashed, followed by a green one that dazzled my eyes. I sort of recognized the facial and retinal scanner, but I was a bit shocked that they'd used it on me. "Confirmed," he said, his tone mild.

The other guard seemed to relax, slightly. I wasn't certain why they were so security conscious... or what exactly was going on. Archive and Support sounded like some kind of filing and paperwork job. This felt like something rather different.

The sergeant tapped on his datapad and a moment later, a green light lit up over a doorway down the corridor. "That's your door, cadet," he said with a nod. "You can leave your gear here for retrieval."

"Thanks, sergeant," I dropped my duffel bags and then shoved them out of the way. I wanted to ask what all this was about, but I somehow sensed that neither of these two guards would be very talkative. Instead I kept my mouth closed and walked down the hallway to the door with the green light. It buzzed as I reached for the handle. The handled didn't turn in my hand, but the door opened at my touch.

I stepped inside and the door slammed behind me, making me jump a bit.

The room beyond looked depressingly boring. There was a reception desk and what looked like offices beyond. Yet as I looked up, I froze. There was a crest opposite me, a crest that I recognized from my dream. It was that oddly familiar jagged lightning bolt crossed with a scroll.

"Cadet Armstrong?" The receptionist asked.

I blinked and shook myself, wondering how long I'd stood there staring at it and hoping I hadn't looked too out of it. "Yes," I stepped forward.

She just gave me a nod and pointed at the doorway to her right. "Through there."

"Thanks," I answered, not sure what else to say.

I stepped into the office she'd pointed at. As I did so, the room's sole occupant rose. "Ah, Cadet Armstrong, welcome to Directorate Thirteen," Commander Weisfeldt rose from behind his desk, his wild eyebrows and disheveled appearance oddly reassuring after all the strangeness.

"Sir," I saluted, and only then registered his greeting.

He seemed to catch my confusion. "Directorate Thirteen," he said with a slight smile, "is your *actual* summer assignment, which you should have read as Academy Archive and Support, I believe?"

I nodded dumbly in response. I had so many questions that I didn't know where to start.

"Technically speaking, the work we do here can be archival and you are in support of Academy personnel," he grinned mischievously at me, as if he enjoyed dragging out the anticipation. He paused for effect, "But what Directorate Thirteen does is rather more specialized and specific. In fact, what we do here is classified at a very high level. You will not be authorized to mention any of it to friends or family. You will not discuss any of it outside of this complex, and you will be given a cover story to memorize on your departure from working here every day. Understand?"

I blinked at him, "Yes, sir."

"Excellent," he rubbed his hands together eagerly. "Now, I'm sure you're eager to get to work..." he trailed off and looked around, "where is that processing tablet, ah, here we are." He picked up a datapad off his desk and passed it to me. "Read through all of this and sign. You'll need to do a bio-metric signature for each statement."

"Sir, what is this about?" I asked, almost plaintively.

He sat back down and stared at me, his bushy eyebrows drooping as if he were examining me to make sure that I hadn't been replaced by a doppelganger or something. "Yes..." he nodded. "Perhaps I got a bit ahead of myself."

"Directorate Thirteen is a very special organization within the Academy structure, and within the Militia itself. Typically Academy staff, especially the Engineering Department, are assigned here. We're selected specifically to assist in weapons and engineering research. We make use of the Academy's excess computing power to run a variety of computer simulations."

"Computer simulations?" I couldn't help a disappointed note in my voice.

"Yes, but very special simulations," he gestured at the tablet. "You need to finish signing all of those documents before I can tell you more. But I will say this. Commander Scarpitti's infiltration of the militia, her theft of military hardware, her murder of a cadet... all of that pales in comparison to the damage she may have done by accessing the secrets of Directorate Thirteen before she died."

"I don't understand, sir," I admitted.

"I don't expect you to, not yet," he nodded, his eyes twinkling. "But you will, soon enough."

***

Chapter 16: I Steal My Cake And Have To Eat It Too

I went back into the waiting area to sign the documents on the tablet.

After the first ten pages of legal documents, I stopped trying to understand everything they meant. I couldn't admit to being here. I couldn't talk about what I saw here. I couldn't remove any information from the facility. I was sort of surprised it didn't say that my mind would be wiped at the end of every work day. The layers of security seemed ridiculous, especially for something that Commander Weisfeldt had as much as admitted that the engineering professors ran in their spare time.

Still, I signed the documents. What else was I supposed to do?

After I'd finished, Commander Weisfeldt's receptionist looked it over, making certain I hadn't missed or skipped any. She gave a disapproving sniff at the end, as if upset that she hadn't found anything that I missed. "Through there, Cadet. I'll let the Commander know that you're on the way."

"Thank you," I said, still not certain if the woman had any rank or if she were a civilian.

She didn't respond as she took her seat. As I walked past her desk, I glanced down and saw the handle of a DCP Needle Pistol sticking out of a holster on the underside of the desk. I recognized it only because I'd had to do research on them for one of Commander Bonnadonna's papers. They were electromagnetically accelerated needle-like round, each of which was designed to penetrate body armor and detonate inside. They were something of a joke, though, since the pistols cost a fortune and the rounds for them were outrageously expensive. Just what she had to worry about that she had the weapon so close to hand, I didn't know. Somehow that made everything seem that much more serious.

I stepped into the set of offices beyond. It was a series of cubicles, with about a dozen or so desks. Various men and women, most of them in uniform, but a handful in civilian clothing, worked at those desks. I recognized a few of them as Academy staff, though most of them didn't teach classes, now that I thought about it.

Commander Weisfeldt met me near the middle of the offices and guided me to the far end. Instead of a wall, there was a large set of glass. Beyond it lay a strange room. It was fitted with more holoprojectors than I'd ever seen. As we stood there, a ship started to take form. "We're running the first set of simulations now," Commander Weisfeldt noted. "This is Project Alexandria, which is the main project you'll be working on this summer."

"What is it?" I asked. The ship looked like a relatively standard military hull. The thick, angular and armored frame was fairly standard. The thick, armored warp drive rings lay almost flush with the hull. The scale was hard to guess, but the size of the weapon's ports and lack of turrets suggested to me that it was probably a corvette or possibly a destroyer.

"This," he said in a low, gleeful voice, "is what's going to one day save our world."

I looked at him in disbelief, "Excuse me?"

He grinned at my expression, "Watch and learn, young woman, watch and learn." He turned and led me off to the right. He stopped at a separate office door and knocked politely, "This is the contracting section. Out there," he gestured, "is where all our people do the number crunching and in here is where the contractors look at what they can actually build, since we don't have a militia dock-yard."

I nodded slowly at that. As far as I knew, we didn't have *any* military-grade shipyards in the system. Most of our ships were built off-world from one of the commercial yards in the Harlequin Military Sector or purchased second or third-hand from other militias or the Guard. *Most of our ships fall in the latter category.*

The door opened, "Ah, Artie, good to see you," Leo Champion smiled as he stuck his head out. "And you brought young Jiden Armstrong, that's perfect, come on in, my people were just reviewing the latest set of plans. This is looking very good, the best yet!"

I gaped as I saw him. The last person I would have expected in some kind of top-secret military research lab was the CEO of a company that had been proven to be stealing military equipment for sale on the black market. *Granted, they proved beyond a doubt that he had no role in it, but it doesn't change the fact that his company paid massive fines over it all.*

Champion led the way inside, talking at his normal fast-paced tone, "We went over that latest simulation data from your engineers, and we're still running into issues with the processing loads. The ship's computers *can* manage it, but it still requires the operator to be involved. I'm not seeing a normal human pilot, even one with an implant, managing this in real-time."

"That's why we brought in a Project Quicksilver subject," Commander Weisfeldt said off-hand.

My eyes went wide at that and I looked between him and Leo Champion, "Uh, sir..."

"Oh, don't worry about the non-disclosures," Champion scoffed. "Honestly, that disaster that happened wouldn't have happened if *my* people had been in charge. And I *never* would have let someone like Aisling anywhere *near* people to use as live test subjects. If you ask me, they shouldn't keep her down here in this hole, they should have--"

Commander Weisfeldt cleared his throat and Champion looked over at him. "Oh, right, I guess I shouldn't talk about that. Anyway," he waved a hand at where several long-faced engineers sat, their shoulders hunched as they stared down at their computer terminals, "I don't see how Miss Armstrong's presence would help. I read the file, Commander, you deactivated all of the implants."

"That's what the file says, yes," Commander Weisfeldt nodded. "But it's not *entirely* accurate, you see, because I happen to know that Cadet Armstrong is one of several Quicksilver subjects whose Tier Three implant is still active."

As both of them looked at me, I felt my heart rise in my chest. *I'm in trouble,* I thought.

***

Only, I wasn't in trouble, at least, not that I could tell.

"Oh, excellent," Champion was saying, "this will help immeasurably. We can dial her into the main simulation, relatively easily."

"We'll need her as part of the ship concept design team," Commander Weisfeldt cautioned. "That's her official assignment and I've got a lot for her to work on."

"Fine, I can understand that," Champion nodded. "How about during the hardware simulation, then? We normally do that on Mondays, giving the system the weekend to 'build' as it were."

"That should work," Commander Weisfeldt nodded. They

both looked at me, "What do you think, Armstrong?"

I swallowed, "Um, I'm not in any kind of trouble for still having a functional implant?" I asked the question mostly of Commander Weisfeldt, since I figured he would be the one to know.

"Why would she be?" Leo Champion asked, looking in turn at Commander Weisfeldt.

"Well, I'll admit, there was some consternation after we went through the data. The Admiral..." he trailed off, "Well, she had some choice words for me. But several of the program's test subjects showed signs of having operational implants. We monitored all of you and, since the investigation team seemed focused on burying the whole thing..." he shrugged. "We haven't made official notice of it. The Admiral has authorized you to utilize your implant's full abilities here within Directorate Thirteen, but you're to limit your activities here, of course. As I understand that, you and the others have self-monitored rather effectively. It's one reason that the Admiral chose to keep your functional implants secret and not to have me attempt to shut them down a second time."

"Okay," I blinked as I considered all of that. "We thought we'd been pretty good about hiding it."

"You *were*," he noted, giving me a level look, his bushy eyebrows ominous, "but I'm not stupid. Nor is the Admiral. There are any number of tests we could run, unobtrusively, to determine your implants were still active."

"Sir," I nodded, not really sure how to answer that without getting in trouble.

"Now, then," he said, "if you've no further questions in that regard, I'll show you your workspace and introduce you to the team. Then we'll get started."

"But sir," I asked, "what *is* this project? I mean, that looked like a small ship, maybe a destroyer at most. And we don't have military-grade shipyards. What *is* this all about?"

Both Champion and Weisfeldt stared at me. "Right," Commander Weisfeldt nodded, "you've missed a bit and this is all new to you anyway." He gestured at the massive holoprojector room back where we'd come from, "Directorate Thirteen has been working on a number of projects designed to give Century a fighting edge against potential enemies."

"It's quite clever, you see," Leo Champion nodded, grinning

a bit maniacally. "Dabbling in tech that the Guard or Drakkus discarded as too costly or too esoteric, adding in bits of alien technology that we've, uh, acquired."

"Bits and pieces we've been putting together for twenty, thirty years," Commander Weisfeldt nodded. "Improved composites and alloys, better power-transfer materials, construction techniques that are too expensive for wide-spread mass production or single production large vessels."

"Weapons designs that were discarded or where testing didn't go as planned," Champion grinned. "Actually, we've had a lot of progress in exotic matter projection, massively destructive and..."

"But the lynchpin has been focused on small ships," Commander Weisfeldt interrupted, waving a hand at the team of engineers. "Corvette or destroyer-sized, ships we can build at our own yards, with teams we can monitor and prevent our designs from getting out. But the problem we ran into is that some *politicians*," Commander Weisfeldt fairly spat the word, "feel that generating uncertainty in our enemies is worth more than actual functional weapons, so they started hinting to Drakkus and the Guard that we had a developing weapon program."

"That's what Scarpitti was here for," Commander Weisfeldt leaned on a convenient table and twirled a hand as he spoke. "She must have heard something, because she asked for transfer to the Academy. But she hadn't been selected for the Directorate, I've been the, well, director, and she hadn't been pulled into the program. So she was sniffing around the Academy, trying to pull secrets without quite knowing what she was looking for, and trying to cover up any ties to Mr. Champion's problem children."

Leo Champion winced at that, "A particularly apt way to put it. Tony and Isaac were such... disappointing offspring."

"The current iteration, our main focus for the next few months within the Directorate, is flushing out the design of this ship. This is Project Alexandria, the end product, we hope, is a warship the size of a corvette, manned by a small crew, and equipped with a warp drive as deep as a cruiser and with firepower to match."

I wanted to say that wasn't possible. I mean, I knew that technically it *could* be possible, with a big enough power source and sufficient quantities of money spent on it. But I couldn't imagine Century building a ship like that. The expense would be astronomical. The power source alone would have to be massive. *Unless...*

"Kyle's equation," I stared at Commander Weisfeldt in shock.

"Yes!" He gestured at me, then looked at Leo Champion, "I told you she was bright, didn't I tell you she was bright?"

"I believed *I* told you that," Champion noted absently as he leaned over the shoulder of one of his contractors.

"Yes, well, we're both right," Weisfeldt grinned. He looked back at me, "Cadet Regan's formula, which *you* ran the initial data on. A way to modulate the power usage and change the geometry of a drive field. Controlling the geometry of a drive field in real-time leads into so many options... well, that was the key. We had all the rest of this in the works, hull, power systems, sensors..."

"Weapons," Leo Champion grinned, "very impressive weapons. Very *expensive* weapons."

"Eh, the weapons need some work," Weisfeldt corrected. "But almost everything else is ready to go. We needed the ship's drive. We were hoping to, ah, acquire..."

"Steal," Leo Champion smirked. "

"Acquire," Commander Weisfeldt insisted, "a copy of the Drakkus Imperial Space Korps drive, the variant geometry drive, VGT, or what they're calling the Zubaran drive, but this is so much better... if, and I say *if,* we can make it work."

"So if anything good comes of that meddling woman Beckman and that brain butcher Aisling," Champion grated, "at least it will be to move this project forward."

"So I'm going to help you to get Kyle's equations to work?" I asked. "Why not bring him in? I mean, this was all his idea."

"I'd love to," Commander Weisfeldt nodded, "But that would be too much attention. The Admiral let me publish his paper--on the secret side, no less-- but she felt it would be too conspicuous for him and you to both disappear for the summer. So, you're officially on a scut-work detail and he's visibly too busy to be working on this sort of thing."

"You don't think that there's another infiltrator like Commander Scarpitti..." I trailed off as I stared at him in worry.

"I don't think there is," Commander Weisfeldt shook his head, "but I didn't think that Commander Scarpitti was a spy in the first place. I just didn't like her, so I didn't recruit her into the Directorate. Woman ate far too many onions, her breath..." he waved a hand, "but I digress. She *was* a spy, and we have to assume that where there was one, there are others. So despite the secret nature of that paper that you and your boyfriend produced, he's doing a nice, non-technical job that won't draw attention and *you* are down here helping. I could only get one of you and I needed the one with the implant."

"Understood, sir," I took a deep breath. "I guess I'm ready to get started."

"Excellent," Commander Weisfeldt grinned. "I only hope you're that enthusiastic about this after five months of twelve-hour days down here." I hoped that was a joke, but I had a sinking suspicion that it wasn't. "Now, I'll show you your work space and make introductions. After that, I'll map out where your quarters are, for you. You'll be staying in the transient officer quarters just off the Administration section. You'll be the junior person there, as a cadet. Before you take your bags upstairs, swing by the front desk and Janna will give you your pass keys for access through the elevator and security points."

"Yes, sir," I nodded. My head was still spinning at all the shocks. Somehow, I wish the Admiral had been here to tell me at least some of this. *Maybe she's still trying to distance herself.* Yet that felt like an excuse, even to me.

"You'll do fine, Armstrong," Champion gave me a nod and then turned back to his engineers, "We've got a solution to the power modulation problem. Now back to work!"

* * *

Most of my first day was spent figuring everything out. They seemed to have a dozen or more projects going on, besides the warp drive research they'd brought me in to work on. Some of them fell under the overall Project Alexandria, some weren't related at all. The worst part seemed to be that everyone knew about my implant and my ability to process data in almost real-time, time that they otherwise needed to set up filters and interfaces and run system calibrations on.

Half the staff in there seemed to see me as nothing more than a walking tool and wanted to plug me into their projects to speed things up.

The other half seemed to treat me with more distance and respect than I really understood.

After about a week of that treatment, I mentioned it to Commander Weisfeldt, who at least treated me like he did everyone else. That was, he mostly ignored me other than absentmindedly giving directions that often required multiple clarifications.

"Oh, they're afraid of you," He told me without looking up. "Do you think this secondary buffer is really necessary?" He asked.

"Afraid of me?" I asked, even as I ran through the specifications for that buffer. It was a power buffer that seemed to exist to prevent a catastrophic overload from causing a cascade effect straight to the main reactor.

"Oh, yes," Commander Weisfeldt looked up, his bushy eyebrows arched as he studied me, as if curious that I didn't understand. "Not so many years ago, cybernetics were virtually unheard of here on Century. Even ten, fifteen years ago, the idea that they'd force all graduates to get implants wouldn't have made it past the discussion stage. Most of the officers and civilian contractors in here don't have implants. Many of them wouldn't consider it and as far as taking an experimental implant, which has been shown to have had serious negative impacts on the mental stability of at least one cadet..."

He shrugged. "Then there's the fact that you've seen more combat than many of the militia. You killed not just one or two criminals, you took on a smuggling gang. You killed an armed and well-trained spy, with nothing more than a bit of leverage."

I swallowed as I thought about that. "But," I protested, "I'm not dangerous!"

"You are *very* dangerous," Commander Weisfeldt said in a low, focused voice. "The thing they don't understand is that you're not dangerous to *them*. Don't worry about them, though, worry about your job, your friends, your duty, and the rest will sort itself out. It's not *your* problem, it's their problem."

***

"Hey, Jiden, how was your day?" Kyle asked, sitting down across from me at the chow hall.

I blinked at him, feeling tired after the past week or more of working at the Directorate. "Good," I replied. "I'm learning a lot." I hadn't seen Kyle all week, not except in passing. He'd been doing all the standard preparatory work for his incoming section of candidates along with training this year's cadet drill instructors.

"In *archive*?" Kyle asked incredulously.

I froze as I thought about my official cover story, versus what I wanted to tell him, versus what I could talk about here at dinner. "It wasn't exactly what I thought and there's a lot more challenge to it than I expected," I was careful how I phrased it. I wasn't, *exactly*, lying. And I put emphasis on the first part. Kyle wasn't stupid and he considered what I'd said... and what I hadn't said.

He pursed his lips as he considered that... and I saw a bit of frustration go across his face. "You know," his voice was a bit plaintive, "sometimes talking to you feels like I'm only getting about a quarter of the full conversation."

I winced. "I'm sorry..."

He shook his head and sighed dramatically, "Not your fault, Jiden. I suppose I should be used to it by now. So, let me tell you about *my* week, huh?" He grinned at me, his green eyes twinkling, "I mean, it's not like you can complain about me talking too much about myself, given the situation, right?"

I grinned at him, "Sure."

"I've got a good team," he noted. He did make a face, "Though I ended up with Beckman, somehow. I swear, I don't know how she made it through her time as a plebe."

I grimaced, "Yeah..." She'd done great in her academics, from what I'd heard, but she had barely scraped by in her military sections. After the drill with me, she'd received a lot of demerits for disobeying a direct order. More than enough to knock her out of the top tier of her class.

Her performance hadn't improved, either. She'd worked under Sashi for several drills, who at least had seemed to keep her out of trouble. I wasn't sure *how* Sashi had managed to keep the girl from doing anything blatantly stupid, but she had.

But after recognition, they'd moved the plebes around to cross-train them, and Beckman's tendency to want to be right had shown up several more times. I'd had another run-in with her, though nowhere near as catastrophic, she'd still managed to endanger herself and others.

Alexander Karmazin had a worse encounter, where she'd even claimed he'd been prejudiced against her because of his background in the Enclave. Just the accusation had been absurd and from what I'd heard, Ashiri had nearly gone after the idiot, but Salter had decided to take the opportunity to do an administrative transfer... and Beckman had ended up in Dust Company.

"She actually seems to be a *bit* better here," he noted after a moment. "I mean, I still want to strangle her every time she opens her mouth, but she seems to get that she's walking a thin line, so she at least stops to think a bit before she opens her mouth."

"Hmmm," I mouthed around a bite of food. I'd taken to skipping lunch, just because the whole clearing my way out of security and then back in ate up most of my time. Besides, I could bring in a light snack to tide me over. Of course, that meant that by dinner time I was ravenous. "You going to eat that?" I asked, pointing at Kyle's dessert.

"Uh, I was..." he started, but I'd already snagged his cake. I normally didn't go for sugary stuff, but it had been a long day and I felt like I burned almost as many calories running my implant as I did physically running. He snorted, "I guess I'll get another one."

"Sorry," I said around a mouthful of cake.

He got up and came back a moment later. I'd finished his cake and the rest of my food in that time. I felt totally drained. "Have you talked with Ashiri or Sashi?" Kyle sat back down, his green eyes inquisitive.

"No, I haven't really seen anyone outside of work," I admitted.

"They had another run-in," he said. "I thought it was going to get physical at one point. Sashi was relaying some info from the Regimental Training Officer, Ashiri didn't like that she went straight to her Cadet Drill Instructors first... it sort of escalated from there."

I frowned, "I didn't think Ashiri was the type to go off like that."

"Me either," he admitted. "I heard the shouting and came running, since a couple of my company are cadet drill instructors for Sand Dragon, this year. The two of them were really going at it. Senior Petty Officer Kennedy intervened and at first it sounded like they both might be relieved."

I blanched at that. A relief from any position at the Academy was a black-mark. It would be hard to come back from that, doubly hard when both of them were holding positions that Second Class Cadets normally held.

"No one has said anything yet, I think they're going to wait to see how this all resolves itself, but you might try talking to them."

"Me?" I asked in surprise.

"You're friends with both of them, they might listen to you," Kyle shrugged. "I'd ask Alexander to say something, but he's already out at the Grinder, and I don't really know anyone else from Sand Dragon that well."

"I'll see what I can do," I sighed. *Not like I don't already have enough on my plate.*

"Good," he nodded at me, then threw a nod over my shoulder, "because, incoming." He said the last in a low voice and I looked over my shoulder to see Ashiri, she was paused in conversation with Andrews, who was one of Sand Dragon's Drill Instructors again this year. But as I looked their way, she finished talking to him and headed my way with her tray of food.

I looked back at Kyle, who looked down at his tray of food as she got to the table. "Oh, look at that, I'm all done eating, catch you later, Jiden!" He looked over at her, "Hey, Ashiri, how goes?"

He didn't wait for her response and was headed off with his tray... just as Sashi came from the other direction and froze, seeing Ashiri about to set her tray down across from me. *Oh... great.*

Ashiri slammed her tray down on the table with a bit more force than necessary. About half of her drink sloshed out of the cup and the boom of her tray hitting the table and the clink and rattle of her plate and cup echoed through the mess hall.

It was a challenge, one that Ashiri had just made very public. Every eye in the mess hall was on them both. I saw Sashi's face darken as she felt all those eyes on her. Ashiri had just thrown down a gauntlet, dared her to come over to the table... but if she didn't, if she walked away, she'd look like a coward in front of everyone.

It was a remarkably cruel thing for Ashiri to do to the other girl. Yet as I looked at my best friend, I saw her face was set in an angry expression, one that suggested she knew *exactly* what she was doing. She was trying to embarrass Sashi, to give the other woman no way out, other than fighting or turning tail.

I stood up, "Hey, Sashi," I said in a voice just loud enough to carry throughout the mess hall, but not shouting. "Come on over. Have you tried the cake? It's delicious."

It was such a cheesy, silly thing to say that it threw everyone off. The entire mess hall had been holding their breath, half expecting the two of them to start a fight, and I'd just asked one of them about cake. I heard nervous giggles and a smatter of conversation start up again. Sashi shot me a grateful look and then came over, careful to set her tray down softly next to me.

"I haven't much of an appetite," she admitted to me, flashing a glare across the table.

"I'll snag yours, then," I said with a smile. I took her cake and then looked over at Ashiri, who hadn't touched any of her food yet. "Ashiri," I asked brightly, "how was your day?"

My friend shot me an almost disgusted look. "It went fine, Jiden. Yours?"

"Another day in Archive and Support," I shrugged. "Not much to say."

Ashiri's dark eyes locked on my face and something of her angry expression shifted, almost as if she'd expected me to say something else. She looked back at Sashi and then started to say something and seemed to think better of it. She rose from her chair, "I think I'm going to get some cake."

She wasn't out of earshot before I turned to Sashi, "What is going on?" I asked.

"Well, she hates, me, obviously," Sashi stared at my friend's back. If her eyes were guns, then Ashiri would have been riddled with bullets. "I don't much like her at this point, either."

"Do you have to work together?" I asked.

"Daily," Sashi admitted, her voice emotionless. I could sense her dread, though, from the set of her shoulders. That was understandable. Sashi had nearly failed out. She'd brought her grades up this last semester, but getting this summer assignment was a rare opportunity for her. But if it came down to her and Ashiri not getting along, there'd be repercussions for both of them and Sashi was the one who could least afford that.

Sashi started eating, wolfing down her food faster than I would have thought possible. "Thanks," she muttered around a bite of food, "for defusing that. I didn't know what to do."

"That's what friends are for," I replied.

"Am I your friend?" Sashi asked it in such a doubtful, worried tone that it shocked me. I looked over and met her fearful eyes. We'd had plenty of hate, between us, but none of it had really been our own doing. *Well, she* did *shoot me... a few times.* Yet I couldn't *really* hate her. And we'd been through so much together.

Most of all, I understood her, now. I knew the pressures she was under. The family that resented her for continuing, the older brothers who should have encouraged her were bullies who wanted her to fail out and go home. There was a grit and an unwillingness to quit in her that I understood more than anything. It was the same thing that had kept me alive when my life had been on the line.

"Yeah," I smiled gently at her, "I'm your friend, Sashi."

For just a second, I thought I saw tears in her eyes, but she blinked rapidly and stood up, picking up her tray, "Thanks," she all but whispered. Ashiri was just coming back, a plate with cake on it in her hands. "All done, sorry, guys, I've got to run."

"Bye," I said in a sunny tone as she departed.

Ashiri sat down across from me, her eyes hooded as she gazed at me. "You're playing a dangerous game, Armstrong."

It was the first time in years that she'd called me by my last name, only. I actually flinched a bit, as if she'd insulted me. "Why do you say that?"

"You can't trust her," Ashiri hissed. "She's proven again and again that she'll always choose herself over you or anyone else."

I frowned at her, "That's an oversimplification--"

"No," she snapped, her voice angry, but her tone low, "it's a truth. Sashi Drien will always chose herself over anyone else. It's what she knows. It's what her family trained into her from a young age. She doesn't know any other way to operate and if you are soft on her, she's going to bite you."

"You seem pretty sure of that," I snapped back, suddenly angry. "Are you sure you aren't projecting some of that?" I saw Ashiri's face go white and I felt my stomach twist. "Sorry, I shouldn't have said that."

"No," Ashiri stared at me, her expression icy, "you shouldn't have. You know *nothing* of my family." Her expression shifted, "You think we're like the Driens? You don't know the pressures *I'm* under from my family to succeed. And they don't measure success on anything other than being the best. But you don't understand that, do you? You can't even understand how lucky you've been!"

She'd said all of it in that same, low, angry tone. I stared at her, shocked at once by how out of control she seemed and yet she managed to control her tone so that no one nearby could hear what she said. "I've been nothing but your friend and when I try to show you how dangerous *she* is, you assume that I'd betray you like she did?"

"That's not what I'm saying," I protested.

"You don't understand what you're trying to say," Ashiri hissed. "You don't know who your real friends are and this whole..." she waved her hands in the air, "this, all of this, has gone to your head. You're meddling with things you don't understand and you're going to get yourself and others hurt. You *have* gotten others hurt."

My eyes went narrow at that, "What do you mean?"

"I mean that I know you better than to believe you sat on the sidelines while they shut down our implants. You might not have been responsible, but you were a part of it. Whatever happened to poor Boyles and Gnad as a result comes back on you." Ashiri's face grew hard.

"We shouldn't be talking about that here," I said in a low voice.

"No, we shouldn't, but I'm getting tired of secrets, Jiden. I thought we were friends, but I know you've got secrets from me. I know you too well, I can tell when you're lying."

"I haven't lied about anything," I protested.

"No, but you get uncomfortable when someone says something that's not true," Ashiri growled. "And I know you well enough and I'm smart enough to read between the lines. Something else happened, and you didn't come to me, did you?"

"I..." I really didn't know how to answer that.

"You didn't trust me," Ashiri sat back. "Think about that, Jiden. Think about that real hard, while you think about why you should trust Sashi with... all of this."

She rose and her expression shifted just a millimeter, "When you realize who your true friends are, I'll be waiting for you."

She gestured at the cake on the table, "You can have mine. I don't feel like eating after all."

Ashiri walked off, her back straight. I looked down at my tray. I couldn't help but feel like I'd somehow failed a test. The food

I'd eaten lay like a leaden weight in my stomach. I still disagreed with much of what Ashiri had said. I didn't think Sashi was a lost cause. I thought she wanted to do the right thing, to be a good officer, to be a good person. I believed people could change for the better... that's what I'd done, after all, wasn't it?

I looked down at the several plates of cake on my tray. "I don't even like cake," I muttered to myself. Sometimes you just had to deal with what life gave you, I suppose.

***

Chapter 17: My Family Is Weird And I'm Okay With That

I managed to get out of the sub-level to watch the first day of the candidates.

My little brother was in among their number and I watched, with some of the other cadets on assignment to the school but not part of the Indoctrination process. I'd been one of the Cadet Drill Instructors, I'd lived the experience from both ends. Watching it happen from the outside was almost surreal, though.

The buses came in the back part of the Academy grounds, the closest to the medical and administrative in-processing areas. I'd had no idea how many of those slots were filled by cadets, most of the medical positions were from one company, while many of the in-processing was done by cadets in-between their summer assignments or as temporary duties.

If I'd had more time, I would have volunteered to help, but we were in the middle of a number of simulations in the sub-level and I didn't think they'd let me free for even one full day.

But the arrival of the candidates came early-morning, well before I had to be at work. So I got to watch as screaming cadet drill instructors tore into the candidates, driving them off the buses in a swarm. It was shocking, to watch it from that perspective, yet I couldn't help but smile almost fondly at the memories, from both sides.

I picked out my little brother almost instantly. He had my mom's height, combined with my dad's coloring. He'd always been more drawn to the outdoors than me and more able to take the bright sunlight of Century. With his dark hair and tan skin, he almost could have passed for a sibling of Karmazin. I saw one cadet drill instructor rush up to yell at him and then suddenly realize just how tall he was.

That hesitation didn't last long, they had him on his face doing pushups in the sand a moment later. *He looks like he's handling it well...* Clearly he'd paid attention to my pointers, and I felt a bit of pride as I saw that. I wanted him to do well. Not just because he'd been assigned to Sand Dragon Company, either.

He was my brother, and as I watched him doing pushups, until he and the rest of his formation were jerked to their feet to stand while Ashiri made her introductions, I'd never felt closer to him. I knew exactly what he was going through... and I was *proud* of him for trying.

I sighed as they dropped the whole formation. It was a game, almost a formula, but not quite a script as they went through it all. Some of the 'punishments' were just ways to keep candidates busy while the cadet drill instructors broke the entire mass down into manageable groups and then controlled the flow of candidates to their in-processing.

I'd thought it pointless cruelty as a candidate. I'd struggled to understand it as a plebe and still only barely grasped it as a cadet drill instructor. Watching it all from the outside, I had an odd moment of realization. It was all about efficiency. Efficiency of scale, of moving several hundred clueless individuals where they needed to be. Efficiency of getting them to listen, to instill discipline, to get them into the right mind-set, to teach them in a way that the lesson would hopefully stick.

It's a process that continues even now. The thought impacted me as I realized that all this, from the candidates and cadet drill instructors participating, to those of us observing, was all a part of that training. The end goal was to make it so that we understood the system, understood the purpose, and so that we applied those lessons as officers.

As my brother's section jogged down into the tunnels and out of sight, I gave a slight sigh. It was time for me to get ready for work.

***

"That doesn't make any sense at all," Commander Weisfeldt seemed to be staring through me as I spoke. Since I'd just told him about watching my brother in Academy Prep School, I felt a bit hurt.

"Sir?" I asked.

"What?" He looked around and blinked, his bushy eyebrows waggling a bit, almost like two furry caterpillars. "Oh, I didn't see you there, Armstrong. This latest round of simulations don't make any sense, we're seeing a net *drop* in energy even below what the formulas suggest, and it's only for a range of drive field geometries."

I restrained a sigh. I'd just spent almost ten minutes talking through some of my thoughts about service and the Academy. Perhaps Commander Weisfeldt wasn't the best person to share personal revelations with. I centered my mind and considered what he'd said, "Isn't that good, though? I mean, greater efficiency and all that?"

"But it's *not* greater efficiency," he protested. "It's simply drawing less power, across every projection. It's still *using* that power, by every projection we have, but it's not drawing it all from the reactor... and that worries me."

I understood that. Power couldn't simply appear. Energy had to come from somewhere. Since these simulations used up a significant portion of the school's processing power, normally they were relatively glitch-free... unless there was a problem with how we'd run the simulation. "Maybe some kind of error with how I modulated the power?" I asked nervously.

"No, no," he waved a hand, "we checked the simulation programming data and your interactions, already."

"We?" I asked, looking around.

Commander Weisfeldt waved a hand, "Yes, I had most of our programming staff working on this since last night. It's not an issue with the programming. The problem is, power shouldn't come from anywhere other than the reactor. We're going to have to go line by line through the raw code to find where it's coming from and that's going to take..."

"I've got it," I interrupted him. I'd already tapped into the stored simulation data. He was technically right, there wasn't coding set to monitor where all power came from in the simulation, but with how my implant worked, I was able to mesh directly into the raw data, "It looks like some of it is coming... from the field itself?"

"What?" Commander Weisfeldt started to his feet, "show me!"

I brought up the simulation and showed power flow diagrams along the curvature of the warp drive field. "I think it's a function of the curvature of the drive," I said after a long moment. "I mean, the normal geometry, you really don't get any power flow, not unless there's some kind of external surge..."

"Yes, yes," he nodded, "normally the result of an impact or an attack, but this..."

"It's drawing..." I brought up numbers, "ten to almost thirty percent of its power from itself. I'm not sure how that's possible."

"It's got to be the generation of exotic particles," he mused.

"Normal particles hit the space curvature and that imparts radial and torsional forces..." I knew the theory. Normally the drive geometry was designed to sort of vent that, so that dangerous particles wouldn't build up as a sort of shock-wave at the front of the ship.

"The drive isn't self-sustaining," he mused, "but while in motion, you're getting a massive decrease in necessary power. This is truly fascinating. The implications on weapons loadout and cost for a reactor..."

"Wouldn't the ship be more vulnerable to incoming fire, though?" I asked. "I mean, this would amplify the shock from any hit..."

"Not with the variable geometry," he shook his head, "the pilot shifts over before battle and then back. In fact, these geometries are more sustainable for cruising or pursuit movements, where a ship needs to travel in one direction rapidly." He rubbed his lips in consideration. "At some of these, the ship would manage point eight of light speed, as fast as a cutting edge warp fighter or missile."

I hadn't looked at that data and I blinked as it registered. He was right, the geometries were most similar to that of a warp envelope, rather than a standard warp drive. "Could the power siphon work for something like a warp missile?" I asked.

"Now that... that's an interesting idea," He beamed at me. "You're a natural at this, it'll be a pity that I'll have to give you up at the end of the summer."

I flushed, "Thanks, sir."

"No, thank *you,*" he waved a hand, "I've been struggling with this all night and you helped resolve it fairly quickly. I only wish I could bring in more of the Project Quicksilver candidates. It's a shame that we still don't know more about the implants, whether the issues we saw before were unique or whether they'll eventually drive all of you insane."

I froze as he said that, his voice rather detached, as if he were discussing the weather. I looked at him, "Sir, you don't think..." I couldn't finish the words.

His expression was still distant as he looked at me. "We don't know enough," he said simply. "I would like to think that Doctor Aisling cut a few corners and a couple of cadets had issues, because of that. But the truth is that we simply don't know enough.

Not yet."

Something clicked in my mind. "I'm another experiment," I felt shock as I realized it.

"Indeed you are," Commander Weisfeldt said with a sad smile. "You were deemed one of the most stable of the subjects, both by my observations and by those notes of Doctor Aisling that weren't encrypted, mostly the notes she presented to her sponsors."

"If I don't snap, using my implant full time for the summer, then what, you might turn some of the others back on?" I couldn't help but feel bitter about that.

"Possibly, but that's not *my* project. I understand that the Admiral is collating the data for someone with a bit more expertise in all this. I can talk hardware all day, but this whole wetware thing," he actually shuddered, "ugh, the thought of brains and blood actually makes me feel light-headed."

I'm still an experiment... and this time, the Admiral is a part of it... she's using *me!* The realization made me angry. Not as angry as the realization of why she'd kept her distance since all this had happened, though. It wasn't just about me, it was about her, too. She couldn't trust me, couldn't trust my judgment. There was a chance that I could go insane... and she didn't want to put herself in a situation where I could be a threat to her.

I'd never felt as alone as when I considered that. I had thought that Ashiri was my friend, that the Admiral really cared for me, and that Alexander Karmazin and the others would be there for me. But now I didn't know what to believe.

"I think I need a moment," I felt distant as I said the words.

"Oh, sure," Commander Weisfeldt waved a hand. "I'll be here, you've given me plenty to work on." He went back to his work, as if he hadn't said anything of much importance.

He'd shaken my world to its core. I'd come to think that the Admiral valued me, but she was using me. I was her guinea pig, her lab rat, and if something horrible happened to me, if my implant drove me insane, she'd probably lock me up down here, where I'd never see daylight again.

Just like Doctor Aisling. I almost wasn't certain where the thought came from. Yet I remembered, on my first day, what Leo Champion had said. Doctor Aisling wasn't hidden away at some prison or distant facility, she was here. Probably somewhere on sub-level four.

I stepped out of Commander Weisfeldt's office and past Jonna, with her holstered pistol hidden under her desk and then into the cubicles, finally sitting down at my desk. I felt an icy chill run down my spine as I realized what I was thinking about.

I'd become familiar with the layout and security of Directorate Thirteen. The rest of the sub-level couldn't be much larger. I could almost guess where they'd keep a prisoner, especially a dangerous one like Doctor Aisling.

I had options from there. I could try to sneak in, to use my implant and my knowledge of the security to slip through into that area of the sub-level. I could find the Doctor, the woman who may have sentenced me to insanity, and I could ask her for the truth.

Only, would I really settle for no answers? Would I be satisfied if she refused to answer my questions? I'd have crossed a boundary just in going into that section. While I was certain I could get inside, I was far less certain that I could get out again, much less that I'd remain undetected.

Odds were, that going to confront the doctor would be a one way trip... or at least, that it might well cost me my freedom, possibly my life in the doing. The obvious answer, then, was that if I did it, then I'd have to force the Doctor to give me answers. I would have to compel her, somehow. Probably through either force or the threat of force.

Could I do that? Was it worth it?

The nagging question as I considered all of it, was that this might well be the first steps of my slide into insanity.

***

I stepped through the doors of the elevator, my heart seeming to want to beat its way out of my chest. I nodded at the guard and then went down corridors that were familiar by now. I wasn't sure how many times I'd come this way, before. Somehow this time felt different.

I stopped outside the familiar doors. "You know why I'm here, you might as well open up," I said.

The doors to the Admiral's office opened and I stepped inside.

The Admiral sat behind her desk. Not for the first time, I

realized that she looked weary. I wondered just how many balls she was juggling... and how much of a toll it all took on her. "That was another test, this morning, wasn't it?"

"Everything is a test, Jiden," the Admiral noted. "Life constantly tests us all."

I glared at her, "Would it kill you to treat me as a human being?"

"I gave you options, Jiden. I couldn't risk that you'd been... compromised."

"That I'd been driven insane by my implant and that I'd try to kill someone?" I asked, gritting my teeth.

She shrugged and rose from her desk, her hands crossed behind her desk. "Girl, I wish I could even give you a bit of the puzzle I'm fighting against every day." Her blue eyes, so much like my mom's, went distant. "Doctor Aisling is only a part of it. Charterer Beckman is only a part. These implants, I don't know if the goal was as stated, or if it was to subvert a key population of officers, or Doctor Aisling's experiment just cut too many corners... I don't know what I don't know, and these 'tests' of mine are to find out how many traps our enemies have set about us in the dark."

"You used me to try and find one," I objected.

"I did," she nodded, "but in the assumption that if you found one, you'd already been compromised."

I took a moment to think about that. The implants, if I understood the Admiral right, might have been designed to subvert key people. I considered who had been selected. "Karmazin, me, and Drien?" I asked.

"A Champion, a Drien, and an Armstrong. Thirty percent of the other candidates come from well-connected political or military families. It's a high enough margin that it seemed a valid data point."

"So... what, you were worried that she'd turned us into some kind of robot cyborg or something?" I shook my head, "Doesn't that seem a little, I dunno, like something out of a cheap holovid?"

"It's been done before," the Admiral said grimly. "The Drakkus Empire subverted the leadership of Tenure through kidnapping and drugs. They officially welcomed in the invasion and stood down the military."

I remembered reading about that, now. "You thought that

I..."

"I didn't know what to think," the Admiral stated and her gaze was hard. "But I had several cadets with active implants, including you, Karmazin, and Drien. None of you came forward upon that realization. That was grounds for deeper inspection."

I sighed, "Did I pass your test, then?"

"As much as is possible," the Admiral went back to her chair. "Have a seat, Jiden."

I sat. "What do we do now?"

"Again and again, you use the word 'we,'" the Admiral quirked a real smile at me, "I'd caution you against having an over-developed sense of responsibility, but I can't level that accusation against someone else without feeling hypocritical." Her expression went serious, "I've tested you, and you seem to have passed, so I continue under the assumption that either you can be trusted or I haven't yet figured out the angle of how they subverted you."

"Great," I said. "So either way, what should I do?"

"Continue your assignment at Archive and Support," the Admiral said. I noted to myself that she hadn't mentioned Directorate Thirteen, not even in this office. "Keep an eye out for other activity."

"What am I looking for?" I asked.

The Admiral didn't answer for a long moment. I wondered if she hesitated because she wanted to protect me or because she didn't trust me. "Last week, there was a serious attack on the network, from inside the Academy grounds. It was focused on the Admin section sub-network. We weren't able to track it, the signal was bounced through too many relays and too much of the connection data was wiped clean."

I swallowed as I thought through the implications. "Diamond or Metal Man."

"Or both," the Admiral nodded.

"What happened with the investigation?" I asked.

"Officially? The entire project has been closed. Charterer Beckman led several of the Charter Council to vote to seal the records. The two affected cadets have been transferred to a special hospital and their families have been informed that they were injured in a training accident."

I blanched, "But that puts the blame on you!"

"It does, but they were my responsibility," the Admiral said. "So I took the opportunity to apologize to their parents." Her gaze went distant, "It didn't go very well. But it seldom does."

The Admiral went on, "Doctor Aisling has proven remarkably uncooperative, which is why I suspect that she did something to several of the project's subjects. That's why she is where she is."

"Is she bait?" I asked.

"That, and I want her where I can keep an eye on her. If she did try to compromise key people, she may have methods to trigger them, methods that a normal prison wouldn't necessarily prevent her from using," she gave me an arch look. "Even the implants being shut down isn't a full clearance, by the way. There's the very likely possibility that should she get free, she could reactivate the implants remotely. Additionally, it has proven remarkably difficult to detect when an implant is live at full capacity versus merely in its powered state. You and a couple others we only detected because of rather intensive scrutiny of the network."

"Which others?" I asked.

She stared at me, as if she were considering whether or not to tell me. Eventually, she spoke, "Karmazin, Drien, yourself for certain. Data transmission and general activity in the network has suggested at least two more, though they haven't used their implants in a location where we can isolate them from you three."

It took me a minute to think about that, "So they must be aware that the three of us are still active?"

"Or else the data transmissions and breach attempts have been from you three," the Admiral said in a calm voice. "That would have been far simpler, though you can imagine why I personally hoped it wasn't the case."

"Can I see your data?" I asked.

She transferred it to me over my implant, and I remembered then that she, too, had an implant. I wondered about that, now. When had she received one? Had she been part of some experimental project too? Had she done it before they were socially accepted? Had it been an easy choice... or had she faced some of the same morality issues that I had? *I wish I had half as much confidence as she possesses.*

I reviewed the data and I saw the clusters she'd mentioned.

They most often occurred while we were in classes, though there'd been one in the barracks, almost a month ago, late at night. I felt a chill as I considered that and I examined the date, comparing it to my nightmare.

"The event in the barracks," I said, feeling my stomach twist as I considered it. "It corresponds to a set of nightmares I had." The Admiral arched an eyebrow and I went on, wondering if I was about to incriminate myself or provide information that was helpful. "It happened just before the summer assignments came out. I felt... a connection, of sorts. Someone or something was trying to tell me something. There was anger and... other emotions, I couldn't really understand them all. It didn't seem to last long, but just before I woke up, I saw a symbol, a crest." I hesitated, realizing that if the Admiral hadn't mentioned Directorate Thirteen, then I shouldn't, not out loud. I sent it to her via my implant, instead, the scroll crossed by a lightning bolt.

The Admiral's eyes narrowed. "You say you had this dream *before* the summer assignments?" I nodded. She sat back, "There's... far too many possible reasons for this for me to know where to go with that information. I've been trying to bring in an implant expert on this, but Charterer Beckman has blocked me, for now. The only one I have access to and trust won't pass the background checks required, and cutting edge neural-hardware specialists don't exactly grow on trees."

"Even if they did, there aren't a lot of those on Century, ma'am," I said with a slight smile.

"True," the Admiral quirked a rare smile, but her expression went hard again. "Until we know more about what Doctor Aisling did, we're not going to make much progress and I don't want to spend hours analyzing what *could* be just a nightmare." I opened my mouth to protest, but she raised a hand, "I didn't say I thought it was just a nightmare, I said that we don't have enough information to go on. Until and unless we can get Doctor Aisling to talk or at least decrypt her files, we might as well be debating the price of hydrogen in the Parisian sector."

I sighed, but I couldn't argue. "Could I get a chance to look at her files, I might be able to..."

"No," the Admiral shook her head, "I don't want you or any other Quicksilver subjects involved. For one thing, that's expressly forbidden by the Charter Council." She rolled her eyes, "While I might ignore that given pressing concerns of safety and security, I cannot ignore the risk that she may have put... traps, there for those with neural implants."

I swallowed, "Traps?"

"Even those of us with a 'standard' implant can be adversely affected by software viruses. There's a particularly nasty set that's designed to overheat a standard neural implant and cook someone's brain. I can only imagine what kind of traps she could build into her encryption for someone with implants like yours."

I shivered at that and I didn't argue. Somehow I didn't think that any horrible action would be beyond Aisling's capabilities.

"For now, go back to your summer assignment. Keep doing the work you do." Her expression softened slightly, "And so you know, I didn't chose to test you because you were expendable. I tested you this way to be certain beyond a doubt that I could trust you. I'm proud of you, girl, you're doing a fine job... I just needed to know that she hadn't compromised you."

"Thank you, ma'am," I said, my eyes misting a bit. I could have been wrong, but I almost thought I saw the Admiral's eyes mist up, too. *Nah, she's made out of hull plating,* I told myself.

Still, it was good to know that she cared about me.

***

Chapter 18: I Said Something And There's No Taking It Back

I paused on my run and moved to the side as a formation of candidates bore down on me. I switched my books from carrying them under my arm to carrying them in front of me. I had to hide a smile at how hangdog they all looked. There was a sameness to their faces and expressions as they raced past. It was an odd mix of exhaustion, despair, and determination. Things had been quiet when they'd been to the Grinder.

I picked out my little brother at the front of the formation, leading First Squad and I felt a mix of pride and a little jealousy as I saw him. He'd taken to the physical nature of all this so well. From what I'd heard, he'd set a new score for candidates out at the Grinder.

At this point in my time at Academy Prep School, I'd been among the middle tier of candidates. I'd managed to get ahead in my classes and then done very well in the final exercise. It looked like my brother was well on his way to graduating the prep course at the top of his class.

As the Sand Dragons raced past, I gave Ashiri a wave. She looked almost as tired as her candidates. To my surprise, she gave me a nod and then dropped back out of the formation, waving to one of the Cadet Drill Instructors to take over.

"Jiden," she nodded at me, panting wearily.

"Ashiri," I grinned, "you're looking good."

To my surprise, Ashiri flushed a bit. She did look good, though, confident, fit and lean. "I didn't mean to wave you down," I said quickly. I shrugged under the weight of books in my arms, "I was just on my way to work."

She cocked her head, looking at the stack of books I carried. "You really seem into that sort of thing." Her voice was neutral.

I shrugged. I'd had a discussion with Commander Weisfeldt, who'd said that I probably should spend *some* time actually working at the Archive section, so I at least understood the job. After my meeting with the Admiral, I'd been quietly informed that this assignment would be counted as a research position, so it wasn't going to hurt my ranking at all. In fact, it was going to count as a 'broadening' assignment, so it might even help.

Working down deep had been going very well, too. We'd made a ton of progress... progress that I wasn't allowed to tell anyone about. On the other hand... "The Archive is actually pretty neat," I said. "I've only cracked a tiny amount of the books working there. We get calls from Militia officers and civilian researchers three or four times a day, often with some pretty complicated questions. A lot of historical stuff that I've never really even heard about. It's pretty interesting."

"I see," Ashiri almost looked disappointed. "Things are slowing down a bit, the candidates are going to start getting access to the test gaming systems this week and they'll start full-time classes. I'd appreciate it if you have time to help trounce them a bit." She smirked at the last bit.

I smiled in reply, "that would be fun."

Her smile faded a bit, "You hear anything from Karmazin?"

I shook my head, "No, how'd everything go in the Grinder?"

Ashiri shrugged and looked away, "Well enough. No excitement like last year, thankfully. They're good kids, your little brother is a natural at all this." She shot me a look, "I'm really starting to put some weight on the whole military family thing."

"What?" I asked in surprise. "Ashiri, *I'm* clearly the exception to the rule, then."

"She says, when she's still high up in the rankings, you're fifteenth in the class, it's not like you're dead last." Ashiri shook her head. "I've been working *so* hard, and you know where I am?"

I knew. I'd seen how she'd ranked up when I looked up my brother. "Third, right? What's the problem?"

"*Karmazin* is number two. Do you know who's number one?" Ashiri asked bitterly.

I hesitated to ask. I hadn't looked that up. "Drien is number one," Ashiri grated.

"*Sashi?*" I asked in shock.

"Yeah," Ashiri hissed. "I *told* you she was trouble."

"I mean, that's good, for her I guess?" I felt my stomach sink as I considered it, though. That was such a reversal after last year that I immediately started thinking about her implant... and if she were...

"She's been doing a fantastic job," Ashiri admitted bitterly. "They made her the Chief Assistant Trainer for the Regimental Training Officer." I'd heard of the CAT position. From everything I'd heard, it was most often used when the Regimental Training

Officer had a really effective assistant, who he trusted to pretty much act in his name.

The CAT ran around hitting trouble spots in the regiment. I'd thought that Beckman was a problem, but I guess they had issues like her in every class. Most companies managed that internally, but if morale or bearing in a candidate section got bad enough, they'd send in the CAT to directly assist.

"Wow," I said. "That's good for her."

"I guess that there were some issues with Viper Company out at the Grinder, some kind of feuding thing between their squads that got way out of hand. She and Karmazin were working together on that for a few days, and then she and *your* boyfriend were working on a similar thing between Dust and Tiger Company and Karmazin got involved again..." Ashiri wasn't even hiding her bitterness at this point.

"Well, I'm sure she's earned it," I said, keeping my voice neutral.

"I thought this assignment would be my chance, Jiden, and I'm *third*," Ashiri snapped.

I looked around to make sure that no one was close enough to overhear. "Hey, it's okay. I mean, I'm setting back here in fifteenth place..."

"Your *boyfriend* is in sixth place," Ashiri sighed. "It's just not fair, I'm giving this everything I've got!"

"I'm sorry," I hadn't realized just how much Ashiri had begun to stress about her ranking. She'd always done well, but I remembered the conversation I'd overheard between her and her mother. I had to wonder how many more like that had happened over the years. On impulse I put a hand on her shoulder, "It's going to be okay. It's not like we're anywhere near done at this point, right? Besides, I hear that you've got the best candidate in school history in your company, that's got to help things, right?"

"I don't know that I'd go *that* far," Ashiri rolled her eyes, "but your brother's a good kid." She swallowed and looked down, "he actually reminds me of my brothers, you know? And part of me wonders how they'd do here."

"Something to think about," I remembered how her youngest brother had looked when Ashiri had talked about the Academy, last year. "Your sister... Hiroe, she's coming here next year, at least."

"Not anymore," Ashiri grimaced. "Mother decided that she'd be better going into medicine, like her."

"*She* decided?" I asked in surprise.

Ashiri's lips pressed in a flat line. "She thinks that career progression will be limited for us due to our lack of connections."

"That's not how it works!" I protested. The obvious implication was that the system was rigged, and that the Admiral would help my career out. I could admit that I'd expect something like that from Sashi Drien's grandfather, but I didn't think it would be restrictive or anything.

"My parents are used to how things were back at Ten Sisters," Ashiri sighed. "I'm going to talk to her, I'm taking a couple of days of leave after all this," she waved a hand around. "But right now, Hiroe won't be attending next year, not unless I..." she trailed off and cleared her throat. "Unless I can change my mother's mind."

A lot of things clicked in my mind, then. Ashiri's mother must think that Karmazin and I had placed first and second because of our family connections. Part of why Ashiri wanted to rank first was to prove to her mother that it was possible.

"I should get going," Ashiri looked at where her section of candidates had disappeared down a ramp. I saw one of her Cadet Drill Instructors, Andrews, pause and jog in place, waiting for her. "Talk to you later."

"Sure thing," I nodded.

I watched as my best friend jogged off. I ached for her, realizing how much pressure she was under. I wished that she'd let me help her, or at least that she'd share some of this with me so we could talk about it, really talk about it. *I should talk with Kyle,* I told myself.

***

I'd got back to my room and noticed my door was open. I must have left it that way when I'd rushed to work in the morning. Working a shift down at Directorate Thirteen and then an afternoon shift in the Archives meant I felt like I was always rushing to get somewhere.

A red-headed, freckled form tackled me as I came through the door. Before I knew what was going on, I was being spun through the air in a tight embrace.

My first instinct was to lash out in one of Commander Pannja's clasp-breaking techniques, but I recognized the voice and smell of Kyle, so I did everything I could to dampen those instincts, which meant I just sort of froze like a sand lizard in a spotlight.

Kyle set me down on my feet. Somehow I'd managed to keep my books all clutched to my chest and I hadn't lost anything. "Hey Jiden," Kyle grinned down at me.

My heart slowed down a bit. I forced myself to breathe calmly. "Kyle," I began, "I love you, but if you ever take me by surprise like that again, I'm going to break you."

He held up his hands defensively his cheerful smile just the slightest bit teasing. "Sorry, I was just happy to see you, it's been almost seven weeks... I thought you'd appreciate an enthusiastic greeting?"

I set my stack of books down on the end table, "Kyle..."

I whipped a foot out and hooked his ankle and pulled, while I stepped into him and threw an elbow into his midriff. I heard him give a whoosh and then he fell back and landed on his backside. I looked down at him, feeling a bit proud of myself and his startled expression. I arched an eyebrow at him in my best Admiral impression.

His shocked expression shifted to chagrin and he gave me a nod, "You've been practicing, then?"

I nodded, "Commander Pannja does summer sessions of his *kerala* class. A year and a half of it and I've managed to pick some things up." My initial impulse when he'd first picked me up had been an elbow to the sternum, which I'd have followed by some other, rather more painful and damaging strikes.

"Maybe I should switch over to some martial arts to keep up with you," Kyle grinned. "Maybe we can practice with each other, then."

I might like that... The thought of physical sparring with Kyle actually got my heart racing again and I felt a flush climb my cheeks as I thought of him in the tight-fitting sparring clothing. I cleared my throat and changed the subject before my thoughts went too far astray, "I hear you're doing well?"

He had a slightly confused look on his face, but he went with the change of subject. "Yeah, Senior Cadet Drill Instructor has been *so* much fun. I mean, don't get me wrong, I'm exhausted and stressed out to the extreme, but it's just *crazy*. I feel like I'm really helping these kids..."

"I heard there was some kind of dust-up with Tiger Company?" I asked, moving to take a seat at my desk. One perk of the room in the transient officer quarters was that I had the whole room to myself. I had a full size desk and I even had a few spare chairs for if I had guests. Not that I'd *had* guests, Kyle and the others had all been gone.

Kyle came over and sat down the chair next to the desk, his presence close and warm. He had been gone a while and it was nice to have him so close, sitting with our legs almost touching. I was reminded once again at how tall he was, his lanky form folding up into the chair in a way that was both awkward and endearing.

"Alex and Sashi had to get involved. It was a mess... I probably should have managed it better, but that jerk Hodges was Tiger's Senior Cadet Drill Instructor..."

"Hodges?" I asked.

"Stocky guy, he was actually one of Ogre's Cadet Drill Instructors last year... *and* the year before, back when we were candidates. I think he just likes yelling at people."

I raised an eyebrow, I sort of remembered who he was talking about, but I hadn't dealt with Tiger Section's people very much at all. They were almost all exclusively on the ground Militia track, so I didn't even share any classes with them. I was a bit surprised that this Hodges had been a cadet instructor three years in a row, but then again, this year he'd been a Senior Cadet Drill Instructor, so that showed some progression.

"Anyway, Dust and Tiger are something of rivals," he coughed slightly.

I snorted, "I might have noticed."

"Yeah, so one of his squads were *way* off of where they were supposed to be and they started taking pot-shots at my candidates as they were resetting from an ambush. It blindsided my kids, bad. They were already struggling and one of my Drill Instructors got involved, trying to stop it so that my kids had a chance to at least get organized, get some training value out of it, you know?"

I nodded. Despite the disorganized feel of the Grinder, a lot of it was carefully orchestrated. The intention was that there wasn't any wasted motion, that trainees got something out of every minute spent there... even if that minute was slogging across the broken wasteland to try and find their unit.

"Well, they tagged Singh, that is, my Cadet Drill Instructor," Kyle grimaced, "and I can't prove it, but one of my candidates says he heard a *Tiger* Drill Instructor give the order. Only, they were in an area with limited coverage from the monitors, so there's no record, especially since their Drill Instructors 'accidentally' turned off their datapads just before the encounter."

I blinked, "That's pretty dirty."

"Yeah. I called in the Observer Controllers as soon as I got the word, but by then, pretty much my entire squad of candidates was down, and they didn't have a Drill Instructor present to tell them what to do... and then some more Tiger candidates showed up, all by coincidence, of course."

I winced. The implications were pretty clear. At least, as long as Kyle's perspective was accurate. I trusted his judgement. I mean, he *was* a redhead, with the temperament that went with his coloration, but he was also very self-aware. He wouldn't say something like this without at least some self-examination to see if he really believed it.

"Anyway, it got pretty ugly out there. Hodges showed up quick. Too quick, if you ask me, like he'd planned it. He started shouting at me in front of the candidates, his and mine, about trying to rig things and cheating," Kyle looked away, his jaw clenching in anger. "I lost it. I knew I shouldn't have. I dragged him away by the arm and we started having it out, out of sight of the candidates at least. Alex showed up a few minutes later, and he brought Sashi, since you know, she was assigned as the CAT, and she and he have been working together a lot."

"I heard," I said in a neutral tone.

"Yeah, anyway, they pulled up observation data and training data. Hodges got slapped on the wrist for his candidates being so far from where they were supposed to be. He tried to say something about giving his guys room to make mistakes, but there was no excusing it, they were fifteen *kilometers* south of their assigned area and they weren't even doing the mission they'd been tasked with, and his other squad was over ten kilometers from where they'd been supposed to be, and they and he showed up way too quick."

"How did they handle it?" I wasn't sure how to ask what I

really wanted to know. It sounded like this situation had been orchestrated by someone. I didn't know how hard it would be to hack the Grinder's network, but if Sashi had done that, it would have been relatively easy to change orders and to set up a situation like this... one that she could step in and fix.

"Sashi was cold, it was actually pretty awesome to watch," Kyle grinned. "I mean, I know her a bit, she was your roommate, after all... but even I was a little scared. She started dissecting Hodges, who brought up some stuff about his mission set being different from what was on file."

My heart sank a bit at that.

"That's when Alex got involved. They tag teamed him, it was great to watch. I mean, sure there was an issue with a couple of his Cadet Drill Instructors mission sets on their datapads, but they didn't *check* them, they just went with the glitched orders. I get that we all get tired, but mission updates come through all the time, you got to be checking things, right?"

"True," I said. I wanted to dig into that, but I couldn't ask questions without getting into things that I couldn't discuss with him. *I need to talk with Karmazin.*

"Anyway, they straightened everything out, Hodges and his candidates went back where they were supposed to be, Alex actually brought out a medical team and got my candidates on their feet again so they could go through their mission without having to go to the casualty center. I wouldn't have thought it would work out that well, you know?"

"Except for Hodges?" I asked.

Kyle made a face, "I could care less about Hodges. He's a jerk. Honestly, if I had a bit more, I'd make an honor board case against him for lying or trying to cheat out there. Whatever his guys' orders said, he gamed the system hard to try and knock Dust Company down a few notches. It's not the first time I've heard about him promoting that kind of thing. He was the Drill Instructor for Ogre when we were candidates, right?"

I nodded slowly. "Well, I talked with Thorpe when we were out there, and he was saying how when he was a candidate, Hodges was *his* Drill Instructor, and was telling all his Ogre candidates to go after the competition in the final exercise."

"Really?!" I stared at him. I remembered all that vividly.

Especially how I'd had to stop Bolander and Thorpe from shooting Sashi in the back.

"Yeah, and man was he angry that a couple of 'Third Class Busybodies' were taking him to task for his performance out there. He tried to file a complaint with the Regimental Training Officer... that didn't go over well." Kyle grinned, "Let's just say, the RTO seems to think Sashi walks on water. *He* wasn't taking anything that Hodges said and he really tore him up over it. I wasn't there, but Martinez, from our section, is another of the Assistants up there, and she told me all about it. Word is that Hodges might be out of Senior Cadet Drill Instructor, after that."

"Wow," I shook my head. Getting relieved from a spot like that was almost a death-sentence to a cadet's career and standing.

"Yeah, if Hodges were smart, he'd resign and maybe even take a setback," Kyle made a face. "Not that smart and Hodges goes together at all in my mind... I mean, he's a Tiger, after all. But he'd be better off taking the rest of the year and letting the air clear."

I cocked my head, "He's a Cadet Second Class, so that would put him back in our class, right?"

Kyle grimaced, "Ugh, yeah, I really hope he doesn't do that. Our class year of Tiger section isn't totally jerks. Having to deal with him, though..." He shuddered and let out a deep breath. "Nightmare fodder, Jiden, nightmare fodder."

I laughed at his expression, "Surely things aren't so bad?"

"Much better, now that I'm back here," Kyle's expression softened and he stared at me. "You know. I really missed you."

I felt my heart flutter as he said that. "I missed you too."

He quirked a smile, "So... did you mean what you said?"

"Did I what?" I asked in confusion.

"You used the 'L' word, Jiden," Kyle winked at me.

My face blanked and I stared at him, feeling suddenly trapped. I felt fireworks going off in my head and my heart fluttered as I realized *exactly* what I'd said to him after he'd tackled me. I opened my mouth, half way to deny it and half way to say... something. I wasn't sure what I was going to say. I *couldn't* have said that out loud... could I have?

"It's okay, Jiden," Kyle said gently, "I love you, too."

My heart melted and my brain seemed to stop working. I found myself leaning forward and Kyle was too. We kissed and I felt electric tingles go up my arms and down my spine. I found myself pulling him in, clasping him behind his neck in a kiss that I hoped would last forever. I felt hot and excited and completely out of control. He could have done anything in that moment and I would have let him.

So of course, that was when someone knocked on the door.

We broke apart and looked sheepishly at each other. I realized that we needed to have a discussion, a real discussion, before this went any further. He stood up and straightened his uniform and I did the same, even as I called, "Enter!"

It was Karmazin, and in that moment, I wanted to kill him.

"Hey, Jiden... oh, hey Kyle," he looked between us and he adopted a slight smirk. "Am I interrupting anything?"

I very much wanted to kill him.

"Not at all," Kyle answered smoothly, his words saying one thing and his tone saying something else entirely.

"Oh, good," Alexander Karmazin's smirk broadened into a full smile. "Now we're even for that whole thing last week."

"What happened last week?" I asked.

Kyle laughed, and Karmazin actually flushed a bit. "Well, it seems that Alex and Sashi have been spending a lot of time together. A *lot* of time. And one thing led to another and I stumbled on them kissing in one of the bunkers."

"Wait..." I blinked at Alexander. "You and *Drien?*"

Alexander sighed, "We've got some similar background, Jiden. And there's some other things we share, too." He tapped the side of his head, then made a slight gesture at Kyle. *The implants, I realized, it's a common thing that they can talk about with each other and can't discuss with anyone else.* Still... "You're seeing, Sashi... really?" I couldn't help the incredulous tone. The thought of them together was... well, it was just odd.

"It sort of happened," he said somewhat defensively. "And don't look at me like that, it's not like I was chasing after her..."

"Oh, God," I threw my hands in the air, "does Ashiri know?"

"Ash?" Alexander looked confused. "Why would she care, we haven't been seeing one another like that in a year..."

"She's going to care," I stared at him. I looked over at Kyle who had a confused expression. "The two of them don't get along, Alexander. The... thing between the two of you might be over, but..."

"Hey, she broke up with me," Alexander protested. "Then told me we could just be friends. She accused me of snoring... I mean, you've been her roommate, she snores like a freight train. I'm her friend, I like her and all, but she's got no claim on me." His voice was a bit too defensive, though. He still had feelings for her and he was still hurt over it all. *Men...*

I tried to find the words to explain it. "It's not going to go well. Not well at all." Kyle still had a confused expression. "Look, call it a girl thing, you don't need to understand it, but *Sashi* will. Has she told you there might be an issue?"

Alexander shrugged and looked at Kyle and then me, "We've been keeping things quiet. I'm just back for a week helping with the transition of candidates out of the Grinder and for..." he coughed and looked down, "Uh, an interview on an assignment shift."

My eyes widened, "What?"

Karmazin shrugged, looking uncomfortable, "It's not something I can talk about, not right now."

"Okay..." I nodded, "But you and Sashi?" I persisted. This could be something totally innocent... or it could be some kind of revenge thing to make Ashiri lose her temper, or it could be that Sashi was Diamond and this was part of her effort to turn Alexander. *Can I trust him? Has he been compromised?* The Admiral's test for me had seemed paranoid at the time, but now I understood her level of concern.

Alexander shrugged, "We're keeping it quiet, for now. The only one who *knew* was Kyle." He nodded at him. "We've been too busy to really do much, but we worked together so much at the Grinder and the long hours and just talking together..." he shrugged. "At one point we were just tired and barely able to stand and sort of leaning on one another and then the next thing that happened was I sort of kissed her." He shot Kyle a look, "Then mister bad-timing came in. It's not exactly a thing we've had a lot of time to work through to see if it's going to last."

"Oh, man," I ran a hand through my hair. "The headaches that guys cause..."

"Hey!" Both of them blurted.

"I need to talk with you more about this," I said, pointing a finger at Alexander. I looked at Kyle and my heart pitter-pattered.

This wasn't fair. We'd both said words that had set my heart to fluttering. I wanted to spend the afternoon talking with him.

"It's fine," he said. He gestured at my stack of research books. "You've got work to do, anyway, don't take on too much of your friend's problems. He shot Alexander a strange look, then he leaned in and kissed me, very thoroughly. It was at once rough and passionate and I didn't know what to do with my hands, painfully aware that we weren't alone.

I had to gasp a bit to catch my breath and my face was flushed as he stepped back. He gave Alexander a final nod, "Alex," he said, and then he stepped out.

"That was..." I trailed off and the realized that Karmazin was still there, staring at a wall, giving me a moment to collect myself. *He's a good guy, too good for Sashi.* I didn't know where the thought came from, but I squashed it. Sashi wasn't a bad person. I understood her a lot better now than I had. It wasn't my place to judge, either.

"Alright," I took a seat behind the desk and gestured at the chair near Alexander. "So... have you seen anything that suggests someone else has an active implant?" I asked.

He cocked his head, "I thought we were going to talk about Sashi and I?"

I couldn't meet his eyes, "Alexander, there's been some more data breach attempts here at the Academy. The Admiral gave me the access attempts. They remained active after finals, and then they dropped off when the candidates went to the Grinder. We don't have any data on what might have happened out there..."

"You think it's Sashi," Alexander crossed his arms and glared at me. "Really, Jiden? I mean, sure, her implant is active, but so are ours..."

"She's a suspect, that's all I'm saying..." I trailed off as I brought my implant live. "Okay, so there's six possible suspects," I admitted. "You, me, Sashi, Ashiri, Thorpe... Andrews, and Ahmed."

"There's three girls and three guys on that list," he said. "You said the Admiral gave you information... does she know that your implant is live?"

I nodded, "She's known since sometime before finals. She knows about you, me, and Sashi, as well. There's been a series of access attempts and network surges that suggest at least two more, based on our activity."

"Only one of those might be our mystery hacker, though," Alexander mused. "The data points after the summer assignments could all be from just one person."

I bit my lip, "That one person could be Sashi. Lots of the evidence suggests..."

"Sashi isn't the one," he shook his head. "Look, Jiden, we've been talking a lot over the past six weeks. We've been talking about the implants, about school, about family... *stuff.*" He said the word distastefully, as if he wanted to use a different word.

I realized, then, that his father, Leo Champion, was working in a lab here at the Academy, or at least directing work. I hadn't seen the CEO of Champion Enterprises over the past week and it wouldn't surprise me to hear that he'd grown bored of the day to day and decided to go back to his company headquarters. I wondered if Alexander knew or if his absentee father had even said anything to him. Given Champion's record as a parent and grandparent, I wondered if it had even occurred to the man to talk to his son.

It struck me that I'd always sort of seen Karmazin as being a solid and stationary guy. He always seemed to have the answers. *Maybe Alexander Karmazin isn't as together as I'd thought.*

"Anyway, she's working her backside off. I mean, she's *totally* driven to prove her brothers and the rest of her family that they're wrong. But it's more than that, Jiden," he flushed, "she'd probably kill me if she finds out I told you this, but she *really* respects you."

"Me?!" I stared at him. I'd have been less surprised to hear that Sashi liked to listen to girly music or had a collection of pink dresses. *Or for that matter, that Karmazin has a collection of pink dresses...*

"Look, she was this," he pinched his fingers close together, "close to resigning at the end of last year. She was going to swallow her pride, go back to her family, marry the guy that her mother picked for her, and just give it all up. Then you came in, and despite everything, you gave her a way to move forward. Just the fact that it was you meant that pretty much nobody in Sand Dragon can say anything about it..."

"Except for Sashi," I noted.

"... which gave her a chance to focus on her studies and her duties," Alexander went on. "You helped her, and you always do the right thing, even if it's not easy for you to do. She really respects that. She actually has based a lot of what she's doing as the CAT off of what she thinks you'd do in the situation."

"That's crazy," I shook my head.

"Maybe, but it works for her," Karmazin said. "And trust me, it's working really well for her."

I looked at him, wondering if he were joking, but he seemed so earnest. "Okay, fine, you don't think it's Sashi." I let out a tense breath, "I don't think it's Ashiri..."

"Not Ash," he shook his head, "she's..." he looked at me and I could tell that he was thinking better of what he wanted to say. "There's no way she'd try to kill you. The sabotage of the skimmer knocks that out."

"Okay," I nodded, "so..."

"That leaves Thorpe, Andrews, and Ahmed." I said after a moment. Their numbers didn't include a female and Thorpe was Ogre Company while Andrews and Ahmed were both from Tiger Company. I couldn't imagine any of them taking the identity of a female, especially not with how Diamond had known so much about me.

"I'd want it to be Thorpe, but he's really not that bad a guy," Alexander said.

"It may not be *them*," I admitted to him. "There's the chance that whoever it is has suffered some kind of psychotic break from the implant. Then there's the chance that Doctor Aisling is controlling them somehow. Or worse, that their implant has taken them over somehow."

"If that's the case, then we can't eliminate ourselves," Karmazin noted. "If the implant's gestalt is behind it, it could take over without us knowing. We might just have a blackout and not even remember what happened, or false memories."

I stared at him, thinking of the nightmare that I'd had, the one where I'd seen the symbol of Directorate Thirteen before I'd been assigned there. I couldn't tell him about it, though, in part because I couldn't talk about Directorate Thirteen and in part because I didn't want him to focus on me as a suspect.

"That's kind of horrifying," the admission was the only response I could manage. "How is it that you've come up with those? The Admiral's got some suspicions too, but hasn't been able to bring in a specialist."

"My father," Karmazin grimaced, "Leo Champion. I guess he got read in on this project some time and he sent me an encrypted packet, from reading it, I gather he... crossed some boundaries on what's strictly acceptable as far as discussing theoretical information. He didn't mention any names, but he talked with a neurosurgeon and sent me the basics. In all my great amounts of free time, I've been reading through it." I snorted at his sarcastic tone. "Without digging into exactly what Doctor Aisling did, or examining one of us, they're just guessing though."

"Even then..." I shook my head. "I wish the stupid Charter Council would let them bring in someone..."

He arched an eyebrow at that, "I hadn't heard that much, even."

I quickly explained how the Admiral had told me that the files had been sealed. "Charterer Beckman doesn't want any word getting out. The Admiral already took the blame for Boyles and Gnad."

Karmazin winced. "This sucks. I thought they were at least continuing the investigation."

"No, and Doctor Aisling is locked up," I didn't specify where. Not that I didn't trust Alexander, but who knew who might be listening?

"We need to do something," he said, his voice strained. "I'm sick of always looking over my shoulder."

"Tell me about it," I nodded. "Okay, hopefully things ease up a little bit and we do a bit of searching ourselves." He looked like he wanted to say something but seemed to think better of it and just nodded in reply. I wondered if it had something to do with his interview... and just what position he was interviewing over.

I suppose he'll tell me if it's important.

He rose and took a deep breath, "Alright, Jiden. At least you're not too busy doing the archive stuff," he nodded at my stack of books. "I'm glad you've been able to have so much free time to work on this."

I stared at him. I worked six hours a day down in the Directorate Thirteen labs. I spent another four hours or more at the archives in my 'cover' job. I spent two hours a day training with

Commander Pannja in the evenings. I wasn't sure I knew what free time meant, anymore. "Yeah," I muttered, "I'll see what I can turn up."

***

Chapter 19: I Get That Old Familiar Feeling

It had been so long since someone tried to kill me that I almost forgot what it felt like.

One moment I was running through a final simulation of the power modulating warp field, and the next I was on the ground. Lying on the ground from that first explosion was what saved my life as a second explosion ripped through the lab, this one driving a hail of debris and shrapnel through the room at chest height.

I heard shouts and screams cut off suddenly. I hoped it was just that I'd lost my hearing, but some part of me noted that people were dying around me and that I had to do something.

I rolled over onto my hands and knees and worked my way towards the far end of the room, away from the smoke and billowing flames. I'd been working in the back areas of the lab, furthest away from the elevator. The blast had happened near the forward areas, but there was a corridor that ran from the back of the labs towards the front.

I'd just reached the door when I heard the unmistakable sound of gunfire.

I froze, trying to make out the type and decide whether I was mistaken. Yet the rattle of gunfire was unmistakable, as was another choked off shout.

We're under attack. The realization twisted my stomach, yet I didn't really feel surprise. My brain went into overdrive as I thought through my next steps. There could be any number of reasons for the attack, but somehow I knew why these attackers were here.

The explosion had happened as they breached the level, probably from some of the lowest maintenance corridors. I pulled up the security monitors on my implant, even as I opened the door and eased into the corridor. The main lights had gone off and the corridor's only lights were the emergency lighting, a dull red glow that illuminated just enough for me to find my way.

I found the attackers almost exactly where I'd expected them. There were five of them, and they'd just breached the doors on the section where they kept Doctor Aisling. There were three security doors between them and her cell, and somehow I knew that they were here to extract her.

I followed the corridor quickly, reaching the reception desk. I saw a blood-soaked and still form behind the desk and I looked away, even as I reached for the holstered pistol under the desk. The DCP Needle Pistol was light in my hands, a thin composite form. I hadn't ever shot one, not even in training. But I knew that the small, needle-tipped rounds were designed to penetrate standard body armor, just as the explosive charge in each round was designed to detonate just after impact.

I checked the pistol, ejecting the magazine and fumbling a bit with it between the darkness and my unfamiliarity with it. I counted twenty rounds in the slots of the magazine before I slid it back in. An indicator on the side told me that it had another round already in the chamber.

I moved out of the waiting room in a low crouch, the klaxons of alarms and the smoke making the entire area surreal. Down by the elevators, both duty guards were down, but I saw the black-clad bodies of three attackers as well. I mapped out the attack even as I followed after the attackers.

They'd explosively breached the lab section, probably using one of the old maintenance tunnels that connected in to the Admin section environmental systems. They'd hit the waiting room and main access corridor from there, then moved into the prison section. I heard sporadic rattles of gunfire as the remaining guards continued to fight.

Some part of me whispered that going up against five armed and armored attackers with just a pistol was stupid and possibly suicidal, but I ignored that. The attackers were almost to where Doctor Aisling waited. I could see her on the monitors as I used my implant to follow the attackers. They'd already ripped apart the security systems, bypassing the access controls so that they could tap into those same systems. I just followed them in and I carefully shut down monitors as I moved in behind them, so they couldn't see me coming.

The last of the guards in the prison section went down, but she took two of the attackers with her as they rushed her position. The attack team moved up to the last set of doors before the cell and I could see them emplacing the breaching charge.

I didn't have much time and I rushed down the corridor, trying to move as quickly and silently as I could, no easy thing in boots on metal deck plates. I was one corridor off and less than ten meters away when they blasted the door open. Two of them took up guarding positions while the third one stepped into the cell block. The only barrier between Aisling and freedom was a single transparent armored door.

I slowed as I reached the final bend, pausing to take a deep breath and waiting for my chance to attack, weighing it against the actions of the attacking team's leader.

"It took you long enough," Doctor Aisling said. Her voice was cold and her odd, lilting accent was thick. Oddly enough, the team leader spoke with the same, strange accent.

"We weren't able to locate you until a week ago. We had assumed you'd been transferred to one of their Enforcer prisons," the team leader replied. He moved to the wall and extracted an odd-looking datapad. I wasn't able to make out the details on the security monitor, but there was something strange about it. *I have a minute or so while he hacks open the security door and then Aisling will be free.*

Somehow I knew that I couldn't let that happen. The entire lab was on lockdown, possibly the entire Academy, but that meant no one would be able to get down here. The attackers might be able to get back to their access point and escape before anyone could bypass the lockdown.

I edged to the corner and then poked my head around to get eyes on the two attackers outside the prison cells. Seeing them with my own eyes was jarring. The monitors had shown them --*still* showed them-- in standard black tactical armor. Yet when I saw them, their armor was entirely different from what was on the monitors. The armor they wore was sharp and angular, the black, curving edges of it wicked looking. Each of them carried thin rifles of some kind, which seemed far too thin to be real. They had an almost insectile look, for all that they were humanoid. I was careful to store an image of them on my implant, even as I ducked back.

"Was your project successful?" the leader asked of Aisling.

"Moderately, the *chinaka* worked, my research was incomplete, but several of the subjects were very promising. We should consider extraction of some of them for further testing," Doctor Aisling went on. "My research notes?"

"We destroyed the originals last night and eliminated the

team the *minahvak* had analyzing them. You have your copy?"

Doctor Aisling tapped her arm and a section of her skin raised. She held up a data crystal, "Of course."

The leader of the attackers drew off his helmet, but I had a difficult time making out his features, it was like something blurred them into in-distinction. "Excellent, let me tell the rest of the team to prepare for extraction. He will want to hear your full debriefing," He turned away and started to speak into his radio.

Glancing out again, I saw both attackers shift in posture as they listened to him. This was my chance. I leaned out and lined up the sights on the first of the two, my world centering on my breathing and bracing my arm against the wall. I squeezed the trigger so slowly that it seemed to take forever.

Either I hadn't remembered that the DCP was fully automatic or else Jonna's had been modified. Half a dozen needle-tipped bullets blazed out of the barrel and scythed down the corridor. The electromagnetically accelerated rounds went supersonic before they left the barrel and the recoil made the pistol swing high.

The attacker I'd targeted stumbled and fell. The other one moved faster than I would have thought possible, turning and firing her weapon in a sweeping arc down the hallway. Her rounds hissed through the air over my head like a swarm of malignant wasps and only the fact that I was down near the floor saved my life.

I brought the DCP down, fighting the recoil and this time there was no finesse to my shooting, I lined it up on the angular, predatory form and squeezed off another burst.

The second attacker fell back with a pained shriek, her weapon dropping as she fell. I was up and running forward, part of my mind watching the cell block with my implant while my eyes watched the two attacker I'd downed.

The first one lay limp, sprawled out, but I kicked its rifle away just in case. The second one was trying to crawl backwards and I kicked her rifle away too. As I came up, though, she rolled over, drawing a pistol.

I fired on instinct, before I even really registered the weapon and my automatic pistol roared in the confined space. The attacker jerked and then lay still.

I didn't stop to look, I saw the leader in the cell block starting to move and I dove through the doorway just as a black object landed in the corridor behind me.

The detonation threw me forward, slamming me hard into the wall. I bounced back, somehow staying on my feet even as I stumbled. I saw the last of the attackers raising a pistol and I squeezed the trigger on mine, firing blindly from the hip, allowing the recoil to swing the barrel around through the room.

The pistol clicked angrily only a few heartbeats later, the electromagnetic coils trying to find rounds to fire but the magazine was empty.

I stared at the attacker. He'd removed his helmet, just as the monitors had shown. Like his companions, his form didn't match what the monitors had shown. He was tall, taller than my mother, taller than the Admiral. His hard, angular face was almost serpent-like, lean and gaunt, his features sharp and angular, but still somehow very human in basic appearance.

Erandi, I recognized the alien with shock and a trill of fear. His body armor was the same featureless black, all sharp curving edges and overlapping plates, just like those of his companions. Except he had a single, small ragged hole in the center of his chest.

His arm fell to his side and for a second he seemed to give me a slight nod, almost in congratulations or salute. Then he sagged to his knees and then fell back, his body still.

I dropped the pistol and moved over to kick his weapon away, but I needn't have bothered, he lay still, his eyes open and sightless.

"Well," Doctor Aisling said, her voice still the same odd lilt, her green eyes bright and her red hair stark against her pale skin, "that was unexpected. Not entirely unfortunate, though. Inavar always was too bound by sentiment." She stared at me, "Child, open the door." She pointed at the datapad on the wall nearby. Up close, I could see that it was clearly of alien origin as well. A strange, crystalline thing, which had glowing sections within it.

"Press the green one and let me out," Doctor Aisling smiled.

"No," I said. I went over and picked up the fallen guard's rifle and checked the magazine. Just in case any more of these attackers were coming.

"Listen to me," Doctor Aisling hissed, her green eyes blazing. "I command you!" I felt the oddest sensation, then, almost like someone had thrown a wet tissue over my brain. It was oily and cold, yet it came apart without much resistance. "No." I repeated, taking up a guard position at the door.

Doctor Aisling snarled something in a strange language. She didn't sound happy. She snapped out at me, "I didn't want to do this, but initiate Eidelon Protocols."

I felt another strange sensation, almost as if some bit of programming in my implant were trying to wake up, yet I didn't allow it to. My implant and I were one and I simply buried the impulse and isolated the programming. "Shut up," I snapped.

Aisling stared at me for a long while. She seemed confused more than angry at this point. She went to her bed and sat down, staring at me. "What are you?" She asked, finally.

"That's what I want to know, myself," I said in a low voice. Somehow, though, I figured the answers wouldn't be as easy as I'd thought.

***

"They are Erandi," the Admiral said as she stood over the bodies of the alien attack team. Commander Bonnadonna had led the team that cleared the floor, also led by Petty Officer Kennedy and several other senior non-commissioned officers that I recognized from training.

A similarly made up team of medics had come through and evacuated the injured and dead from Directorate Thirteen. I'd stood and watched, the rifle clutched in my hands, refusing to leave my self-assigned guard posting. I'd already back-briefed Commander Bonnadonna, and I'd just finished doing the same with the Admiral.

I looked down at the lean, strangely armored bodies and I barely repressed a shudder. It wasn't revulsion, not really, simply an uncomfortable alien feeling. The videos I'd seen of the culmor and some of the other alien species that Humanity had encountered was one thing. The culmor, humanity's foes for over seven hundred years, looked passingly similar to humans in that they were bipedal and laterally symmetrical. Their eye placement, lacks of noses, and mouth placement were alien enough. They also had joints that went different ways and a vaguely avian-like gait, along with feather-fur manes. Combined with their diminutive size, no one would really confuse one with a human.

Erandi, though...

"The monitors showed them as human," I noted.

"We think they modified the monitor input," Commander Bonnadonna pointed at the alien device, still mounted on the wall near the control panel for the cell block. A team had begun to, slowly, attempt to remove it. They were checking it for traps and part of me wanted to be out of the room, just in case.

"Make way," someone said from out in the corridor. The three of us stepped out of the doorway and a team came in, carrying a heavy set of equipment that they began to set up outside of Doctor Aisling's cell.

I frowned as I watched them unfold it. It looked like a weird cross between a medical scanner and a radar dish. "What is that?"

"It's a deep tissue scanner," the Admiral said, as she stared at Doctor Aisling. The Admiral had a distant, emotionless look to her face that made me nervous.

Doctor Weisfeldt looked up from where he was setting it up, "It's a product of Directorate Thirteen, actually, designed to scan for *humans* who've made use of extensive body modification or surgery. There's been persistent rumors of certain organizations making use of body modification implants, so Directorate Thirteen cooked this one up, well, a few years ago, actually. We've used it a couple of times, it's designed to scan through a concealing object, so it's actually perfect for this situation."

"Feel free to open the door," Doctor Aisling smiled. "I promise not to cause trouble."

"I think I'll stand right here, thank you," Commander Weisfeldt replied, without looking up from the control panel from the scanner. "After all, your friends left such a mess..."

How he was so lighthearted about it, I didn't know. I'd seen far too many people dragged out of the level, people I'd worked with every morning for weeks. I was the only one who'd survived uninjured, and I didn't know how.

"So," Commander Weisfeldt went on, "all I need to do is... this, and... ah, here we are."

The scanner began to hum, a faint vibration that I felt through the soles of my uniform boots more than anything. A moment later, the display flashed and red text appeared. *Non-human.*

"She's erandi, too, then?" I swallowed as my suspicions were confirmed.

Commander Weisfeldt looked over at me, his bushy eyebrows raised, "Um... maybe. The machine wasn't designed to identify alien species, it was designed for analysis and scanning of humans. It will take a little time to analyze the data, and unfortunately, the creator, Doctor Aroguthra, well..."

"He was in the section that the team breached through," The Admiral finished for him. I winced. Even in the rear lab, the initial breach had knocked me down, while the secondary charge had blasted lethal shrapnel. Anyone in close vicinity of those two blasts was probably very, very dead.

"Collating the data will take some expertise and time," Commander Weisfeldt continued, "but it's a valid assumption to go on, which will require some additional precautions..."

"That... thing, she did, where she tried to tell me what to do?" I asked.

"Yes, some erandi have made use of capabilities that, whether technological or otherwise, resemble telepathy," Commander Weisfeldt nodded, rubbing his chin, "it's very interesting, some humans apparently aren't vulnerable, either because of their brain chemistry or some kind of latent..."

"We're increasing security," the Admiral interrupted. "Commander Bonnadonna, I want that access shaft sealed. Get with Commander Weisfeldt and identify any other structural weaknesses and seal them off as well."

"Ma'am," Commander Bonnadonna nodded. He looked at me, "Miss Armstrong, perhaps you should go get yourself cleaned up?"

I looked down at the dirt, blood, and sweat that had pretty much ruined this uniform. I was exhausted and the confirmation that Aisling was an alien of some kind had taken the last bit of energy out of me. "Yeah... I mean, yes, sir."

Petty Officer Kennedy stepped forward and I passed over the rifle. I swallowed a bit as I did so, "The guard, she took two of them down before I could get here..."

"I'll treat her weapon with respect, Cadet," Senior Petty Officer Kennedy nodded formally at me.

"Thank you," I turned away as I felt tears well up in my eyes. I followed the Admiral out as she headed for the elevator. "Ma'am," I spoke up, stepping over rubble and bloodstains, "what happened up top?"

"Nothing," the Admiral looked around, her face bleak. "The depth of this facility meant that no one on the surface even noticed the explosions. Even on the lower levels it only set off some vibration sensors. The attackers had hacked the monitors and cut the transmission cable to the surface, as well. If you hadn't stopped them, they would have been long gone before we knew what they'd done."

I swallowed. "Then... how did anyone come?"

"My implant pinged me with a warning on the vibration sensors. I put the entire school into a lockdown and sent Commander Bonnadonna down here... just in case." There was something iron-hard in her expression. "We lost twenty-three personnel in this attack. We would have lost far more if they'd attacked later in the morning."

"Was that the point?" I asked, as we came up to the elevator shaft. As far as I knew, the response team had rappelled down the shaft. After they'd secured the floor, they had put the elevator back in working order, but for now, the doors remained locked open.

The elevator came down and the Admiral and I stepped aboard. "We don't know. Extraction of Doctor Aisling appeared to be their primary purpose, but with the erandi..." She shrugged. "We don't know whether they're affiliated with the Erandi Republic or the Erandi Empire, or if they're renegades operating outside of the boundaries of either. I have no idea what they're doing so far from their common border with human space."

I didn't really know much about the alien species. They lay almost on the far side of human space, near the Rose Nebula Military Sector. They looked somewhat human, similar enough to creep out anyone who saw one. Their two polities, the Republic and the Empire were in a state of war, though the interrelations of their member worlds and factions was too complex for humanity to identify allegiances, which seemed to shift based upon so many factors that any kind of alliance with either nation was considered impossible.

What I remembered was that they were very technologically advanced. They had faster, more powerful ships and a complete disregard for human life. Erandi slavers were the bane of the Rose Sector. Raider ships had been seen far afield of both nations, as far as culmor space, even. The little bit of military training we had to counter them was to concentrate as much firepower on individual ships as possible and hope it was enough to drive them off.

I didn't know if anyone had fought them on the ground successfully or what this meant. *This is way beyond me, I'm just a cadet.*

I felt a moment of panic, though, as I thought of the Alien and Telepath Act. "Are we in violation..."

I didn't have to finish the sentence. The Admiral looked at me, "To the knowledge of anyone outside of Directorate Thirteen, Doctor Aisling is a renegade and criminal. Nothing more. Do you understand?"

"Yes, ma'am," I snapped. Implicit with that order was that I wouldn't discuss it any further.

I decided not to ask any more questions to which I didn't want to know the answers.

The elevator doors opened and the Admiral led the way out, into the Academy Control Center. I wanted a shower and to sleep, but I paused, "Ma'am, about what happened, what should I..."

I didn't have time to finish. A woman swept into the Academy's command center, her tightly pressed business suit a stark contrast to the dark uniforms of the Enforcers who flanked her. "Admiral Armstrong!" Charterer Beckman demanded, her voice nasal and overbearing, "I demand to know the meaning of this unacceptable behavior!"

Lieutenant Commander Corgan stood next to her and I had no doubt as to who had summoned the woman to the Academy.

"Charterer Beckman, my apologies," the Admiral said in a tone that didn't sound remotely apologetic. "I've just come from an emergency inspection."

"Emergency?" Charterer Beckman shot a look around, "I should say so! There's been reports of injured and even dead being removed from here. If I didn't know better, I would think you faced some kind of mutiny!"

"Reports?" The Admiral asked, her tone icy.

Charterer Beckman didn't meet her gaze, "I came as soon as I'd heard, to make certain that things are well in hand, Admiral." *Her niece,* I realized, *Cadet Beckman, the little rat called her aunt to report... she's spying on the Admiral, on everything we do.* I fought down the impulse to go find the girl and shake her, scream at her. That wouldn't do any good right now. Nor would shooting her with a training round, though that might have been a bit more satisfying.

"A power conduit in the lower level led to a major power short. An engineering team went to fix it, when a power coupling detonated," the Admiral said it all in a calm, matter of fact, tone. "Unfortunately, twenty-three men and women were killed, the entire engineering team and several from a second team which was en-route to assist, plus the guard detail on site. Several more were injured."

"That's terrible," Charterer Beckman's voice was sour. I had no doubt that she wished the Admiral had been among that number. "Is the situation in hand, then?"

"It is now," the Admiral replied. To my surprise, she laid a hand on my shoulder, "Cadet Third Class Armstrong was present and assisted in getting the situation under control. Without her help, further lives might have been lost."

The Charterer's blue eyed gaze locked on me. There was hatred in that look. Hatred and calculation. She didn't see me as a young woman, not even as a person. I was nothing but an inconvenience. "I see."

Her expression shifted slightly and she spoke up, "I seem to remember the Academy detention facility is on those levels. I have Enforcers with me, if you want, I could take any prisoners down there back to a different, secure facility?"

I saw the Admiral's face darken and her gaze go across the crowded Command Center. There were dozens of officers, enlisted, and even cadets present. The secret of the cell block buried deep down below was now out.

"I think not," the Admiral answered. "Especially as I understand there was something of a security issue at the Enforcer headquarters, I'd hate to add additional burdens to the Enforcers when they're, no doubt, under a lot of pressure to find answers." Her voice was generous, her expression friendly, but the words were a slap to the face and I saw the Enforcers surrounding the Charterer stiffen in response. She'd just called them out on the fact that they'd been successfully attacked... and she knew about it.

Charterer Beckman gave a wooden smile. "Well, then, give my official condolences to the families of those personnel who you've lost. I understand you're very good at that."

The room went very, very still. No one breathed. No one moved.

"Charterer Beckman," the Admiral said, "thank you for your condolences, I'm certain my people and their families will take them for what they're worth. Now, I'm afraid that I have to manage the aftermath, so if you and your people would be so kind, Lieutenant Sobani will escort you, Lieutenant General Corgan, and your Enforcers to your skimmer."

A security team practically materialized around the Charterer. I watched as they efficiently escorted the woman and her Enforcers out of the Command Center. As they went, I caught a hesitant motion and then spied Cadet Beckman near the doors, trying to slip out. A red haze went over my eyes and I started to advance on her. The back-stabbing, malicious little--

"Cadet Armstrong!" The Admiral snapped and I froze. Her voice was like a rope that jerked me up short and spun me around to face her.

"I believe I gave you an order to go get yourself checked out at the infirmary and then to get some rest?" Her words were calm, but they were as much of an order as if they'd been carved out of stone.

"Yes, ma'am," I saluted sharply. To hell with Beckman. To hell with *both* Beckmans. I respected the Admiral and I was sure the rest of the Academy did, too.

The Admiral saluted back and I turned sharply and marched out of the Command Center.

***

Chapter 20: No One Tried To Kill Me, Really, I Promise!

"Your bed is right there, waiting," Doctor Fuesting said with a tone of resignation.

"I don't think I need a bed--"

"Right. There." The woman bit out, without looking up from an unconscious woman.

I didn't argue. I went to my room.

Kyle was waiting, his face pale and his expression worried. "Jiden!" He stood up quickly and rushed to embrace me.

"Kyle," I protested, "I'm fine, and I'm covered in dirt and--"

"I don't care," he hugged me tight. My face was buried in his chest and I didn't really care either. It felt good to lean on him. He held me for a long while and I was just happy to be there. After a moment, he pushed me back and looked at me, his face still lined with concern, "Are you sure you're okay? I can go get the doctor..."

"I'm fine, really," I rolled my eyes, "there's lots of people worse off than me."

"I heard," he shook his head. "A power surge down in the lower level, blowing a power coupling." His voice was neutral as he said it and stared at me. "I thought you were working in the Archives?"

"I was helping out an engineering team," I hedged. "Of course, that's when... when things happened."

"Right," Kyle didn't look convinced. Then again, he wasn't stupid. "There's some burn and shrapnel victims out there," he noted. "But some of the injured look like they have bullet wounds."

"That's odd," I answered. I was glad that some of those shot by the erandi had survived. Most hadn't. Despite the delicate looks of their weapons, they'd punched right through the guards' body armor.

"Yeah, and that you just happened to be there to help out..."

I turned away. "Kyle. Please, don't do this right now. It's been a very, very rough day."

He went still and I felt like a horrible person. Then, to my surprise, he came up behind me and hugged me. "You're right. Now isn't the time. But sooner or later we need to talk about all of this."

"I'll tell you everything that I can," I whispered. He didn't say anything in reply, he just squeezed me a bit tighter and, for the first time since the explosion had thrown me to the floor, I started to feel like things would be alright.

***

A few days later, in the recently repaired waiting room of Directorate Thirteen, the Admiral, Commander Weisfeldt, and a few other officers were present while I stood at attention.

"Attention to orders," Commander Bonnadonna read off in his deep voice. "For valor under fire, Cadet Third Class Jiden Armstrong is hereby awarded a Bronze Cross for valor in combat, during the events of the tenth day of May, when working under Directorate Thirteen, and her work area came under attack. During the firefight, Cadet Third Class Jiden Armstrong acquired the weapon of a fallen guard and engaged three intruders, killing all three of them and stopping them from achieving their mission. She did this despite being outnumbered and out-gunned and having had the opportunity to seek safety, she instead engaged the enemy. Signed, Admiral Victoria Armstrong, Century Military Academy, Commanding."

I swallowed back tears as the Admiral pinned the award on my dress uniform. "The award is classified," she noted, "so you can wear it, but you can't say where you earned it. You understand?"

"Yes, ma'am," I nodded. They'd just finished giving similar awards to the three guards who'd died fighting the attackers. I felt guilty for receiving the same award. After all, I'd survived. But I saluted sharply after the Admiral shook my hand and stepped back out of the way.

"We suffered a terrible attack," The Admiral said. Almost all of the military and many of the civilians for Directorate Thirteen were gathered to listen. Most of them hadn't been on duty that early in the morning. Of those that had, all six of the survivors were still in the hospital.

"It is not the first such attack that the Militia has suffered. It won't be the last. I'm proud of all of you for the work that you've done and that you will continue to do. As of this morning, I've received permission to increase our staff and funding levels. The attack here as well as the earlier one against the Enforcer headquarters, has reinforced the concerns of the President and the

Charter Council that we need every advantage that we can give ourselves." The Admiral looked around at us and I felt myself stand straighter as her eyes went over me.

"Those we have lost will not be forgotten, but we will not let such tragedies stop us. As a part of the funding increase, we're going to be bringing in a number of new people and new projects. I challenge you all to make them feel welcome, to help this organization grow, to never forget those who died in this terrible attack, but to continue to look forward in honor of those we've lost."

She gave the assembled officers a sharp salute. "Dismissed."

We stepped out of formation and I stood there, feeling sort of lost as everyone else went back to work. I'd be starting in the archive section in a few minutes, but leaving after her speech felt wrong.

"Walk with me, Jiden," the Admiral said, gesturing towards the elevator.

"Ma'am," I nodded and fell into step to her side and a slight respectful distance behind.

"Part of the authorizations I received are to bring in the neurosurgeon expert. Doctor Schoeffelk will be joining Directorate Thirteen as soon as he has time to finish off his civilian obligations," the Admiral said it in a low voice. "I doubt he'll join the staff until after the end of the summer period, but when he arrives, I'm going to have him begin analysis of the implant program and try to find answers as to what Doctor Aisling did to you all, and what really happened as a result."

I felt a knot of tension at her words. "Do you think he'll be able to find answers? I mean, if Doctor Aisling is really..."

"He'll be able to provide some good guesses, at the least," The Admiral managed to sound confident, but I didn't see how. Working with cutting-edge technology was one thing. Even the work that my parents had done in analysis of the ancient alien materials, the smart material that we'd reverse engineered to act as an implant, which was at least something I would think that others could understand.

But to figure out what an alien had done to human minds, to try and figure that out in living, breathing people? To try and isolate if the implants were going to drive us insane or if they already had driven some of us insane... *I don't see how it's possible, not without*

Aisling's cooperation and she's not talking...

"We'll get through this, girl," the Admiral said softly as the elevator doors opened. "Trust me."

I nodded. After all, it wasn't like I had much of a choice.

***

Life and school went on.

Kyle and I had that talk that I'd been both looking forward to and dreading at the same time. It came up suddenly, one moment we were talking about the next semester and then he sort of trailed off and stared at me. "So," he swallowed, "what about next year?"

"Next year?" I asked, feeling equally nervous.

"I mean, I've finished a Senior Cadet Drill Instructor position, so odds are that I should take a Militia assignment. And getting a Senior Cadet Drill Instructor or even a Chief Assistant Trainer spot would be good for you. So we wouldn't see each other for five months," Kyle chewed his lip.

Commander Weisfeldt had told me that my rating for my "Archive and Support" position would be weighted as heavily in the system as a Senior Cadet Drill Instructor position, so I wasn't too worried about that. But I knew that he didn't just mean next year. We were on the catwalk running track near the top of Bunker Seven, with the cool air and the great view and I reached out and took his hand. "I don't want to be away from you too much, but there's going to be times we can't avoid it."

"Yeah," he replied, his voice getting rough. "But I don't like that."

I thought about it as I held his big, warm hand in mine. There was a strength in Kyle, a solidarity that I really appreciated. "I don't like it either. Next summer we can work out, maybe we both do Militia assignments? Then see what happens our First Class year?"

He seemed surprised by that, but I wasn't sure if it was the implication that I'd give up a training position to be with him or that I assumed we'd both make it that far. After all, we'd seen plenty of our classmates fail out already.

"I get my implant just before classes start again," he noted. "Any advice?"

"Be sure they have a good doctor for you," I grumbled. He

shot me an odd look and I changed the subject, "Now," I began, "what about after graduation?"

He let out a whooshing breath. I knew I'd put him on the spot, but I wanted to know what he thought, what he felt... and what he expected of me. "Jiden..." he sighed, "I don't know, really. I mean, if you're talking, well, if you're talking about marri--"

"Ack!" I interrupted. "Don't finish that, I don't, that is, I'm *not* ready for that discussion!" I found myself blushing furiously. Granted, I had friends my age from Black Mesa Outpost who'd gotten married, but I wasn't ready for that. Not yet. I liked Kyle a lot, even loved him, but thinking about weddings made my stomach and heart flutter in opposing motions that left me a little light-headed.

"No, I meant assignments, what are you planning on doing in the Militia after graduation?" I went on. I was not going to start picturing myself in a wedding dress and Kyle in his uniform. Especially not in the Academy chapel...

Kyle's expression was every bit as relieved as mine. "Oh. Good. I mean, not that I wouldn't want to... I mean, with you, maybe! But..."

"Assignments," I interrupted him again, "Militia Assignments."

"Yeah," he scratched his head. "Um, my dad is Active, but he actually sort of regrets it, he says all the fun stuff is done by the Reserve, any more. I figured I'd apply for one of the Reserve fighter squadrons, maybe?"

"Okay," I thought about that. "I could live with that." It didn't sound all that exciting, but we'd be together and fighter patrols did occasionally intercept pirates and smugglers.

Kyle gave me a relieved grin. "Good, me too."

I gave his hand a squeeze and we went back to watching the sunset.

***

The Plebes did their final exercise not long after that. I sat in the stands, above where they sat, and watched. At this point, my little brother had almost a ten-point lead over any of the other cadets there. Since the most anyone could get was fifteen points, unless he really messed up, he was going to at least place well in his class, if not first by a wide margin.

I'd seen his scores, between his academics and his performance in the grinder, he was near the top ranking of the school *ever*. If he did well in the final exercise, he was going to set a new record. I wasn't sure how I felt about that. I mean, I wanted him to do well, but he was still my little brother. Little being a relative, word, of course. If anything, he'd shot up another few inches over the past five months of training and he'd put on muscle. I was glad I'd taken Commander Pannja's classes and I'd be able to put him in his place if necessary. After all, he still was my *little* brother...

After the past couple of years, I couldn't help but feel that this year the First Class hadn't quite managed to make a memorable final exercise. I mean, granted, I'd nearly died both years. Well, last year, anyway. The year before that I'd only dislocated my arm and broken some fingers, then been shot point blank by a training round in the face. Come to think of it, that had been pretty painful.

My Academy Prep Course, there'd been a mountain with lanes leading up towards the center, and an honest to god forest with plants and everything. Last year, Cadet Lieutenant Webster had engineered a basalt maze that had just happened to be based off of a million year old alien ruin in Century's Black Mesa.

This year, it looked like lots of piles of rocks and sand.

There *were* lanes, but the entire thing was set up to be a sort of mass melee. I'd actually asked Sashi about it, since I'd had a peek at it earlier in the week and she'd been involved in carrying out the construction as the CAT. I'd thought it was still a work in progress at the time. She'd adopted a pained expression and explained that it was actually a goal of the Regimental staff. Apparently it had been pushed pretty hard by Ogre Company's Commander, Cadet Commander Drien, Sashi's oldest brother.

The resulting product was a large, open area, several hundred meters across, with sporadic cover. Each rock pile had a flag on it, corresponding to a Company. In my opinion, Ogre Company's pile looked just a big bigger and a little better positioned with cover, but it wasn't my place to bring that up.

Each of the sections had to defend their flag while fighting across the mostly open space to capture the flags of the other sections. Knowing what I did about the other sections, especially those that were far less combat focused, I understood a bit better why teams like Ogre and Tiger tended to do so much better at these sorts of competitions. After all, medical personnel all came from one company and they had to compete with the rest of us.

Of course, I kind of *wanted* Tiger to succeed, or at least to do alright. Karmazin's surprise had been that he'd interviewed to be Hodges' replacement. Apparently Hodges had been smart enough to realize he'd pushed things too far, and he'd stepped down to take the rest of the year off. The downside being he was joining our class, of course.

Seeing as Kyle was in charge of Dust, things had been interesting. Granted, the rivalry had died down a lot with Karmazin in charge of the candidates. From what I'd heard, he'd done a great job of turning them around. And now, my two best friends and my boyfriend were in direct competition. I almost didn't know who to root for. *At least I can cheer when they shoot down Ogre candidates, I guess...*

The whole thing began and immediately the lights dropped to twilight. Then, there was a burst of different lights, in pulses. It almost induced a headache as the lighting on the battleground shifted across the spectrum. *Ah, it's supposed to be the challenging part.*

It certainly looked disorienting. Then everything sort of settled out. The firefight began as skirmishes as one section or another would try to advance and multiple other groups would open fire. There wasn't room to maneuver, there wasn't room to hide. It became a battle of attrition. Anyone who showed any bit of movement was fired on by anyone in range. Since it wasn't a ring and the different rock piles were irregularly spaced, anywhere from twenty to nearly a hundred candidates had fields of fire on anyone who tried to move.

Viper section tried a rush after a couple minutes and pretty much the entire section was scythed down. A handful made it back into cover, and a squad from Scorpion jumped up and made a dash for their mostly undefended flag... only for them to be gunned down in turn.

After that, it became a slow, painful experience. I kept looking down at the ranks of the training officers for all the companies and a lot of them were looking over at Drien from Ogre. Sashi's older brother had a scowl on his face. I thought I saw him mouth something to his Senior Cadet Drill Instructor, my lip reading wasn't up to it, but there was a monitor nearby...

"They're not doing it right," Drien said.

"I know, sir, but I don't know what to do about it," his younger brother was his Senior Drill Instructor, I realized, seeing them from close up by the monitor. I felt a bit guilty about it. "It's not like we can tell them what to do at this point."

"They're making me look stupid!" the elder Drien hissed.

I think you managed that on your own, I thought.

I went back to watching the fight down below and I was watching *my* brother just as he decided to change things. He edged up to the front of his line and tied a cloth to the tip of his rifle and waved it at the nearest group. "I'm coming over to talk!"

"No tricks!" one of the Dust Company candidates shouted back.

I watched nervously as my brother edged across the open ground, but everyone seemed curious as to what was happening more than anything else. Once over, he ducked down in cover and he and the candidates from Dust Company talked for a long moment. Then he rushed back to cover with the Sand Dragons.

I started hearing mutters in the upperclassmen around me. There was confusion, but there was interest. Somebody was up to something and that piqued people's interest.

"What was he saying?" I heard over the monitor near Ogre's Company Commander. I wondered that he hadn't taken another summer assignment, that he'd retained his position... or had it been an assignment?

"I'm not a lip reader, Nahka," his brother hissed at him.

"Fine, just let's hope one of *your* candidates shoots him down. Father will be upset if an Armstrong wins first place again, doubly so if he breaks records doing it!" I saw them both shoot glances up at the senior officer balcony, where their father and grandfather no doubt sat watching.

My brother popped up on the other side of the Sand Dragon mound, again waving his cloth, this time at Tiger Company. They let him across, though he was close enough to Ogre that several of them took shots at him as he dashed across the gap. He made it into cover, though and my eyes narrowed as I looked at where Dust Company, Sand Dragon Company, and Tiger Company lay. They were almost in V shape, with another company at the center of that

V was... Ogre Company.

A moment later, my brother dashed back out. This time, a half dozen Ogres were waiting for him and they rose to take shots at him.

Tiger, Dust, and Sand Dragon Companies all opened fire in return, however. At least three Ogres went down, and the rest dropped into cover. But no sooner did my brother reach cover than he shouted, "Let's go!"

His squad followed him, clearly they'd planned this far ahead, at least. The squad raced across the open ground while the other two companies laid down suppressive fire.

His squad hit the Ogres as they scrambled to find cover or put up a defense. The Ogre candidates fought hard, and they took down several of his squad, but with fire from the flanks and enemies among them, the entire section went down in only seconds. A moment later, my brother pulled down the Ogre flag and a cheer went up from Dust, Tiger, and Sand Dragon companies.

I looked down at Nahka Drien. The First Class Cadet's face had gone wooden. He didn't look up at his father or grandfather, he stared down at his boots. I felt a moment of pity for him, but then I thought about how he'd treated Sashi and I looked over at *her*. She was seated near the Regimental Training Officer and she had a slight smirk on her face. *Part of their rating is class cohesion and building them past their rivalries...* This was making her look good and I couldn't help a smile. Right now, *everyone* I liked was winning.

The fighting continued, but now it became far less of battle of attrition and something more like mopping up. With three sections combining their firepower, they were able to flank and pin down their targets, moving one to the next. Two more sections waved makeshift signals at each other and joined up, working on the other side, but most of the other sections didn't have time to react. One minute Tiger would lay down covering fire while Sand Dragons attacked, the next Dust was doing the same on the other side while *Tiger* attacked and the Sand Dragons covered their rear.

Within an hour, there were only five companies. The two who'd teamed up waved signals and sent out representatives. I saw my brother and candidates from Tiger and Dust go out. They stood around and talked for a long minute, then they all made a big show of counting flags. Sand Dragons had four. Tiger and Dust both had three. Of the two that had teamed up, Hawk had three and Scorpion had two. The section leaders all shook hands and they went back to their sections, the candidate laid down their rifles and formed up. *They're done... they're not going to fight each other anymore, they're happy with how it ended.*

I had no idea how the First Class Cadets were supposed to judge this one. This had gone from an individual performance into something rather like the Grinder, with team performance providing the necessary boost to win. Ogre and other sections had been dominated, not because they weren't good, but because they hadn't thought to work with the other sections.

I had no doubt that my brother had just cinched first place for himself, and possibly broke the records I'd worried about earlier. He'd earned it, though. He'd turned the entire final exercise on its head and trivialized an unsolvable problem. When the fight is impossible: don't fight, work out a deal. I decided that maybe even an older sister could learn a lesson from that.

***

Chapter 21: I Go Back To The Trenches And I Like It

I'd been proud of my brother at his graduation from Academy Prep School, but that seemed like it had happened years ago as classes swept in. My brother had broken every record on scores for a candidate. My mom and dad had shown up for Graduation and had been suitably impressed especially as my brother described this or that event. I could only smile, the proud older sister... though I caught the worried looks from my mom. She thought about what I'd been through and what it had cost me.

Soon enough, though, my brother was headed home for five months prior to his start as a plebe in the coming spring. In the meantime, I had lots of classes to make sure I passed.

The fall semester seemed to start off quickly and just go faster and faster as it went on.

Commander Bonnadonna's group military history classes were over. Now we had one-on-one sessions with him in various military simulators. Since he had classes on top of that, it meant my section and two others were split out over the nights and early mornings, with appointments at odd hours and intervals, along with one-on-one discussions and, of course, his ever-present papers.

I really began to enjoy those sessions. Last year I'd thought he was trying to kill me, only to find out that it was Commander Scarpitti. It had been a weird thing for me, in that I'd gone from hating his classes to enjoying the material, but still not trusting him. This year I'd been able to just enjoy the class discussions, even if the weekly, ten-page papers still remained something of a chore.

"Very interesting, Miss Armstrong," he noted to me on the end of week review. "Particularly your choice to engage the terrorists in two of these exercises, despite the risks of civilian casualties."

I took a moment to answer. At the time, it had been a split-second decision and I hadn't had time to really consider it, not in either situation. "The initial briefing suggested the terrorists tended to use and then dispose of hostages," I met his dark eyes with as much confidence as I could muster. "I felt that the risk to those hostages was acceptable given the odds that the terrorists would kill them all anyway."

"A hard choice to make," Commander Bonnadonna nodded.

"And much easier to make in a simulation when you're dealing with digital lives rather than real ones." I wasn't sure if that was a dig or not, so I kept quiet. "Something else to remember, too, is that if our enemies believe we will disengage due to risk to hostages, they'll use them more often. It's a counter-piracy tactic that the Guard uses, when they deal with pirates. They're totally willing to ignore any threats to hostages in order to recapture ships boarded by pirates. Any casualties taken by hostages are added to the charges those pirates face. They've seen a remarkable increase in surrenders of hijackers and pirates in the past few years since they adopted that tactic."

I nodded, though as he'd said, I wondered if I could be as calm about it if they were real people. *Not afterwards, afterwards there would be a price to pay... but I suppose that's a part of duty too.*

"All in all, I'm impressed with your performance. You've been out of the tactical element for most of the past few months," he shrugged, acknowledging my actual combat encounter and the fact he couldn't mention it, even here. "Most Third Class Cadets in your situation have needed some refresher training. You've come along well enough that I think I'll have to step up your challenge rating."

I bit back a groan in response, but I wasn't entirely successful.

"Don't worry, Miss Armstrong, everyone likes a good challenge. And, since that will require more hours in the simulator, I'll waive the weekly military tactics papers... instead, you can assist me in reviewing some of the military history papers from the Fourth Class Cadets." He grinned in good humor. "I'll warn you, reviewing some of them can feel like watching a dying animal stagger around. Rather pathetic and disheartening."

"Oh," I didn't think they could be *that* bad.

He seemed to read my expression again. I'd hate to gamble with him. "I'll send over the first twenty or so. It's Friday, so you should have plenty of time to read through them all and give me your impressions for our Monday."

I stared at him, wondering if he were joking. Twenty papers at ten pages each would be over two-hundred pages of reading. Worse, it sounded like he wanted me to remember individual papers and keep them all separate for discussion. That was on top of

Saturday's drill and all my other homework. I didn't know what to say or how to object.

"Good, I'm glad we worked that out," he smiled in satisfaction. "Now, I've got my next counseling coming up, this one with Mister Andrews. Dismissed, Miss Armstrong."

***

"Too slow, you're dead again," Commander Pannja said offhandedly as one of the other cadets vanished to incoming fire.

I noted it, but I didn't look away. I didn't have time to be distracted, I was going through my own attack *preparations*, using my implant and my hands to upload course changes and update attack parameters as my simulated Mark Five Firebolt dove at an enemy formation.

The attack parameters were so narrow for the fighter that it was akin to trying to curve a bullet to hit another bullet in mid-air. Worse, with limited maneuverability in a warp envelope, a Firebolt made a relatively easy target as it came in on its final attack run. And since a Firebolt's main anti-ship weapon was Mark III antimatter bombs, I had to get *very* close to engage an enemy ship.

I swept past the enemy ships, far faster than I could even register them as visible specks I would be past them. They were icons and projected possible vectors, nothing more, and then they were past me and the attack parameters I'd set had taken effect.

The fighter's attack computer had released all four of my bombs as I'd swept across the enemy formation. Only one of those had hit and--

My screen darkened and I sighed. "You got too caught up in the attack, Biohazard," Commander Pannja grinned at me, leaning over my simulator. "But you took down one enemy ship on the way through. That's *almost* a pass. But they shot you down on your way out, since you followed a nice, clean trajectory trying to get a battle damage assessment." He was referring to me scanning the enemy ships to see how many hits I'd managed on the attack run, a normal tactic for warp fighters, which often operated as scouts after they dropped their bombs.

"You get to start over again, but not bad at all," he clapped me on the shoulder as he walked away.

I sighed and brought up the simulator again. We were well

past the single tactic drills or even the more complex battle drills. We'd begun the class plotting full patrol routes, then progressed into updating mission parameters due to enemy contacts, and last week we'd integrated attack runs after we managed intercepts. What I'd managed just now would have been a passing grade on the training... last week. That would have meant I could go back to my room and get some sleep.

Instead... instead I had to start over again. I didn't bother to pull up a clock on my implant. I didn't want to know how late it was at night. It was Friday. I'd keep at it until either I completed it, or until Saturday drill started, whichever came first.

For just a moment, I was tempted to use my implant, but I banished that thought as my Firebolt materialized around me in the simulator. That would have been cheating, using an ability that none of the rest of my class could use. *Besides, I have no idea how dangerous it could be... not yet.*

***

"Move left, left!" I shouted, shoving Fourth Class Cadets out of the way as an 'enemy' gunship swept down on us. "Take cover!"

I dove for the ground, tackling one of the slower cadets under my command as the combat skimmer 'strafed' our position. It fired gas canister munitions, which detonated in orange billows of smoke on the position we'd occupied only a moment ago. "Counter-fire!" I shouted, even as I rolled over on my back and fired at the skimmer as it roared overhead, close enough that the hot gasses from its gas turbine engines tore at my uniform and body armor and blew some of my blonde hair out from under my helmet.

I didn't know if our small arms fire counted as a threat or if we'd even been lucky enough to hit, but the combat skimmer roared up and away. A moment later, I rolled to my feet, "Move out!"

We were on an attack mission, today. Sashi, Ashiri, Karmazin and I had all been selected to lead attack teams against fortified positions on the Academy grounds. It was almost totally opposite what we'd started the year doing, and since the defenders had access to the full Academy resources, I felt pretty darned outnumbered and out-gunned.

I hadn't lost anyone, yet, though, so there was that at least.

I'd somehow managed to end up with Beckman on my team.

That alone had left me irritated, especially since I'd spent most of the night in the simulator. Worse, though the other five cadets I had were sort of the poster-children of 'excess personnel' from several different Companies.

Bellmore and Reese were moderate in ranking, but they at least listened and kept their heads down. Bellmore was borderline and was already on probation for academic performance. Chu was doing fine academically, but she was on probation for her physical fitness and she'd be failing out if she didn't manage to get back in shape soon.

The last one was Tinney, a cadet from Ogre Company. He actually seemed like a decent, sort, for an Ogre, but he didn't seem to understand the idea of taking cover. He was a big, heavy-set guy, and he'd been the one I'd tackled to the ground when the skimmer had attacked. When he'd first been assigned to my team, I'd seen that he had the dubious honor of having been hit in every single engagement he'd ever been in, including the one I'd led him in as my first as team leader. He'd even been rendered unconscious in two engagements where cadets weren't supposed to be hit by training rounds at all... somehow he'd managed to be in the wrong place at the wrong time and been shot by people on his own side.

"Ma'am," Beckman panted as we came up near the crest of the ridge and I called a halt. "Our orders have us going straight in. If we delay, we're going to mess up the timing of the other teams."

I knew that, but I was also in communication with the other teams and I knew that Sashi and Karmazin had both run into heavier resistance than expected. They were behind as well, and Ashiri's team was off on the flank, least likely to be effected by this scenario. Since we'd just run ten kilometers to get in position and I wasn't totally confident of my troops' capabilities, I was willing to stage a moment and let them get their bearings. *I hadn't thought I'd miss ammo loading detail at Bunker Three.*

"We're staging here," was all the answer I gave her. Beckman seemed to take any explanation as a point to argue. The less I explained to her, the less she fought with me. Sashi Drien had been right about that, even if it made no sense to me.

I dropped to a belly crawl and edged up to the crest of the ridge. Our orders had us attacking the south end of the Academy grounds, which was a bit more rocky and hilly than the other areas. I was a bit less familiar with the perimeter here, and I wanted to see what we would be up against.

I picked out several enemy positions and dropped back, thinking through an attack route even as I evaluated my team. "We're going to work our way up the left side," I said, drawing a quick sketch in the dirt. A part of me wondered how many other cadets had stood in this same spot and done the same thing. The Academy grounds had to be the second-most fought-over section of the planet after the Grinder. "Once we get to our attack positions, we'll wait for the other teams to get in position and then attack these firing positions. Chu, you and Beckman will lay down covering fire while Bellmore, Reese, Tinney, and I advance down the left side..."

"Ma'am," Beckman interrupted, "shouldn't we press the attack quickly? That skimmer probably reported our position--"

"We're attacking fortified positions," I interrupted. "They already know we're coming. Our best advantage in this case is to attack in sequence with our other teams and mass fires." Despite myself, I had to explain my reasoning and I saw Beckman's face darken. She started to open her mouth to argue and I went on, "That's an order, Beckman."

Her mouth shut like a trap and she glared at me. *Well, it's not like there was any chance she'd like me anyway...*

I restrained a sigh. "Move out."

I led the way out, using the ridge-line as cover as I headed down to the low gully that I'd seen before. I felt an odd sense of familiarity as I reached it and I had to think about it, as we moved up. *This is a lot like my first engagement with Beckman earlier this year, only we're the attackers.* I hoped that wasn't some kind of omen.

I waved Beckman and Chu to their positions and the two girls split off, while the rest of us continued up the gully. *Almost in position,* I sent to Karmazin and the others.

I'm bogged down, Karmazin sent back to me. *There's a forward patrol out here, I think Sashi is tangled up with them too.* That wasn't good. If there was one patrol out, there might be others. The defenders already knew we were coming...

"Spread out," I ordered to my team. "Tinney, you're center with me. Bellmore, you're on the right flank, Bellmore, the left. Get in position, get ready to move." I got on my team radio, "Beckman,

Chu, get ready to kick it off, it looks like we may be alone."

I heard a rattle of gunfire to the right, distant enough that it had to be the others, tied up with the patrol. Now it was just my team against a fixed position. *At least they have to be low on personnel, several of them are out on patrol...*

"Covering fire," I snapped. I heard Chu open up followed a moment later by Beckman. I didn't *think* that delay was intentional, but then again, I wouldn't have put it past her.

"Move out!" I yelled and dashed up and out of the gulley with the other three of my team.

As we did so, I knew something was wrong. No fire erupted from the positions ahead of us.

Instead, a moment later, fire erupted from our right flank. The only thing that saved any of us was that everyone saw Tinney and opened fire on him. Dozens of practice rounds struck him, so many that as he fell, I saw his whole side was covered in paint rounds. "Ambush, take cover!" I barked as I dove to the ground

The only cover I could find was Tinney's comatose form. I winced as I heard multiple more training rounds strike him, the dull thwacks signs of the massive amounts of bruising he was going to have. I rolled to the side and got eyes on our ambushers and as I did so, I saw movement to the front as well. "Contact, front, contact right! Fifty meters!"

My implant told me that Reese was down. The enemy in the fixed positions opened up with a crew-served weapon and Chu's icon on my heads up display went amber and then red.

I was low enough down that I didn't think the machine gun could shoot at me, but I was pinned. Bellmore was still up, but looking over, I saw that he was pinned down, the rocks he used as cover were stained from the impacts of multiple training rounds.

Beckman was still outside the ambush area, but that hardly gave me confidence. "Beckman, can you put down fire on the right?"

There was a long pause, "Negative, ma'am, not from here."

I didn't have a good enough mental image of the terrain over there. "Do you think you can work to the side and take them under fire?" I asked, even as I started to edge forward.

"I'll try, ma'am," Beckman sounded sullen, but I didn't really care, I was the one out and exposed.

I said a silent apology to Tinney and then rolled him over on his other side. The sound of meaty thwacks told me that he'd soon have a matching set of bruises on his other side.

He let out a soft snore, though, so at least he was getting some rest.

I'd have to roll him over again to get to any real cover, but from there, I *might* be able to assault the machine gun nest. I edged up further and tucked my shoulder into Tinney, careful not to let any of the paint round residue touch my skin or non-body armor. The tranquilizer mostly evaporated after exposure to air, but some always stayed in the paint and Tinney had been hit by a *lot* of rounds.

I rolled him over and then crawled the last bit of distance to cover. I was just below the machine gun nest, now, and I had cover from the flanking force. If they'd rushed out to finish us off in the initial seconds, they would have taken all of us down, but they'd stayed stationary, which had given me a chance to move up at least.

"Bellmore," I said, "I'm about to rush the machine gun nest, when I do, I want you to move forward and get into their trench system. Beckman, I need you to lay down suppressive fire on the flankers."

"I'm out of position for that," Beckman protested.

"The machine gun won't be able to fire on you or Bellmore, they'll be worried about me," I snapped, "On three: one, two, three!"

I scrambled up the slope on my hands and knees and then rolled over the top, swinging my rifle around and engaging the two defenders as I rolled down onto the fighting platform. Slamming into the concrete floor drove the air out of me, but I'd managed to tag both of them before they'd realized I was in the position. "I'm in, Bellmore, what's your status?"

"I'm in, too, ma'am," he replied. "Moving to your position."

"Beckman?" I asked.

"Flankers are engaging me, I'm pinned down," she reported.

I grinned as I looked up at the stationary crew-served weapon. It was time to give them some of their own.

I hopped up on the weapon, and at least a few of the flankers seemed to know that I'd taken the position, because incoming fire thwacked into the concrete and steel around me. I didn't flinch, though, as I swung the machine gun around and then opened fire, driving a number of bursts across where the enemy positions were. I didn't try to pick out individuals in their positions. The machine gun fired big rounds, the training rounds for it hit with terrific force and I fired off the belt in five and eight round bursts, walking the fire across the enemy position until the ammunition belt was gone.

There wasn't any return fire when I let up. "Status?" I asked.

"I've got your six, ma'am," Bellmore had a respectful tone of voice.

"I'm clear, ma'am," Beckman reported. She sounded annoyed or angry. I wasn't certain which.

"Come up on my position, I'll cover you," I ordered. "Drop medical beacons on Tinney, Chu, and Reese as you come up." My heads up display had marked them as killed in action, which meant they'd be low priority for pickup and evacuation. Still, I didn't want them to have to lay unconscious in the sun all day.

Most of the enemy presence must have been concentrated between the ambush position and the forward patrol that the other teams had run into. We swept through the defensive position and then up to the next one. We cleared the other two quickly and I messaged the others of the assault force. "We've seized the bunker section, what's your status?"

"Finishing off the patrol," Ashiri reported, her voice clipped and her tone irritated. "You made it through their defense line?"

I was a bit surprised by her response, but it wasn't like I'd faced a cake-walk. "Yeah, they had a pretty good ambush position, I lost half my team, but we've secured the objective."

"Roger," Ashiri growled. "Karmazin's down, along with most of his team. Sashi hit the patrol from the flank, though and took most of them down. I secured the right flank and we took out the remainder as they fell back."

"That's it, then?" I asked. A moment later, ENDEX flashed across my helmet display. Apparently, that was it.

***

Chapter 22: It Seems Things Run Deeper Than I'd Thought

The after action for that drill was interesting. Ashiri seemed irritated and didn't want to say much. Karmazin and Sashi sat so closely together, chatting and laughing, that I figured I could guess the cause of Ashiri's irritation.

Salter had rotated out of company command, and our new Company Training Officer was hard-faced young man, DiAugustine, who I hadn't dealt with very much over the past few training exercises, and not at all earlier in the year when he'd been on Regimental Staff. "Walk me through the ambush," he said to me.

I did so, and he nodded, "Anyone have anything to add?" he asked of my team.

Tinney raised a hand. He looked like someone had beat him all over with a baseball bat and I genuinely felt bad for him. "I think there was excellent use of cover after the ambush, sir."

Everyone stared at him in disbelief and he gave a wry grin. "I get hit almost every exercise, I'm a big guy." He shrugged. "This is the first time I've been all that useful after I go down. Most of the time, people just complain about how heavy I am to get to the medics. If I get a choice in the matter, I'd like to be on Biohazard's team again."

I was shocked to hear that. Not only had he been hit multiple times, but I'd used his unconscious body as a meat shield to keep myself in action. *Besides, he's Ogre Company, his commander is really going to hate him speaking in the positive about me.*

"I'll second that," Bellmore spoke up. "I was sure we were done for, but Biohazard really pulled us out of it."

DiAugustino gave a nod, "Noted, both of you." He looked at Beckman and Chu, "Do either of you have anything to add?"

"Uh," Chu looked down, "I wasn't very careful about the position I chose. I sort of figured the defenders would be keeping their heads down or focused on the assault element. Then when the ambush triggered, I was so startled that I stopped covering fire, which gave their crew-served weapon a chance to open up on me."

"Noted," DiAugustino nodded. "And your honesty is just what I was hoping to hear. I know that none of you," he nodded at them, "are Sand Dragon, you're here as additional forces for this raid, but you all performed well." He hadn't been looking at

Beckman when he said that, but now he did. "Cadet Beckman, do you have anything to add?"

"I think Armstrong should have waited until *after* the others finished with the patrol they ran into. We would have had the advantage if we hadn't rushed into the ambush," Beckman sounded far more confident about that than she should.

DiAugustino stared at her, "Did you have information that you didn't pass along to her?"

"Sir?" Beckman didn't seem to understand.

"Was there some key bit of information that you had, something you saw or heard that led you to believe that the other three teams would successfully fight past the patrol and that the enemy ambush force wouldn't have time to put together a counter attack or fallback defensive position?"

"Well, no, sir," Beckman answered. "But Douglas, Chu, and Tinney..."

"Your team leader lost only three personnel to a complex ambush against a numerically superior foe with the benefit of a fortified position," Cadet Lieutenant DiAugustino said. "She then proceeded to counter-attack and defeat the ambush *and* take the objective while the three other raid teams were decisively engaged by the enemy's forward patrol. Under the circumstances, that's not something to criticize."

"She walked us right into the ambush!" Beckman protested.

"Did you see the ambush? Were you aware that they were there? Did you know that this section of the defenses had been reinforced for this drill exercise so they'd have the forces to conduct a defense in depth?" DiAugustino's voice was calm as he verbally dissected Beckman. As she stood there, a sullen look on her face, I saw his audience wasn't her, though. *He's already written her off.*

He was talking to the other cadets, and he made that clear as he looked around the briefing room. "Remember: *anyone* can look back at a decision and judge it with greater knowledge after the fact. Being the person on the ground, making the decisions, is the thing that matters... and sometimes, even a bad decision, made in time, is better than no decision at all."

He waved a hand at Beckman, a gesture so dismissive that Beckman's face went white. "Cadet Fourth Class Beckman, I've discussed and administrative transfer with the Company Training

Officer from Viper Company. She thinks you'll be a better fit over there. I was inclined to keep you within Sand Dragon until I've seen more of you, but after what I've seen so far, I think you are personally prejudiced against personnel within your chain of command. I don't think your performance will improve under these circumstances and, as of this moment, I've authorized the transfer. Our Company Commander has agreed with my evaluation and your orders will follow shortly. You are dismissed, Cadet Beckman."

The briefing room had gone completely silent. DiAugustino could have pulled Beckman aside at any time. He could have saved that information for after the meeting. Instead, he'd made it public. The message was clear. *You don't belong here, go away.*

No one spoke as Beckman stood up, grabbing her gear and weapon and starting for the door.

"Cadet," DiAugustino said, his voice dangerously calm, "That rifle belongs to Sand Dragon Company."

Beckman froze and for the first time, some emotion besides bitterness or anger went across her face. It was a moment of shock, followed by chagrin. She looked down at the rifle she'd carried since she was a candidate. I vividly remembered when *I* had received my rifle, in the small ceremony outside of the shrine-like armory. Each of our weapons had been carried by fallen heroes. Beckman unhooked her rifle from her armor and then, with surprising gentleness, set it down on a briefing table. Without a word, she left the room.

"Now, then," Cadet Lieutenant DiAugustino said, his gaunt face calm, "Cadet Takenata, between you and Cadet Drien, you flanked and destroyed the enemy patrol..."

I sat back as the Company Training Officer went on with the review, but I couldn't help looking at the closed door through which Beckman had left.

***

I stared at the text I'd read three times already, wondering if I was just tired or if it really said what it did.

To be sure, the use of high velocity kinetic munitions against a populated world is rarely acceptable, however given the right circumstances...

Nope, it said what I thought it had. I rubbed my eyes and set the datapad down. I'd worked my way through almost five papers now and part of me was glad the names were blanked out on the copies that Commander Bonnadonna had sent me. So far, I had a depressing feeling that half of the Fourth Class Cadets were either brain-damaged or sociopaths.

Please, tell me I didn't write drivel like this... Part of me wanted to pull up one of my old papers, but I wasn't sure I could take that right now. Instead, I skimmed through the rest of the paper, which seemed to hedge around the idea that sneak-attacking a populated planet full of enemies and bombing their cities without warning was the most humane way to fight a war.

I put that one aside and stared at the remainder of the paper titles. Most of them looked depressingly generic, the type of thing that someone threw on a paper they'd rushed and just hoped it wouldn't stand out and cause them to lose points. One of them piqued my interest, though, a paper about military families. Since I technically came from one and I'd seen Sashi struggle with it and Kyle seemed to enjoy it, it seemed like an interesting enough topic.

The introduction was fairly standard, with writing that had me fighting to keep my eyes open, especially after the intense drill exercise combined with the late night working through warp fighter attack runs, but I skimmed through that, cheating a bit with my implant to make sure I picked out the main points.

I froze, though, as I got to the paper's first example. *Lawrence Armstrong was a first-generation arrival to Century. A native of Old Earth's North America, Armstrong had served in the military, fighting in Solar Tariff Wars of 476 and 489 SP. While he emigrated as part of the initial First Wave with the intention of being a businessman and tradesman, he was called to serve in the first stand-up of the Century Colonial Militia after the pirate raid of 492 SP, where he was given the rank of Colonel of Ships. His initial command included only his personal freighter, which he took out a loan to arm.*

I read through a run-down of his actions against those pirates. There was more, but I had to sit back and stare at the ceiling for a moment.

I'd thought that my military lineage had started with my grandparents. The Admiral and the grandfather I'd never met, who'd died in the Three Day War against the Dalite Confederacy when my mother was still a young child. Most of my military history readings had focused on the United Nations Star Guard, who acted as a military hegemony over most of human space. I'd read up on the Three Day War after learning that my family rivalries went back to that. Depending on which histories you read and who the authors were, they painted the Admiral as either a hero or a reckless commander who'd put her ships and world at unnecessary risk... and those same histories painted Admiral Toshi Drien as either a coward or a clever officer who'd retained a military force in position to counterattack the enemy at a moment of weakness.

I had done a bit of reading into the Battle of Rowan III, mostly because Kyle's grandfather had fought there. But I hadn't read anything about any Armstrongs involved in that fight. Nor had I remembered reading any more about the Armstrong family name in history.

I went back to reading. *After his successes, he was promoted to Colonel-Commander of a flotilla of defense ships in the Century Colonial Militia, which was made up mostly of refitted freighters with a single pair of surplus cutters. It was this force that intercepted the Star Guard convoy bringing the Second Wave. After an initial challenge was rejected, Lawrence Armstrong's force was attacked by the Guard escorts for the convoy. While several of his ships were damaged, he drew the fire of the majority of the enemy long enough for the Century Colonial Militia force to withdraw with the only total loss being his vessel. Colonel Commander Armstrong was subsequently captured and arrested on charges of piracy and insurrection and sent to trial at Harlequin Station.*

Apparently, piracy was in the family tree, too... though I'd contest that.

Charges were upheld, despite Armstrong's justified defense being that his ships challenged the Star Guard's arrival at Century as a sovereign star system. After Armstrong's trial, he was sentenced to five years confinement. Meanwhile, the Guard force used his trial as further justification for their peacekeeping force to remain in orbit and oversee the forcible unloading of the Second Wave.

Armstrong was released after only one year of confinement, corresponding with the loss of the Star Portal and subsequent unrest throughout Guard Space. He returned with a group of refugees, sometimes referred to as the Third Wave, which included the woman who would later be his wife...

Apparently war brides were a thing back then, I noted. I skimmed over some of the suggestive details. After the new Charter, my ultimate great-grandfather had been selected to head the duly authorized Century Planetary Militia, which was very careful to stay within the official bounds of what was considered legal. *No wonder, if he'd been arrested and convicted of piracy...*

I skimmed through that, to a section that noted that he'd had four children, all of whom had followed him into the Militia. He'd missed the initial confrontations between the First and the Seconds it seemed, as well as the founding of the Century Charter, seeing as he was in prison at the time, but he had a part in standing up the Militia on his return afterward.

Lieutenant Commander Lawrence Armstrong Junior, his eldest son, was killed in action when Century's first corvette, the Independence, *suffered a drive malfunction on patrol. He'd served for ten years before his death as the commander of Century's first true warship came only two years after his father stepped down as the Militia's senior officer, replaced by Brigham Drien.*

Lawrence Armstrong was very public in his accusations, up until his death three years later, that Brigham Drien's focus on Militia ground forces had led to maintenance shortfalls aboard ship that led to the accident that killed his son.

His three other children all served full careers within the Militia. His eldest daughter was the only child to marry and have children, leading to a family tradition in which the women of the Armstrong family retained their family name after marriage...

That explained my mother's decision, then. Apparently stubbornness was hereditary.

The Armstrong family has served in every major and most minor military engagements in Century's history, but the cost to the family has been stark. Of all of the Militia's military families, the Armstrongs have borne the brunt of the wars in which they have fought. The Militia Cemetery in Duncan City has an entire row dedicated to the family, in which almost no generation has gone by without losses...

I set the datapad down, the words hitting a little too close to home as I considered it. It was the unspoken cost of what we trained for, of course. I'd come near death several times now. It wasn't something I could say that I was comfortable with, but it was something that I'd accepted. For all my happy times with Kyle, and all my nervousness about the idea of commitment, there was a not-insignificant chance that I would die in the Militia, fighting to defend my world.

I pulled up the time and sighed as I realized how late it was. I still had plenty of homework to do and it was already, technically, Sunday. I yawned and set the datapad aside. I probably shouldn't read anymore until I had some sleep and things were a bit less grim.

I looked around Sashi's desk and saw that my roommate was still at work. I fought down a sudden impulse to ask her if she'd known our family rivalries went back so far. *Probably best to let those wounds heal...*

"Still working?" I asked.

"Yeah..." Sashi looked up and blinked owlishly at me. "I hadn't realized you were still awake. Sorry, am I keeping you up?"

"Reading for an assignment," I replied. "How're things?" I realized that I really hadn't talked with her much since classes had started. Or really that much at all, outside of class and drill, for all that we shared a room. I started around the corner of the desk to take a seat next to her on the edge of her desk, since I felt too tired and aching to stand.

She waved a hand at her datapad and closed it out as I came around, her actions so quick that I couldn't help a spurt of suspicion... had she been trying to hide something from me? Maybe it was what I'd read or maybe it was that I was tired, but I couldn't shake the certainty that she'd been up to something that she didn't want me to see.

"Classes are going well," Sashi replied. "Hard, but my work load isn't quite as bad as last semester and I'm almost caught up." That felt like she was dodging my question.

Two can play at that game, I thought to myself, splitting off a fraction of my focus into my implant as I talked to her. It took only a moment to pull up the room monitor and go through the recordings. I saw that she'd been reviewing the exercise from the day. She'd been examining positions, movements, and footage from the battle.

"How are things with you and Karmazin?" I asked as

neutrally as I could, even as I examined the data she'd been reviewing. I saw right away that she'd been using her implant to do that... and that she'd been focused almost entirely on my team's actions. In fact, much of her focus had been on *me* in particular. She'd been going over every part of the fight, examining my every action in detail... and I didn't know why.

Sashi gave me a smile, but I didn't trust it, not after seeing that she'd been watching me. "Good," she replied. "Not that we have any time to do more than talk in class or passing one another in the hall. Which is rough, you know?"

Despite myself, I nodded feelingly. I had four classes with Kyle, but it seemed like we barely saw one another. We had a study session tomorrow and I had an impulse, "Kyle and I are doing the study session for Commander Pannja's next exam, would you like to join us?"

"What, me and Alex?" Sashi asked with a frown, "sure, but isn't Takenata going to be there?"

I blinked at that and then winced, "Yeah... yeah, she is."

While Ashiri's attitude had improved slightly, there was no hiding the fact that she and Sashi simply didn't get along. And while I'd like to think that Sashi and Karmazin had been a natural attraction, I couldn't help but wonder if Sashi had gone after him deliberately, as a way to hurt Ashiri. "Well, I'll talk to her, maybe it would be good to study together."

It would give me another set of eyes to watch Sashi. *It was stupid of me to trust Karmazin over this...* He wasn't thinking with his brain. I wished that Ashiri's implant was active so I could bring her into this, but maybe I could talk to her about some of my suspicions, anyway...

"Maybe..." Sashi hedged. But I knew if I invited Karmazin, then he'd go for it. He was still clueless as to why Ashiri might be angry about him dating Sashi, after all.

"Well," I said, "I'm pretty tired, I'm going to bed. Good night."

"Want me to get the lights?" Sashi asked.

"I got them," I toggled them off as I went past the door. I climbed into the top bunk and lay there, taking deep, slow breaths and letting my body relax, even as my mind raced. Sashi was using her implant and she hadn't told me. She was examining the drill from the day... why?

My first thought was that she might be trying to find a weakness, but that seemed like paranoia talking. I'd been extremely lucky in that engagement and Sashi had plenty of opportunities to stab me in the back before now... so what was her angle?

Why was she trying to figure out what I'd been doing during the drill?

I lay awake, reviewing everything she'd reviewed, wondering what it all meant, before I finally managed to fall into a troubled sleep.

***

When the nightmare came, I was expecting it.

It was the same dark, oily sea and Diamond hovered above it, though in her human form. This time, though I wasn't about to let her pull me down. "I'm not playing your games anymore," I snapped. I focused, and either because of the nature of the dream or because this was artificial, I floated up to hover in front of her.

"Of course you aren't," she hissed back at me, her hair covering her face in rain-drenched shadows. "You never play by any rules but your own, do you, *Armstrong*?" She almost spat the name, like it was a curse word. "Playing by rules is for those without the advantages."

"You're the one who's cheating, aren't you?" I asked, waving around at the dream-state world, the simulation built to hide her identity from me.

"Tell that to those whose lives you destroyed," Diamond hissed. "Like Boyles and Gnad? Or maybe Ted Meeks?"

"How dare you..." I shook my head, the cold heavy raindrops running down my face and into my eyes and mixing with the hot tears I felt welling up. "How *dare* you! Not a day goes by that I don't wish I could have prevented those deaths!"

"But you *caused* them, didn't you? Because you're arrogant, because you always have to be right, you always have to be the best! Boyles and Gnad would be fine if you hadn't gotten involved in something that was never your business!"

"You came after *me*!" I snapped. "You tried to kill me, you saw *me* as a threat, long before I even knew you existed," I threw my anger at her and in this world that anger shoved Diamond back with physical force. Her form wavered and the rain about us froze in mid-air.

"Everything is always about you, isn't it?" She growled. "We didn't want to have anything to do with you. Aisling was always the threat. She's the one who..." Her voice trailed off. "But why bother telling you? It's not like you ever listen. Not when you can stand back and judge, not when you can always be the best, always be right... not when you *never* fail, not even when you're supposed to!"

I had no idea what she meant. At this point, I really didn't care. Diamond was crazy and I couldn't trust a thing she said. I was half-convinced it was Sashi, especially with some of what she'd said, but I didn't know why she hadn't just come out. Maybe she didn't want to risk exposing herself where others could see.

"Why are we even talking?" I asked with resignation. "Why don't you just try to kill me again? Why not remove me from the picture, huh? I mean, that's what I am to you, right, nothing more than an obstacle?"

She stared at me and I wondered if she was going to try to do just that. "You really don't understand, do you? I don't want this, I don't want to fight you. I *never* did. We could be friends, if you'd just... if you'd just stop trying to be right all the time."

"I doubt it," I said tiredly. "You're clearly crazy and I'm going to do everything I can to stop you from whatever it is you have planned."

"Why... why won't you get out of my way, why don't you ever listen..." Diamond howled the words at me, but at this point, it felt like I was talking to a recording. She wasn't listening to *me*. Why should I listen to her?

"Get lost," I growled, "It's been a long day. I need to sleep." With that, I waved a hand and the entire simulated world vanished... and I slept.

***

Chapter 23: That Point At Which I Start To Doubt Myself

I wasn't able to set up a combined study session. Ashiri was busy with a different assignment and Karmazin bailed as well, since he and Andrews had some kind of group project due for one of their classes. Since Kyle didn't know about the implants, I couldn't bring him in on it and so I shelved my plan to confront Sashi.

Instead, I spent the day studying for classes and trying to figure out what Sashi/Diamond was up to. I kept coming back to the exercise footage she'd been reviewing, but I couldn't understand why. That kept me irritable all the way through Sunday and into my morning review with Commander Bonnadonna. "Miss Armstrong," he greeted me as I sat down across from his desk. He had what was the most eclectic office of all the Academy Instructors. He had actual swords mounted on the walls, and antique guns, and there was a helmet from one of Old Earth's pre-space wars on his desk.

"So, how did you enjoy the papers?" He asked.

I couldn't quite restrain a sigh, "Sir, some of them..."

"Terrible, aren't they?" His deep voice held boundless mirth over my revelation. "Don't worry, Miss Armstrong, my job as an instructor is not to get them to produce works of art, it is to get them to think about these topics."

"Original thought?" I asked, considering some of the first few papers I'd turned over to him as a Plebe.

"Original might be asking a bit much," Commander Bonnadonna leaned back in his chair, his expression cheerful. "Nothing is truly original, as they say. No, I'm looking for them to individually consider things on moral, ethical, and philosophical grounds... though the latter might be asking a bit much." He rested his hand on the antique helmet on his desk, "As I've stated before, sometimes it is the very ability to question the orders we must give that gives them some validity. To question what we do is what separates us from animals, after all..."

I wasn't sure I really agreed with that... put maybe that proved his point.

"Now then, did any papers stand out to you?"

"The one on military families, did, sir," I admitted.

"Yes, I thought that one might, after reviewing it. Did you gauge it for accuracy?" He asked me directly, as if he expected a certain answer.

"No," I admitted. "A lot of it was new to me. I hadn't ever heard of Lawrence Armstrong, not before reading the paper."

He seemed surprised by that, "You haven't researched your own past?"

"I haven't exactly had a ton of free time here at the Academy," I admitted. "I suppose my best opportunity would have been working at the Archive, but I was pretty busy there."

"You had no curiosity about your past before the Academy, then?" He shook his head in disbelief.

"I did a paper on my genealogy at one point, but that was kind of... muddled," I admitted. "I'm mostly descended from the First Wave, but my father's family is half First and half Second..." I trailed off as he stared at me.

"That's not what you meant, I take it?" I asked.

"No," Commander Bonnadonna said gently. "I'm sorry, it's something of a passion of mine, history, as you see." He waved at some of the weapons on the walls. "Military history, in particular. It's a family tradition, as well. I can track my family back to Old Earth, where several of my ancestors were military historians, while others served. Records that go back as far as the Napoleonic war."

I was fuzzy on Napoleon. I thought he came from Europe, but I wasn't certain which of Old Earth's Great Wars he'd been a part of... or whether he'd won or lost.

"Your family, which apparently you didn't realize, goes back nearly as far. The Armstrongs..." he shook his head, "Well, their names have changed but their careers have almost always centered around the military. It just surprises me that you were unaware."

"My parents like history, but military history wasn't a big aspect for them," I admitted. I thought I remembered my mother telling me I was related to some famous people on Old Earth, something about the Daughters of the Revolution or something like that, but I couldn't remember for certain.

"Well," Commander Bonnadonna said, seeming a little disappointed, "I suppose we'll go into some of the content of the other papers. What did you think of Mister Humane Genocide, as I like to think of him? The one who advocated for destruction of biospheres in surprise attacks to limit the spread of warfare?"

I snorted with laughter at his remarkably apt description and settled in for the discussion.

***

"Hello, class," a tall, gray-haired man said as he came into the classroom. Since we'd been expecting Doctor Fuesting, who'd been leading us through training on our implants, I was a bit shocked to see a man in civilian clothing. He didn't look military at all. He was tall, stoop-shouldered, and gray-haired. "I'm Doctor Schoeffelk, I'll be taking over your classes on neural implants."

He looked around and gave us all a friendly smile, but I felt nervous. I wasn't sure why he was here or who had sent him. Somehow I knew this had to do with the Quicksilver project. I just didn't know if he was here on Charterer Beckman's behalf or if he'd been assigned by the Admiral.

"Now, then, I'll also be conducting neural plant installation on all cadets going forward, as well as doing periodic check-ups. My previous assignment was head of Century Medical's neurosurgeon department, and I just finished a stint at the children's wing, where I was installing implants designed to heal children who've suffered brain injuries, generally through the use of implants designed to augment or stimulate or bypass those damaged parts of the brain." His smile was gentle and friendly in a way that I just couldn't shake. "I'm excited to be joining the Academy staff and working with all of you over the next few months and hopefully years."

He waited looking around, "I must say, I'm used to rather more questions in the civilian field. However, moving forward, I'm canceling these large-scale classes and I'm going to one-on-one assessments with all cadets who've received implants. We'll try to get you the full use of your implants as well as make sure that your installed implants are functioning correctly and that there aren't any issues with installation." He made a face, "I've been reading up on Doctor Aisling and I can't say I'm terribly impressed with her teaching and coaching methods, so I promise you there will be a lot of changes moving forward. My goal is to get all of you comfortable with your implants and healthy in the long-term."

"Now, I know everyone's schedules are very busy, so I've scheduled the first three sessions during class today, and I'll get to the rest of you over the week. After that, we'll shift to bi-weekly sessions and by the end of this semester, I want all of you thoroughly comfortable with where you're at. If Cadet's Armstrong, Karmazin, and Drien would remain behind, I'll see you three first. The rest of you are dismissed."

I jumped a bit as he said my name. I wasn't looking forward to this and I found myself crouching a bit in my chair, my muscles going tense. His selection of us three eliminated any doubt at all that this was entirely above-board. This was about the special implants we had... and he knew exactly which three of us had active implants.

The class filed out. Kyle gave me a worried look as he left, and I could tell that he'd realized from my reaction that something was wrong, but he didn't know what. How could he, when I couldn't tell him. The thought burned like acid in my brain. I was tired of looking over my shoulder, tired of secrets, tired of lies... both the ones people had told me and the ones I had to uphold.

As the doors shut, Doctor Schoeffelk looked at the three of us, seated near the front. "Now," he said, "I'm certain that none of you require me to explain that I'm aware of the full range of Doctor Aisling's research. I'm here because I was invited by Admiral Armstrong to review Doctor Aisling's notes and research, or at least, what is available... and to run a complete neuro-physical on all of you, everyone she operated on, as well as the Cadet who refused the procedure."

I jumped a bit at that. I'd forgotten about the one cadet who'd walked out, rather than volunteering. His gentle smile faded into something more serious. "I tell you this ahead of time. I think the decision by Doctor Aisling and those who authorized her, to conduct these experiments on young people is inexcusable. What I've read of her methods and her ideas are extremely risky. That said, I *do* have some good news for the three of you in that I was the primary physician for Boyles and Gnad. I was able to restore their minds, bypassing some of the trauma they received, without having to resort to a mind-wipe or mental conditioning. I feel confident that both of them will make a full recovery and, from talking with them, they both want to return to the Academy and I've helped them both receive clean bills of health to accomplish that."

I gasped in surprise and relief at that. Every bit of information I'd heard about the two of them before they'd left was that they'd been effectively brain-dead, with zero brain activity. *If he could save them, then maybe he can help us.*

"Until now, this project operated under very tight secrecy and Doctor Aisling shared little, if any information with you. I am not Doctor Aisling. Nor am I a military doctor. You are not my test subjects, you are my patients, and your safety and health is far more important to me than any short-term benefits your implants provide you. I'm going to be doing a full gamut of testing on you three, since your implants are active. Some of those tests will be *very* invasive. Some will probably be painful. My goal, however, is your long-term mental and neurological health."

Despite my fears, the doctor's blunt honesty was winning me over. "Now, up front, there's two more bits of information that I've been able to ascertain from Doctor Aisling's data readings, which is the only set of information that they've been able to decode as of yet. The first is that her initial Sensory and Cerebral Interface Mapping was used to identify viable and safe subjects for her full cerebral integration, the implants that you all have. We've matched only three subjects as being viable in that initial round of testing... you are those three."

Some things began to make a lot more sense, such as why the three of us still had functioning implants. "From that point on, she modified her viability pool, adjusting the parameters to get a larger pool of test subjects. I also believe that in her second and third rounds of testing and calibration that she attempted to modify the brain function of all of her subjects. This could be as simple as making your minds more receptive to integration with the implants... or it could have some very dangerous implications. I don't know yet, but I do know that the three of you were the least altered. Cadet Armstrong, in fact, reacted in an unpredicted fashion while Cadet Karmazin and Cadet Drien," he nodded at them, "shifted your neural activity outside of her desired parameters."

I remembered that session, thinking back. I remembered that the Admiral had come looking for us, since I'd been in the system for hours. I remembered the puzzle that Aisling had wanted me to solve, a puzzle that had only one solution... until I'd forced a new one.

"The other data point I uncovered was that her initial round of testing and several of her subsequent ones, involved several failures. Cadets who suffered neurological issues: micro seizures, memory or personality breaks, and in at least one case, a full mental collapse. The proper response would have been to conduct a full rehabilitative effort on each of those cadets. Instead, it appears that she wiped the affected portions of the brain and overwrote them, sort of like a band aid or writing over a bit of corrupted data on a computer."

That didn't sound good. In fact, it terrified me to consider that she'd had that capability and the willingness to use it.

Doctor Schoeffelk nodded somberly at us as we saw the implications. "There were at least five such events, including one during the actual implantation procedure. I think those events were restricted to no more than three of her subjects, but I only have the data readings that indicated that she did this, I don't have sufficient data to identify the Cadets she did it to, or at least not all of them. I *did* confirm that Boyles was one of them, based upon neurological damage that matched some of those readings."

"Diamond, Metal Man, and Inkblot," Karmazin said softly.

"Possibly. Judging on some of the... modifications to Boyles, I would guess that she used external neurological patterns to overwrite damaged sections of the brain. Some of those *could* be from the gestalt she created based upon all of you, but it could be from other test subjects or even herself."

"Wait..." Sashi Drien stared at him in horror, "you're saying that Aisling wrote parts of herself into our heads?"

"I don't *think* you three are in that category," he cautioned. "But the three who seemed to have the most issues? I suspect that may be the case. The gestalt patterns in Boyles' implant was different from the neurological pattern in Gnad. Those differences could be answered by the use of another person for the neurological pattern."

"So, your neural patterns both with the implants active and without will be one of the things I'll be studying on you three as well as my other patients here," Doctor Schoeffelk finished.

I was even more horrified than the others, because I knew the truth. Aisling wasn't even human. She was an alien, masquerading as human. Who knew what kind of horrid things she'd put in our heads?

"Now then," he said, "I'd like to get started with the first series of tests..."

***

"You need to get me out of here."

I knew I was asleep and this must be a dream. Yet it didn't feel like a dream, or like my encounters with Diamond. It wasn't dark so much as absent of light. Nothing had form, and yet I could hear, the words, like I was somehow between the people talking... or they were talking *through* me, somehow.

"I'm doing what I can."

I recognized the first voice, it was Doctor Aisling, her lilting accent carrying obvious irritation. What surprised me was that I also recognized the second voice, thought it took me a while.

"Armstrong keeps blocking me," Charterer Beckman explained. Somehow I knew she was talking about the Admiral, and not me or my parents. "And her precious little granddaughter," she snarled, "is acting as her spy on the Academy grounds. My eyes there report that she's in Armstrong's offices almost every week. Neither of them are aware of the full extent of our agreement, but if I push too hard, too fast, I'll tip my hand. Please, give me time to work on my allies. We can salvage this situation."

"We are coming dangerously close to me rescinding our initial agreement," Aisling growled.

"I'm doing everything I can!" Charterer Beckman protested. "I have the advantages, it's just going to take time!" The pleading note in her voice made me shudder. This was one of the most powerful people on my planet. I'd seen her arrogance before... and here she was, sounding almost like she was begging.

"Several of my people died attempting to get me out of here already, and their lives will be added to the cost," Aisling said.

"I'm sorry," Charterer Beckman's voice was almost frantic. "If I had known about their attempt, I would have helped--"

"We were not certain that you were still willing to uphold your end of the bargain," Aisling said. "But if you are, then I need a show of good faith."

"I arranged to get this link to you--"

"A communications link that goes only to you, one which is designed to self-destruct if I attempt to modify it. Hardly a show of good faith... more a sign of either desperation or an attempt to gain my favor only to betray me." Aisling's voice had gone cold and hard. "No. I need something more, Charterer, something that you cannot discard so easily."

What I was overhearing, if it was real, sounded an awful lot like treason. Yet I didn't know *how* I could be hearing it. *This must be a dream.*

"I want what is owed to me. Have it delivered to my people," Aisling said. "At the normal location."

"But, how would you know..."

"I will know," Aisling's voice practically purred. "In the same way that my people found me. You will have it done and I will know. And then, as promised, I will continue our work."

"You'll wait for me to get you out?" Beckman asked, her voice breathless.

"I will. And, when you do, I will complete your project, as desired. You will have the tools you need and I will have the ones that I desire," Aisling's voice was soft, but there was something terrifying about it, like a dread, malignant, confidence. *She's keeping her end, but only to the letter, not to the spirit of whatever agreement they had...*

Aisling was a snake, I'd already figured that out. She didn't care about people, she didn't really care that her people had died trying to get her out and she saw humans as little more than pawns.

"Thank you," Beckman's voice was filled with relief. Whatever she thought to get out of this agreement, it was important.

There was a feeling of disconnection and then, somehow, I knew the conversation was over. *What is going on?* I didn't have voice to speak aloud in this place.

A form appeared. It was a fleeting, temporary thing... and I realized in shock that it was me. There and gone, just my face, my blue eyes glowing. Then it was gone.

I woke up gasping, in the darkness before morning. I could hear Sashi's soft breathing on the bunk below me. What I'd heard, what I'd seen, had been so vivid, yet so odd. I didn't see *how* I had heard it. But I somehow felt it was real.

I didn't see how to tell the Admiral, though. I hadn't been able to record the conversation, not in that strange limbo. I tried to bring up the memory of it, to see if there was any way to do that, but as vivid as it felt to me, it didn't seem to translate over, it was like pulling at cobwebs, they only came apart as I tried to make them into something substantial for my implant.

That was no use, and it seemed like Beckman had the Admiral under observation. I had no doubt that her niece was a part of that, but there might be others. The Admiral didn't seem confident in speaking freely even in her own offices about some things, such as Directorate Thirteen.

That meant I couldn't take this to her. I might try to tell Doctor Schoeffelk, but I wasn't sure that I trusted him fully, yet. And besides, this was all so surreal, even compared to some of my other dreams. The last part, where my face had materialized, truly unnerved me. I didn't understand it... and that made me even more nervous.

That presence, which had somehow enabled me to overhear it, had some tie to me... and I didn't know what it was.

***

"Something big happened a few nights ago," Karmazin said to me as he sat down at the table across from me. I hadn't slept well over the past few weeks, my worries and concerns all catching up to me and keeping me awake at night. When I did sleep, all too often I had more dreams like the last odd one. I overheard bits of conversation or sometimes sections of text. Some of it didn't make any sense, but one of them were between Charterer Beckman and her niece, with a detailed schedule of my daily activities and far more information about Kyle than I really liked. I'd had nightmares about something terrible happening to him for almost a week after that one.

I looked around the chow hall. It was late on Saturday, most of the cadets had gone out on pass to Bahta Town. I hadn't felt up to it and Kyle was too busy for that anyway. We'd finished our last set of major drills before the finals week. "What do you mean?" I asked.

Sashi sat down her tray next to him and I couldn't help but adopt a guarded expression.

We'd gone a few more weeks of classes and my concerns about Sashi had only grown. Her ranking had gone to number one. Karmazin was right behind her. Ashiri was third, and I was fourth. I didn't even care about my ranking, not right now. Part of me had started to see classes and drills as obstacles, just things to overcome as I tried to figure out what Doctor Aisling's plan was, who Diamond was, and how this all tied in to Charterer Beckman.

Sashi was still my number one suspect for Diamond. A full month of Doctor Schoeffelk's testing hadn't revealed any other cadets with active implants. By default, that meant it had to be one of us, and I was pretty certain it wasn't me. *Mostly certain.* The voice in the back of my head reminded me about the misty vision from my dream, and how Diamond had taunted me with my own image before.

"I've been seeing some increased message traffic on the network, especially late at night," Sashi said, her voice level. "Some of it seems to be from the outside, I'm not sure what that's about," she noted, "but some is on the inside. Someone, or *several* someones, has been very active, all the signs of someone with one of our... advantages." She didn't specify our implants, but we weren't exactly in a secure place to talk.

"You've been monitoring the network?" I asked in surprise.

Sashi nodded, her dark eyes bored into me, as if she were trying to read my mind. I kept control over my expression as much as I could. I didn't know how this tied into my dreams, but I had a pretty good idea that I'd been one of the causes of that increased traffic. But I couldn't exactly come clean on that, not when I thought Sashi was Diamond.

I hate this. I wanted to trust Karmazin's judgement. I mean, they were *dating*. I tried to imagine deceiving Kyle, the way Sashi had to be deceiving Karmazin... and I just couldn't. I couldn't even consider it, not pretending to be close to someone while manipulating them. *She did it to you before*, I reminded myself.

"I've been able to plot some of the activity," Sashi nodded. "There's a lot of it centered on our barracks area."

"Well, the three of us are in Sand Dragon," I noted. "That could distort things."

"Some of it, yeah," Karmazin said. "But I haven't been using my full capabilities for classes, well, not besides our sessions with Doctor Schoeffelk. Neither has Sashi." She nodded at that. I bit back a snort of disbelief. Sashi's grades and performance had shot up. There'd been an increase the last semester and that improvement hadn't stopped. I didn't say anything, though. Not yet.

"Neither have I," I answered the unspoken question. I couldn't help a sigh, "I *wish* I could, sometimes. It would make things so much easier. But I have avoided using my full... capabilities on anything we're graded on." I shrugged, "Not only to keep down on the noise, but also because it doesn't seem right."

"Yeah," Sashi nodded, her voice small, "I thought about it a couple times, God knows, my work load has been high, but seeing how hard everyone else is working, it doesn't seem right." Those words almost convinced me. Her attitude exactly mirrored how I felt, yet I told myself that it had to be an act. There was no other explanation. *Either she's lying and she's Diamond... or I am.* I banished that thought.

"Anyway, a lot of it is concentrated around drill events and classes. A *lot*," Karmazin transferred me the information and I read through it. I wish I knew how to whistle in appreciation. It looked like both of them had done a *lot* of work putting this all together as a sort of map. "Have you shown this to Schoeffelk or Commander Weisfeldt?"

They stared at me, "Schoeffelk, I could see, but what would Commander Weisfeldt have to do with this?" Sashi asked the question intently.

"Um," I blinked at them. "He was involved in the implant design, right?" I asked lamely. I couldn't talk to them about Directorate Thirteen. There were too many secrets and I was just too tired to keep them all separate. I wished I could talk to someone about all of it. Kyle came to mind, but I couldn't tell Kyle about any of it.

"I guess, but I don't think he's involved in this anymore," Karmazin frowned. "At least, Doctor Schoeffelk hasn't mentioned talking to him."

I'd actually overheard a conversation between the Doctor and Commander Weisfeldt in one of my dreams, where they'd been in one of Directorate Thirteen's labs, talking about how the implants functioned. So I knew they were working together. But again, I couldn't say anything. *Too many secrets...*

"Well, maybe you're right," I shrugged, looking down at my food and scraping at it with a fork. I hadn't really eaten much. I hadn't been eating enough in general. I dropped my fork on the plate and pushed my tray to the side. "Anyway, so these increases in the classes and drills, have you localized them?"

"Some, they correspond in a few points, but they're all where there's three or more suspect cadets in one place," Sashi replied. I looked at the data and saw she was right. In fact, most often it happened when all three of us were present. The couple times it didn't, Sashi and I were always there. The biggest spike had been today's drill.

"There's a lot of correlations," I noted, "but there's no way to isolate it, there's no one person that it centers on. There's not even *two.*" That was my big concern. Diamond hadn't been alone. There had also been Metal Man... and if Sashi was Diamond, then Alexander Karmazin might well be Metal Man.

If that was the case, then I didn't see a way to win.

"We had an idea," Karmazin said with a glance at Sashi, "what if Diamond has been triggering others? What if she activates her implant and accesses the network *through* them, maybe even as a time-delayed thing?"

"You're saying she's running some kind of deception operation?" I asked sitting back as I tried to force my tired mind to process it. The technical implications made my head hurt, a bit, but based off of our simulated worlds we created between our implant networks... it might be possible. I nodded slowly as I considered it. "Geez. That's... that's *devious.*"

The two of them stared at me, almost as if expecting something more. I looked back at them, blinking tiredly. "Have you thought of some way to track it? Maybe we can tie into this somehow, figure out how she's doing it?"

Karmazin gave Sashi an odd look. Sashi nodded slowly, but her expression shifted slightly as if she hadn't heard what she wanted to hear. *Some kind of test on her part, maybe, to see how much I know or suspect?*

"We could," Sashi said. "I have an idea about that. Maybe we can meet early in the morning, tomorrow, someplace... out of view?"

I looked around the chow hall, picking out the ever-present monitors. I understood the idea of being cautious, yet I was getting tired of the layers of secrets. I was almost certain Sashi was Diamond, and I figured she knew that. Part of me wanted to just confront her here, but I wasn't ready. *Tomorrow.*

"Sure," I said. I nodded at Karmazin, "Remember where we first met up and talked?" That section of corridor wasn't frequently traveled and it had fewer monitors. It was also close by to the Admin section and Directorate Thirteen, so after I got Sashi to reveal herself, I could get her someplace secure and figure out what Diamond's endgame was.

Karmazin nodded in response. He seemed uncertain and I wished I could trust his judgement and him enough to tell him everything I suspected. Yet there was a chance, too large of one, that he was Metal Man.

I gave them both nods, then and picked up my tray, "Well, then, I'll see you in the morning, zero six, sharp."

I cleared my tray and dropped off my plate and silverware at the chow hall kitchen and then went back towards the barracks. I felt as if a weight had been lifted off my chest, like I could finally breathe. I was done with hiding in shadows and looking over my shoulder. One way or another, I'd reveal Diamond's identity. Even if it wasn't Sashi, then at least I'd eliminate her as a suspect. Karmazin, too, and we could actually move forward. Maybe I could get the Admiral to bring them both in on Directorate Thirteen.

I looked at my list of homework assignments left to do and then at the time. I decided that I'd done enough for the Academy for the day. I crawled up into my bed and I went to sleep early. It was glorious.

***

I met Diamond for what I somehow knew would be the last time under the rain and wind-swept skies of her dream-state world. She was staring at the sky, her back to me. "I miss how it's never dark here. I miss the rain."

The cold rain drops and the oppressive waves left me on edge. I looked to the sky, noticing for the first time that there were multiple stars shining through the ragged gaps in the clouds. *How odd.* "Why are you here?"

"I know this is a trap, you know this is a trap, why are you so determined to go into it?" Diamond's voice was tired. There was an edge of exhaustion to her, almost as if she were as tired as I felt.

"I want an end to this," I said. "I will reveal you. Then we'll hook you up to Doctor Schoeffelk's machines and we'll fix whatever is wrong with you."

"You know who I am, already," she said tiredly. "Even if

you don't see it. This isn't about what Aisling made me, this is about *you*. You always have to be right. You always have to be the best... you can't let me win, just *once*."

"You're doing better than me on rankings, don't think I haven't noticed," I growled.

"Is that why you're coming after me, because I'm doing better than you?" Diamond hissed angrily. "You don't even understand the pressures I'm under. You don't know how hard I've worked and how much I have to prove."

I stared at her, thinking of Sashi's family, feeling vindicated to know that I'd guessed right. "Just because you have things to prove, it doesn't justify doing things the wrong way."

She spun, her dark hair dropping in a curtain over her face. "Really?! You have hounded me from the beginning. I have *always* supported you, Armstrong. I have *always* been there, and not once did you even think of what it cost me. I'm doing this for *me*, but I'm also doing it for others. You don't understand that. You *can't* understand that, because everything always comes back to you... you and your blasted Armstrong sense of duty and honor."

I recoiled from the venom in her voice. Her words burned me like acid the simulated world seemed to shudder under her anger.

I stood straight, though, in the face of that anger. "You have hurt people. You tried to kill me. You've used your abilities to get ahead, you've *cheated*."

"The honor code, yes..." Diamond's head drooped, "I took the advantages I was given. But we all did, at first. Your new-found morality about it doesn't change the fact that we were given tools and if we don't use them, then why have them in the first place? I've given up *so* much... gone through so many terrible things... I just want this *one* thing, to accomplish this for myself and my family, Jiden." She said my name almost gently. "Please. Don't do this, tomorrow. Don't force my hand."

"I'll see you there," I said and waved my hand to end the link between us.

***

Chapter 24: I Really Should Have Seen This Coming

The lowest levels of the Academy all pretty much stayed the same temperature, mostly due to their depth. It was slightly chilly, just enough so that I rubbed my bare forearms as I stood in the empty section of corridor. I'd slept deeply, after my last confrontation with Diamond. I'd woken up early, feeling refreshed, and left the room and Sashi sleeping to go make preparations for this confrontation.

I'd met with Commander Weisfeldt, meeting him at Directorate Thirteen in the early morning shift that I knew he worked and getting what I needed from him, with a request that he and Doctor Schoeffelk would be ready.

I paced back and forth a bit, feeling the heavy weight of the pistol tucked into a concealed holster in my belt. It felt awkward, but it was my insurance policy, just in case I had misjudged Karmazin. The training rounds should be enough to stun both of them if it came to it.

I heard footsteps down the corridor and I turned, taking a deep breath and letting it out slowly. I felt nervous, but I also felt relief. This was going to be over, soon, and maybe I could get on with my life.

Karmazin and Sashi came around the curve and walked towards me. They both wore slung rifles and my heart started to beat fast as I saw the alert looks on their faces. "Jiden," Karmazin nodded as he came up.

"Uh," I looked between them, wondering if I was really in trouble. "Guys... what's with the weapons?"

They looked at each other and then, in unison, they brought their weapons up, aimed squarely at me. "Sorry about this Jiden, but it's over."

"Well," I said, raising my hands slowly, not daring to go for the concealed pistol at my waist, "that's really unfortunate."

***

"So you decided to do it this way, did you?" I asked of Sashi. "So, what's your plan, kill me? Don't you think that there will be a few questions asked when someone finds the body?" Since I'd told Commander Weisfeldt who I'd be meeting and why, there'd be more than a few questions asked. Still, I'd rather be alive and around to help with answering those questions.

"We know that you are Diamond," Karmazin said calmly. He might as well have said that he liked eating crayons.

I blinked at him, "I'm sorry, what?"

"The data points, they almost all directly correspond to you," Sashi said. "It's the only explanation. If you cancel out the noise that someone could generate from remotely activating implants, then you have to be Diamond. Or else you're using your implant to cheat."

"You're crazy," the words came out of my mouth on their own volition. I looked at Karmazin, "And you... don't you realize that *she* is Diamond?" My hands dropped a bit and I almost thought about going for my pistol, but they both tensed and I had no doubt they'd shoot me.

"The data doesn't correspond," Karmazin said, his voice implacable. "She hasn't been present at a majority of the network events. Plus, she's taking make-up classes, where there have been *no* events. Even if she were triggering other implants, it doesn't make sense."

"Her ranking has shot up like a rocket," I hissed in frustration. "You don't think she's using her implant, not even a little bit?"

I saw Sashi's face darken and her finger dropped down onto her trigger. Alexander reached out his free hand and put it on her shoulder, "I know she hasn't been, I've watched her working. I've been listening to her, day in and day out. She's doing things right, Jiden."

I rolled my eyes, "Look, you two can drop the act. She's got to be Diamond, which means you're Metal Man."

Karmazin's eyebrows shot up and he returned his hand to his rifle. "Sorry, what?"

"There's no way you'd be stupid enough to believe her if she's Diamond, so that means you're Metal Man and she's Diamond," I said bitterly. "So you two can stop toying with me. I suspected it, from the first, but I didn't want to believe it."

I had my implant recording all this and transmitting it to Directorate Thirteen. The problem was, I doubted they could get to me before these two killed me. I closed my eyes. This really wasn't how I'd wanted to die. Alexander had been my friend. Sashi had almost become a friend. "I just have to ask, why? Why did you guys try to kill me? Why try to earn my trust after I stopped you before? I mean, what's your end game? What does this have to do with Aisling?"

They stared at me and then looked at each other. "You don't think..."

"Got to be a trick," Karmazin muttered.

I didn't understand. As far as they knew, they had me dead to rights. The least they could do was drop the act.

"Maybe she really doesn't know," Sashi lowered her weapon slightly. She stared at me, "Jiden. There's always been a chance that the implant has been the culprit, that Aisling put something in the programming or did something to our minds to let it take over. Have you been experiencing any black-outs, any strange dreams?"

I stared at her and I felt my stomach clench. *No.*

I felt all the blood drain out of my face as I realized that she and Karmazin genuinely believed that I was Diamond. This wasn't an act. They weren't going to try and kill me. They didn't want to hurt me. "No," I shook my head stubbornly, "You have to be Diamond, it's the only thing that makes sense."

"Maybe the implant has been triggering others remotely," Alexander said softly, "Maybe there's something wrong with your gestalt, maybe Diamond *is* your gestalt, only it takes you over sometimes."

"No," I protested, "Diamond tried to kill me. I had that dream and then someone sabotaged my skimmer!"

"You came out of that alive," Sashi said, her voice taking on almost a pleading tone. "And your skimmer black box differed from your implant readings. The investigators ruled it was an equipment malfunction... but it could have been that you sabotaged yourself and ejected. That way no one, especially not you, would suspect *you.*"

That made a twisted amount of sense, but I shook my head, "No, if I could covertly be controlled by my implant, why couldn't either of you?"

"We've been watching each other," Sashi replied instantly.

"We've been, uh, very close, a lot of the time. And I know I'm clear because none of the data points correspond to when I was in the Grinder by myself." Karmazin added.

"The Admiral didn't have data on that," I objected.

"We... cheated a bit," Sashi admitted. "We hacked their database and took that information."

I could have gotten it for them, but I didn't say that. "The other thing, we saw that you were using your implant a lot during the summer session. Plus there was a huge spike in connectivity around the time of the power surge, the one that killed twenty-three people."

"Wait, what?" I asked in surprise.

"You had no reason to be there. You were on a dead-end summer assignment... I mean, you were working in the *Archive*." Sashi shook her head. "That could have been enough to torpedo your ranking. Then there's this big explosion, and you happened to be close by? And you got an award a few weeks later, the contents of which are sealed. You think that's all coincidence? Jiden, you have to face the truth, especially on that one. People died, Jiden. I didn't want to consider it, but that alone is a big, nasty pill to swallow."

I stared at them both. "That's not what happened." I felt a bit relieved that their main point of evidence was something I could easily disprove. I actually found myself smiling in relief.

My smile clearly unnerved them and I saw them tense. My smile vanished as I saw just how deadly serious this was.

Sashi spoke, her voice hard, "You may not realize it, but if Diamond is part of you, maybe part of your subconscious, she could have arranged all of it. Your summer assignment, to throw off any suspicion, your presence on that engineering team, the power surge and the coupling exploding..."

I shook my head, "Look, now you two are just getting paranoid. What happened that day is very well documented and it's not at all what you think!"

"She's in denial," Karmazin said. "We should do this and be done with it."

Oh my god, I thought, *I'm going to be murdered by my friends because they think I'm a psycho...*

I'd been so focused on them that I barely caught motion behind them. My eyes widened a bit as I saw someone step out of the shadows behind them, though.

Both of them tensed as they saw my expression. But they hesitated, clearly not certain if it was a trick or not.

In that moment of hesitation, Ashiri walked out of the shadows behind them and fired training rounds into their backs. Three in each, her shots quick and precise. As Alexander Karmazin staggered a bit, not quite going down, she adjusted her aim and hit him twice more in the back of the neck, just above his body armor.

He dropped limply to the floor next to Sashi. "Hello, Jiden," Ashiri said calmly. She looked at the two prone figures for a moment, "we should be going."

"Uh," I looked at her in confusion, "not that I'm not grateful and all, but what the hell?!"

"We should go, someone will have heard the shots," Ashiri gestured with her weapon and I realized that it wasn't, quite, a request. I realized that the weapon which had taken out my two friends was now aimed, more or less, at me.

"Ashiri?" I asked, starting to back up.

"Keep your hands where I can see them, Jiden. I'm not sure where all you went this morning, you dodged the monitors fairly well, but I'm sure you had some kind of plan for all of this," Ashiri said as she stepped over the unconscious forms of Alexander and Sashi. "That's part of why I'm jamming your implant right now."

"You're, *what*?" I asked in surprise. I reached out and sure enough, all I got was static.

"I'm doing this for your own good, Jiden," Ashiri said. She gestured at me to turn around. "Let's go. Don't worry, it's not far."

We went down the corridor and I felt my stomach sink. "Wait, Ashiri, you..."

"I'm Diamond," she answered. "Which you would have known if you weren't so focused on your stupid family's drama. I mean, granted, I didn't trust Drien and I'm a little proud of you for thinking it was her, but you have some serious blind-spots."

"You..." I shook my head. "But, your implant..."

"Has been inactive, every time we get scanned. I've run tight beams and uploaded data files to the network remotely. I've kept myself hidden and I've flown under the radar. And yes, I've used every advantage I could whenever I had the opportunity. I have to finish first in our class, Jiden. I have to do it for my family, to prove to my mother that it's possible. To open up things so that maybe my brother can come here..."

"So you tried to kill me?" I asked in shock, looking back

over my shoulder at her. I saw that she'd lowered her rifle a bit, but I still didn't see an opportunity to go for my concealed pistol...

"Use your brain," she growled. We stopped at the end of the corridor, near the stairs. Somehow, I knew that she was jamming the monitor.

Andrews stepped out of the stairwell, "It's clear." *Metal Man,* I realized.

"What are we doing now?" I asked.

The two of them moved close together and Ashiri started to talk in a low voice to Alexander. He leaned in close to hear her and for just a moment, their attention wasn't entirely on me and in that fraction of a second my hands dropped to my waist.

I drew my pistol as they both swung towards me. Andrews' rifle came up and I knew that I wasn't going to get my pistol up before he fired.

"No!" Ashiri shouted, dropping her own rifle and batting his barrel aside, just as he fired. The sharp thunder of real bullets being fired and the malignant whine of them flying past me told me how close I'd come to dying. I didn't hesitate. I centered my pistol on Andrews and fired, then shifted to Ashiri who had a look of resignation as I centered the sights on her.

"I'm sorry," I said, and then I shot her.

***

Chapter 25: I Really Need To Be Careful About What I Kind Of Answers I Try To Learn

I stood outside of the Directorate Thirteen cell block, staring into the cells that contained Ashiri Takenata and Morgan Andrews. I felt empty. I had never really suspected her. I didn't really care about Andrews. But the betrayal by Ashiri cut me deeply. *She tried to kill me...*

She was responsible for the damage to Boyles and Gnad. She and Andrews had gone rampant across the school networks, doing who knew what. She'd cheated, using her implant to manipulate the ranking, to score better on tests, and who knew what else.

All of that, though, paled in consideration of one fact. She'd tried to kill me. I had thought of her as my best friend and she'd seen me as nothing more than an obstacle.

What is wrong with me? Did I simply attract people who would use me? Did I have some kind of sign that warned sociopaths to take advantage of me? First there had been Tony Champion, then there'd been Sashi Drien, then Commander Scarpitti... and now Ashiri. Somehow I felt that it had to be my fault. At what point was it a pattern of my own failures?

"Very interesting," Commander Weisfeldt said, his bushy eyebrows rising in surprise as he read his datapad. "Now that they're unconscious, I'm getting accurate readings on their implants. Not at all what I expected."

"You are right, Art," Doctor Schoeffelk nodded, "I mean, look at this! The implants, they're practically alive, sending traffic both ways. Very different from what we saw in the other cadets. In Armstrong, or Karmazin, or Drien, their implants are integrated, amazingly so... but in these... I mean, look at *where* they're tied in."

"I can't look at that screen or I'll lose my lunch," Commander Weisfeldt waved a hand. "It's all brains and tissue and..." He shuddered. I looked over the screen, but I didn't see any differences.

Doctor Schoeffelk looked at me, "They're tied into different regions of the brain, regions that wouldn't make any sense for their stated purpose. I saw *some* of this with Boyles, but nothing to this extent and certainly not enough for me to draw full conclusions."

"You amuse me," Doctor Aisling said from behind us.

We all turned. I'd forgotten about her and I repressed a shiver as I realized that she'd been watching us all, silently appraising us. I looked over at the two guards who stood by, their faces hidden behind their armor and visors. Their presence reassured me somewhat.

"Care to explain?" Doctor Schoeffelk went on, his normally gentle voice now cold with anger.

"Oh, no, this is far too entertaining," Doctor Aisling smiled. Her toothy grin seemed to have too many teeth and this time I *did* shiver.

"I'm glad that our efforts are accomplishing something," Commander Weisfeldt said. "But I'm more than a little angry that my efforts on designing these implants have been corrupted for your purposes, whatever they are." I glanced at him and he said in a low voice, "This is the first time she's spoken, I hope to get something out of her."

"Oh, you have no idea, little man, no idea at all," Aisling's grin stretched wider, in an inhuman fashion that just looked *wrong*. "But do continue, your pitiful attempts to understand my art are most fascinating." She went back and sat on her cell's cot, going cross-legged and her arms relaxed to either side. Her green eyes twinkled with inhuman mirth. Somehow I suspected that she'd smile that same way if she was covered in human blood, dissecting our brains for her own amusement.

Not dissecting, child, vivisecting. I heard her voice in my head, broadcast straight to my implant. I jumped and looked around, but no one else seemed to have heard. The fact that she'd heard *my* thought terrified me.

I pulled Commander Weisfeldt away and explained what had happened, even as Doctor Schoeffelk went back to his study of Ashiri and Andrews.

"Interesting. I'm not sure if it's an element of the implant or her abilities," he murmured.

"The whole erandi telepathy thing you mentioned?" I asked.

"Maybe," he looked uncomfortable. "Look, we haven't, uh, exactly identified what she is… not yet."

"What do you mean, sir? You've had her down here for almost twelve *months*. You've run tests, right?" It came out as more of a demand than a question, but I didn't care at this point. Aisling terrified me and somehow the realization that even Directorate Thirteen didn't know what she was left me even more afraid.

"He means," the Admiral said as she stepped inside, "that we are not yet certain exactly what she is, in part because she's been very heavily modified to look human, but in part because she's also undergone additional extensive modifications to her physiology."

Aisling shrugged, "We all have our hobbies."

It shouldn't have surprised me that she'd overheard our conversation. I looked at the Admiral and my eyes widened a bit as I saw Sashi and Alexander behind her.

"Uh, hey guys," I said sheepishly.

They looked around, their eyes wide, "Jiden, what is this place?"

"We can do explanations later," the Admiral said. She walked over to the cells that contained Ashiri and Andrews. "Doctor, do you have any answers for me?"

"I have lots of additional questions, but it seems that one of my patients is waking up, so perhaps we can ask her," he replied gesturing at Ashiri.

My friend sighed and sat up. Her head went in her hands. "I forgot how much getting tranked hurt, especially when you don't get the antidote."

"Sorry about the headache." I'd shot her in the head, so she already had a massive bruise across her forehead and I knew at least part of her headache would be from that. I watched as she felt at the purple bruise and winced.

"So," the Admiral said. "Now that we have all the interested parties, I think it is time for explanations."

"Why bother?" Ashiri said in a resigned tone. She gestured at me, "Whatever she says is what you'll believe."

"I like to think I'm a bit more objective than that," the Admiral said. "Let's start with what you know of Doctor Aisling and what she did?"

My friend's face went stiff. She glared through the armored glass of her cell across at Doctor Aisling. "She's a monster. I learned that from my gestalt. She wasn't satisfied with things, so she tweaked them. She took bits and pieces from other people, some of them were victims from her previous experiments, and she put them together to make our minds more suitable."

"You know this, how?" the Admiral asked.

"Because I rushed things a bit and some of those neural patterns carried more than methods of thought, they carried *memories*," Doctor Aisling said from across the corridor. "I suspected, but I wasn't certain. Most of my subjects required *some* modification, of course, your pathetic little human minds just aren't up to the strain. But some of you required more work than others."

I turned and glared at her, but she still sat calmly on her cot.

"Doctor?" the Admiral asked.

"That makes some sense," he admitted. "It doesn't explain the differences in where the implant ties into their minds."

"We were closer to what she wanted," Andrews said as he opened his eyes and got to his feet. "Which is why we hid. She used our gestalts in the planetary networks to gather information and to monitor her allies. But those gestalts tied back into us as well, and ours are more like partnerships. They told us some of what she was doing, they told us that we were different and that we needed to hide it."

"Interesting," Weisfeldt, Schoeffelk, and Aisling all said at the same time. Commander Weisfeldt and Doctor Schoeffelk stared at each other for a long moment and then looked at Aisling, but the alien simply sat there, her expression of exaggerated amusement apparent.

"So your gestalts, they're not like us?" I asked, gesturing at myself, Karmazin, and Sashi Drien.

"I wish they were," Andrews said bitterly. "Mine is constantly talking to me, trying to take over, trying to do things or get me to do things. It's like sharing my head with another copy of me... one that was tortured over and over again by that *chikaken*." He waved his hand at Aisling.

"Mine's a bit quieter, calmer," Ashiri said in a soft voice. "We're partners. It's why we were able to stay hidden for so long, they aren't trapped in our implants, they can go out, hide in anything with enough storage. The Academy network, the other special implants, anything."

"So that's how you avoided the shutdown. Plus, you were hiding from her as well as the rest of us," the Admiral said. "You were also trying to do well here, in the process. Why the attack on Jiden?"

Doctor Aisling laughed. "Oh... oh, this is so *rich*. So very amusing."

Everyone turned to face her. "Do you care to elaborate?" The Admiral asked it in such an icy tone that even I flinched. The woman had been torturing her cadets and whatever Ashiri and Andrews had done, they were still her responsibility, and her duty was to protect them. I understood that on a level that I couldn't explain.

"Little Jiden Armstrong asked me a question, which made me think that *she* had information about *me*. I misunderstood her innocence and naivety. I thought she sought to blackmail me with information she'd uncovered with her implant. So my two little birds here didn't try to kill her... *I* did."

"But I overheard them!" I protested, "They talked about removing me!"

"We were trying to sabotage your ranking," Ashiri said bitterly. "So I could score better. We figured that if I scored highest, then maybe I could go to the Admiral, lay it all out, and show her how effective we could be... and maybe she could protect us from Aisling. I should have known it would never have worked. You delivered us right to her..." She glared at me, her face empty of hope. "All because you just couldn't let me win."

"But she's in a cell," I stared at her.

Ah, child, I've only been here so long as it suited me.

I heard the words in my head and then I understood. I turned to shout a warning as the cell door clicked open.

Aisling moved so fast that she was nothing more than a blur. The guards raised their weapons but she was in among them before they could line up shots. Her blows struck them, smashing one of them into the wall hard enough that his armored visor shattered and hurling the second one down the corridor at us, bowling over Doctor Schoeffelk and Commander Weisfeldt.

The Admiral drew her pistol, firing from the hip. I saw Doctor Aisling stagger as bullets tore into her side. She didn't go down, though, charging at the Admiral and swinging at her.

The Admiral fired a last shot from point blank, right in Aisling's face, but the alien didn't so much as stagger, she batted the Admiral into the wall and then she was coming at me.

I drew my pistol but Aisling smashed it out of my hands and

into the wall before I could even squeeze the trigger. She picked me up by the neck, her diminutive form far stronger than it should have been. "I owe you," she said, "twice over. For the removal of the team that sought to retrieve me, you gave me my freedom, though you didn't realize it. But for delivering these two to me... yes, I think I'll spare you, child."

I heard weapons rack and then suddenly I was flying through the air to hit the wall. Gunfire roared and I dazedly saw Sashi and Alexander firing the fallen guard's rifles at Aisling.

She dodged left and right, though, ripping the rifle out of Sashi's fingers and then driving the butt of it into Karmazin's face. He fell back and she kicked out, moving too fast to see and Sashi flew back into the wall before dropping limply to the ground.

"No," I croaked.

"Oh, I didn't kill them," Doctor Aisling dropped to a squad to almost gently caress Karmazin's unconscious face. He groaned and I realized he wasn't unconscious, just dazed like me. She lifted a bloody finger to her lips and smiled. "They're far too valuable to me alive. You and these other two are far outside of what I intended, and I'll need to thoroughly study you. Just as I'll use these other two as I've always intended."

She had at least a half-dozen bullet holes in her torso, and the Admiral's last bullet had punched through her right eye. Blood and strange green, glowing ichor dribbled out, but Aisling didn't seem to care. Alarms had begun to sound, and I knew the response team would be on its way soon. Yet Aisling gestured and the alarms cut off, followed by the lights.

The emergency lighting came on and she gestured and Ashiri Takenata and Morgan Andrews' cell doors came open. "Come children, we have work to be done."

I looked over at them, my vision still blurred from the impact with the wall and adjusting to the emergency lighting. To my horror, I saw Andrews and Ashiri step out of their cells. They didn't go for weapons. Their shoulders were slumped and their expressions were hopeless. They came up to stand before Aisling. "Take them," she gestured at Sashi and Karmazin... and me. "We'll have such fun, together."

"Don't help her!" I protested, fighting my way to my feet. I looked around for a weapon, but I didn't see anything in reach.

"We've no choice," Andrews said, his voice dull. "You can't fight her. What she can do..."

Ashiri stared at me, her expression forlorn, "I'm sorry, Jiden. I really am, I didn't want this. I was trying to *stop* this... I wish you'd listened to me."

"I gave you an order," Aisling growled. "Or do I need to demonstrate my power to you?"

Andrews screamed and dropped to his knees, clutching at his head. The look on Aisling's face, one part pleasure and one part detached interest, told me that if we let her take us out of here, it would be a terrible, horrible mistake. It would be better to die than let her take us. Even besides what she would do to me, I couldn't let her do that to Ashiri, Alexander, and Sashi. Not even to Andrews.

I couldn't fight her physically. She'd just taken down all of us in the span of a few seconds. She'd been shot in the chest and head and didn't seem to even *notice*. But I had a sudden thought and I reached out with my implant, connecting to Sashi, Ashiri, and Alexander. *Help me, help me to fight her.* I didn't wait for them, I threw my mind down that barely sensed link, through which she'd talked right into my mind.

In the real world, I saw her go still and her eyes widened.

In the artificial world, I drove into her mind driving everything I had into her. Her mind was every bit as alien as I could imagine, a thing of crystalline perfection, where every thought, every emotion, had a razor edge. I was entering through *her* implants, I realized, and I could feel them inside her mind, clustered in different parts of her. I attacked inwards, using that moment of her surprise to hit her as hard as I could.

Yet she reacted far faster than I hoped. One moment I burned everything I had, smashing at her crystalline thoughts and tearing into her mind... and the next an overwhelming blackness smashed into me. Terrifying laughter enveloped me. *Oh, child... that was beautiful, truly. I think I shall treasure you... your defiance, your stubbornness... one day, you will serve me with those traits. But you are unprepared for this fight and very much alone.*

"She's not alone," Sashi grunted and then she stood beside me in Aisling's mind. And then Alexander stood next to her. And then Ashiri stood there, next to me. Her avatar looked afraid and she wavered, but she was there.

The darkness recoiled slightly and as it did so, we attacked.

It was a thing of chaos and confusion. We didn't know enough to combine our attack. It wasn't like going into a computer. It was alien and it was terrifying and we abandoned anything resembling finesse. I drove into the darkness while Ashiri blazed brightly, causing crystalline structures to vibrate and then shatter. Sashi seemed to move in a blur, like a human pinball, bouncing off everything in her path and leaving a wake of destruction.

Alex moved like a hammer, simply smashing everything in his path. I heard Aisling howl in frustration and anger. "I will destroy you all!"

"No," I growled, clenching my fingers into the darkness that was her conscious mind, holding her while Alexander smashed her and Ashiri and Sashi ripped into her mind. "You're done."

I felt her reach out, back across the link. I realized what she was doing, even as she sought to attack us through our implants in return. I let her go and intercepted those tendrils of thought, even as the others continued to smash into her. I split my attention four ways, each of me engaging her efforts one on one.

She was trying to overheat our implants, to cook our brains, but I wasn't going to let her. Every time she reached out, I smashed at her, like a digital hydra, slicing off each head as it came at me.

Aisling weakened, her attacks becoming jerky, and uncoordinated, and I was able to split my attention once again. This time, I staggered over to one of the fallen rifles. She tried to raise a hand, but she shuddered and green ichor spurted from her empty eye socket as something inside of her ruptured from the damage that my friends were doing.

I didn't say anything, I just raised the rifle, aimed it at her torso, and started firing. After the first dozen impacts, she fell to the ground and then I stepped over her, adjusted my aim, and met her single intact eye. "This is for hurting my friends," I said. Her eye was unfocused, I didn't know if she heard me or not. I didn't really care.

I emptied the magazine into her.

***

Chapter 26: Kyle Makes An Honest Woman Of Me... Mostly

It was a rather battered group that met a few hours later. The Admiral had her arm in a sling and Doctor Fuesting had sniffed in disapproval and said that she expected to see her in physical therapy. The doctor had simply given me a look of disapproval, but gauged me as having nothing more than bruises and superficial injuries. Commander Weisfeldt had a concussion, and he was still having difficulty getting his eyes to focus. Doctor Schoeffelk had a bandage on a gash on his head and he kept feeling at it, as if bemused by the injury.

Andrews had been taken upstairs. While I'd managed to protect my friends, Aisling had attacked him and Doctor Schoeffelk thought that the most humane thing would be to try and restore his mind and undo what had been done to him.

"What am I going to do with you all?" the Admiral stared at my friends and I. She looked tired and I could see lines in her face, lines of pain and stress.

Ashiri stepped forward, "Ma'am, I want to formally apologize. I just... I was afraid, and then Jiden thought I tried to kill her. I should have come forward. I shouldn't have used my implant the way I did." My friend swallowed, "I realize that what I did amounts to an honor board and is grounds for expulsion." She straightened, "I'd like to formally offer my resignation..."

"Oh, stop that," the Admiral waved a hand.

Ashiri stared at her in shock.

"I won't accept it, girl," the Admiral growled. "Leaving aside the honor board violations for a minute, you violated over a dozen regulations, between you, Boyles, and Andrews. You hacked secure military networks, you violated planetary security, and you put lives at risk when you did it. Your little stunt when I tried to flush you out also nearly cost the lives of Boyles and Gnad."

We all went still as she said that. The Admiral looked at us all with cold, blue eyes, her expression stern. "I would be well within my duties as the Superintendent of this Academy to put *all* of you on formal charges, including my granddaughter, for numerous violations of regulations. Some of you would face serious prison time as a result, especially if a board found you guilty of collusion, even indirectly, with that little monster and whatever she was trying to do."

The room had gone deathly silent. I wasn't breathing, I felt like the air had been sucked out of the room. No one spoke, no one moved as the four of us realized that our careers, our lives, might be forever destroyed.

"I'm not going to do any of that," the Admiral said, her voice flat. "Instead, I'm going to bury all of this under sufficient classification that it won't see the light of day until we're all safely dead."

I finally was able to draw breath and I gasped. I wasn't the only one. The Admiral smiled a little as she stared at us, our relief evident. "I won't say I approve of your tactics, but I understand your position, at least, girl," she said to Ashiri. "And as for your cheating... the Honor Board does allow for extenuating circumstances in sentencing, which falls to me, normally. I think we're inside that area... but I warn you now that you had best finish the rest of your time here fairly or I will *bury* you, do you understand me?"

Ashiri nodded quickly.

"I'm going to probably assign you some probationary work, as well, but that's for when we're not all concussed and I'm not in pain. I tend to be a little harsh when I'm in immediate pain, just as I tend to be a little magnanimous when someone just saved my life," the Admiral said in a dry tone of voice. I couldn't help but snort in nervous laughter.

"Now, as to the rest..." She looked at Doctor Schoeffelk, "Doctor?"

He took his hand away from the bandage on his head, almost as if he'd been caught picking his nose or something equally embarrassing. "What, yes?"

"Can you give me clean bills of health on their neural implants?" The Admiral asked.

The doctor looked at Commander Weisfeldt and they both shrugged. "Mostly, well, yes. I mean, the neural work that Aisling did to Mister Andrews and Miss Takenata is particularly disturbing. The fact that their gestalts are separate, discrete individuals... that's not healthy either. It could cause something like cognitive dissonance leading to psychosis or something rather like multiple personality disorder, except of course, these are two different individuals..."

"Small words, Doctor," the Admiral sighed.

"I need to do some patching, to try to heal their minds. I'm also concerned about the way that Aisling modified their implant architecture. It's hooked into parts of their, well, what you might call their lizard brain. I don't think she intended for those portions to activate, I think she was just playing with possibilities, but they're integrated and I don't know if I can disconnect those connections without causing severe damage."

"What kinds of repercussions are you talking, as far as leaving them?"

"The way they're tied in, they'll naturally amplify impulses, maybe even lower inhibitions. Both Andrews and Takenata exhibit higher levels of adrenaline, which suggests they're kept at a state of fight or flight, almost like artificially induced post-traumatic stress disorder. It's going to wear on them both. Some of their actions," he waved a hand, "were probably driven by that."

The Admiral looked at Ashiri, "You're saying they're not going to be mentally stable?"

"I am *not* saying that," Doctor Schoeffelk protested. "I'm saying there's issues. I can probably... tone things down a bit. Dialing back the stimulus of their implants to those regions will go a long way. Counseling, anger management, that sort of thing can also help. I think I might be able to dial back Andrews' implant the most, just with how it's plugged in. Combined with integrating his gestalt and maybe some restructuring, I think he'll have a good recovery."

I moved up and stood next to Ashiri, "What about her?" I put my arm around her shoulders. No matter what, I would be there for her. I tried not to think too much about how miserable she must have been, the horrors of trying to stay hidden to avoid further torture. She tensed at my touch at first, but then she leaned on me and I felt her relax a little.

"Ashiri's implant architecture is far more integrated into her brain and the neural reconstruction that Doctor Aisling performed is far more extensive," he spread his hands, "It's going to take me months to see what I can do. I think she can function, yes, I think she's going to take years to fully recover."

I heard Ashiri sob slightly and I tightened my arm around her. "It's over for me," Ashiri sobbed, "I..."

"If you monitor her and help her, can she still stay here?" I demanded.

The doctor looked between us and the Admiral, who stared at him with an unreadable expression. "It's going to be hard. She's going to be going through a lot."

"I'll be here for her, she's my friend," I said.

"Me too," Alexander came up on her other side.

"Yeah," Sashi said simply as she came up next to him. "We all have hard times, we'll help her through them." I'd never felt so proud and I wanted to kick myself for ever doubting her.

"Doctor, as long as you monitor her and as long as *you,*" she looked hard at Ashiri, "let people know if you're having issues, I'm willing to accept those risks. God knows, you won't be the only cadet with issues." She took on a distant, tired look. "Frankly, if the past three years are anything to judge, I don't know how much more of this I can take."

The words caught me by surprise. The Admiral had become a fixture of my life. I couldn't imagine the Academy without her.

She shook herself, "Alright. The four of you are dismissed." She snorted slightly, "Give yourselves a day or two to recover. I'll have someone put in a form for it. But I believe you have finals in two weeks, so don't fall behind on your classes." She shook her head bemusedly, looking at the green ichor staining the floor where I had finished off Doctor Aisling. "What a strange world we live in."

"Cadets," she nodded at us, "dismissed."

***

"So," Karmazin asked as we stood waiting for the elevator to arrive and take us to the surface. "This was your summer assignment, huh?"

"I can't talk about it," I answered, rubbing a hand on my face.

"Does Kyle know?" Sashi asked, cocking an eyebrow at me.

"No," I sighed. "Oh, god, I have no idea what I'm going to tell him about... all this. I don't know if I *can* tell him anything."

"Boys, they get so sulky when you don't tell them things," Sashi laughed. I started to giggle in response and Ashiri joined in. Alexander just stared at the three of us with a suffering expression.

Our laughter trailed off as the elevator doors opened. We stepped aside to allow several security personnel to step out and then stepped into the empty elevator. "Do you think it's really over?" Ashiri asked in a small voice.

"What, the deal with Aisling?" I asked as I used my key card to take us to the upper levels. She nodded.

"Well, Jiden made very sure that she's not going to be a problem anymore," Sashi grinned. "I think the reload and second magazine was a *bit* much, but I'm not going to complain."

I grinned sheepishly, "I just wanted to be sure, that's all." My grin faded as I thought about the rage and anger that had gone through me. Killing Aisling had been an execution. It had been necessary to protect my friends, but I'd still ended it all by killing her when she was basically helpless. I didn't regret it in the slightest, but I sort of worried about the fact that I didn't regret it.

"Don't worry, Jiden, you've got friends to keep an eye on you and keep your violent tendencies in line," Ashiri clearly read my expression.

"Says the one who shot us in the back," Alexander grumbled. "Back of the *head* for me."

"You deserved that," Ashiri sniffed. "Thinking that Jiden would kill innocent people, *really*!?"

"Well, that's sort of what the data suggested," Sashi noted. "And we still don't know how you got that award..."

"I can't talk about it," I said. I wondered just how much I'd have to say that in the future. Looking down at my uniform, I saw it was stained with blood, powder burns from the rifle, and green ichor. The elevator doors opened and we stepped out.

Kyle was there and he grabbed me in a hug, "Jiden, oh my God, I've been so worried. They had a medical team come running this direction and I couldn't reach you..." He pushed me back and looked down at my stained uniform. "What happened to you?"

I sighed, "I can't talk about it."

**

We finished out the semester, somehow. There were all kinds of questions and rumors. Near the end of the semester, the Admiral gave Doctor Schoeffelk the go-ahead to turn on the implants from the other cadets. There was even some talk of possibly continuing the program within the realm of Directorate Thirteen.

The remainder of my classes and finals were nothing more than a blur to me. I got through them, but I couldn't remember individual events. I was just too wrung out. The bit of brainpower I had outside of classes I spent with my friends and with Kyle.

I had to give him credit, he knew that we had some shared experience outside of what he knew and I could tell he was a bit envious, but he never once pressured me to tell him what had happened. I got permission from the Admiral, finally, anyway, to tell him some of it. It was after finals, but before we had our grades, that awkward stage of limbo while we all waited to go home on Christmas break. Kyle had invited me to spend Christmas with his family this year and I was actually looking forward to it. I was nervous, too, especially to meet his mother. But I knew that no matter what, even if his parents hated me, we'd work things out.

Sashi had finished out the year in first ranking. There was no doubting that she'd earned it. She'd worked harder than any of us to not only make up lost ground, but she'd done it while spending hours every week trying to find out the identity of Diamond. She'd guessed wrong, but then again, so had I. She and Karmazin had mentioned something about visiting the Enclave over Christmas Break. I assumed that meant I wouldn't have to put her up at my parent's place, so that was nice.

Karmazin had finished up the year in second place. He seemed comfortable with that, and I couldn't blame him. Bolander and Thorpe had both edged up, taking third and fourth after Ashiri's scores had all been penalized. Kyle had come out ranking fifth overall for our class. I'd ended up sixth and there were other names behind me that I recognized, both from Project Quicksilver and just as faces in my classes. Ashiri, after taking her penalties and punishment from the Admiral, had received a painful one hundred demerits *and* her grades and ratings for all her drills had been dropped twenty percent overall.

That had put her far down the rankings. It was a blow that I knew she could recover from. Sashi had done it, and I knew that Ashiri was every bit as capable. It was going to take her a lot of work, though. Still, I had promised her I'd be there for her... just as I had promised I'd be there for her when she told her mother, if she needed some support. She'd asked for some time alone to do that and I'd given her that, while I'd went to find Kyle.

I'd finally had a chance to get permission from the Admiral and Commander Weisfeldt to tell Kyle some of what had happened to me... which was why we stood outside of the Admin section elevator, Kyle reading through the datapad loaded with its page after page of legal disclosure statements.

Kyle's expression was dogged, especially as he got to some of the really convoluted legalese. At one point he looked up, "I'm pretty sure this section says if I think about whatever secrets you tell me, around anyone I suspect of being a telepath, I'm in violation of several regulations and I'll go to jail."

"Really?" I asked. "I never made it that far. Just sign the thing. I'm dying to tell you."

Kyle ran a hand through his red hair, "I'm almost afraid to know at this point. I mean, I swear sometimes my mother is, like, psychic."

I giggled at that. "It involves some of the equations we worked on earlier this year," I said. "And a lot of the crazy stuff that happened to me. Oh, and that award I got that I'm not allowed to talk about..."

He muttered something under his breath and signed the forms. I walked him into the elevator, showing the guard the signed documents and then using my pass-key to toggle the elevator. As the elevator doors closed, I began, "So, let me tell you about the WAR drive, the Weisfeldt-Armstrong-Regan warp drive."

"Wait, my name's last?" he asked suspiciously.

"WAR sounds cooler that RAW or RWA, sorry," I kept my tone offhanded, waiting for full realization to dawn upon him.

"Wait... warp drive?" Kyle's eyes went wide. "As in, not *theorem*, not *research*, but *actual* warp drive!? You *solved* them--"

"All these interruptions," I grinned, "will you let me finish?"

Kyle glowered at me and I giggled. Just to comfort him a bit I leaned towards him and tilted my head up for a kiss, "I love you."

He grumbled, but he kissed me back. "I love you too," he smiled.

The elevator doors to Directorate Thirteen opened, "Come on, Kyle, let me show you a world of wonders..."

The End

The Children of Valor series continues with Valor's Cost

About the Author

Kal Spriggs is a science fiction and fantasy author. He currently has five series in print: The Valor's Child YA series, The Renegades space opera and space exploration series, the Shadow Space Chronicles military science fiction and space opera series, the Fenris space opera series, and the Eoriel Saga epic fantasy series.

Kal is a US Army combat veteran who has been deployed to Iraq and Afghanistan. He's a graduate of a federal service academy and used a lot of his experiences from there in writing the Valor's Child books. He lives in Colorado, and is married to his wonderful wife (who deserves mention for her patience with his writing) and also shares his home with his son, and several feline overlords. He likes hiking, skiing, and enjoying the outdoors, when he's not hunched over a keyboard writing his next novel.

CPSIA information can be obtained
at www.ICGtesting.com
Printed in the USA
LVHW020622161218
600644LV00019B/3340/P

Making an Ecosystem

MW00891971

Lisa Holewa

Smithsonian

Contributing Author

Allison Duarte

Consultants

Jessica Lunt, Ph.D.
Marine Biologist
Smithsonian Marine Station

Stephanie Anastasopoulos, M.Ed.
TOSA, STREAM Integration
Solana Beach School District

Publishing Credits

Rachelle Cracchiolo, M.S.Ed., *Publisher*

Conni Medina, M.A.Ed., *Managing Editor*

Diana Kenney, M.A.Ed., NBCT, *Content Director*

Véronique Bos, *Creative Director*

Robin Erickson, *Art Director*

Michelle Jovin, M.A., *Associate Editor*

Mindy Duits, *Senior Graphic Designer*

Smithsonian Science Education Center

Image Credits: front cover, p.1 David Clode/Unsplash; p.7 (top) imagesandstories/picture alliance/blickwinkel/Newscom; p.9 (top) David Doubilet/National Geographic/Getty Images; p.10 Dennis Kunkel Microscopy/Science Source; p.11 (top and bottom left), 19 (bottom left) Dennis Kunkel Microscopy/Science Source; p.13 (bottom) Ann Ronan Picture Library Heritage Images/Newscom; pp.16–17 Glenn Beanlan/Getty Images; p.18 LeonP/Shutterstock; p.20 Reinhard Dirscherl/Science Source; p.22 (top) Paulo Oliveira/Alamy; p.23 (map) Carol and Mike Werner/Science Source; p.24 (bottom left) John De Mello/Alamy; p.25 (left) Citizen of the Planet/Alamy; p.27 (top) Peter Bennett/Science Source; back cover (top left) Gerd Guenther/ Science Source; back cover (right) © Smithsonian; all other images from iStock and/or Shutterstock.

Library of Congress Cataloging-in-Publication Data

Names: Holewa, Lisa, author.
Title: Making an ocean ecosystem / Lisa Holewa.
Description: Huntington Beach, CA : Teacher Created Materials, Inc., [2019] | Audience: Grade 4 to 6. | Includes index. |
Identifiers: LCCN 2018022267 (print) | LCCN 2018024511 (ebook) | ISBN 9781493869602 (E-book) | ISBN 9781493867202 (paperback)
Subjects: LCSH: Marine microbial ecology--Juvenile literature.
Classification: LCC QR106 (ebook) | LCC QR106 .H65 2019 (print) | DDC 579/.177--dc23
LC record available at https://lccn.loc.gov/2018022267

☼ Smithsonian

Teacher Created Materials

5301 Oceanus Drive
Huntington Beach, CA 92649-1030
www.tcmpub.com

ISBN 978-1-4938-6720-2
© 2019 Teacher Created Materials, Inc.

Table of Contents

Underwater Worlds

There are many worlds to explore under water. They can be in shallow, sandy lakes. Or they can be deep within the ocean. Entire ecosystems exist when you venture off land.

Marine ecosystems exist along coral reefs. They exist within mangrove forests. They are along limestone ledges. They're within seagrasses close to the coastline.

Scuba divers explore these worlds. Sometimes, they are shallow enough for snorkelers to see. Other times, only scientists in submarines can reach them. Or they might be displayed for everyone to see at museums or zoos.

A pygmy seahorse blends in with red coral.

Aquariums have tanks that model marine ecosystems. They re-create underwater worlds. People often enjoy watching the biggest creatures in these tanks. They notice the most unique or most colorful creatures. Jellies and sea stars are fun to watch. It's hard not to wonder about seahorses and sea urchins. Blue crabs and spiny lobsters draw attention.

But, what about creatures too tiny to see? Do bacteria exist in the sea? Do microbes affect ocean life? Can the smallest creatures in underwater worlds also be the mightiest?

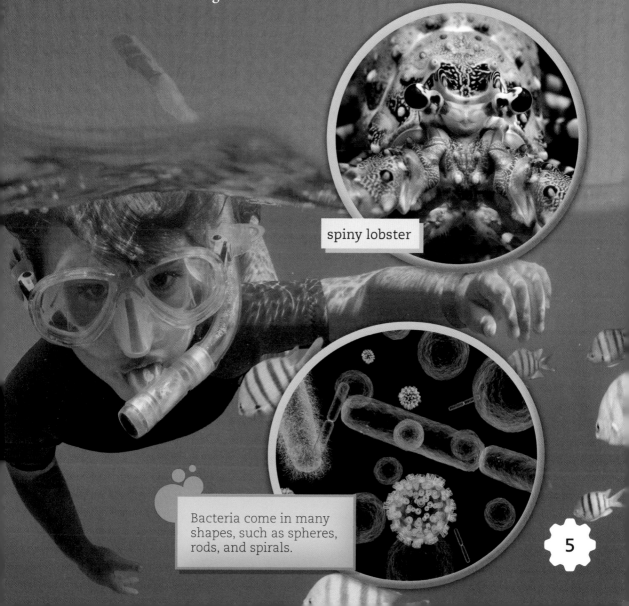

spiny lobster

Bacteria come in many shapes, such as spheres, rods, and spirals.

Studying the Marine Environment

Aquarium tanks allow people to see marine environments more closely. They help people understand more about underwater worlds. Hopefully, they also inspire people to take care of oceans and lakes—and the creatures that live in them.

Tanks also help scientists. Sometimes, they study model ecosystems to learn more about how certain changes affect marine life. Many big aquariums hire researchers. Their job is to learn more about life under water. Researchers work with aquarists. Aquarists take care of creatures at aquariums.

Sea lions swim in an aquarium filled with giant kelp.

ARTS

A Display for All

Aquarists want fish in a tank to act as they do in nature. Having the right plants and rock formations can make sea creatures feel right at home. But aquarists must balance this with the need for the public to easily see the animals. If there are too many places for fish to hide, visitors won't see them and won't want to come back.

Untangling the Food Web

Aquarium researchers study marine food webs. A food web is a bit like a food chain. But it shows many different ways marine plants and animals are connected.

Sea jellies, for instance, were once thought of mainly as predators. They eat the eggs of many sea creatures. They didn't seem as though they would be good food for other fish because they are mostly water. Now, we know that many sea creatures *do* eat sea jellies. Penguins and sea turtles consider them a good snack!

Researchers also know that some squid are cannibals. Their research shows that swordfish, whales, and seals eat squid too. This is just another way in which marine food webs are very complex.

A sea turtle eats a jellyfish.

7

Changes in the Water

Aquarium researchers also study how marine creatures find their food in the water. But pollution can change water. That makes it hard for animals to eat and stay healthy. And scientists are learning about other threats.

Scientists know that carbon dioxide (CO_2) levels have changed the **atmosphere**. But are they changing underwater worlds too? Researchers are trying to find out by measuring levels of CO_2 in samples of water. Levels are increasing. This might be bad news for some coral. They need certain conditions to grow. And CO_2 makes seawater more **acidic**. It affects the conditions that let coral grow.

Some aquarium researchers are trying to learn more about how CO_2 affects freshwater lakes. Does it make the water harmful for creatures who live there? Does it make it harder for them to find food? There is much to learn.

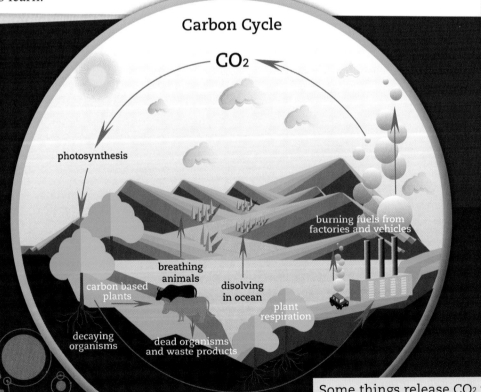

Carbon Cycle

CO_2

photosynthesis

burning fuels from factories and vehicles

breathing animals

carbon based plants

disolving in ocean

plant respiration

decaying organisms

dead organisms and waste products

fossil and fossil fuels

Some things release CO2 into the atmosphere. Other things both absorb and release CO2.

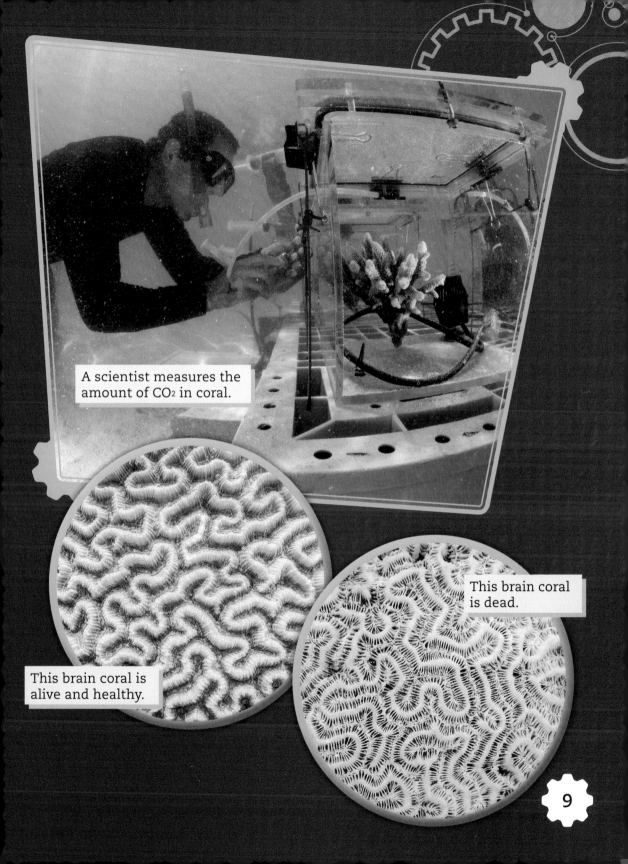

A scientist measures the amount of CO_2 in coral.

This brain coral is alive and healthy.

This brain coral is dead.

9

Marine Microbes

Creating a marine ecosystem on land is not easy. It requires an understanding of underwater worlds. Small changes have big effects.

Bacteria Are Everywhere

Microbes are creatures so small they cannot be seen without microscopes. But they are everywhere. In fact, microbes make up 98 percent of the **biomass** of the planet's oceans.

Many of those microbes are bacteria. Scientists have known for a long time that bacteria affects life on land. But they are now working to understand the role of bacteria in lakes and oceans. New technology is giving them tools to study bacteria's effects. This is a growing field of science. It is called marine microbial ecology.

One thing scientists know is that bacteria are key to life in the ocean. They are necessary in the nitrogen cycle. This is true on land and in water. Nitrogen makes up most of the air we breathe. But this type of nitrogen cannot be used by most organisms. In the ocean, marine bacteria help change it into a type of nitrogen that other marine life can use.

This single bacteria cell has been magnified more than 2,000 times.

Part of the Land Nitrogen Cycle

bacteria

animals

plants

Part of the Marine Nitrogen Cycle

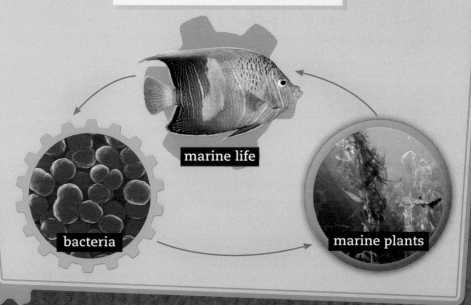

marine life

bacteria

marine plants

One milliliter (0.2 teaspoons) of sea water can hold up to a million microbes. Eight liters (2 gallons) of seawater hold more bacteria than there are people on Earth.

Decomposition is another important part of the nitrogen cycle. Marine bacteria decompose organisms that have died. These organisms can be as big as whales. They can be as small as tiny microbes. Either way, bacteria help break down molecules that made the creature. This makes their nutrients available for other organisms to use.

Many different types of microbes live in the oceans. They all play different and key roles in the nitrogen cycle. They are vital to the marine CO_2 cycle too. Microbes also help in other ways. Some elements, such as iron, are hard to find in the ocean. Microbes can catch iron released by dead organisms and make it available for others.

Microbes themselves can also be food for bigger creatures. The role of microbes is a tricky part of keeping an aquarium. Water can have too many microbes. When this happens, water might look like a mess of green algae (AL-jee). Or, water can have too few microbes. That is bad for the creatures that rely on microbes. Keeping the right balance of microbes is hard.

Whale Shark size
compared to human

TECHNOLOGY

Making a Microscope

Microbes were first discovered in the 1600s by Dutch scientist Anton van Leeuwenhoek (VAHN LEY-vuhn-hook). As a teenager working for a cloth merchant, he saw a simple microscope. It was a basic magnifying glass on a small stand. He learned to make his own microscopes. Soon, he discovered how to make very small glass spheres to use as lenses. These provided very strong magnification. He used his simple but powerful microscope to look at drops of water, where he discovered single-celled microbes.

Leeuwenhoek's microscope

Putting It All Together

There are many things to consider when putting an aquarium together. These include lighting, food, filters, temperature, and water movement.

Lights and Action!

The sun provides light and heat for Earth. Plants use light energy to make their own food. This process is called photosynthesis. Aquatic organisms, such as algae, use photosynthesis too. They have to live in parts of the oceans that get sunlight. Deeper in the water, light becomes dimmer. And even deeper, there is no sunlight at all. Creatures live in these depths, but there are fewer of them.

In tanks, people have to create artificial sunlight. It's a complicated job. There are different types of sunlight that organisms need to use as energy.

Distance in Meters (m)
Sunlight Travels in Ocean Water

sea level

sunlight zone
sunlight reaches;
photosynthesis possible

200 m (~650 ft.)

twilight zone
some sunlight reaches;
photosynthesis impossible

1,000 m (~3,280 ft.)

midnight zone
sunlight does not reach;
zone is completely dark

10,000+ m (~32,800 ft.)

jellyfish in an aquarium tank

These types of light come from the visible spectrum—part of the electromagnetic spectrum. Different organisms need different parts of the spectrum for photosynthesis. For instance, green algae need mostly red light. But red algae use blue light. So, the lighting in tanks needs to cover most of the visible spectrum. Aquarists need to check light levels often to keep microbes happy and healthy.

SCIENCE

All the Colors of the Spectrum

Each color in the visible spectrum has a different **wavelength**. Red has the longest wavelength. Violet has the shortest. Water easily absorbs red light, so it does not travel very deep. But blue light reaches farther into the ocean. For this reason, a snorkeler's view under water looks much like the view above water. But scuba divers see a world of blue and black.

Aquarium lights also have to be strong. Electric lights are not nearly as bright as the sun. This means they have to work harder. In some aquariums, lights are on for as many as 15 hours each day. Aquariums that model coral reef ecosystems need the brightest tank lights. Those showing deep-water ecosystems need much less light.

Feeding Time

Many living creatures move to a new place if their current home doesn't have enough food. But moving is not a choice for creatures in tanks. And moving is not a choice for marine creatures such as coral, which cannot move at all. This can make feeding tank creatures a difficult task.

Ideally, a marine ecosystem exhibit would show an underwater world as it really exists. But most visitors want to see a lot of big, colorful animals. This means tanks have more creatures in small spaces than those habitats could normally support on their own. There are more fish, and the fish are bigger. There may be a lot of coral too. Many species have to compete for food. To prevent food shortages, aquarists regularly add food to tanks. This way, animals won't eat each other and visitors get to see a lot of sea creatures.

An aquarist feeds fish at Bueng Chawak Aquarium in Thailand.

Aquarists feed animals at the Melbourne Aquarium.

Many aquarium coral reefs are modeled after the Great Barrier Reef—the largest coral reef in the world. It is more than 2,000 kilometers (1,250 miles) long.

Adding extra food to tanks is known as supplemental feeding. The food might be frozen, freeze-dried, or even still alive. Fish will often get the most food. They are usually fed twice a day. Many types of coral feed on plankton. Plankton are organisms of any size that drift in a body of water and cannot swim against tides. But aquarium tanks are small and packed with animals that eat plankton. That can make it hard to keep enough plankton around for animals to eat.

The extra food added depends on the type of habitat in the exhibit. A coral reef exhibit may get a lot of extra baby shrimp every day. A seagrass ecosystem may need grass shrimp so slower animals, such as seahorses, get their share of food too.

Feeding schedules are an important part of keeping animals fed. They keep track of what type, how much, and when food is added to exhibits.

An aquarist feeds fish in the Coral World aquarium in Israel.

Having a Filter

Aquarists have another obstacle to overcome in tanks' enclosed spaces—a lot of waste products. This is why tank water must be filtered. The nitrogen cycle helps remove waste from water. Marine microbes, such as bacteria, change nitrogen into a form of the gas that phytoplankton use. Then, bigger creatures eat the phytoplankton, and the nitrogen moves through their bodies. But the nitrogen cycle can't remove all the waste products. That is where filters come in to help.

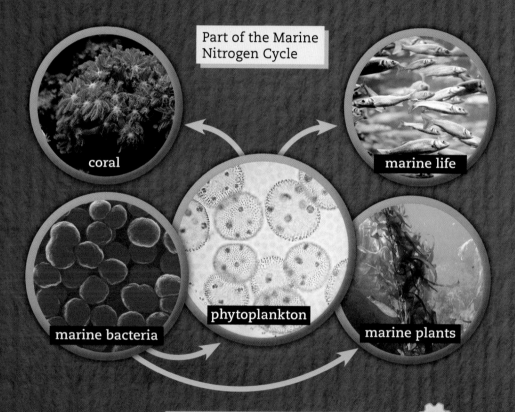

Part of the Marine Nitrogen Cycle

coral

marine life

phytoplankton

marine bacteria

marine plants

MATHEMATICS

How Many Fish Will Fit?

The general rule for home aquariums is that they should have no more than 5 cm of fish for every 7.4 liters of water, or 1 inch per gallon. But volume isn't the only thing to consider. The surface area of a tank is also important. A tall, thin tank has less surface area, which means more pollution from waste. A longer tank has more surface area.

Tank filters help remove aquatic animals' waste. Without filters, chemicals from animal waste can quickly reach **toxic** levels in tanks. High levels can cause algae blooms. Algae blooms happen when a lot of algae grow very quickly. They can disrupt entire ecosystems.

To prevent waste issues, water must be filtered. Many aquariums use turf algae—a type of microbe. They act as a biological filter. First, water from a tank moves along trays of turf algae outside the tank. Bright lights help the algae grow quickly. Then, the algae capture the extra nutrients, such as nitrogen. This helps to clean the water. Aquarists then harvest the algae. This removes any extra nitrogen. Finally, clean water is pumped back into the tank.

Algae filters also serve another important role. They produce oxygen and remove CO_2 from the water. This is important because fish need oxygen to breathe. And too much CO_2 can harm marine life.

Sometimes, aquariums use chemical filters instead of microbial filters. These filters often use charcoal. The charcoal captures waste and toxins from microbes. But chemical filters can remove useful nutrients too.

Since parrotfish eat coral, their waste is sand.

These pipes carry water to a filter outside the tank.

algae bloom

Adapting Turf Filters

Turf filters were created over 20 years ago by a scientist named Dr. Walter Adey and his team. However, they take a lot of space and can be noisy. People who have aquariums at home found them hard to use. So, engineers made changes to the design. They created a screen that hung vertically, with a waterfall-style pump. Today, these filters are engineered for home aquariums to be used in smaller spaces.

Temperatures and Tides

Water temperature is another important part of tank upkeep. Tank water needs to be the same temperature as the water where creatures live naturally. If water gets too warm or too cold, animals will die.

Sometimes, tanks have heaters to warm the water. Other times, aquarists have to chill water to keep it from getting too hot. It is not always that simple, though. For instance, coral reefs need cool water and bright light to grow. Overhead lights can be installed for coral reefs. But these lights give off a lot of heat. So, the water must be chilled to keep it from getting too hot.

A mudskipper swims in warm water.

A seal hugs a beluga whale in cold water.

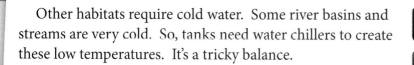

Other habitats require cold water. Some river basins and streams are very cold. So, tanks need water chillers to create these low temperatures. It's a tricky balance.

Aquarists also have to consider water movement. In nature, tides, **currents**, and waves move water. Ocean water is constantly moving. The movement brings in fresh supplies of food and oxygen. It carries away dead matter and excess nutrients. In aquariums, pumps and filters keep water moving. They can also **simulate** waves and tidal cycles.

Ocean Currents
→ warm
→ cold

This pole measures the height of tides in different years.

Water around Antarctica can be as cold as −2° Celsius (28° Fahrenheit).

Changing Water

Ocean water contains salt. *Salinity* is the word that describes the amount of salt in water. The salinity of ocean water stays about the same all the time. But the salinity of places such as **estuaries** might change. It depends on tides and other factors. It's important that tanks have the correct salinity. Many factors can change the salinity of water in a tank. To make up for this, most aquarists need to add water and check salt levels frequently.

Once salinity is under control, aquarists have to make sure water in a tank stays clean. Filters and microbes help keep water clean, but aquarists still have to replace the water. Some aquarists replace about one-fifth of their tank water each year. To do so, some of it needs to be pumped out. Then, new water is filtered before it is pumped in. This helps add more nutrients. It makes up for those that marine creatures have used up. And it helps remove loose algae.

After aquarists have checked the salinity and cleanliness of a tank's water, they have to keep watch. They monitor these and other properties of water. Aquatic creatures depend on working equipment. Aquarists can help make sure that happens.

An aquarist checks the water at Waikiki Aquarium in Hawai'i.

This test shows the level of acidity in water.

Workers at Aquarium of the Pacific in California can test water from this private area.

An aquarist measures coral growth.

Most of the salt in ocean water comes from land. Rainwater carries salt particles from rocks into rivers, which flow into the sea.

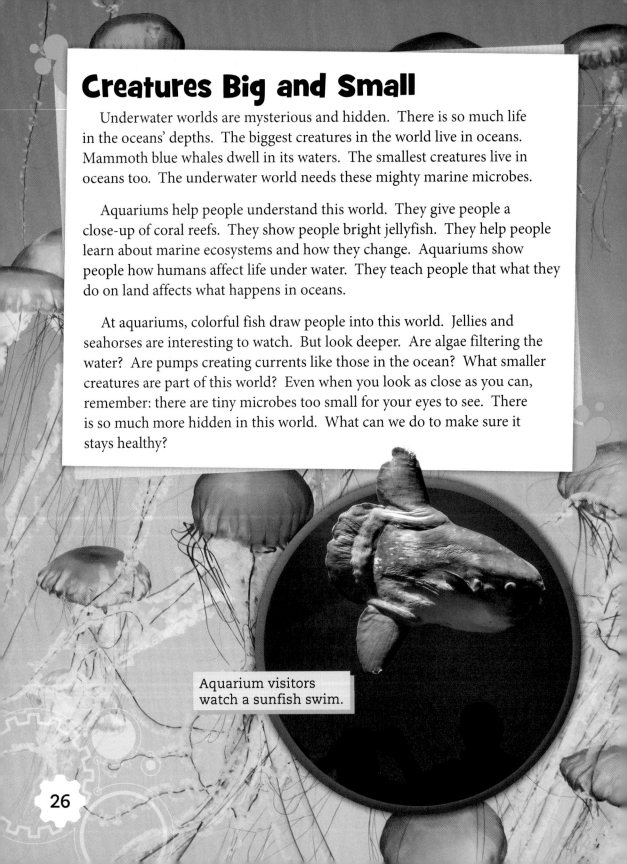

Creatures Big and Small

Underwater worlds are mysterious and hidden. There is so much life in the oceans' depths. The biggest creatures in the world live in oceans. Mammoth blue whales dwell in its waters. The smallest creatures live in oceans too. The underwater world needs these mighty marine microbes.

Aquariums help people understand this world. They give people a close-up of coral reefs. They show people bright jellyfish. They help people learn about marine ecosystems and how they change. Aquariums show people how humans affect life under water. They teach people that what they do on land affects what happens in oceans.

At aquariums, colorful fish draw people into this world. Jellies and seahorses are interesting to watch. But look deeper. Are algae filtering the water? Are pumps creating currents like those in the ocean? What smaller creatures are part of this world? Even when you look as close as you can, remember: there are tiny microbes too small for your eyes to see. There is so much more hidden in this world. What can we do to make sure it stays healthy?

Aquarium visitors watch a sunfish swim.

Scuba divers explore ocean life near Monterey Bay Aquarium in California.

marine microbes under a microscope

Humans have explored only one-twentieth of the ocean biome!

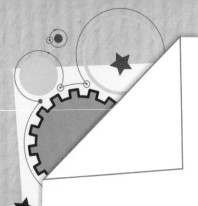

STEAM CHALLENGE

Define the Problem

Imagine you are an aquarist at the Georgia Aquarium, the largest aquarium in the United States. Your task is to maintain the coral reef exhibit. The fish are fed a meal of frozen brine shrimp twice daily. The frozen shrimp are stored far from the exhibit, and you are looking for an effective way to transport the frozen shrimp.

 Constraints: The interior of your container must be at least 20 centimeters (8 inches) across to maximize the amount of shrimp you can carry in one trip.

 Criteria: A successful container will prevent ice from melting for 15 minutes.

Research and Brainstorm

How do aquarists make sure that all organisms in an exhibit are fed? Is it important for a container to be closed during transport? How will you carry the container?

Design and Build

Sketch your container design. What purpose will each part serve? What materials will work best? Build the model.

Test and Improve

Place an ice cube in the container and allow it to remain undisturbed for 15 minutes. Then, measure any water in the container. Did it work? How can you improve it? Modify your design and try again.

Reflect and Share

Which parts of your model worked best to slow the melting of the ice cube? Could your model be used to prevent ice from melting for a longer period of time? What do you think would happen if you added multiple ice cubes to your model?

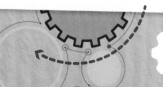

Glossary

acidic—an imbalance in water that contains potentially harmful chemicals and can affect plant life

atmosphere—the entire mass of air around Earth

biomass—the amount of living matter in a certain area

cannibals—animals that eat other animals of their own kind

currents—continuous movement of water in the same direction

decomposition—the process that causes something to slowly be destroyed and broken down into smaller parts

ecosystems—all the living and nonliving things in particular environments

electromagnetic spectrum—a way of grouping all energy and light waves

estuaries—areas where rivers meet seas

mangrove—a type of tropical tree that grows in coastal swamps and shallow seawater

marine—relating to the sea or the plants and animals that live in the sea

molecules—the smallest possible amounts of things that still have all the things' characteristics

simulate—to look, feel, or behave like something else

supplemental—acting to complete something

tides—the regular upward and downward movements of the level of the oceans

toxic—poisonous

wavelength—the distance between energy or light waves

Index

Do you want to help aquatic animals?
Here are some tips to get you started.

"In school, I loved learning about animals and how healthy ecosystems worked. I earned my degrees in marine biology—studying the animals of oceans and estuaries. To understand ecosystems, you need to learn biology, chemistry, geology, botany, behavior, and math."
—*Jessica Lunt, Marine Biologist*

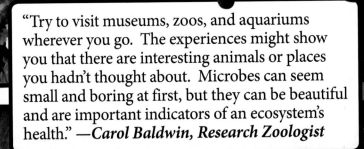

"Try to visit museums, zoos, and aquariums wherever you go. The experiences might show you that there are interesting animals or places you hadn't thought about. Microbes can seem small and boring at first, but they can be beautiful and are important indicators of an ecosystem's health." —*Carol Baldwin, Research Zoologist*